SOMETIMES AT NIGHT

SOMETIMES AT NIGHT

Ben Sanders

SEVERN
HOUSE

First world edition published in Great Britain and the USA in 2021
by Severn House, an imprint of Canongate Books Ltd,
14 High Street, Edinburgh EH1 1TE.

Trade paperback edition first published in Great Britain and the USA in 2022
by Severn House, an imprint of Canongate Books Ltd.

severnhouse.com

British Library Cataloguing-in-Publication Data
A CIP catalogue record for this title is available from the British Library.

ISBN-13: 978-0-7278-5053-9 (cased)
ISBN-13: 978-1-78029-818-4 (trade paper)
ISBN-13: 978-1-4483-0556-8 (e-book)

All Severn House titles are printed on acid-free paper.

Typeset by Palimpsest Book Production Ltd.,
Falkirk, Stirlingshire, Scotland.
Printed and bound in Great Britain by
TJ Books, Padstow, Cornwall.

ONE

Marshall said, 'So what's the problem, Ray? Tell me a story.'

Ray Vialoux drained his wine and picked up the bottle with his other hand before he'd even set the glass down. The place had only been open for two months, and Marshall thought that Vialoux might be setting an early precedent in terms of consumption. He watched Vialoux fill his glass to the rim and then lean forward to sup the first mouthful, like taking the foam off a pint of beer. Last time they'd seen each other was 2010, but Vialoux seemed to be aging in overdrive: bloodshot and pale, neck and jowls too stringy for a man not yet fifty. He looked like he'd eaten nothing for a week and then driven here at a hundred miles an hour with no windshield.

Marshall said, 'Going off body language, I have to assume it's pretty bad.'

Vialoux slid his glass aside, looked at his arms folded on the table. Shirtsleeves pushed back and a shabby bloom of cuff at his elbows. He scanned the room slowly, hunched and looking out from under his brow, like the burden of things going wrong was too much for normal posture.

He said, 'I didn't know who else to talk to, so you're it.'

He gave Marshall half a smile, like his situation – whatever it was – still had a funny side. They were in an Italian restaurant down in Sunset Park. The dining room was the converted bottom floor of a two-story clapboard house on a corner site, fronting Fourth Avenue. Marshall hoped the place would survive. He and Vialoux were the only customers, and Marshall's presence didn't count for much as far as the check was concerned. He was still on his first beer, some kind of micro-brew label he'd never heard of, but no doubt a sensible offering in gentrified Brooklyn, where the local denizens would take a photo of the can and then put it on Twitter. They had a table near the back of the room, Marshall in the forward-facing chair so he could see the door, a row of windows on his right showing the cross street: quiet and dark, the blacktop shiny from late-evening rain. Every now and then a car went by with a hiss of groundwater.

Vialoux looked at his arms some more, seeming embarrassed. 'Anyway. Thanks. I know it's been a while, so I appreciate it.'

'I haven't done anything yet.'

'Yeah, well. You showed up. That's a start. Where you been, anyway? You were UC, right?'

NYPD, undercover.

The worst years of his life.

Marshall nodded.

Vialoux said, 'I heard . . . man, I heard all kinds of stories.'

Marshall didn't answer.

'I mean . . . I heard your op went pretty bad. Everyone heard about your shootout, up by the park. And then you just seemed to disappear and . . . yeah. People said maybe witness protection, maybe you'd left the country or something.'

'I was in New Mexico a few years, but I've been back up here since 2016.'

'And no one's murdered you.' Vialoux managing a smile.

'Yeah. Knock on wood. I do a fair bit of looking over my shoulder.'

Marshall slid his can aside, like it might open up the conversation, get them to the heart of the matter. He'd had to wait ten minutes for the dew line to draw down below the rim, giving him space to get a thumb on there without disrupting the moisture pattern. He didn't know why he had to do it that way but he did. Situations came at him with information, parameters for action. He didn't know why. Some part of his head gave him rules and he followed them.

He said, 'All right. Lay it out for me.'

Vialoux's shirt was open two buttons. He jutted his chin and tugged some more slack out of his tie. Marshall saw his Adam's apple dip and come back.

Vialoux said, 'I got in sorta deep with guys I shouldn't have.'

'All right.'

He waited, but Vialoux was taking his time, rolling his wine-glass stem between his thumb and forefinger, giving that small motion a lot of focus. Back in 2010, he'd been a narc detective at Brooklyn South, and always seemed sure of himself, the way people do when they're on a path that means something to them. Right now, sitting hunched and thirty pounds lighter, missing that magic weight of a gold shield and a gun, he looked as if everything central to his happiness was being slowly crossed off a list.

Marshall said, 'I'm not going to see it any different, whether you say it fast or say it slow.'

Vialoux looked up. 'You probably figured this isn't something I can take to the front desk of the precinct.'

'There are other people you can call. Even if you're not completely spotless on this. But I don't even know what we're talking about yet. There's no point saying it in riddles. Just lay it out plain for me.'

Vialoux didn't seem to hear him. He said, 'I just want to let you know before we get into it. So you know what kind of circus you're showing up for.'

Some guys were like this with bad news, edged up on it slow like a kid at a diving board. Marshall leaned to his left and looked past Vialoux's shoulder to the maître d' station and the front door. A clean break would be as easy as getting up and walking out. But being asked for help is a special kind of entrapment. To say no would be to forfeit moral fiber. Then again, to say yes would be to forfeit even more, potentially. There'd be a line somewhere. A point of optimal involvement.

Marshall said, 'What's happened?'

Vialoux's foot was pumping under the table. He said, 'Guys down Brighton Beach running a sports book I been into. Sixty-k deep. Sixty-seven, actually. I owe sixty-seven.'

He glanced over his shoulder as the owner approached their table. He was a tall, beefy guy in his forties who had to walk sideways to get between the tables.

'You guys good, Ray? You need anything? Another bottle?'

Vialoux stroked an eyebrow with a thumbnail, looked at the tablecloth. 'We're good, Paulie. Appreciate it. Maybe just the check, when you got a minute.'

The guy sidled off again, trailing hand raised, finger aimed at Vialoux. 'Sure, you got it. Don't you guys hurry, though – all the time in the world.'

Marshall drank some beer. He said, 'Who's running the book?'

Vialoux gave it a moment and then looked up again. 'Mob guys. Italian mob guys. I thought . . . you know, I thought you might still have some phone numbers.'

'I have some phone numbers. But I don't have any seventy-thousand-dollar favors owing.'

Vialoux didn't answer.

'Give me some names. Who's running this thing?'

Vialoux sighed, held his hands edgewise on the table, ten inches palm-to-palm. It seemed to Marshall he could see the whole dilemma framed there, overlapping wineglass stains like a Venn diagram of how life goes wrong.

He said, 'I talked to a guy. You ever meet D'Anton Lewis?'

Marshall shook his head.

'Finance guy, gets involved in various things . . . anyway, he got me in.'

He was nodding slowly to himself, looking out the window, as if trying to sum up how things could start OK and then veer off the rails. He said, 'I had a . . . I'd sorted it out with them, I was paying it down. But, yeah . . .' He shrugged. 'They called it in. They called in the whole debt.'

Vialoux waited as Paulie put a pen and a wallet with the check on the table. The guy sidled off again, and Vialoux said quietly, 'I'm maxed out. Man, you got no idea. I used to think . . . I never could understand how people could be poor, you know? It's like: get a job, work your way out of it. But shit: I feel like . . . it's like I'm walking a tightrope, and I got a bucket in this hand, and a bucket in this hand, and another fucking bucket on my head, and in a second I'm going to lose the whole lot.'

He closed his eyes, massaged his temples.

Marshall said, 'Who's running the book?'

'Frank Cifaretti. He must be capo level, now. You know Frank?'

Marshall nodded. He recognized the name. His undercover work had been with the Asaro family. They thought he was a bent-cop-cum-bodyguard. He'd sat in on a couple meetings between them and Frank Cifaretti.

Marshall said, 'I think we've met. You got a number for him?'

'Yeah, I got a number, but it's got to the point, he's not even picking up the phone. I mean, he's not even talking.'

He looked away, pumped his leg some more. Marshall's beer can rattled faintly with the vibration. He set it on a napkin. It was empty now, and the stalagmite dew pattern would draw down whichever way it pleased. Marshall didn't have a role in it. He was off the hook.

He watched Vialoux twist and reach in the pocket of the coat hanging on the back of his chair. He came out with a folded envelope, letter-size, flipped it on the table.

Marshall waited a moment before touching it. He knew he had to see the contents, but then everything he learned posed a risk of trapping him. Data has a gravity. There'd be a point where he'd learned too much, and couldn't just walk away from the problem. Something would chime with that inner current, that inner guide who says, You should fix this.

Vialoux was leaning forward again, elbows on the table, the envelope's fold easing slowly open.

Marshall picked it up.

Vialoux's gaze was faraway and bright, his eyes starting to fill.

Marshall opened the flap and slid out the contents.

Two photographs. A shot of Vialoux's wife, Hannah, side-on to the camera and opening a car door. And a headshot of his teenage daughter, Ella. Hair across her face, quarter-profile. Zoom-lens shots with foggy backgrounds.

Marshall said, 'When did you get these?'

'Yesterday.' Vialoux cleared his throat, blinked a few times. When he spoke again his voice was steadier. 'They were taken out front of the house. There's a note, too.'

He didn't see it at first, but then he moved apart the photos and found the strip of paper: MONEY BY TUESDAY. NO COPS.

Today was Thursday.

Five days to get him out of it.

Marshall slid everything back in the envelope and closed the flap and placed the envelope in the center of the table. Like that small point of order was step one in bringing order to the bigger picture.

Vialoux massaged the bridge of his nose, dragged his hand down his face. 'I didn't sleep last night. Kept hearing break-ins, you know? People showing up early to collect.' He shook his head. 'Jesus.'

Marshall said, 'If he's not answering the phone, how do you tell him the money's ready?'

'He used to just call, I'd meet him in his car somewhere. It's almost like a hobby for him, you know? Go for a drive, pick up a few k. Plus it's harder for the law to keep an eye on him. Does business somewhere different every time. He used to have this bagel place, Neptune Ave, but I only ever dealt with him in the car.'

'Who else have you told?'

'No one. Just you.'

'All right.'

Marshall picked up the pen and tested it on a napkin, and then flipped the napkin over to the clean side. He could see it wasn't quite square. He laid the pen neatly on the principal transverse axis of the napkin with an equal pen length projecting on each side and slid the napkin across the table to Vialoux.

Vialoux said, 'My writing's not that small.'

'I don't need it in scenes with dialogue. Just give me the names.'

Vialoux didn't answer.

Marshall said, 'I'm not saying I'll do anything. But I can't make up my mind one way or the other until I know the players. So.'

He nodded at the paper.

Vialoux's eyes dropped to the table. He fortified with some wine and then raised the pen. Up front, Paulie was fussing with the register, trying to be unobtrusive, making a stealth job of killing time. Beyond him on Fourth Avenue the nighttime traffic was just floating lights running back and forth, puddles picking up the tint, an electric mural with each passing. Marshall leaned to pull his billfold from his pocket, and as he moved he had a broadened view of the window next to them, and on the sidewalk beyond the weak reflection of the tablecloth and its candle flame, he saw a man in black, face hidden by a ski mask, gloved hands bringing up a shotgun.

The barrel swung to target Vialoux as Marshall rose from his chair, and as he came upright he grabbed the table by its edge and flipped it toward the window. The tabletop was vertical as it struck the glass, the pane dropping out as a curtain of white pebbles, and then the shotgun boomed.

Quiet after that: splinters and blood exploding through the room in near-silence under the ringing in his ears. Marshall crouched and dived and caught Vialoux in a tackle chest-high, crashed him backward off his chair and onto the floor. The second shot blew out more glass and wood chips. Paulie was on his stomach beneath another table, hands crushed to his ears like a skull vise. Marshall risked a glance, saw the man with the gun cross the street to a car idling at the far curb, lights off, exhaust misting at its fender. The guy jumped in back and the car took off hard, cutting right onto Fourth through a red light.

No chance of catching them.

No chance of helping Vialoux, either: he lay on his back bleeding from the chest, eyes open in that distant stare the dead have, looking all the way to heaven.

TWO

Paulie had turned very white. Marshall kept him on his side under the table and called it in on the phone at the maître d' station, told the operator what happened and gave a description of the car: silver Impala, maybe an oh-four model.

Six minutes later, a couple of uniformed guys from the seven-two precinct showed up in a radio car, full lights and noise. They came in with guns drawn, one guy staying up by the door while his partner came down for a look at Vialoux and decided, yeah, they definitely needed detectives.

Three more radio cars from the seven-two and an ambulance arrived. The paramedics took Paulie out on a stretcher and gave him oxygen, and twenty minutes after that, two detectives showed up.

One guy was Hispanic, early thirties, looked to be something of a bench-press enthusiast. His partner was a black guy nearing sixty, tall and lean enough the act of getting out from behind the wheel of the unmarked looked mechatronic: joint and limb motion like the sequenced unfolding of some prototype robot.

They took a look at the broken glass and the table out on the sidewalk and then came into the restaurant.

Marshall was at a table by himself up front. The younger cop paused at the maître d' station, like reflex obeyance of the WAIT TO BE SEATED sign, but the older guy came straight through without breaking step, everything about him dialed in on Vialoux.

Outside, one of the uniformed cops said, 'Kinda looks like they overcooked his steak or something, tossed the table out the window.'

The younger detective smiled, and it got some chuckles going around cop-to-cop for a moment – 'I asked for it fucking *rare*' – but the older guy didn't laugh or say anything. Marshall liked that. He was probably into his fourth decade of police work, maybe sacrificed plenty, but he hadn't lost any deference. He knew walking up to a body and standing over it demands a certain attitude, certain manners.

He talked the younger cop through the scene examination – start at the body and work out, drink in the detail, don't disrupt the blood spatter going for his pocket contents – and then he came back down the aisle to where Marshall was sitting.

'You the guy that saw what happened?'

In the interest of completeness, Marshall was of a mind to tell him there were five guys who saw it: one was dead, one was outside in an ambulance, one pulled the trigger, one drove, and he was the fifth. But from the cop's demeanor, Marshall gathered he was abreast of the semantics.

Marshall said, 'Yeah. I was drinking with him.'

The detective sat down in the chair opposite, knees coming almost to table level. He wore a blue suit and a tie and small rimless spectacles. A thin beard disguising old acne scars, pockmarks, as if he'd been hit in the face with a load of number 10 birdshot. Marshall figured he must've been six foot six at least, maybe a hundred seventy pounds if you hosed him down in his suit and he kept his shoes on. He had a pen and a bound notebook with him.

'I'm Detective Floyd Nevins, NYPD.'

He took a business card from his coat and slid it across the table, as if to prove the statement.

'Are you happy to answer some questions?'

Marshall read the card and leaned to slip it in his pocket, the same reflex motion that had maybe saved his life thirty minutes ago, and said that he was. Nevins found a clean page, flipping past half a book's worth of notes from other nights, other murders. He took down Marshall's name and address, and then asked him what had happened. Marshall gave him the crux of it, said they were having a drink at the table down the back and a guy came up and shot Vialoux through the window. Got in the back of a waiting car and escaped uptown on Fourth.

The detective called Nevins looked down the aisle to where the damage was, as if making sure the story fit. He said, 'Ray Vee-loo, huh? What's the spelling on that?'

Marshall told him.

Nevins took it down, and seeing the name written seemed to spark something in his memory. He looked at the paper a long moment, fanned his pen absently in two fingers.

'You get a look at the shooter?'

'Lean guy, short, maybe five-seven with his boots on, one-fifty.'

'You see his face?'

'No. He wore a mask.'

'No hair or skin exposed?'

Marshall shook his head. Outside, one of the uniformed cops was saying backup might be a while. The President was staying at his Fifth Avenue place. Half of NYPD was on guard duty in Manhattan.

Nevins said, 'So nothing at all that stood out?'

'Nothing physical. They knew what they were doing, though. That's pretty distinctive with this sort of thing.'

Nevins didn't answer, giving him room to unpack.

Marshall said, 'A shot through the window's hard, but probably the best option given the setup in here. We were way down at the far table, so if the shooter came in the front, we could've gone out the back. Percentages from their point of view were way down. I think they sat out there and thought about it and then made a final call. And I think that means they had a couple of different guns with them.'

Nevins just looked at him.

Marshall said, 'No one shows up for a hit with just a

pump-action Mossberg. The gun was as big as he was. I think they would've planned to do it close-in with a pistol, but then swapped to plan B. Which wasn't necessarily a worse option. I mean, reflections on the glass, I didn't even see him until he was six feet away. He fired twice – slugs, not buckshot, obviously. Then he walked across the street, got in the car, and they drove off. Car was a nothing-sedan, basically invisible. You add every-thing up, I think the bottom line says hired guys who've done this before. It was dispassionate and relaxed.'

Nevins said, 'Anything else?'

Nothing in his tone, as if the conversation was essentially consistent with his last thirty-five years of witness interviews.

Marshall said, 'The six-eight precinct's only a few blocks away, so they needed to lose the car pretty fast. They went north, so I figure they went up to maybe Thirty-ninth Street, something like that, dropped the car off by the railyard. They could've had a swap-vehicle, or maybe just walked over to Ninth, took the subway. That's how I'd do it, anyway.'

Nevins regarded him flatly. The pen nib hovered, two inches off the paper. It made a couple of small motions, as if circling in on a concise summary. Then it touched down, and Nevins wrote: DISPASSIONATE AND RELAXED. His handwriting was even and careful. He wrote only in capitals. The ink was police-blue. He applied visible nib pressure. Marshall liked that. Maybe like the man himself, every new page carried the ghost of prior cases.

Nevins said, 'You notice the car when you got here?'

Marshall shook his head. 'There are vehicles almost solid on both curbs. It could've been here and I didn't notice.'

'You see any exhaust smoke?'

'Yeah, a little.'

Nevins looked out the window again. Marshall saw him chewing on possibilities. Fumes implied a cool engine, no fumes implied a warm engine. He wanted to know how long they'd sat out there, thinking about the hit. He was murder police. He didn't come out to do the work, only to let someone squirm out of culpability, plead down to Manslaughter in the Second. He needed death, and the proof of human planning: Murder in the First Degree. He came out looking for Murder One.

He said, 'How'd you know this guy? Friend of yours?'

'Yeah, former colleague. We were NYPD.'

He told Nevins about his and Vialoux's history, the taskforce back in 2010, Brooklyn South narcotics.

Marshall said, 'Then I got moved to a different unit, and I didn't really see him again until today. He called me up about two o'clock, said he needed to meet.'

Nevins nodded as he listened, and then he wrote: VIC X/MOS and WIT X/MOS, which was a shorthand meaning both victim and witness were ex-members of service, ex-NYPD.

Nevins said, 'So he knew someone wanted to clip him?'

Marshall told him about the sixty-seven-k debt.

'And let me guess: he couldn't pay?'

Marshall stretched a leg down the aisle, reached in his pocket for the envelope Vialoux had given him. He placed it on the table.

'What's this?'

'He said he had until Tuesday to make the payment. They sent him that as encouragement.'

He watched Nevins examine the contents. The two photos, the written threat. Money by Tuesday. No cops. For a moment, the pen hovered again above the notebook, and Marshall sensed his internal debate, whether to transcribe the message or not. He obviously deemed it sufficiently memorable.

'Wife and daughter, I take it?'

'Yeah.'

Nevins leaned back in his chair, looked at the broken window. 'O'Malley?'

The cop who'd made the steak joke glanced over. 'Yeah?'

'Put a unit on the victim's address when you get it. Hold until further notice.'

'You got it.'

Nevins returned the papers to the envelope. 'No cops. But he told you.'

Marshall nodded. 'We go back. He thought I could help him on the quiet.'

'But you hadn't seen him in a while, right? How'd he make contact?'

'Through a lawyer I know. Harry Rush. Vialoux went to Harry first, and Harry put him on to me.'

'And who suggested this place for the meeting?'

'Ray did. He lives around here – Fiftieth Street, something like that. Haven't been there in a while.'

'And how do you know Mr Rush?'

Marshall worked for him as an unlicensed P.I., but he didn't want that going in Nevins' notebook. He said, 'I know him from my cop days.'

Half the story, at least.

Nevins said, 'So who was leaning on Vialoux? Who'd he owe?'

Marshall looked outside to the ambulance. Paulie was still in the back getting oxygen, but he was upright now, sitting on the edge of the stretcher. Marshall wasn't sure how much the guy had overheard, but he was erring toward nothing. The man had come on too friendly for someone who sensed a life-and-death issue being outlined in his orbit. So it was tempting not to give up the names – D'Anton Lewis, Frank Cifaretti – and just look into it himself. It would be nice to find whoever killed Vialoux and drop them off maybe a four- or five-story fire escape. But Nevins was looking at him with such a steady, neutral stare, it was like he could see through Marshall's face to that imagined narrative as it unfolded. In any case, reticence wouldn't be any kind of service. The more people hunting, the better.

Marshall said, 'He told me a guy called D'Anton Lewis got him involved with the betting operation, and that it was run by someone called Frank Cifaretti. The debt was with Cifaretti.'

That obviously warranted a notebook entry. Nevins wrote down the names. He said, 'Who else?'

'That's all he gave me. You look outside, there's probably a napkin and a pen trapped under the table. He was in the process of writing down the details.'

Nevins watched him. 'Keep his mouth free for drinking, huh?'

His pen hovered. The nib made its circular motion, but it didn't land. He closed the notebook, cupped one hand in the other and cracked his knuckles in clean and measured sequence, one-two-three-four as he looked out the window.

He said, 'I'm retiring next week. Last shift's Tuesday.'

Tuesday. The same day as Vialoux's deadline. Marshall let that small parallel go unspoken.

Nevins said, 'I did two years down in Baltimore – CID

homicide. Worked ninety-seven murders total, lead and assist, not once did I work a dead police. Not even once. CID handles cop shootings, but I never caught one. Now I got a dead gold-shield, five days to go.'

He shook his head, and then his eyes came back, and Marshall saw the story wasn't so much a digression as evidence: there was nothing else in the world that he took more seriously than what he was doing right now. He watched Nevins stand up, slide his chair back in.

'Wait there a moment.'

Marshall said, 'I know the family. If you're doing next-of-kin, I'll ride with you.'

Nevins thought about it. 'Wait there.'

'If you're checking up on me, personnel's slow this time of night. Talk to Lee Ashcroft at organized crime.'

Nevins looked at him for a moment, like maybe the name meant something. Maybe he knew what flavor of operation Ashcroft liked to run. But he didn't say anything. He went outside, stood by the table and the broken glass and began dialing on his cell phone. He had it to his ear when the cop called O'Malley interrupted him.

'Detective?'

Nevins put the phone to his lapel.

The cop said, 'We ran the vic's details, dispatch says they had a nine-one-one call from his address just tonight, twenty-two hundred. Wife called it in, said she had a guy at her living-room window – guy in a mask just standing there, waving at her.'

THREE

Nevins told the other detective to stay at the scene and interview the restaurant owner, sign the body release once the M.E. showed up. When he reached his car, Marshall was waiting at the passenger door.

Nevins said, 'Uh-uh. Sorry.'

'I told you I know the family. I'll ride with you.'

'You haven't been cleared. No offense, I've no idea who you are.'

'Yeah, but Hannah Vialoux does. So it's an easy test, isn't it? She'll either vouch for me, or she won't.'

He opened the passenger door, but Nevins cut in again: 'Hey. No.'

Aiming a finger at him across the roof. 'You ride with me, you're going in back. Any problems, you're staying there.'

Marshall didn't argue. He got in the back and Nevins took off, pulling out onto Fourth and gunning it, grill lights flashing. The traffic seemed to unzip as cars ahead swung curbside to let them through, people on the sidewalk turning to watch, low brick buildings whipping past, signage advertising LAUNDROMAT and ROTISSERIE CHICKEN and LAW OFFICE – an exhibit of perfect randomness that Marshall felt only New York City would conspire to arrange.

It was only a three-minute trip up to Fiftieth Street. The whole block was brownstone town houses, all of them near-identical – a short flight of concrete steps and a bay window at each level. The Vialoux place was obvious, though: two NYPD radio cars were double-parked out front.

Nevins pulled up behind them and got out without a word. Marshall was in the center seat, one foot each side of the drive train in an attempt at nominal comfort. He ducked forward to watch Nevins walk up the front steps and knock at the door. It took a certain leg strength to do that: make the ascent with the burden of awful news, year after year after year. He had his badge wallet out, up and ready, but it was a uniformed cop who opened the door, and she let Nevins straight in.

The door closed.

Marshall sat watching the house, shadows visible in the gaps between the drapes. Ten minutes. Twenty. Shadows coming and going, fluid and random, ghost-motion. Ghosts talking about the dead, he figured.

Rain began to fall. Mist at first, and then fat drops that wormed and shivered and crawled on the glass, blurring Marshall's view, a steady hiss like signal-loss as the rain drummed the car roof.

He took out his cell phone and called Harry Rush. It was true what he'd told Nevins. They knew each other from Marshall's cop days, when Rush Law specialized in defending drug dealers. These days he was smaller scale, and used Marshall for repo work and tracking down witnesses. Occasional cash jobs that helped keep Marshall in the black.

The call went to voicemail.

'Harry, it's Marshall. Ray Vialoux's dead. Give me a call.'

Light now from the direction of the house, droplets on the glass turning molten-gold, and he heard muffled voices. Then a shape loomed up darkly in his window, and the door opened, and Nevins leaned down, rain flecks on his glasses.

'She says she knows a Marshall, so we'll see if you're it.'

Marshall slid across the seat and got out. Ahead of him, the brownstone houses and the row of sidewalk plane trees were matched by mirror-house and mirror-tree on the other side of the street, the twinned arrangement extending without variance and without apparent end into the dark. He went up the concrete steps to the Vialoux house, the door open and releasing warm light and the smell of coffee: perversely homely, perversely welcoming in this context.

Inside, the cop he'd seen earlier stood with her chin ducked, listening to a dispatch update from her lapel mic. Another cop of about forty was posed similarly, grim but deferent, and beyond him in profile stood Hannah Vialoux: a figure of concerted but tenuous composure with her jaw clenched and hands pressed together with white intensity, fingertips to chin.

He saw the surprise come into her face as he stepped through the door. Like he was some storied figure, rumored lost or dead, and now returned. Greek odyssey, with a New-York-undercover twist. And then she lost it. Face slackening, mouth drooping, the horrible expression of the recently bereaved, as if flesh itself was being sucked away by misery.

She said, 'Oh, Marsh, Jesus Christ . . .'

She came to him with arms wide, so desperate it was like for a moment he would need to catch her. He held her as she sobbed, her words disappearing into his shoulder and Marshall whispering into her hair, telling her it would be all right: he'd find who did it. He was going to find who did it.

*   *   *

They sat in the kitchen. Marshall and Nevins said no to coffee, but Hannah Vialoux gave it to them anyway. She was bustling on autopilot. Some people were like that, in Marshall's experience. Sheltering in the groove of the mundane.

She'd be nearing forty now, but she hadn't been on the same aging graph as her husband. Hannah's curve was shallower, more graceful. She still had that nice figure, still had her hair color. A few fine lines around her eyes and mouth, but that was nothing. Compared to Ray, it was like she'd been on a regimen of honey baths and yoga while he was off staring into blast furnaces without a mask.

She poured a cup for herself and joined them at the table. 'I knew something was wrong, but he wouldn't tell me. He wouldn't tell me anything.'

Nevins had his notebook and pen out. Marshall watched his little routine, turning pages, looking for clean space. He paused at the last page of notes – still half-blank – and Marshall sensed his thought process: turn to a new page, or make this interview part of the thing at the restaurant, part of the Vialoux saga. In the end, he turned the page, studied Hannah Vialoux, and asked her when she'd last seen her husband.

She slid a phone from her pocket, checked it, put it on the table. 'For God's sake, why can't she just call . . .'

Nevins said, 'Like they told you, there's a unit been sent to collect your daughter. The best thing you can do is just not worry.'

He gave it a couple of seconds and then repeated his question: 'When did you last see your husband?'

Hannah said, 'I don't know, frankly. Two, three days ago. I mean, I *heard* him tonight. He came in, I don't know. Seven thirty? I heard his car, and I heard him thumping around down here.' She blinked carefully, exhaled. 'Seemed to hit . . . honestly, he must've bumped into every wall in the house. I was going to come down, but then I thought it'd just turn into a fight. So, yeah . . . I stayed upstairs, and he went out again, took my car. I don't know whether he meant to or not. Probably grabbed the wrong keys and couldn't be bothered coming back . . .' She looked away. 'I could feel everything sort of ending. I don't mean like this, I don't mean with him dead. I mean he was never here. More often than not he wouldn't even come in at night. At first

. . . you know, I'd lie awake, wanting to hear him come home, but . . .' She smiled thinly. 'You don't get much sleep that way.'

Nevins said, 'Did he tell you where he was?'

'Work. He always said work. He wasn't creative with his excuses.'

'Why. Where do you think he was?'

Hannah just shook her head. She said, 'It's terrible, but I just had this bad feeling for months. That something awful was going to happen. But then you think: well, it's arrived, why didn't you do anything?'

Nevins shook his head, holding her gaze. 'None of this is your fault.'

'I know. I just mean, so often in life, there's a feeling that comes before the thing itself. You know what I mean? But how often do you act on it?'

No one answered.

The seating configuration was wrong. The table was round, and the three of them should have been positioned with equal circumferential spacing. But they weren't. The Nevins–Hannah offset was too small. In a coordinate sense, the positioning was isosceles, as opposed to the infinitely more pleasing equilateral. But there was nothing Marshall could do about it. He'd just have to sit there and accept it was going to be on his mind. He drank some coffee.

Hannah said, 'I'm sorry, I don't know what to tell you. He went out Tuesday morning, I think it was, didn't hear from him at all the last couple days. I mean, other than tonight. And then you showed up.'

Nevins said, 'Did he seem stressed or anxious recently?'

'Well, I don't know . . . like I said, something wasn't right, because I never saw him. But he wouldn't talk to me about it. I remember last week, he finally came in one night – two, three a.m. maybe, and I just said to him, What's going on? And it was literally like talking to a wall. He just rolled over and I was talking to his back. He reeked of booze, I mean he *stank* of it. It was like he was sweating alcohol. But I just said something like, Whatever, or, Suit yourself.' She shook her head. 'Funny when you look back, it really feels like you're telling the universe to do its best, you know?'

Nevins didn't have a response to that. His pen nib touched the paper a few times, as if marking an ellipsis, noting the pause.

Hannah jutted her lower jaw, caught a tear with the tip of her tongue, looked at her phone again. 'Kids, honestly. Always on their phone unless you're trying to reach them yourself . . .' She looked away, as if seeing a thought come together in the middle distance. She said, 'It's terrible, but I know he's done something. This isn't some kind of freak event that might've happened to anyone. He set it in motion somehow. I don't know how and I'm not . . .' She caught another passing tear. 'I'm not saying he deserved it. I'm not saying that. But something was happening.'

Nevins said, 'Tell me again about the man in the mask.'

Hannah blinked, made wide eyes at the ceiling, clearing her vision. 'Do you think he's the man who killed Ray?'

'I'm not sure yet. But I need to find out what happened.'

She shook her head slightly, eyebrows raised. That vacant look people get, as if baffled by the power of hindsight.

'I was in here cleaning up, and I heard this tapping at the window in the front room. Very precise – you know: one-Mississippi, two-Mississippi . . . Maybe, I don't know, five or six times. I went to see what it was, looked out through the drapes, there was just this guy standing by the front steps, looking up at me. He was . . . I already told you he was wearing a mask, but there's a streetlight right there outside our door, and I could see from the shape of it – the shape of the mask – I could tell he was smiling. It's such a bizarre thing to see out your window, I kind of stood there for a second looking down at him. I mean, there was nothing unusual about him other than the mask, if that makes sense. He just stood there looking back, and then he waved at me, like this . . .'

She raised a hand like taking an oath and curled her fingers a couple of times.

'Almost . . . it's strange, but it was almost royal. Completely still, except for his fingers. Anyway, that's when I called nine-one-one. The operator said to lock myself in the bathroom, but I was worried he'd still be there when Ella got home. She's over in Williamsburg at a party, did I tell you that? Anyway, I was on my cell phone, so I stayed at the window with the guy still looking at me, but then I thought he could be just a distraction. You know, keep me at the front window while someone broke in through the kitchen. So I came back here to make sure the door was locked, and then by the time I checked the front window again, he'd gone.'

Nevins said, 'Think back to when you saw him standing outside. Was he tall, short, fat, thin . . .?'

'Shortish I guess, medium weight. He was wearing quite a heavy coat, waist length. Gloves on, too. Couldn't tell his skin color. And he was standing . . . he was standing almost side-on, with his hip forward, almost like a boxer might. So maybe that's something . . . looking for a shortish guy who stands sideways.'

All three of them smiled, trying to coax something out of that little spark.

Nevins said, 'Yeah. That should narrow it down.'

Hannah said, 'Honestly, I don't know what to feel. I mean . . . I'm devastated. But then, it almost felt like this was where he was heading. He wouldn't talk to me, he wouldn't tell me what was wrong. I'd hear him come in, hear the door close, and then the next thing was the stopper coming out of the wine. He was drinking so much he could never seem to remember anything – he couldn't even keep the days square. I was worried . . . I literally thought maybe he was getting Alzheimer's or something, early onset, but I think he was just loaded all the time. Lucky he was into wine and not whiskey, he'd be dead years ago. He's had diabetes the last five years, type one. Childhood-onset diabetes at forty-three. I guess sometimes it just goes that way. It was hard, because Ella's actually had it since she was two, so it seemed . . . well, I don't know. You never know what's going to happen. But it just seemed extra-cruel that they both ended up with it. I'd thought maybe they could help each other, but it never seemed that way. They were kind of on independent tracks, really. But the thing was of course, when Ray was diagnosed, he had to retire from the PD, and I think that really knocked him. I think losing his career was a bigger blow than the condition. Some people . . . they really need a structure and a . . . well. They need a formal purpose for getting up in the morning, and that was his. He was police. He never came out and said it, but you could tell. Even his car, he drove one of those old Fords – a Crown Vic. He was adamant it had to be a Crown Vic. He never said it, but it was obviously part of the connection. He drove the car, he felt like he was still on the job, still on the inside.'

Nevins said, 'Did he ever mention having trouble with anyone?'

'Well, I mean, it was his job, wasn't it? Some people were easier than others, I guess. I don't know.'

'But you weren't aware of anyone threatening him?'

'No, like I say, we just . . . he wouldn't talk to me. It was like . . . well, to be honest, I don't know what it was like.' Her mouth trembled and then steadied. 'He looked like he was in trouble, but he wouldn't talk about it. He just would not talk about it.'

'You aware of any financial trouble he might've had?'

'You mean like loan sharks?'

'Anything like that. Loans, gambling . . .'

She shook her head. 'It's the same answer to every question, really.' She shrugged. 'He wouldn't talk to me. There's not a lot I can tell you.'

'So he didn't mention the type of work he was doing?'

'He wouldn't ever talk cases. It was the same when he was on the P.D., he wouldn't ever talk cases. But I guess, in general, last six or eight months, it was office-based stuff, mainly. Fraud investigations, more and more I.T.-related work.' She laughed. 'God. He used to be . . . setting up a T.V., or downloading photos from a camera, it'd be a three- or four-hour saga.' She stayed in the memory for a moment, smile slowly fading. She said, 'But I think he actually developed an affinity for it. He looked like he knew what he was doing, anyway.'

From the front of the house came the sound of a key scraping in the lock. Hannah rose from her seat. 'Ella, I'm here. Ella.'

Marshall leaned in his chair and saw the girl step in through the front door. She was maybe nineteen or twenty, a younger version of her mother. Superficially, at least. Same hair and height, maybe five-eight, same facial structure, but Ella still had an adolescent smoothness, features not yet sharpened by age. She wore jeans and an oversize hooded sweater, a fat satchel hanging from her shoulder. Rain had plastered her hair tightly around her face. She resembled someone peering out through a dark thicket.

Hannah said, 'I was trying to call you . . .'

The girl looked back through the open door to the police cars at the curb, the cops in the hallway busy listening to their collar mikes and studying the floor.

She said, 'He's dead, isn't he?'

Neutral, like she was unfazed.

Hannah hugged her, and the girl's chin settled on her shoulder.

Hannah said, 'Yes, he's gone. Someone shot him.' Voice shaking. 'He was sitting in a restaurant and someone . . .' Deep breath. 'Someone shot him.'

Ella just stood there, one thumb hooked in the strap of the satchel, face blank and pale, eyes on Marshall now.

She said, 'I remember you. You worked with Dad.'

He smiled. 'I remember you, too.' He wanted to tell her he was sorry, but he knew whatever he said would be inadequate. He didn't trust himself to summon the proper level of condolence, even if it was sincere. Some things you couldn't wrap a phrase around.

She shrugged. 'It was going to happen. Almost like he wanted it.'

'Sweetheart . . .'

Hannah pulling back now, holding her at arm's length.

'It's true. I'm serious.' She stepped away. 'I can't do this now, honestly. I can't do this.' Her voice breaking up.

'Ella . . .'

The girl's feet a leaden trudge on the stairs. Marshall looked at Nevins, saw him scanning back through what he'd written. Or maybe looking at what he *hadn't* written: the information between the lines, things that would get in his head and wake him at three a.m. one day. Marshall got up from the table. His coffee was only partially consumed, and he felt that when he parted ways with it, the mug should be either empty, completely full, or half-full. The challenge was in the fact the mug's horizontal cross-section varied, curving inward at the base, and so the half-capacity mark wasn't evident by inspection. All he could do was leave it empty, or perhaps top it up with coffee from the flask. But that would trigger the obvious corollary problem of identifying the proper flask volume. Better not to get involved. He rinsed the mug and set it on the counter and went through to where Hannah was standing in the hallway, hands tented across her nose and mouth like a breathing mask. She turned to him, blinked carefully a couple of times.

He said, 'I'm more than happy to stay, but I'll get out of your hair if you like. Whatever you want.'

She moved her hands to her hips. 'No, no, you're fine. Thank you for coming. I appreciate it.'

'It's no trouble. It's the least I can do.'

'It's been . . .' She looked at the floor, and then back at him. 'God. I haven't seen you in years. Ray said you were undercover, and then we just . . . It seemed like you disappeared.'

He smiled. 'Yeah, I did, sort of. But I'm glad I put my head up again.'

She nodded, studied him carefully. Concern and maybe even pity in her face, and Marshall wondered what she'd heard that she could spare those emotions for him on a day like today, so cataclysmic for her own life.

She said, 'We umm . . .'

She was looking upstairs, hands back to her mouth. She combed her hair with her fingers. 'I think I just need some time with her. But I don't even know how you talk about this kind of thing. I don't know what to tell her.'

Marshall said, 'Tell her we're going to find who did it. Maybe that's a good way to start.'

As soon as he said it, he knew it was wrong. He couldn't guarantee anything like that. He shouldn't be claiming otherwise. But it sounded better than a promise that he'd do his best. Maybe it was what *he* needed to hear. Hannah just hugged him again, cheek against his chest and rocking slightly, foot-to-foot. He rested his chin on her head, not sure what else to tell her, and when he looked up Nevins was there, looking back.

'Mrs Vialoux, sorry to interrupt. We're going to get an officer to take you down and make the formal identification. Maybe in about an hour, if that's OK.'

Marshall felt her swallow. She stepped away, wiped her eyes with the heel of a hand. 'Yes. Of course.'

'And ma'am, did your husband have an office in the house? Computer or anything I could take a look at . . .'

She told him Ray had a home office in the spare bedroom.

She led Nevins upstairs, saying she'd been through it before out of curiosity, never seen anything that worried her, other than credit card bills. She leaned out from the landing and said, 'Marsh, honestly. You don't need to stay.'

'I'll leave my number. Give me a call if you need anything.'

She nodded, managed to tell him there was a pen and paper down there somewhere, and then she was welling up again. Kindness was different in these situations, he'd found. The share price went way up. He found a pen and a spiral-bound notepad in the side table in the hallway, turned to a clean page and wrote down his name, address, and phone number, centered carefully to ensure equal margins. He used only burner phones, switching to a different number once per month on average. He flipped through the book. Pages of notes that meant nothing. Names and phone numbers and reminders. Plumber Tuesday. Dr Poole Friday. Routine entries, but it was still all private information, and he felt guilty for prying, even if he was in search of murder clues. It felt like a dubious dispensation. He cleared space on the table and left the notebook open to the correct page, and returned the pen to the drawer. It was full of paper detritus he didn't attempt to review. But there was a fat stack of business cards secured with a bulldog clip. He fanned through them. Plumber, gasfitter, glazier, AC technician, accountant, lawyer. Even a private investigator. JORDAN MORA INVESTIGATIONS. No one Marshall had heard of. Maybe a colleague of Ray's. A magnifying glass logo, and phone numbers for landline and cell. An address up in Queens. Marshall slipped the card in his pocket with Nevins' and left the others in the drawer.

The front door was still open, and the uniformed cops had moved outside. Nothing like silence among strangers to force a move. He stood there a moment, listening to Hannah's muffled voice from upstairs, and then he took the cordless phone handset off the hallway wall and went back through to the kitchen.

The REDIAL button brought up the call history in the little backlit window, and there was another button with arrows that let you navigate up and down the list. The system stored the last twenty outgoing calls, apparently. The most frequent number appeared five times. It was almost midnight, but he tried it anyway, dialing the number on his cell.

The woman who picked up sounded elderly: 'Yes, hello? Is that you, Hannah?'

Her mother, Marshall figured.

'I'm very sorry, ma'am. I've dialed the wrong number. Apologies for waking you.'

The woman said goodnight and hung up on him.

Marshall scrolled through the list again. He could hear one of the cops arguing by radio, telling someone that if the President wanted to vacation on Fifth Avenue, he had to accept they didn't have the staff to look after him: they couldn't pull both cars off the Vialoux place.

The next most frequent number showed up four times. Marshall thumbed it in on his cell.

This time a man answered: 'Bagel shop.'

He remembered what Vialoux had said earlier: Frank Cifaretti the mob man, with his bagel shop down in Brighton Beach. He figured Ray had been calling up, trying to renegotiate his debt payments.

Marshall said, 'Is Frank there?'

'He's out of town.'

'When's he back?'

'Who are you, pal?'

Marshall went out into the hallway. He said, 'Tell him Marshall's looking for him.'

He ended the call and pocketed his cell. Then he hung Hannah's phone up quietly on the wall and went outside to wait.

He stood on the sidewalk next to what he guessed was Vialoux's car. The old Crown Vic that Hannah had mentioned. The rain was fine enough it seemed to hang in the air like mist, streetlights haloed and suspended as if by magic in the dark. One of the patrol cars had departed, the final ruling being that only one unit was required for guard duty. He put his collar up against the cold and jammed his hands in his pockets. A block away on his right, the Brooklyn Queens Expressway was stilted above Fourth Avenue like some kind of iron mantis, green and rivet-studded. A minute later, Nevins came down the steps and joined him.

He said, 'You need to be careful with your pronouns.'

Marshall didn't answer, not wanting to be drawn in by a line the guy was obviously pleased with. Probably been working on it the last few minutes while he said his goodbyes.

Nevins said, 'You told her *I'm* going to find who did it, and then you told her *we're* going to find who did it.'

Marshall said, 'Did you remember that, or did you have to write it down?'

Nevins said, 'You're a witness. You're not part of the investigative process. I need to make that distinction clear to you.'

Marshall gave that a second. He said, 'You're not going to be part of the process, either. You've only got until Tuesday. And it'll probably take half a day to clear your desk.'

Nevins turned and looked back up the concrete steps at the house, as if needing a reminder of context. He said, 'I spoke to Lee Ashcroft at organized crime. He and I actually go back. Did some time together at Manhattan North.'

'Good for you.'

'He tells me you were undercover for a long time with the Asaro family.'

'I'm pleased that he's so committed to secrecy. Was he at home, or was he shouting to be heard over bar noise?'

'He says you have a vexing propensity for unilateralism.'

Marshall smiled. 'Glad he's learned to talk and hold his thesaurus at the same time.'

Nevins didn't answer.

Marshall said, 'I can assure you, I don't have any delusions of officialdom.'

Nevins gave a few small nods, keeping his gaze level. He said, 'Great. I just want to make sure you understand you don't have a license to withhold anything from me.'

Marshall said, 'I knew there was some kind of rule like that.'

Nevins shrugged. 'So is there anything you want to tell me?'

'Yeah, actually there is.'

He could see he'd caught Nevins off-guard: just a flicker there in his eye, half a second.

Nevins said, 'Go on, then.'

Marshall said, 'That windowsill's nine feet high. I think the guy stood out here and reached up with the shotgun to tap on the glass, and then waited to see who looked out. That's why he was standing side-on: he wanted the weapon out of sight from the house. If Vialoux had come to the window, the guy would've killed him. As it was, they found him at the restaurant. But then how did they know he was there? We know they weren't lying in wait, because otherwise why come here first? They established he wasn't home, and then left. But then the timing suggests they went *straight* to the restaurant. Which is significant, too. Because they didn't just stumble across him: this is New York City. It's probably ten thousand to one they'd find him, even if they knew he'd stayed in the same neighborhood. So I think in their minds, it was almost binary: you know, he's either here, or he's there – at the restaurant. And they were right. But then why would they know to frame it like that?'

Nevins didn't answer.

Marshall said, 'Because either they'd watched him long enough to establish his restaurant visits as some kind of reliable habit, or someone tipped them off.'

Nevins still didn't have anything to say.

Marshall said, 'Do you need to write any of that down?'

'I don't want the pages getting wet.'

Marshall said nothing.

Nevins said, 'You think the owner was in on it?'

'No, because otherwise Vialoux wouldn't have asked to meet me there. I think more likely, someone went in, handed over a few hundred bucks and a photograph of Vialoux, and said call us if you see him.'

Nevins looked back at the house. 'He told you he had until Tuesday. Is that right?'

'Yeah.'

'So how come it's only Thursday and he's dead?'

'Hannah said he couldn't even keep the days square. Maybe they meant Tuesday just been, not Tuesday coming. Frankly the state he was in, I can imagine that being the case.'

Nevins didn't answer. He dragged a hand down his face. He said, 'What's your interest in this anyway? You said you hadn't seen him in ten years.'

'My interest? Are you kidding?'

Nevins didn't answer.

Marshall said, 'He asked me for help, and then he was shot right in front of me.'

Nevins was still looking at him, maybe sensing there was something else.

Marshall said, 'What else did Lee have to say about me?'

Nevins looked past him to the traffic on the BQE. 'He told me you blew your undercover op when you shot the target of the investigation. He said you took a quarter million dollars cash from the target's wall safe, but the FBI couldn't pin it on you.'

'Yeah. They could never quite make that one stick.'

Nothing.

They looked at each other. The silence of reciprocal analysis.

'He also said if you find these guys first, you'll kill them, and I won't be able to pin it on you.'

'I'm glad he still holds me in such high regard.'

'Is it true?'

Marshall said, 'It's moot. You wouldn't want to pin it on me.'

Looking at Nevins for a tell, but the man was inscrutable: blank and patient, like he could stand there in the rain all night. Marshall thought maybe it was best to come clean, give him the background.

He said, 'There's something else I should mention, too. Before you find out by yourself and get all excited.'

Nevins took off his glasses and cleaned them on his tie and put them back on again. 'All right.'

Marshall nodded at the house. 'Hannah and I had an affair ten years ago.'

Nevins seemed like he might comment, but he just stood there, looking faintly vindicated. Like he'd felt there was something else.

Marshall said, 'I'd rather you did your conspiracy thinking sooner rather than later.'

'The conspiracy being what, exactly?'

'Well. Maybe I had Vialoux shot to get him out of the frame. Maybe by being a witness, I have a better excuse to reconnect with Hannah. Maybe I paid the guy with the stolen cash from my undercover op.'

Nevins let that have a second, and then he said, 'We've cleared up delusions of officialdom, but we need to clear up delusions of using your old undercover contacts to find out who'd murder someone over a debt.'

Marshall shook his head. 'It's far more complicated than that.'

'In what way?'

'Think about it. Why kill someone who owes you money? Makes no sense. Be pretty hard reclaiming anything now, won't it?'

Nevins cleaned his glasses again.

Marshall said, 'I saw him tonight, he looked like a guy who thought his life was ending. So what are the chances that a gambling debt with the mob was his only problem?'

Silence for a moment. Nevins said, 'You need to come in and make a formal statement.'

'No I don't. I've already told you what I know.'

'Have you forgotten how policing works?'

Marshall shook his head. 'I have the opposite problem. I remember too well. I was undercover with the mob for two years, and whenever I sat down in a briefing and said we needed to wrap things up tomorrow because I was going to get a bullet in the head, no one listened. They just sent me back in and said, Don't worry. I ended up having to exercise my vexing propensity for unilateralism.'

Nevins didn't answer.

Marshall said, 'Anyway. Now I like to say things once.'

He turned and walked away toward Fourth Avenue.

FOUR

His place was over in Flatbush, a straight shot east with no direct subway line from Sunset Park. A cab would've been the fastest way home, but his MetroCard was two days from expiry, and for reasons inchoate but nonetheless compelling, he felt the need to maximize its usage during the final forty-eight hours of validity.

He caught an R train all the way up to the Barclay Center, and then came back south on a 2 train toward Flatbush. He had a car to himself, but he stayed on his feet in the aisle, the train going through its normal subway anguish, screaming and clattering through the dark, Marshall swaying hands in pockets and thinking about Ray Vialoux, thinking about Hannah. It had been a strange feeling to hold her again, transported by sensation back through time with perfect clarity. With Nevins there, it had felt as if their history was apparent, as if they'd hugged beneath a bright-red sign reading PAST AFFAIR.

It would've been 2009 when he met her. It was a dinner at Alan Moretti's for some of the task force people. Moretti and his wife, Ray and Hannah Vialoux, a handful of others – whatever their names were. Marshall was there by himself. This had been back in his undercover days, acting out Lee Ashcroft's grand plan as a supposedly dirty cop in Tony Asaro's operation. Lee's plan worked. The mob thought Marshall was their pet lawman. He fed them tip-offs, stolen drug evidence, low-value-but-legit intel files from One Police Plaza. But feigning corruption took a lot of work. For a long time, he'd lived at the cusp of his mental limit, scared he'd be found out, scared someone else would get killed, scared that he was way beyond permissibility, and that he'd end up in prison. It dulled his capacity to question bad ideas, so when he showed up for that dinner in 2009, and became aware that Hannah Vialoux kept looking at him, all he thought was maybe this will lead somewhere.

On a false pretext, he called their house on a night he knew Ray was on a long surveillance shift. He had a story prepared about wanting to pass on a message from a CI, but he didn't even get to it. Hannah told him straight off that Ray wasn't home, and then didn't seem in any hurry to get off the phone. They transitioned from small talk into something awkward and stilted about how evenings alone are hard, and he remembered she'd segued pretty cleanly into asking him where he lived, and then ninety minutes later she was at his door, and ten minutes after that she was in his bed.

She visited him on three more occasions. She told him their marriage was ending, and she was looking for someone else. That confession doused the fantasy pretty quickly for him. He'd been looking for escape. He didn't want to run off with a colleague's wife in the middle of an undercover op. He told Hannah he wanted to draw a line under the arrangement, and then waited for news of her separation.

It never came.

He blew his undercover role, and moved to New Mexico as part of federal witness protection. In 2016 he left the program and moved back to New York, and when Vialoux got in contact, he was half-expecting a confrontation about past indiscretion. If only.

He got off the train at Beverly Road. On the platform, a trio of young guys fell into step alongside, one left and two right, wanting to know if he was in the market for crack cocaine. Marshall said that he wasn't. For a second he toyed with explaining he'd been a subway user for at least as long as they'd been alive, and during that time the NYPD had been consistently proactive and humorless even in regard to lowly turnstile jumpers, so with that in mind, why did they think they had a show trying to push hard drugs? But he didn't bother. He kept walking. He wasn't going to trigger any great Eureka moment. They were down at a level where the luck-currents weren't in their favor. If they didn't take a hit on a drug charge, something else would get them. As he walked through the platform exit, they'd moved on to someone else.

His place was south of Clarendon on a block of two-story town houses. This part of Flatbush had more variation than Vialoux's street over in Sunset Park – some brownstone, some brick, some clapboard. Even granted his fondness for regularity, he still appreciated the mix in architecture. The street didn't just look like barracks for clones. His own house was a clapboard place that he rented from his neighbor, a Russian woman named Vera Boykov.

He let himself in with his key and locked the door again behind him. The added problem now was he didn't know how closely Nevins would look at him. The guy was smart. Leaving aside the fact Marshall's admission was self-implicating, his involvement should have struck Nevins as remote. But *smart* and *thorough* sometimes worked against each other with police. Nevins might be the type of guy who couldn't sleep until he'd run a theory into the dirt. He could picture him in an armchair somewhere: brooding in a darkened room, wondering if a guy like Marshall could seem short if you viewed him from an elevated window.

He turned on the light in the front room. On a table under the window, and presided over by a gooseneck lamp, was a thousand-piece puzzle of Jackson Pollock's abstract expressionist painting, *Convergence*. He'd bought it at a yard sale from a kid over on Thirty-first Street. The kid was nine years old, and a puzzle-enthusiast of evident zeal. He'd explained to Marshall that despite the mid-century appearance of the packaging, this was actually a fortieth-anniversary reissue of a 1964 original, which itself had been a mere 340 pieces. As the kid put it, 'the full 1000' was something of a gold standard in demand and complexity. Marshall was unsure as to the veracity of the historical claims, but he figured that actually completing the thing would take him a while. He gave the kid five bucks for it, on the basis there were no missing pieces, and the kid, somewhat affronted, told him he wasn't in the business of giving out light product.

He switched on the gooseneck lamp and stood there for a moment, reviewing progress. It was always the first thing he did after coming in the door. The jumbled pieces were in such precise and extensive disarray, it was like a change in the house would manifest as a change in the pieces on the desk, under the scrutiny of the light. He'd completed the whitespace at the border of the image, and an inch-thick perimeter of the artwork proper. But this was just base camp. Still a big climb ahead.

In the kitchen he turned on the light, and then almost walked into the black cat that was standing on the floor looking up at him.

Marshall said, 'Whyn't you say anything when I came in?'

He poured a glass of water and stood drinking it at the counter. The cat watched.

Marshall raised the blind and looked out the kitchen window. An alleyway separated his house from Vera's. A light was on in her upstairs office. He took the phone off its wall charger and called her number. He used burners for business, but the house had a landline in Vera's name, and he was happy to use it in situations that didn't incur a security risk.

She said, 'Uh. You know what time it is.'

He figured she was maybe seventy-five. She'd told Marshall she came to America twenty years ago, worried about this ex-KGB guy named Putin attaining power, wanting to get some distance

on him. She'd been in Flatbush since she got here, running a
blog about Russian politics from her spare bedroom. Marshall
would see the light on in there every other night. She'd told him
that's when she wrote. Sometimes too she gave interviews via
Skype to dissident political commentators who published stuff
on YouTube. Occasionally if he went outside he'd hear her, this
faint voice holding forth in Russian, guttural and exuberant.

Marshall said, 'I saw your light on. I just wanted to let you
know Boris is over here.'

'You feed him nothing. Understand?'

'All right.'

'You say all right. But that cat, he look like Giuliani. And it's
not from what I feed him.'

Marshall smiled.

'Yes, I hear you thinking it's funny.'

'Vera, I don't feed him. I promise.'

'And you are up at this hour late for what, precisely? The
time is . . . it is after two a.m.'

Marshall said, 'Just living a strange old night.'

'Mmm. By design that is cryptic, yes?'

'I just wanted to let you know Boris is here.'

'I know where he is.'

'I know you know. I just told you.'

'No. I know prior to admission of the fact.'

'OK.'

She said, 'I and Boris, we visit vetinary. Veterinarian. He inject
Boris with a tracker. I see him right now, on my screen. Boris,
not the vetinary.'

'Very sensible.'

'For pets, yes? But you listen: in world's mind they are the
unimportant lives, but they are the canary for what is next. For
everyone. You know this phrase? Canary in the mine?'

'Yes.'

'OK, yes, good. Pet get ill, euthanize, yes? Wonder where
pet is, inject tracker, yes? These are symptoms of how things
change. Watch: your children will be born, and trackers there
will be for them also. The doctor will do it: weigh him, and then
inject. Bam.'

Marshall said, 'I'll leave you to it.'

'Good. What do they say in the films? No, you hang up.'

The gooseneck lamp was still on in the front room. He sat at the table and studied the layout. From an assembly standpoint, the edges of the painting had the advantage of limited colors – black over tan – whereas the central portion of the art included streaks of yellow, orange, blue and white. The groupings alone were a sufficient challenge. He'd created informal categories of loose reserves – edge pieces and internal pieces – with the internal ones sub-categorized depending on color inclusion. He nudged a few around, marrying colors. On a couple of heady occasions, he thought he saw a lineup. Even on nights where he'd pre-committed to organizing color groups only, he couldn't resist the urge to try pieces on the working edge. All puzzle guys knew the feeling. You chased the rush: the moment when correct shape and correct position meant compatibility, and a given piece went in flush with its neighbor. That was perfection. That's what you showed up at the table for.

Nothing for him tonight, though. He turned out the light.

The cat followed him upstairs, stood in the bedroom doorway and watched as Marshall opened the closet and unlocked his document safe. He took out his Colt 1911 pistol, checked the load, and then carried it with him into the bathroom. The cat kept its distance now, watching, planning something in the depths of its cat head. Marshall showered with the bathroom door open and the gun in arm's reach on the vanity beside the stall, wrapped in a towel for moisture protection. The cat paced the hallway and checked in on him every so often. Maybe it had pegged this as unusual behavior, but it wasn't prejudiced. It waited until Marshall had brushed his teeth and got into bed, and then it jumped onto the mattress and curled up against him.

'Boris. This isn't going to work, pal.'

Nothing.

'If Vera could see this, you'd be in a ton of trouble.'

He remembered the tracker, and thought maybe she could see it. Maybe it reported elevation and velocity. Maybe it could interpret a leap onto furniture.

Then he had another thought.

He held his breath on it, as if trying to pause any mental currents, hold the notion steady for inspection.

He let the breath out slowly and said, 'Huh.'

The cat raised its head and looked at him and then settled back down.

'Don't go moving around in the night, or you're out of here. You got a perfectly good Russian lady next door.'

Silence for a minute, and then it settled into a purr: low and rhythmic, almost a crackle. Marshall lay in the dark listening to it – rain with a bass note of cat – thinking about the past and the dead, what to do about everything.

FIVE

Marshall only slept for three hours. Five thirty and he was awake again, something in his blood. It was still raining. Up on Clarendon, the traffic was sparse, cars slow and black-windowed and hissing along through the groundwater. He knew he should take the subway – he could feel the heat from the MetroCard in his pocket – but he felt that efficiency was the governing concern right now.

He crossed Clarendon and waved down a westbound cab. The driver was off-shift, and gave him an off-meter fare: fifteen bucks across town to Sunset Park. The guy let him out on Fourth Avenue, under the BQE, and Marshall walked down to Fiftieth and stood at the corner. The Vialoux place was halfway along the block. An NYPD cruiser was still parked out front, tight in behind Ray's car.

Marshall checked his watch. The graveyard shift ran until seven fifty. He had eighty minutes to kill, unless this guy planned to clock out early, factor in the drive and paperwork delays.

He walked south on Fourth until he found a coffee shop. He liked the way coffee was heading in New York. It used to be that if you wanted something elaborate, they'd give you a splash of cream, or a container of half-and-half on the side. As far as Marshall could tell, that had been the zenith of fancy. Now you could get a cappuccino just about anywhere, and every so often he'd find a place that did a kind of Antipodean take on it

– something called a flat white, which Marshall approved of greatly. This place on Fourth didn't know about flat whites yet, but the cappuccino they made him was pretty good.

The neighborhood was well awake now, stores open and the traffic getting heavy. No one paid him any notice. In an alley off Forty-third he found a mound of empty cardboard boxes, kicked through them until he found an offcut of plastic strapping. A good specimen: three-and-a-half feet. He stuffed it in his pocket and headed back up to Fiftieth.

At seven twenty-five, the cop car finally started up and pulled away toward Fifth Avenue. Clocking off early, but he probably figured if the last eight hours had been uneventful, the next twenty minutes would be similar. Marshall left his cup in a trash can and walked over to where Vialoux's Crown Vic was parked curbside, dropped to a push-up position so he could see beneath the chassis. Nothing out of place. He checked the wheel wells in turn. Clear. Nothing under the front or rear fender. He took the length of plastic strapping from his pocket and halved it, went around to the driver's side and passed the fold in the strap in between the window frame and the door pillar. He fed in another six inches off one of the tailing lengths, and the inserted portion separated to form a loop. He eased the loop down over the lock button on the top edge of the door, pulled the loop closed, and yanked upward. The button popped up, and Marshall opened the door and got into the car.

He smelled booze immediately, and he wondered if it was the product of a single spill, or just gradual buildup: months or years of maintenance pops. In any case, the culprit was in the glove compartment: Southern Comfort, a few inches remaining. Not just a wine man, after all. He placed the bottle on the seat while he sorted through detritus. Insurance documents, mechanics' invoices and work summaries, a handful of receipts. Liquor, liquor, liquor. Appliances Connection. Maimonides Medical Center Parking. He wondered if Ray had been ill. He didn't look himself last night. Then again, Marshall hadn't seen him for probably a decade. Thin and frazzled might've been the new normal.

He checked the door pockets, leaned across to check beneath the passenger seat. A Snickers wrapper and an empty bottle of

Southern Comfort. When he sat back upright, Hannah Vialoux was standing at his window.

When he was a cop, he used to marvel at these guys who didn't recognize the stupidity of a given action until after the fact. Even then, a lot of the time they weren't putting it together. And now here he was.

They looked at each other for a moment. Then Marshall cracked his door. He didn't know what to say, so he went with, 'Good morning.'

Hannah said, 'I have a key, you know.'

'Sorry. I wanted to look for something, I thought I could just be in and out without disturbing you.'

'Something.'

He didn't answer.

She said, 'Come inside. Make sure you lock it after you.'

The entry hall smelled like toast and coffee. She went into the kitchen, but Marshall stayed by the door, unsure of himself, feeling like an idiot.

She said, 'You're lucky I saw you actually get in, and didn't just glimpse you in the car. I might've had a heart attack. Or did you factor that into your risk assessment?'

He didn't have anything for that straightaway. She emerged from the kitchen with a pot of coffee in one hand and two empty mugs in the other, eyebrows raised as if in mild curiosity. The overall effect was to reiterate his blunder, feigned breeziness drilling the message right to his bone marrow. He checked the time. Seven forty-two. Not a brilliant start to the day.

She nodded past his shoulder. 'We'll go in the living room.'

He moved in ahead of her and sat down on a sofa, making an effort not to go straight to the window. It had a pull for some reason: the place she'd seen the gunman.

This had been Ray Vialoux's living room, but it didn't feel like it, somehow – even if the photographs in the glass case and on the mantelpiece were of him, his family. Too soft, too intimate, too personal. Mismatched furniture in mismatched colors – heirloom pieces, Marshall thought, retained out of filial duty. An old tea wagon with a pink china tea set, a dark landscape painting, visibly textured with oil, a heavy faux-gilt frame. A busy feature wall of photographs: Ray and Hannah and Ella through the years. He tried to picture Ray in here, maybe in that armchair in the corner: a skewed window-shape of sunshine on the floor, Ray with the *Times*, up and open. He couldn't make it fit. He thought about the Hannah Vialoux he knew in 2010, and he couldn't make that fit, either. A woman who'd told him her marriage had run its course shouldn't have a living room like this, a shrine to the happy life. He thought maybe it was all a prop. A diorama for how things should be.

Hannah put everything down on a low table in front of him, poured herself a mug of coffee. 'Help yourself.'

She took a chair opposite, the table between them, and mirrored his pose: leaning forward, elbows to knees. He had the sense that every pause, every silence had this special quality to it, energized somehow. The charge of common history. The question was whether to acknowledge it or not.

The burner phone in his pocket buzzed. That would be Harry Rush, calling him back. Marshall ignored it. He said, 'Look, I know that was dumb. I thought you might be still asleep, and I didn't want to wake you for the sake of a theory that was wrong anyway.'

She gave a small shake of the head, kept her eyes on him. 'I didn't sleep.'

A patter of feet on the stairs, descending. Hannah said, 'Ella, I'm just in here. Marshall's back.'

He poured himself some coffee, parsed the line carefully, those last two words: Marshall's back. Good thing, or bad thing?

He said, 'I kept thinking about the timing last night. They were here, waving at you through the window, and then they were at the restaurant. So somehow they knew where Ray would be if he wasn't home. I told Nevins they might've been tipped off, or been watching him long enough to establish some kind of routine, if he'd been going there regularly. But then I realized there was an easier option. They could've been tracking your cars.'

He sipped some coffee, not wanting to drown her in dark maybes, but she was sitting quietly, waiting for the rest of it.

Marshall said, 'He took your car to the restaurant. Assuming they were tracking the vehicles, it made sense that they came here first. And then it would just be a case of, if it's not this car, it's the other one.'

His phone was buzzing again.

Hannah said, 'I'll give you a minute.'

'No, don't worry.'

But she was already walking out.

Marshall answered the phone.

Harry Rush said, 'I got your message. Police have been calling me, too. I'm going in this afternoon to make a statement.'

'I'm with Hannah right now.'

'She doing OK?'

'I don't know. You checked out those names for me?'

'Not yet. I wrote them down, though. D'Anton Lewis and Frank Cifaretti.'

'I guess that's a start.'

'You think they hit him?'

'I don't know. I'm trying to square up the basics before I talk to them.'

'Right. Did you have a package delivered? From eBay?'

'Maybe. What is it?'

Quieter now, Harry talking offline: 'Marlene, what was that package that came?'

A pause, and then Harry came back, full volume. 'A jigsaw puzzle of a Jackson Pollock painting.'

Marshall said, 'Is it *Autumn Rhythm*? Otherwise it's not mine.'

Harry said, 'You know, maybe you could get stuff sent to your own place? Or, no, tell you what: I'm going to open it, take out a random piece – just one. Call it a handling fee.'

'I'll drop by later.'

Harry hung up.

Marshall sat listening to voices through the wall, muffled but tense, a staccato rhythm, back-and-forth. Footsteps in the entry hall, and Hannah's voice said, 'Just keep in mind that *I'm* not the problem.'

Then she was back in the living room. She sat down across from Marshall again and said, 'I had the same theory. That they were tracking the cars, I mean.'

She placed a small black rectangular object on the coffee table.

Two inches to a side, maybe half an inch deep. Slender LED windows labeled GPS and POWER. An on-off button and another labeled SOS.

She said, 'You're the expert, but that to me looks like a tracking device. Don't you think?'

SIX

M arshall picked it up. Some kind of sending unit, definitely. The technology had moved on since his day. Improved slenderness, and improved longevity he guessed. This was more compact than the stuff he was used to. You could just about swallow it with water if you needed to.

He said, 'Where was it?'

'In his car, the glove compartment.' She shrugged. 'I told you I couldn't sleep. I found that at about four a.m. Nevins said he was going to look at Ray's office first and then come back for the car, and, you know, just made me think: what's so interesting about the car?' She smiled faintly. 'That might be a start, anyway.'

He held it flat on his palm for inspection. It was edged thinly with rubber. Maybe for shock absorption, or maybe so people thought they were buying something Pentagon-approved.

Hannah said, 'I turned the power off. I thought they might assume the battery died.'

'Who knows about it?'

She shrugged. 'Me, you, whoever put it there.'

'What about the cop on scene guard?'

'All he knows is I got in Ray's car last night and then got out again.' Her mouth downturned, innocent. 'Maybe I was getting a phone charger.'

Marshall opened his coat and dropped the device in a pocket. 'Can I hold on to this?'

'It's already in your pocket.'

He didn't answer. He leaned back in his chair, and for a moment when he looked down, he could see the material of his shirt bouncing minutely, a tiny amplitude in time with his heartbeat.

He realized too he could hear it in his ears: the thud of growing anger. He took a breath and released it gently, let himself grow still and quiet and calm, and in the absence of other things there remained the certainty and the clarity about what he was going to do.

He said, 'If they were tracking both vehicles, there'll be a device in your car, too. The police probably have it by now, and they're going to wonder why there isn't one in Ray's car when they search it.'

Hannah said, 'Do you still want it?'

Marshall nodded. 'Yes. I just want you to keep in mind they'll be asking about it.'

'It might not be an issue. They might assume Ray found it and got rid of it. But why do they need both, anyway? They can have one, and you can have the other.' Looking at him carefully. 'See who gets answers first.'

Marshall didn't answer.

Hannah said, 'I was so relieved when you showed up. Last night, I mean. Police will do their job, say "thoughts and prayers" and that kind of thing, but you're the only one who *needs* to know what happened. I mean . . . you're the only one who wasn't paid to show up.' She shook her head, took a moment putting something together in her head. She said, 'It wasn't debts. Why would he be killed over a debt? You can't pay when you're . . . you know. He's not going to be paying anyone now, is he?'

He didn't want to answer that, no point taking her deeper into the gloom.

He said, 'Was he having any health trouble?'

'He was drinking a lot. Other than that, I don't know. I think if he did have anything, the bullet would've cured it.'

He wasn't sure whether to smile or not.

She shut her eyes, shook her head briefly. 'I didn't mean it like that. Why do you ask?'

'He had a parking receipt from Maimonides Hospital.'

'Oh, right. Yeah. I know what that was. A friend of Ella's – Jennifer Boyne. It was terrible. She committed suicide. Her parents asked Ray to look into it. I think they were worried there'd been some encouragement. Bullying, maybe. In the end, he didn't find anything. It was just one of those awful tragedies.

No note or anything. It was . . . well, it was funny actually. It was like they saw a different side of him. Her parents, I mean. He wouldn't take any money because they knew Ella, and they thought he was just the sweetest, most generous guy. All these different sides to him, you know? One of them's got all the others in trouble.'

Marshall let that one slide past him. He found that was the thing with encouragement. You had to hang back, really go in hard when you saw an opening.

He said, 'I know Nevins asked you this last night, but can you remember any specifics about what else Ray was working on?'

'Well, like I said, it was mainly office-based stuff, I think. Fraud and auditing. But . . . I remember six, seven months ago I guess it was, he was hired by a gallery owner. Sounded like a vaguely interesting one. Upper East Side. Something like . . . I can't quite remember the details. I think there were two owners, and one guy was worried the other was using sales to launder drug money.'

'And was he?'

'I don't know. Like I say, Ray wouldn't talk shop with me. But I'd hear him on the phone now and again, and put things together. The other one I can remember – you know that company Plethora? Online shopping?'

'I've heard of it. Like Amazon, right?'

'Sort of, yeah. One of their executives, his wife hired Ray to find out if he was cheating on her. He was worth like two billion dollars or something, and I think Ray was following him for a while, taking photos.' She smiled. 'I think he actually got some good ones in the end. Ray had a guy helping him with it. Ex-cop. Jordan . . . Mora, I think?'

As in Jordan Mora Investigations. The business card he'd taken from the side table last night.

Marshall said, 'I'll see if I can call him. He might have some more details.'

'Right, sure. Ray probably has his number somewhere . . .'

The phone in the hallway rang, and she went through to answer it.

He heard her say, 'Vialoux,' and then, 'Oh, yes. Good morning.'

Stilted, a bit too formal. The kind of thing you'd say when a

police detective calls to talk about your dead husband. Marshall
didn't want to sit there, feeling like an eavesdropper. He got up
and went through to the kitchen. Ella was still in there, at the
table. She had a vial of something colorless raised to the light,
a hypodermic syringe inserted in its base. That's right: diabetes.
Hannah had mentioned it last night.

He said, 'Sorry. I'll leave you to it.'

She caught him mid-turn as he was going out the door: 'Don't
worry. Medicine, not drugs.'

He thought he'd handled things quite well, coming in and
then heading straight out again, giving her privacy, but now
her reply had trapped him. He couldn't walk off and leave her
hanging. But small talk had never been Marshall's forte, and
there was more at stake now: he didn't know what avenues of
conversation were open, given the context. Murder shuts things
down. The part of his brain in charge of interactions was
telling him to say something, but the speech department wasn't
giving him anything usable. It was all inane and awkward.

He was still standing there, not saying anything.

She looked at him.

Marshall said, 'You and your dad both had it, huh?'

That wasn't too bad. But it had been easier talking with Nevins
last night, trading clipped lines with no feelings at stake. Too
much to navigate, here.

She said, 'Yeah. Awesome coincidence.'

Behind him in the entry hall, he heard Hannah wrapping up
her call.

Ella kept her attention on her task, flicking the syringe to
encourage bubbles back up into the vial, and now Marshall
had something. He knew he should've opened with this line,
gone in strong and simple: He said, 'I just wanted to let you
know, your dad was a friend of mine, and I'm going to do my
absolute best to find out what happened.'

Nothing.

He said, 'If you want to talk sometime, or if you need anything,
you're welcome to give me a call. Your mother has my number.'

She removed the syringe from the base of the vial, touched
the plunger to bring a pearl of fluid to the tip of the needle.

Still not looking at him.

She said, 'Well, that makes me feel a million times better. I'll keep that in mind.'

From behind him: 'Ella, that's so rude. Apologize, please.'

Marshall stepped out and headed for the front door. 'No, don't worry. Forget it.'

'Ella, for God's sake. He's trying to help.'

Marshall said, 'Hannah, honestly, it's fine. I was just on the way out . . .'

'Her attitude, I'm serious. Last thing I need . . .'

She came past him raking her hands through her hair, biting her lip, appearing in every sense to be right at the limit. She opened the front door and stood outside on the top step. Marshall gave it a moment before he joined her. He scanned the street. The scene was basically unchanged. A few cars had been replaced, but they were all clear-windowed and vacant.

She said quietly. 'They burned his office.'

'What? When?'

She shook her head, eyes shut. 'Last night. That was Nevins on the phone. Someone burned his office. Ray's office. They poured gasoline over everything and burned it. Even the file cabinets. He said they opened the cabinets and poured gasoline on his files. There's nothing left. He said it's . . . they burned everything.'

'What time was this?'

'He said around half-past ten. They must have . . .' She bit her lip, looked at the sky. 'They must've shot him and then gone to his office. It's just up in Park Slope. It's a street-front unit. He said they just broke the glass and went in.' She shook her head. 'All he had, it was just a desk and a computer and some papers. It's like . . . was it not enough that he's dead? Have to destroy his office, too . . .'

She raked her hands through her hair again, face distorting with the strain. She whispered, 'Why would they do that?'

He had a theory, something along the lines of what he'd told Nevins last night, that Vialoux had more problems than just a gambling debt.

He said, 'Battery life on those trackers probably isn't long. Maybe a week, something like that.'

Hannah said, 'Five days on that model, on average. I googled it.

Depends how much the car's moving. I think when it's stationary they go dormant, essentially.'

'So if it still had power when you found it, it must have been placed recently, maybe only a few days ago.'

'But it was just in the glove compartment.'

'Right. So you need to think carefully about where the cars have been during the past week, and we might be able to work out who had access to them.'

She didn't answer.

Marshall said, 'Two options. The device was either planted by someone who broke in, or someone who was a passenger.'

'A passenger? What, you think we *know* them?'

'Ray definitely did. He knew who put the contract out, anyway. So we need to know who he's given rides to.'

'Well, I've no idea. He used my car all the time.'

'We can still try to narrow it down. Depending what days he used your car.'

She said, 'Is it a crime, giving it to you? The tracker?'

He thought about that. At the very least, he was in a legal gray area. He said, 'The only thing I'm worried about is who shot Ray. If that's your position, too, I think we're good to go. I'll hold on to it for a day, talk to some people. If I don't get anywhere, I'll give everything to Nevins.'

This far in, he was pretty sure that was the truth. That was his honest intention right now, anyway.

He said, 'Don't go out today. Keep the doors locked. If anything looks off, call the police.'

'You think they're still watching?'

Marshall didn't answer that. He said, 'We'll find out what's going on.'

He'd told her that a few times now, maybe not in those words, and the look she gave him as she stepped inside seemed to reinforce the fact. Like getting answers needed to be a case of when and not if. He waited for the sound of the bolt sliding home, and then he turned and walked away.

SEVEN

He was tempted to head up to Park Slope and look at Vialoux's office, except it was more than likely still an active crime scene. And that meant it was more than likely he wouldn't be able to take a quiet tour. Better to do something away from scrutiny.

He'd covered the western leg of the block on the walk in – Fourth Avenue to the Vialoux house – so Marshall crossed the street and turned left, eastbound. The curb space had opened up since he arrived. Every third or fourth parking spot was available. He checked cars as he walked, looking for signs of prolonged occupation, a red-eye surveillance shift. He was thinking of the photos Vialoux received, the photos of Ella and Hannah: most likely taken from a moving vehicle, but potentially shot from a static position. Nothing obvious caught his eye. No backseat mounds of fast-food containers. No gallon bottles of urine.

He paused for a moment and scanned houses. They were all basically homogenous. The front courtyards were the only real source of variance. A few of them held a kid's bicycle, or a miniature swing set. A guy riding a mobility scooter came past, a Kurdish flag flying from a pole on the rear tray. A minute later, a woman with a Labrador went by on the opposite sidewalk. The dog had a plastic bag of shit tied to its collar, but seemed happy enough with the arrangement.

Marshall resumed walking, noticed a guy in a window across the street, watching him. He had a beard, and a T-shirt printed with #DAD. A small pink bicycle with silver tassels on the handlebars was chained to his front fence. Marshall threw him a wave, more out of risk-mitigation than friendliness, not wanting his photo being sent to Crime Stoppers.

He made it to the end of the block without seeing anything that made his heart skip a beat. An old timer in a newsboy cap was having a smoke on his front steps. He took his cigarette from his mouth and raised it an inch in greeting and returned it

to his mouth. Marshall dipped his chin by a corresponding incre-
ment and turned around and headed back west. The guy with the
#DAD shirt hadn't moved. Still there at his window, still looking
at him.

Marshall paused for a second, decided it might be best to
square this up before it turned into a problem. He gave the guy
a big smile, all the wattage he could muster in the cold and under
the circumstances, and then he crossed the street, and walked
up to his front door. The guy had it open before he got there,
just a three-inch gap. He looked out at Marshall above the curve
of the security chain.

'Hey there. Can I help you?'

Marshall said, 'Sorry, I didn't mean to cause any concern.
You may have seen some police cars on the street last night?'

'Oh, you're with the police?' Thawing out already.

'Ex-police, actually. I'm a friend of one of the residents.' He
offered Nevins' card through the gap. 'Feel free to call Floyd. I
didn't mean to cause any alarm.'

That seemed to hit all the right notes. The guy slid the chain
off and opened the door. 'Oh, no, no, no. That's fine. I'm Bruce
Linney, by the way.'

'Marshall Grade.'

'Sure, hi. Yeah, I just wondered what you were doing. Come
in. Was it Hannah's place? I saw something happening.'

'Yeah. She had a guy outside her front window last night.'

'Oh, God. Doing what?'

He wasn't sure how to euphemize it, but a kid's voice from
the front room saved him: 'Daddydaddydaddy!'

The guy's brow knitted for a second, pained tolerance. 'Here,
sorry, come in.'

Marshall followed him into the living room off the entry hall.
He saw a two-year-old in a high chair, eating toast. Peanut butter
was smeared amply on all surfaces within the kid's reach. A
TV was showing a discussion panel on ESPN, and there were
approximately one thousand pieces of Lego on the floor. By the
window, a little girl maybe eight years old was peeping out over
the sill into the courtyard. In the kitchen, a boy of maybe ten
was sitting at a table, a workbook open before him, expression
vacant and aimed at the TV in the living room.

Bruce Linney tore a wet wipe from a pack on a chair arm and started attending to peanut butter. 'Oh, dude. This is a situation. Baxter, I want to see you crushing that homework, not watching the TV. OK?'

Marshall navigated through Legos to the window. The little girl didn't move. Marshall said, 'These cars parked out here, are there any you don't recognize? Or any that might've showed up in the last week, and haven't moved?'

'Uh . . .' He was still in clean-up mode. 'Well, I mean, this is New York. Cars everywhere, so I couldn't really say. What happened, anyway?'

Marshall said, 'Just a prowler.'

'And sorry, you're a friend of Hannah's, is that right?'

'Yeah. I worked NYPD with her husband.'

The little girl said, 'The cars are all the same.'

She tipped her head back to see Marshall standing behind her. He liked how little kids could do that: strike an unusual pose but do it poker-faced and earnest.

Marshall said, 'That's good to know. What about people? Have you seen anyone you don't recognize?'

'Just you.'

Bruce Linney said, 'Sweetheart, come away from the window and get ready, please.'

'But I'm watching my bike.'

'The bike is fine. The bike is chained to the fence. No one is going to take the bike.'

Marshall said, 'Yeah. It looks pretty safe to me.'

The girl put her chin on the sill, stared at the bicycle. 'You should check the Facebook page.'

Marshall said, 'Oh yeah? What's the Facebook page?'

The kid at the table obviously thought this was all pretty interesting. He said, 'There's like a Facebook page and people post stuff about if there's something weird. Like, on the block.'

'Dad, show him the Facebook page.'

'Yeah, Dad, show him the Facebook page.'

'Guys, guys, guys. Everyone please be task-focused.'

Marshall waited.

The girl tipped her head back again to see him, and then resumed her bike-watch. The kid in the kitchen watched ESPN.

Bruce Linney gave up on the peanut butter and took a smartphone from his pocket.

He said, 'All right,' and then sighed, like this was one of those days where he'd need to tackle one thing at a time. 'Facebook page.'

He moved his finger on the screen, scrolling. 'Man, makes you realize people are nosey. A lot of stuff on here . . . uh. Couple of people noticed a guy going door to door. Said he was realtor, apparently.'

The girl said, 'Dad, that was likc a month ago. You have to swipe *down* so it loads the new stuff.'

'Sweetheart, you can just speak nicely, please.'

'Well, you do.'

Marshall waited.

Bruce Linney scrolled on, in a daughter-approved manner. He said, 'The only other mention . . . someone called . . . someone called Sandra, I'm not sure where she is—'

The girl said, 'She's that place,' and pointed: a place across the street, five doors east.

'Oh, right. Anyway, Sandra says . . . Man, there's so much baking group stuff here. Honestly.'

Marshall waited.

Bruce Linney said, 'Sandra posted saying she saw a guy coming and going from Lydia's – shortish guy, dark hair, blue coveralls. But then actually . . . someone else on the thread, Mrs Lopez—'

'She's nice!'

'Yeah, she's nice.'

'Guys, excuse me. Please don't cross-dialog.'

Bruce Linney did some more finger-scrolling. He said, 'There's a post here from Mrs Lopez saying that she spoke to the guy, and he told her they're Lydia's nephews.' He looked up from the phone. 'Is that helpful? What happened anyway? Is everyone safe?'

Marshall didn't answer, seeing in his mind the figure with the gun outside the restaurant. A small guy, light and compact. And then Hannah's description of the man outside her window. She'd used that same word. Shortish.

Marshall said, 'Nephews. With an S?'

'Uh . . .' Looking at the phone again. 'Yeah.'

'So how many people did she see?'

'Well, I mean, I don't know. There's nothing else on the thread. There's just the mention of the one guy, but Esther – Mrs Lopez – definitely said nephews, plural. Might've been a typo, I guess.'

Marshall said, 'Which house is Lydia's?'

'Is everything OK?'

'I hope so. Like I said, Hannah had a guy . . .' He pivoted slightly, midsentence, not wanting to get too heavy in front of the kids. 'Hannah noticed a man outside her house last night.'

The girl said, 'What was he doing?'

'Shh, sweetie.'

Marshall said, 'Which house is Lydia's?'

'Uh . . . Lydia, Lydia . . .'

The girl said, 'She's next to Jeanie. She's right next to Jeanie.'

'Yeah, that's right. Ah . . .' He came to the window and pointed. 'That's Jeanie there, so that must be Lydia, to the right of her.'

Marshall said, 'Appreciate your help.'

'Do you need me to come over?'

'No, don't worry. I'll let you know.'

Bruce Linney walked him to the door and saw him off with a handshake and a worried look. When Marshall crossed the street and glanced back, there were three faces at the window, watching him: Linney, and the two kids chin-to-sill.

He walked over to the house they'd identified as Lydia's, went up the front steps and stood listening. Nothing. The drapes had been pulled across the windows. The glass showed a faint sweat of condensation. Marshall knocked at the door.

Another moment's silence, and then he heard a cat: a meow, very faint, and then silence.

Marshall knocked again. The cat answered once more, weak and plaintive.

It took a few seconds, but then the details combined, and the adrenaline hit him: the chemical jolt of a bad feeling.

The cat, the moisture on the glass.

Maybe nothing. Maybe a very bleak picture.

He went back down the steps and stood on the sidewalk, scanning windows, knowing he had to go into this calm. He looked to his right, westward toward Fourth, and on the north side of the street, sixty yards away, he could see the Vialoux place. An oblique vantage, but the entry was visible, and the front windows, and Ray's car sitting there at the curb.

He went up Lydia's steps again and tried the handle: thumb and first finger in a pincer grip, minimizing contact area, not wanting to disrupt prints if there were any.

Locked.

They wouldn't make it that easy. He knocked one last time, wanting to be wrong, wanting a harmless reality to intervene with his suspicions.

Silence. Then the cat meowed again.

Marshall glanced behind him, across the street, and saw the Linneys still watching him. He took a long pace back, stood on the edge of the top step and balanced on the balls of his feet, boot heels hanging off the tread. He bounced there for a moment, getting some tension in his legs, pictured the masked face of the man with the gun. He superimposed the little asshole on the door handle, and then lunged forward with a kick, heel-first. A big man, a Doc Marten, a lot of practice: the door smashed open and bounced off its stop and swung back, almost closed.

Marshall shouldered in.

He was ready for the smell: putrid, cloying, unmistakable. He zipped his coat and ducked his nose inside the collar. The cat was upstairs, meowing frantically now. Marshall knew the men would be long gone, but training and habit made him clear the ground floor first. Deserted. He went upstairs, following the stench.

The old woman – Lydia, he presumed – was in the bedroom, on the bed. Marshall guessed she'd been dead three or four days. The cat was a gray tabby, and it was up there beside her, keeping guard, mewing.

Marshall clicked his fingers gently, beckoning, and then picked it up carefully under one arm.

'Here you go. It's all right.'

It squirmed in his grip, looked at the woman on the bed. Her wrists and ankles were bound behind her with duct tape. More tape covered her mouth. It had been looped several times around her lower skull for surety of muteness. A plastic drinking straw protruded from the tape at the corner of her mouth, the stem carefully lapped into the wrappings. The straw was in six pieces, tape-spliced to form a single tube leading to a bucket beside the bed. The bucket was empty. She was long since out of water. She looked to be at least seventy-five, very frail. Taped up like that with her wrists behind her, she'd have never had the strength to make it off the bed. Her eyes were wide, as if surprised at the sudden push that sent her over the edge. Marshall tried to put himself behind those eyes, and he knew he couldn't. He looked around, and he just couldn't.

He stroked the cat, trying to quiet it. 'It's all right. We'll find you new friends. We'll find you some nice people.'

The cat settled down a little, but it was still tense and twitchy under his arm. They went and looked in the bathroom. A shower stall and a toilet and a vanity. A strong mold smell, but it was better than the smell in the rest of the house. The bed in the guestroom was just a bare mattress. Marshall went downstairs and did another circuit of the ground floor. The living room appeared as if untouched for twenty or thirty years, not two or three days. Lime-green wallpaper and faded pink furniture. The walls were covered with photographs and embroidered art, everything protected by dusty glass. The photos all featured Lydia, and a man Marshall assumed was her husband – dead too, he guessed. Earlier checkout, nicer circumstances.

The embroidered pieces were all six-by-six-inch panels. Ducks and dogs and fruit bowls, in the pixel-language of coarse thread. There was a larger piece, maybe twelve-by-twelve, unfinished on the sofa. A tiger coming together quite nicely. That one detail anchored Marshall in place for a moment. Sometimes it was like that. He remembered from his police days, seeing corpses, murder victims, and feeling almost unaffected, in a way. Like the horror was abstract. Then gradually he'd see the details, all those little pieces that go into building up a life, and he'd know what had happened, what had been taken from the world.

The cat meowed.

'It's all right. We're just figuring out what happened.'

He moved to the bay window. The dew on the glass was decomp gas, slowly condensing on the cold surface. Marshall crouched, and the cat mewed again with the descent. There were indentations in the carpet, three of them, a triangular arrangement, not quite equilateral. Scalene in a strict sense, and lacking symmetry. He figured they'd had a tripod set up here, a camera aimed along the street at the Vialoux house. He couldn't help wonder how people could operate like that. Configure a thing and then leave it, all the while knowing it wasn't perfect.

He found nothing in the kitchen that looked useful. Nothing that looked like it might yield DNA. No used dishes or cutlery. He expected the crime scene people would spend a day or two scouring the place, and arrive at the conclusion he'd already made: these guys were pros.

As he went out, he closed the front door as best he could. The odor was an element of the crime scene. He knew the forensic techs wouldn't thank him for airing the place out. He went down the front steps, and a voice said, 'Are you another nephew, or are you someone else?'

Marshall glanced toward the noise – leftward, the adjoining house – saw a woman in her seventies standing at the top step beside her open front door. Short, heavy build, and a bit of authority in the way she held the balustrade: a wide, firm grip, like riding a Harley. He figured this was Esther Lopez.

Marshall said, 'I'm someone else.'

'Is Lydia all right?' She had her hair in a bun, so taut it looked like you'd get a tune if you strummed it.

Marshall said, 'What did her nephews look like?'

'Excuse me? Who are you? What are you doing with Maurice?'

He wondered if she'd been like this with the ersatz-nephews. More indignation with more haste might have changed something.

'He's fine, Esther. He came and saw me earlier. Friend of Hannah's – the Vialouxs.'

Marshall turned and saw Bruce Linney in the middle of the street.

Esther Lopez said, 'Yes, but what is he doing in Lydia's house? Look at the door. My Lord.'

Bruce Linney said, 'Is she OK?'

Marshall said, 'What did her nephews look like?'

'Why, what's happened? You haven't said what's happened?'

She looked over at Linney: a strange one-man tableau, hands on hips in the traffic lane. The worried face at odds with the warm wholesomeness of his silly T-shirt: #DAD.

Mrs Lopez stood there for a couple of seconds, just looking at him. Then she seemed to get it, and her hands went to her face, and her eyebrows went up. 'Oh my God. Oh my . . .'

Marshall said, 'What did they look like? Just relax, it's OK. Tell me what they looked like.'

She shook her head, as if desperately sorting through memories. 'There was a . . .' She held the rail with one hand and kept the other to her mouth. 'He was such a polite man. Small, much smaller than you. Very tidy—'

'What about his face. What did he look like? Hair, eyes.'

'Black hair – black hair combed back. Always smiling, very polite. So polite. I just didn't think . . . what have they done? I thought they were her nephews. He was just . . . he smiled at me the whole time.'

'How many were there?'

'I'm . . . what?'

'You said nephews. How many men were there?'

'I . . . I only spoke to one. I only saw one man. But he said they were her nephews. I thought . . . it was more than just him. There was another man.'

'When was this? When did you see him?'

'Uh . . . Weds – no: three days ago. He said they were just leaving. He said they'd helped with some things around the house and now they were leaving.'

Marshall figured that was probably true. He wouldn't want to be seen there again, having told her he was finished. But three days ago was at least forty-eight hours before Vialoux was killed. Marshall wondered why they'd bailed early on the surveillance.

Esther Lopez said, 'Please tell me what's happened?'

He couldn't keep putting it off. Everyone knew. They were just waiting for him to say it. He said, 'She's dead. I'm sorry.'

Esther Lopez' expression turned completely tranquil. Then she sat down on her top step and put her hands over her mouth. She didn't say anything. She sat there shaking her head, breathing carefully into her fingers. Bruce Linney was still in the middle of the street, hands on his hips, like a background artist in a stage play.

Marshall said, 'Sorry, I can't hang around. Can I give you the cat? He'll need some water.'

Bruce Linney glanced around, as if surprised for a moment to occupy his own body and not another. 'Of course, yeah. It's the least . . . yeah. Pass him here.'

As he walked toward his house, he kept looking back at Lydia's, as if gauging distances, working out the safety margin between his own happy sphere and whatever had happened on the opposite side of the street.

The children met them at the door. Bruce Linney went in first with the cat, and Marshall followed uninvited.

The girl said, 'Does she not want him anymore?'

Marshall found Nevins' card on the sofa arm beside the wet wipes. It had picked up some peanut-butter smears, but it was still legible. He stood in the kitchen, listening to the kids talking to the cat, working up a list of names: they didn't like Maurice. Strange to be here in the midst of a family scene because someone was dead. What a tradeoff. He used the Linneys' landline to call Nevins and tell him what he'd found.

EIGHT

I n addition to caffeine, the coffee shop on Fourth offered a limited food menu. Marshall went back and ate some of their fried eggs on ciabatta toast and drank a cup of their specialty brew. Black this time, no frothy dairy additives. He took a stool at the bench along the front window where he could watch the street and the door at the same time. It occurred to him that surveillance of the Vialoux place could be ongoing, in which case there was every chance he was on someone's radar. But everyone looked like a natural and benign element of the scene. No dark-windowed cars lurking, no one shady hanging out in doorways. He watched a trio of patrol cars head uptown on Fourth with lights flashing, off to see dead Lydia, presumably. Ten minutes after that, a morgue van. Marshall drank more coffee. He was there an hour before Nevins came in and sat down beside him at the window bench.

Marshall said, 'You working double shifts, making the most of your last few days?'

Nevins said, 'When you were a cop, did you like it when witnesses just wandered off, or did you generally prefer that they stay around the crime scene?'

'I told you where I'd be.'

'Yeah. Very courteous.' He brought out his notebook. Marshall could imagine him in a couple years' time, post-retirement: still writing things down, still feeling that connection to the life.

Nevins said, 'What?'

'Nothing.'

Nevins asked him what had happened, and Marshall ran through his morning. Meeting the Linneys, and then finding Lydia.

He said, 'I heard they torched Ray's office.'

'Let's stay with this for a moment. Why were you out here?'

Marshall said, 'Looking for surveillance.'

'What made you think there may have been surveillance?'

'I don't know. Because I thought there might've been.'

Nevins looked at him.

Marshall looked back. He shrugged. 'Why did I think of the thing that made me think of the thing that I chose to do? The antecedents are infinite. You'll need another notebook.'

Nevins still had room on the current page, but he turned to a new one anyway.

Marshall said, 'The neighbor, Mrs Lopez. She spoke to one of them.'

He told Nevins about the friendly-nephews ruse. He watched Nevins write SMILEY, and underline it. He said, 'You know anyone like that?'

'Grinning hitmen? No. What about you?'

He was drawing a box now around SMILEY, pretended not to hear. 'What did you touch?'

Marshall said, 'The front door, and the cat.'

'That's it?'

'That's it.'

'You didn't touch the vic?'

'I didn't touch the vic.'

He watched Nevins write. On the far sidewalk, a couple of homeless guys were playing chess, cross-legged on the pavement, the board set up between them.

Marshall said, 'Did you know there're more possible games of chess than there are particles in the universe?'

Nevins said, 'More ways for people to be cruel to one another than there are particles in the universe. I'll have to take your word for it about the chess.'

'You been through the house?'

'Briefly. I had to come looking for you, of course.'

'It isn't going anywhere. You see the marks by the window?'

'Yeah. They must've had a tripod or something.'

'So what do you think he was into?'

'Sorry?'

'These guys killed a woman, used her house for surveillance, shot Vialoux in a restaurant, and then burned his office. They didn't go to all that trouble because of a gambling debt.'

Nevins didn't answer. Then he said, 'I was her, I'd prefer they killed me when they walked in the door, rather than take the chance someone would find me in time.' He shook his head. 'What a way to go.'

Marshall said, 'These guys aren't squeamish, though. They could've killed her sooner, but they didn't. So what's that tell you?'

Nevins didn't answer. He was leaning forward now on folded arms. The window bench was too low for the posture: the hunch looked too extreme, as if adopted out of physical necessity, the demands of marrow-deep fatigue.

Marshall said, 'Getting rid of bodies is hard. Would've been difficult getting her out of the house in one piece, and then they'd have to take the body somewhere. Really, they'd want power tools, or an acid bath. But there's no tub in the house, you notice that? And the neighbors would've heard a power saw. I think they knew they'd be there three, four, five days, didn't want to be living with a body slowly turning ripe.' He shrugged. 'Better to do it like they did, tape her up, put her on a slow fuse, wait until they were out the door before she died.'

Nevins was good at listening to theories without giving anything away. Nothing in his face to say if he agreed, or if he was holding his finger on the delete button.

Marshall said, 'The bed in the spare room had been stripped. I think maybe they were sleeping shifts, obviously needed to take the sheets with them. For evidence.'

Nevins didn't answer.

Marshall said, 'What did the office look like?'

Nevins shrugged. 'Soaked and charred. Lucky FDNY got there when they did, could've lost the adjacent units, too.'

'Hannah said they burned his files.'

Nevins nodded. 'They broke the front window to get in. Alarm went off, obviously. The cabinets were all crowbarred.'

'So it's like I said. There's more to it than just a debt. Destroying files is pretty telling. There's a big difference between, say, throwing a Molotov through a window, and breaking in to then light a fire.'

'In what sense.'

'In the sense that a Molotov could be plausibly dismissed as vandalism. But the forced entry implies something deliberate and targeted.'

'So if there's more to it than a debt, why didn't he tell you about it? If like you say, the whole point of meeting you was to ask for help?'

Marshall didn't have an answer to that just yet. He said, 'Did you run those names I gave you?'

'Which names?'

'Frank Cifaretti. D'Anton Lewis.'

Nevins shook his head. 'I can't discuss it.'

'Yes, you can. We're two guys sitting in a coffee shop. No one would know what you've said and what you haven't said.'

'*You* would know what I said. That's the whole problem.' He looked over. 'And you were wrong about the car, too. If they dumped it, it's not anywhere around Thirty-ninth Street, or the railyard.'

'What happened to you can't discuss it?'

'I can't discuss confidential information. There's nothing confidential about which cars happen to be parked on Thirty-ninth Street.'

Marshall let that one go. They sat there for a minute or so, looking out the window, cars and people going by: a scene that despite its disparate elements was pleasing to Marshall in its

balanced randomness. By virtue of pure fluke, for every direction of movement there occurred a counter-movement in
counter-direction.

Nevins said, 'You got anything else potentially useful you
might want to part with?'

'Anything else? Didn't realize my theories had any merit.
That's real encouraging.'

Nevins' head made a slow pass above his forearms, elbow to
elbow and then back, in apparent examination.

Marshall said, 'I'm the one who's made the break so far. So
do you have anything you want to tell me?'

'It's not really how it works.'

Marshall said, 'If you hadn't run the names yet, you could've
just said so. There's nothing confidential about that. So if you can't
talk about it, you must have come across something interesting.'

Nevins said, 'I thought I was speaking English. I said I can't
talk about it.'

Marshall said, 'All very well playing it New York Confidential
while you have a badge. But this time next week we're on the
same team. You might need to be a bit more collaborative if you
want to solve anything. I never met this D'Anton Lewis character,
but I ran into Frank Cifaretti while I was undercover. I wouldn't
describe him as particularly law-abiding. And he's obviously a
person of interest now. So if you can't give me a clear answer
about whether or not you've talked to him, I'm happy to go see
him myself. And this D'Anton guy, whoever he is.'

Nevins was back to looking out the window. He said, 'Here's
a radical idea. Why don't you leave me to do my job?'

'I could do. But we're making good progress with the current
arrangement.'

Marshall stood up and slid his stool in under the bench.
The stool was circular, and care needed to be taken. To his eye,
perfect placement was the point at which the stool, when viewed
from directly above, was fully concealed by the bench, with the
bench-edge forming a tangent to the stool-edge. A precise align-
ment, pleasing to achieve, a small but nonetheless satisfying
victory on a day of bad events. He trapped cash under his mug
and walked out.

*   *   *

Heading uptown on Fourth, he dug out the card he'd found for Jordan Mora Investigations, and used his burner to call the landline and cell numbers. No answer on either. The cell had been disconnected, and the landline went to voicemail. No greeting, just the beep. Marshall left a message saying he'd try to see him in person, and then took the subway up through Manhattan and east into Queens.

The address on Mora's card led him to a six-story brick building over in Jackson Heights. The ground floor had a drycleaner's, and an optometrist's that appeared to be using promotional material from about 1987. Mora was in unit 501, according to the card. Marshall didn't get an answer when he tried the intercom by the street door. He hit buttons for random units, and on the fourth try someone buzzed him in. He took the stairs up, and knocked at 501. The door opened two inches, and a lady in her seventies looked out at him with one eye.

'You the man who left the message? For Mr Mora?'

'That's right. Is he in?'

The woman shook her head. 'Hasn't been in for two years. Which is how long I been here. I never even met him.'

'Do you know where he moved to?'

'No.' She smiled. The eye looked him up and down. 'I get all these calls, people leave messages saying their wife's cheating, can I help, all this sort of thing. At first I thought, maybe I'll get a new number, but then I thought, you know: actually kind of entertaining. Hear all these predicaments. Get ones you'd never think of in a million years.'

'I bet.'

'You think you have troubles, but then these people call up, leave a message proves you dead wrong. Anyway. You see the super downstairs, maybe he can help. I got something on the stove, sorry.'

He found the super's apartment on the first floor. A handwritten notice reading NO SE PERROS was taped to the door. A guy in his sixties answered Marshall's knock. Tortoiseshell glasses, short-sleeve buttoned shirt tucked into belted trousers ironed razor-sharp: he looked like he'd emerged from a 1972 sales conference in Des Moines.

'Yes?'

'I'm looking for Jordan Mora. Used to be in five-oh-one.'

He was shaking his head halfway through the sentence. 'Jordan moved.'

'Do you have a number for him? Or a forwarding address or anything?'

The guy smiled.

Marshall said, 'What?'

'Wait here.'

He left the door half-open. Somewhere in the room beyond, a TV was playing a sports game. Baseball, maybe. The sound of the commentary oddly jubilant in the dull, dim corridor with its Spanish dog-ban. No se perros.

The guy came back and handed Marshall a Post-it note with a handwritten phone number.

'Good luck.'

The door closed in his face.

Marshall walked along the hallway and stood looking out at the street while he dialed the number on his burner.

Three rings, and then a woman's voice said, 'Hello?'

Marshall told her he was trying to reach Jordan Mora.

'Yes. Speaking.'

The mental gender-swap took him a second. He said, 'Are you able to meet in person? I'm a friend of Ray Vialoux's.'

Quiet for a beat. Maybe she'd heard something in his tone, or maybe she had some additional context. She said, 'What's happened?'

'I'm sorry, I didn't want to do this on the phone. Ray's dead. He was shot last night.'

Silence for a few seconds. Then she said quietly, 'I don't think I got your name.'

'Marshall Grade. I was a colleague of Ray's at NYPD.'

'Where are you now?'

'In your old building. The super gave me your number.'

She said, 'I work at the Junior High up the block. I'll meet you on the corner of Eightieth and Thirty-fifth in twenty minutes.'

He got there early. Not exactly a vibrant scene on a cold morning. Brick apartment buildings in all directions, tan and brutal and studded with AC units, sidewalk trees leafless and skeletal coming into winter. A 114th precinct car slowed as it came abreast of him, the two cops up front giving him a good long stare before driving on.

Jordan Mora showed up after exactly twenty minutes. She was in her late thirties probably, shortish and trim, looking pretty stylish by most Junior High standards, Marshall figured. Jeans and a knit sweater and a tan coat that were all pretty flattering to his eye. He'd imagined some approximate replica of Ray Vialoux. Mid-fifties, male, ex-homicide, running on nicotine and statins and warfarin.

A few people were standing at the corner waiting to cross, but she picked out Marshall with no trouble, walked up to him and said he looked like an ex-cop. Marshall smiled at that and shook the hand she'd extended. Obviously her preconceptions had been more useful than his own.

She said, 'I heard all about you. You worked with Vialoux at Manhattan North, right? With Jeff Lewis?'

Testing him.

Marshall shook his head. 'No, Brooklyn South. With Alan Moretti and Angela Luciano in those days.'

She made no reaction to that. She stood looking at him, hands in her coat pockets, a leather bag slung on one shoulder. She said, 'What happened?'

'We were at a restaurant last night, someone shot him through the window.'

She took that in with a deep breath and then looked away, cupped one hand to her mouth, as if trying to keep her re-action contained. He saw her eyes fill, but she blinked it away. Breathed carefully through her lower teeth.

'Do they know who or a why, yet?'

Marshall said, 'Still working on it.'

Jordan Mora looked back the way she'd come, wind laying her hair across her face. She said, 'I think we better sit down.'

NINE

S he hadn't moved far. She had an apartment on Thirty-fifth Street, in a brick building more or less identical to the one Marshall had just visited. It was only half a block away, visible from the corner with Eightieth. He felt awkward, walking along next to her in silence, but he didn't want to come on too heavy with the Vialoux stuff. He asked if she was still a P.I.

It took her a moment to respond, probably trying to drag her thoughts out of murder. 'No. In fact, I never was, technically. My husband had the license. We ran the business together. He was CID with the state police, up in Massachusetts. Drugs detective. He got out early, we moved down here eight years ago. I actually started out as a cop, too. Plan was we were going to work together . . .'

The story went on hold while she sorted through her keys and let them into her building. She led the way through the lobby and then up the stairs, telling him that they'd named the business after her, Jordan Mora Investigations, because it sounded better than Henry Mora Investigations. Better ring to it, somehow. She had an accent he couldn't quite place: flattish, maybe a slight drawl, neutralized somewhat by New York exposure. He asked how long she'd known Vialoux.

'Since we moved down from Boston. So, seven or eight years, I guess. I met him through Henry. We're separated now, actually. We closed the business, but there're obviously a few cards still floating around. Sorry, it's a climb . . .'

Her apartment was on level four. It was a small space, but Marshall liked the style. The floor had been stripped back to the original wood, and one wall in the living room was exposed brick. Scorch marks and cracks and daubs of paint all over it. He wasn't sure if it was genuine wear and tear, or the result of that trend to make things look distressed. These days, half the places he bought coffee seemed decorated to imply imminent collapse.

A boy of maybe twelve or thirteen was seated at the kitchen table with a pad of paper and a couple of textbooks. Jordan took off her coat and hung it on the chair beside him. 'Any progress?'

'Yeah. Sort of.'

Jordan went to the TV in the corner and slid her hand behind it. 'Nice try. It's still warm.' She nodded at a door. 'Hang out in your room for a minute. I have a meeting.'

The kid slumped, jutted his head forward with a slack face. 'Can't I just sit here?'

'No, I don't want to argue. Put your music on, treat it as a math holiday. Go on.'

'Jeez, honestly . . .' But he managed to drag himself away from the table. His bedroom door closed firmer than was strictly necessary.

Jordan said, 'Music, please.'

Nothing for a moment. Then a stereo began playing. Jimi Hendrix, 'Voodoo Chile'.

'He told me he needed a day off school. I don't think home-work was in the plan, somehow. Have a seat.'

They sat facing each other at the table, errant pages of algebra between them. Jordan tamped them together and slid them aside with the textbooks.

'So you saw it. You were with him.'

'Yeah. I was with him . . .'

He hadn't been sure how much to tell her, but it didn't feel right, holding back. So far, the burden of trust was on her. She sat watching him as she listened, pensive and a little deflated now as she took in the details of his story. The shooting, the man at Hannah's window the same night. The surveillance house with the old woman dead upstairs.

'Oh, God. This was today?'

'Yeah. Couple hours ago.'

He told her about Mrs Lopez' description of the little guy with the smile.

Jordan shook her head, looked away. 'A mob-run betting ring.' Putting weight behind each word, like trying to drag it out of its own absurdity. 'What the hell was he thinking?'

'Did he ever mention to you that he was in trouble?'

She hesitated. Her eyes cut across to him, and he saw with sudden clarity what he was doing.

'Look, sorry . . .' He took Nevins' business card from his pocket, slid it toward her. 'I didn't mean to come in here and grill you. That's the guy looking into it, Floyd Nevins. Give him a call if you like. I've spoken with him a few times.'

'No, don't worry . . .' Faint smile. 'You don't seem too crazy.'

She slid the card back across the table. 'I hadn't actually seen Ray for . . . well. Probably a year, I guess.'

That made him pause. He said, 'Hannah was under the impression you were still working cases with him.'

She shook her head. 'No. It's been at least a year. I wouldn't have had the time, anyway. The school job's a full-time role. I'm on their admin team.'

He wondered if Hannah had simply been mistaken, or if Vialoux had seen a need for a small mistruth. Claiming he was out on cases while he was doing something else. Through the wall, Jimi was still going. He'd moved on to 'All Along the Watchtower'.

Jordan said, 'They wouldn't kill him over a debt. They'd want him alive so he can pay. Surely.'

'That's what I thought, too. But he's definitely dead.'

He regretted that as soon as he said it, and Jordan didn't seem to know where to go from there. She stood up from the table and took a lighter and a pack of cigarettes out of a drawer in the kitchen. She offered him the pack, one tan filter protruding.

'No thanks.'

'I'm trying to quit. I'm down to one every twenty-four hours. I think I'm allowed two today, though. All things considered . . .'

She went to the kitchen window and lifted the sash a few inches, sat on the sill as she lit up. The building was in a U-shape, built around a rear courtyard. He could see a metal swing set and a slide down there.

'You said you met Ray through your husband?'

'That's right.' She seemed to hesitate, and then she said, 'They were in AA together.'

Obviously Ray had fallen off the wagon pretty hard.

She said, 'Ray was one of those people, he always seemed to be walking uphill. Drinking problem, and I think maybe a *purpose* problem, eventually. I think he loved police work so much, and then, you know: going through paperwork on insurance fraud cases wasn't really the same. Didn't really cut it.'

'Hannah said something similar. How many cases did you work with him?'

'Not many. Five? Six? Henry worked with him quite a bit over the years. I think they just liked hanging out. You know . . . stake out some guy cheating on his wife, pretend they're on a murder case or something.'

'What sort of work did you do with him?'

'This and that. Fraud, surveillance. To be honest, when Henry and I split, I was going to close everything down. Like I say, he was the one with the license, so I couldn't really keep it going above-board. But then I didn't have anything permanent at the time – other work, I mean – so Ray said I could do some cases with him. But it just got to the point, it wasn't worth it.'

'Why not?'

She shook her head, tapped ash out the gap in the window. He could see why cigarettes used to sell so well. Make a commercial with someone who looked like Jordan Mora smoking, people would buy them by the crate.

She said, 'There was some funny thing with Hannah. I think . . . well, I'm not actually sure. Ray said he was worried about telling her he was working with me. I don't really know what the situation was, but, yeah. For whatever reason, he was pretending Henry was still on the scene.'

He took a second with that, looking out the window, down at the courtyard. 'She definitely told me you're a Mr Mora.'

'Right, well there you go. There was some kind of odd dynamic. At first I kind of thought, whatever: not my problem. But then I had other work coming in, I was part-time at the school, I could do without anything complicated.' She shrugged. 'I stopped taking on jobs with him.'

'So you don't know what he had on the books recently?'

She shook her head. 'Sorry.'

'Hannah said he didn't like talking shop at home—'

'Yeah, that sounds like Ray—'

'But she said he'd been hired by an art dealer or something? You hear anything about that?'

She nodded. 'Yeah. I did, actually. He said it was two brothers who owned the place, and one thought the other was using the business to tidy up cartel money. I think he said he got about a week into it, and then the guy's daughter called and told him her father was delusional, more or less. Apparently he'd been reading a book about drug money, started seeing laundering schemes everywhere. Kind of thing that can happen I suppose, when you're old. Guy was about eighty-five, I think.'

'Something to look forward to.'

'Yeah.'

'The only other one Hannah remembered from recently was a divorce job. Some billionaire executive. Plethora, I think she said.'

'Oh, OK. That one was horrible. I helped Ray out with it. Don Madden, the guy's name was. His wife was the client. She thought Madden was having an affair, and I think Madden had said he didn't even know the woman involved. That's what he'd apparently told the wife. Ray and I followed him around for ten days, and got a bunch of photos of him and this woman he'd supposedly never met.'

'Nice.'

'Yeah. Good initially. Happy client. Well, vindicated client. Problem was, Madden then went and hanged himself.' She looked away. 'So that was . . . yeah. Sometimes they're a lot harder than they should be. I still think about him. But that was . . . it must've been three or four years, I guess.' She shook her head. 'Not sure why she'd think it was recent. Same with the art dealer job. It'd be eighteen months ago that he mentioned it.'

Marshall considered that, but he didn't answer. He looked out the window. The swings were swaying gently in the breeze, as if ghost kids were playing on them. Man, he was thinking about ghosts all the time. He watched a blackbird descend in jagged frenzy on the crossbar of the swing frame. It ruffled for a second and then stood motionless in silhouette, as if ink-stamped on thin air.

He said, 'You ever know him to hang out with mob guys?'

'Mob guys . . . I'm not sure. He was always around . . . well, *characters*. Just the nature of the work, he'd deal with people who owed something, or wanted something, or said they witnessed something.' She shook her head. 'So often you see them, you think: what angle are you playing? You know. Pretty obvious there's some kind of calculation going on . . .' She shrugged. 'But yeah. Possibly he knew mob guys. But I couldn't tell you any in particular.'

'Frank Cifaretti? You ever hear that name?'

She shook her head. 'Don't think so.'

'What about D'Anton Lewis?'

She nodded slowly. 'Yeah, D'Anton. I've met him. Why?'

'Ray said it was D'Anton who got him into this gambling scene.'

'That'd be right. Ray's done a few jobs for him.'

'And how did you meet him?'

'I went with Ray for a prelim on a job D'Anton wanted. Twenty-seventeen, I think it was. Good money, but in the end I thought I'd keep my distance. I remember Ray saying D'Anton had made money in commodities, but he might've had something extra on side.'

'Illegal.'

'Yeah. I asked him what he'd meant, all he said was he thought D'Anton might be a businessman.' Raising her fingers to make inverted commas. The cigarette left a smoke-trace of the motion. 'I told him if the guy's that dubious, you shouldn't take on the work. I'm not sure whether he did or not.' She shrugged. 'Might've just not told me. You remember that investment banker who got arrested on sex trafficking? Couple years ago, now?'

'I read about it at the time. Jerry Erskine.'

She nodded. 'That's right. Anyway, D'Anton bought his house. Over in Manhattan, Upper East Side.' She came over to the table, faint perfume and smoke coming with her. She took her phone from her coat pocket and went back to the windowsill while she typed. 'Yeah, here you go. East Seventy-third Street. Nice old place.'

She turned the screen so he could see it. A street-shot of a three-story white town house.

She said, 'Looks like you'd need to be in commodities or trafficking to afford it, anyway.' She put the phone beside her on the sill. 'It was funny, these guys – Ray and Henry, I mean – they liked to think they were still police, still part of the law, which in theory put them on a different team from D'Anton. But guys like that . . .' She thought about it for a second. 'I don't know. People seem to get in their orbit, can't help but do a few loops.'

That was a good way to put it. Marshall said, 'I was undercover with the mob for a while. I know the feeling.'

It was out of his mouth before he'd even really thought about it.

Jordan's eyebrows went up, mid-drag on the cigarette. 'Oh, really? Here in New York?'

Marshall nodded. 'They had me with the Asaro family for a while. All those guys, yeah, like you say: they were just a bug light for people who liked power.' He heard the implication of the line and said, 'Even decent guys, you know. There's a certain temptation to see what things look like on the other side of the wall.'

She nodded, still looking at him as she drew on her cigarette. He could tell he'd piqued her interest with the UC mention. He thought she was going to ask him something else, but in the end she looked away.

Marshall said, 'You were a cop, too?'

She nodded. 'Police in New Zealand. Took a year out when I was twenty-four, came here on a Green Card thinking it was going to be a short-term thing. But then I met Henry.'

'It's not all sheep and hobbits, then?'

'No. They definitely need cops. What do you do now? You a P.I., too?'

He shook his head. 'No, I went cold turkey.'

'So this is all unofficial, then?'

He almost told her something about how he was here because of his friendship with Vialoux, and that had nothing to do with what was official or unofficial. But he said, 'I just want to find out what happened.'

The music went quiet for a second, and then Eric Clapton started playing 'Layla'. The boy had good taste in music.

Marshall said, 'Do you know if your husband was still in touch with Ray at all?'

'I don't know. He lives in Cleveland now, so I can't imagine they've seen each other for a while. You ever watched that show *Capische*? About the gangster?'

'No.'

'The woman who wrote it, she brought in Henry as a consultant. And . . . well. They got on just terrific, put it that way.'

That little smile again. He liked it. As if she was in on how the world worked, and it didn't bother her too much.

She said, 'He moved to Ohio to be with her. That'd be three years ago, now.'

The music volume spiked as the kid's bedroom door opened. Clapton tearing into that famous riff before the chorus. He said, 'You're not meant to be smoking.'

'Yeah, I know. This can be tomorrow's one.'

An interesting exchange, Marshall thought. Like they'd swapped roles for a moment. Filial parentage.

The boy said, 'Is the meeting still going?'

Marshall stood up from the table. He said to Jordan, 'Thanks for your help. Sorry to show up with such bad news.'

'No, not at all . . .' For a second it sounded like the news wasn't bad, not that she didn't blame him. She sent more cigarette ash out into the breeze, watched it disappear. 'Nice to meet one of Ray's fabled colleagues. Marshall, this is Jake.'

They shook hands. The kid had a teenage awkwardness that had him touching his hair and studying the floor a lot. But he looked Marshall in the eye and summoned up a decent grip. Then Jordan was on her feet and showing him to the door. Marshall followed in that nice blended scent of perfume with a smoky edge, watching her legs move in the jeans, and he had the sudden feeling that in a moment he would be gone, and he was running out of time. And now here he was out in the hallway, and all she had to do was close the door on him.

But she hadn't. She was standing there, still holding it open, looking at him pleasantly, as if waiting for him to get to something. Except Marshall had a dilemma. If he was going to go for it, he wanted to keep it simple and direct, ask her straight up if she was interested in a drink sometime. But trying the line out in his mind, it didn't fit the situation. He didn't know how to go from dead Vialoux to asking her out. Maybe he was better to leave it, and just call her sometime. Or maybe he was over-thinking it.

In the end, Jordan gave up on waiting for him. She said, 'I

don't know if I can get time off at short notice, but I have some days owing. If you need a side-kick, I might be free for a while.'

His tongue and his brain got things figured out between them. 'Yeah, great. That'd be great. Let me know.'

'He was a good guy, in his own way. A really good guy, actually. Anything I can do, let me know. Do you have a card or . . .?'

He smiled. 'No. I don't have anything. I have a burner phone with about twenty minutes left on it.'

She smiled back, relaxed, looking him in the eye. 'All right. You call me, then.'

'Yeah. I'll call you.'

Good: he'd got there eventually. He could hear Eric Clapton coming through faint – *Lay-la!* – and he couldn't help but stand there enjoying the anticipation, thinking maybe as soon as tomorrow he was going to see her again.

She still hadn't closed the door. 'Don't go looking for hitmen on your own.'

'No. I thought I'd talk to this guy D'Anton first.'

'He might be just as dangerous, in his own way. I'm serious. Take care, Marshall.'

TEN

He headed down to the subway station at 82nd. He liked this part of town, the tracks up on girders above the street, everything hemmed in and vibrant, the old brick storefronts all wanting him to buy something. It had a casino feel, like walking down an aisle of two-story slot machines, except the bright lights said T-Mobile and Starbucks and Citibank, and every so often a train would come smashing down the line on the bridge above the street, and for ten seconds straight, that was all you could hear. He remembered this part of town fifteen years ago, before the corporate branding and the neon started to proliferate, and the drug trade was a more dominant aspect of the economy. He'd been out here a few times with Vialoux when they worked together, following up a lead, Vialoux living at some kind of peak, or at the very least on a longish plateau of competence and certainty. Marshall could picture him with that steady and relaxed manner he always had, amused and skeptical. Like he knew that the world was built on deceit and subterfuge, but with patience he would get a chance to look behind the curtain. And then at some point, he lost his way. Marshall wondered how it happened. He remembered that Hemingway line about going bankrupt: gradually, and then all at once. Maybe Vialoux just woke up one morning and realized it was over.

He caught an F train over to Manhattan. A guy standing in the aisle was freestyle rapping the whole way, forty minutes without seeming to take a breath, throwing in hand flicks and shoulder dips like a boxer working a heavy bag. His face was dripping sweat and the floor around him was pretty damp too by the time Marshall got off at Fifty-seventh, just south of the park.

Rain was pounding down, gray as nails. He made it up to Fifty-ninth and took shelter in the little Strand Books kiosk. A crowd of protestors, maybe a hundred or so, had gathered outside the Trump building and were spilling into the east lane of Fifth Avenue. Police officers were putting out barricades, trying to divert traffic, the whole scene this crazy street disco with car horns blaring and placards in the crowd going up and down at random in the gray rain. Marshall had never been a close follower of politics. He always felt like he lived in a stratum that was essentially unaffected by who was in charge. He'd grown up in Gary, Indiana with a mother who made ends meet with drug sales. Then he came to New York and worked in an organized crime unit before going undercover for NYPD. As far as he could tell, a left or right twitch of the political dial didn't affect the uphill gradient of the day-to-day. But it was different now. There was a burgeoning sense of civic breakdown. It felt like in another six months, it might all come down on his head. He watched a guy wearing some kind of Halloween mask climb on the roof of a parked cab and then shout something through a bullhorn. Too hard to comprehend him. All Marshall heard was shout-echo, harsh and digital, an electronic crackle at the edge, like some government broadcast in a future dystopia.

He watched for another minute, and then as the rain eased

he headed uptown on Fifth, the air cold and park-scented. D'Anton Lewis's place on East Seventy-third Street was on the block adjoining Fifth Avenue, right across from Central Park. Prime real estate. Marshall imagined he'd need ten or fifteen million bucks to move up here and live in something larger than a mailbox. D'Anton's place was French Renaissance style, he was pretty sure. White stone façade, little wrought-iron Juliet balconies on the upper-level windows, a wooden front door like something from a medieval castle, big enough to admit horses. The door was set back a few feet in a little alcove, and on one alcove wall were the initials DL, in brass letters. D'Anton Lewis. Recessed in the stonework nearby was an intercom panel with a miniature video screen. Marshall tried the TALK button and waited.

Nothing. The screen stayed black.

He tried again, and then thumped on the door. Still no answer. He waited with his back against the alcove wall by the DL monogram. The house was probably two hundred years old. The stone step had cupped slightly through the center, worn down by use. He wondered what sort of foot-count was required to do that. He gave it another ten minutes, and then popped his collar up and walked back along the block to the corner with Fifth Avenue. The rain was strengthening again. He sat on the edge of a low concrete wall, and waited. Fourteen minutes past twelve in the afternoon.

Nothing happened for over an hour. The rain kept falling. A light drizzle, persistent enough to soak his hair and collar. He watched tour buses go by on Fifth Avenue, passengers on the top deck shrink-wrapped in their soaking rain slickers. At 1:25, a black Lincoln Navigator SUV turned in off Madison Avenue onto Seventy-third and double-parked outside D'Anton's. A guy got out of the passenger seat and opened the curbside rear door and stood waiting.

Marshall got to his feet and headed back along the block, not dawdling, but trying not to look too purposeful. He saw two guys step out of the alcove and take up positions on the sidewalk, back-to-back but with six feet between them, one guy facing east toward Madison, and the other guy looking this way, west, toward Marshall. Big guys in their mid-forties, tall and heavy under knee-length dark coats, the kind of stern vigilance that comes natural to ex-police.

Marshall kept walking. They didn't seem to have clocked him as anything other than a regular pedestrian. A westbound truck had pulled up now, blocked behind the SUV. The driver blew his horn, and the east-facing guy on the sidewalk gave him the finger: blasé, a good long dose with the hand raised.

Marshall was thirty feet away when a young woman maybe twenty years old exited the house and crossed the sidewalk toward the waiting car. She pivoted neatly and backed into her seat as she collapsed the umbrella she carried – not an easy move in high heels and a tight skirt, Marshall imagined – and then a third man stepped out of the alcove. He was black, maybe fifty, tall and brisk of step, expensively dressed in a fitted coat and gleaming loafers.

Marshall said, 'D'Anton.'

The guy paused in the middle of the sidewalk and seemed to consider him.

Marshall said, 'I need to talk to you about Ray Vialoux.'

The guy stood there another second, and then he resumed walking.

Marshall called his name again, trying to seem neutral and unthreatening despite the volume. He changed course slightly, veering right, toward the SUV, and the west-facing bodyguard moved to intercept him. He sidestepped into Marshall's path, right hand outstretched to block him.

Marshall said, 'Don't touch me. I just want to talk to him.'

He called D'Anton's name a third time, and didn't break step. As he felt the contact on his chest with the security guy's open palm, he laid his right hand across the top of the guy's wrist and twisted clockwise, in the same motion yanking the arm down and stepping left, the man dropping to his knee and staying there, locked in place by the awkward inside-out rotation of his shoulder.

And he saw now that he had D'Anton's attention. He'd paused half-out of the car, watching the action on the sidewalk, the young woman in the far seat leaning across for a view, too.

The east-facing man was still in position, looking back across his shoulder at Marshall, but the man on rear-door duty was coming over.

Eyes on D'Anton, Marshall said, 'Vialoux's dead. I need to talk to you.'

He adjusted his wrist-lock, flipping his grip to give himself more range, free up his stance. He thought if he had to, he'd feign an open-palm jab on the rear-door man and then just kick him in the balls left-footed, and now with the guy only six feet away, D'Anton Lewis shouted, 'Stop.'

The rear-door man halted like he'd been caught by a leash. The truck behind the SUV blew its horn again, the driver shouting mutely behind his windshield, gesturing with one arm – obviously more concerned about being on time than anything else: New Yorker, all the way to the core.

D'Anton ignored him.

He stepped up on the curb and took a second buttoning his coat: that small motion his way of broadcasting grand status. He came over, almost seeming to glide, paused at the rear-door man and said, 'What the fuck are you idiots doing?'

His soft tone making the line seem reasonable. An almost lush pedigree to the whisper.

No one answered.

Marshall still had his man in the wrist-lock, the guy down on one knee, flushed and goggle-eyed, breathing through clenched teeth.

D'Anton said to the rear-door man, 'You see something resembling a threat, why would you do anything except close the door? And yet, you're over here.'

Marshall said, 'It's a good point.'

D'Anton looked at him, came a step closer. He must've been six-four, two-twenty at least. Bigger than Marshall by an inch and twenty pounds. Short hair crystal-specked with rain. Almost vampiric in his dark coat, collar up and the points aiming forward.

He said, 'Let him go.'

Marshall said, 'He's learning a good lesson about keeping his hands to himself.'

D'Anton shrugged, bored, no life in his face. 'All right.' And then smiling a little, keeping his eyes flat and distant. He said, 'Harass me in the street, you think I'm going to sit down with you, listen to what you have to say?'

Marshall said, 'You already heard what I have to say. Ray

Vialoux's dead. Most people I've told, they found that pretty concerning.'

D'Anton kept looking at him, didn't move.

Marshall said, 'So now I have to wonder, are you going for the Guinness World Record in not giving a shit, or are you trying to hide something?'

Across D'Anton's shoulder, he could see the young woman in the SUV still leaning across to watch them. She called, 'Dad, c'mon. Forget about it. C'mon.'

The truck driver leaned on his horn again: a solid five-second blast like a ship coming into port.

No one looked.

D'Anton unbuttoned his coat with one hand, opened it slow, let Marshall see the dagger he was carrying. It hung by the crossguard from a loop in the satin lining. Maybe ten inches tip to tip, bone-handled and some kind of delicate pattern textured in the stainless blade.

Marshall said, 'I tell you a man's dead, you show me that? What am I meant to think, you're a gentleman?'

D'Anton swallowed carefully. 'I don't care what you think, and I don't care what you want to say to me. You step up on me like that again, I'm going to open you up, cock to throat. Get off my street.'

He closed the coat, and the motion of his arm seemed to propel him in a half-turn and then onward toward the car. The man on door duty followed close, shut D'Anton in quietly with the girl and then got in up front.

Marshall looked at the guy kneeling beside him. 'You going to be civilized now?'

He let go of the wrist and then stepped back as the guy came to his feet, flushed and angry, swinging at him with a left hook. It was a loopy, awkward shot with his wrong arm, and Marshall ducked it and skipped backward with his hands raised and ready. The guy followed for a few paces, and then somewhere in his head the judgement came through that it wasn't worth it. He gave Marshall the finger and spat at him, lip curled and vicious, showing teeth. Then he cursed indecipherably and headed back toward D'Anton's place, walking with his arms a little wider now, trying to exaggerate his size.

Marshall turned and walked west toward the park. D'Anton's SUV kept pace with him for a few yards, the quiet dark shape gliding along in his periphery. When the truck behind blew its horn again, the SUV accelerated in a hurricane of groundwater. It paused at the corner, waiting for a gap, and then swung out into traffic through a red light.

All of that warranted some thought. He didn't want to walk back past D'Anton's, in case the security guys felt there was a point to be made. He went a block north on Fifth and then over to Lexington, headed up to a deli he knew at Seventy-fifth Street. He bought coffee and a six-inch pastrami on rye, and took the last available stool at the window: Marshall a relatively youthful addition to a six-strong line-up of elderly male contemplation.

Open you up, cock to throat.

Pretty unequivocal. Maybe that was his standard attitude on any given morning, but Marshall couldn't help wonder if fear was a motivator for the line. Fear, deep behind a mask of ice-cool. He'd got no reaction, telling the man Vialoux was dead, which implied he'd heard the news already. But was that because he was complicit, or because he'd been keeping tabs for his own sake, his own self-preservation? Maybe he thought his name was on the same list as Ray's. But if that was the case, why had he not viewed Marshall as a greater threat? He remembered D'Anton emerging from the alcove and crossing the sidewalk, pausing to assess him and then continuing, apparently unconcerned.

He finished the sandwich and worked on the coffee. The deli's front window faced Lexington Avenue, with a view eastward along Seventy-fifth Street. The southeast corner had a Bank of America, and the northeast corner had a line-up of the kind of fashion stores people shopped in if they owned a ten-million-dollar town house on the Upper East Side. He watched a Ford Fusion sedan pull up on a fireplug outside the Bank of America. Dark paint, dark tinted windows. Unmarked NYPD cars had improved since Marshall's day. No telltale antennas on the rear lid. Consummate anonymity was the only giveaway.

The old guy on his left eased off his stool and departed with a complex rhythm of wheeze and wince and hobble. He'd left the *Times* sport section behind. Marshall flipped through it, just to kill time. Pointless photos and information. Sport had never interested him, particularly. He thought the loyalties involved were the most curious aspect of it. The fact people felt such affinity to teams they had no plausible connection to, other than some nominal commonality of region.

As he finished his coffee, he saw a second Ford pull up on the far curb of Lexington Avenue, this time on the north corner outside one of the fashion stores. Maybe they were pursuing an unrelated matter, but he didn't like the feeling of triangulation: a car left and right of him, now. He placed tip money under his mug and stood up. The most difficult decision was how to handle the paper sandwich wrapper. By its very nature, it was pre-creased in an extensive and erratic fashion. It was hard to understand and quantify the prevailing geometry, and therefore he couldn't say what would be most rational in terms of an imposed fold. Best not to get involved. He left the wrapper in its quasi-natural state, somewhat creased and concave on the bench below the window, and he stayed close to a trio of other customers as they exited. It was probably a false sense of camouflage. The diner's front window wasn't one-way glass.

He walked west on Seventy-fifth Street. It was the best exit strategy available: contraflow to traffic, Lexington and the two unmarked cars behind him. But it was raining, and he had his chin ducked against the weather, so he didn't see the third car until he was twenty feet from it. He sensed motion ahead of him, glanced up and saw a guy in a suit climb out from behind the wheel of a dark Ford Fusion. The suit was the same color as the car. He raised a badge wallet with a gold shield clipped inside it, and with his other hand he gestured at the rear door of the Fusion.

'Sir? We'd appreciate a moment of your time.'

Marshall stopped. 'For what?'

'If you could get in the car please, sir.'

Which was not the same thing as saying, *You're under arrest.*

He could keep walking, if he wanted to. Marshall turned and looked behind him. The second car had moved off the curb and was idling in the middle of the intersection. Watching, in the event backup was required. It was a fairly elaborate prelude to a conversation, if that's all it was going to be.

'Sir?'

Marshall glanced back at the guy. The badge was gone, but he was still gesturing at the rear door of the car. Grimly formal in his dark suit with his arm aslant, outstretched hand gently cupped, almost deferent. Like a waiter who would break your neck if you forgot your manners.

Marshall said, 'Five minutes.'

He stepped to the rear door of the car and opened it and climbed in.

ELEVEN

The lone occupant of the vehicle was a woman who looked to be in her mid-fifties. Marshall didn't recognize her. She was in the back, behind the empty front passenger seat, the opposite side of the car to Marshall. She had her elbow up on the sill, thumb and first finger rubbing together in a slow and contemplative fashion, or perhaps in the first outward sign of impatience. Burning off vexation, a micro-calorie at a time.

Marshall pulled his door shut.

The rain on the glass gave the car a submerged, hermetic quality. The guy he'd spoken to stayed on the sidewalk, his murky shape receding toward the relative shelter of a building eave.

The woman said, 'I'm Deputy Inspector Loretta Flynn. NYPD.'

She opened the black leather purse resting in her lap and produced a badge wallet with a gold shield and an ID.

Marshall said, 'You did well to find me. Or do you have people outside every lunch place in Manhattan?'

She wore a white blouse and a charcoal suit that looked to be fitted rather than off the rack. Marshall guessed tailoring was a justifiable expense, on a deputy inspector's salary. She had the sinewy and slightly drawn look of someone who did fifteen or twenty hours a week on a treadmill cranked to a life-or-death velocity. She said, 'We followed you up Lexington by CCTV. But I did think you'd be more difficult to corner.'

They'd worked him perfectly, he had to concede that. The two cars on Lexington as a visual nudge, prompting him back along Seventy-fifth, directly to where she was waiting.

Marshall said, 'I was more focused on eating my lunch than playing fugitive.'

'I see.'

'How can I help you?'

'What's your interest in D'Anton Lewis?'

The question expelled a mint-scent of chewing gum. Nicorette, maybe. He could picture her smoking her way through some tense operations.

Marshall said, 'I think you know the answer.'

In her pale blue eyes was a faint quality of wariness and contempt. 'Why do you say that?'

'I don't imagine I'm his first ever visitor. And I don't imagine the previous ones got this kind of treatment.' He smiled. 'Or is it standard practice to deploy three unmarked cars and a DI whenever someone knocks on his door?'

'From what I understand, it went a bit beyond a knock on the door.'

Marshall shrugged. 'Even if I broke his nose and pulled his teeth out with pliers, I wouldn't expect the second in charge of a precinct to show up.'

She didn't answer.

'Where are you based? The two-three?'

'I'm second in charge of the one-seven.'

'Right. So you could've stayed in your nice office and signed overtime forms. But instead you came up here. Which means you were forewarned about me. Which means you know what my interest in him is.'

'I understand that Detective Nevins conveyed to you that this is a police matter. The Vialoux investigation.'

Marshall smiled. 'You're not investigating Vialoux.'

Her eyebrows rose. 'Oh, is that right?'

'Yeah. Let's see if I can guess it on the first try. Nevins made an intel request on D'Anton, and because you're investigating him for something else, it sent up a red flag, and you told Nevins to keep his distance.'

She made no reaction.

Marshall said, 'And Nevins said he would, but he mentioned I'd probably show up sooner or later. Is that about right?'

'He told us you'd be along this morning. So you're a little slow.'

Marshall said, 'D'Anton stonewalled me. But given your theatrics, I know he's definitely worth pursuing.'

Flynn's elbow went back on the sill. Her thumb and first finger resumed their circling. She said, 'You worked undercover for Lee Ashcroft.'

Marshall nodded. 'Long time ago, now.'

'Sure. But you can still appreciate the fact that cases take time to build.'

He shook his head. 'No. I appreciate the fact it takes time to convince the desk people that the ducks on the street are all in a row.'

She smiled. No emotion in it. Blue eyes unmoving. Like an executioner looking across the blade of a guillotine. She said, 'I've earned my stripes. I did my time. So you don't need to imply you're sitting here with some naïve bureaucrat.'

'You did your time, huh? What, undercover on a drug investigation, and now you're overseeing one?'

'Nice try. But no comment.'

'OK. I had a hunch he was maybe into drug trafficking. But I guess he could just be a recidivist jaywalker.'

Silence for a moment. Beyond the glass, pedestrians went by in rain-blurred anonymity. The man who'd ushered him into the car was still there in the shelter of the eave, Reaperish in vague silhouette.

Marshall said, 'Maybe you could just explain clearly what you want me to do. Imagine for a moment that your sole mandate is to leave me in no doubt.'

She sighed through her nose, a smooth and visible deflation. Then she opened her purse again and removed a smartphone. Thin and black and glossy, like a piece of limousine glass. She navigated briskly through various menus, and then raised it so the screen was facing him.

A photo was displayed.

A hand, Marshall realized, although it took a moment for the image to register. It looked amphibious, because the digits had been amputated at the first knuckle.

Flynn said, 'A former girlfriend of Mr Lewis. She called him in November 2017 and said she was going to disclose the infidelity to his wife, but for a million dollars she might keep it to herself. They pulled her out of the Hudson eight days later. You'll note those cuts are clean-edged. They think he used a box-cutter. One pass, like slicing a carrot.' She lowered the screen.

Marshall said, 'I'd say he used that dagger he carries in his coat.'

'Possibly. And you have evidence now that he's prepared to use it.'

Marshall said, 'Is this meant to give me a better idea of who I'm dealing with? I had an inkling before I met him that he's not an upstanding citizen. And then he told me himself that he's going to cut me from groin to voice box if he sees me again. I think his phrasing was slightly harsher.'

She didn't answer.

Marshall said, 'But you don't care about dead people, anyway. Otherwise you'd let me ask him about Vialoux. And you'd let Nevins speak with him, too.'

Flynn returned the phone to the handbag. No sign of nicotine gum, but Marshall saw an e-Cigarette. He felt a small and point-less charge of vindication. Flynn pursed her lips for a moment, fine wrinkles emanating radially, and then said, 'Prison is prison.'

'Sure. What does that mean?'

'It means whether you get locked up for murder, or drugs, or jaywalking, at the end of the day, it's the same result. You're alone in a cell. And if you stay out of my way, that's where D'Anton Lewis is heading.'

Marshall said, 'I don't necessarily think that he killed Vialoux—'

'Good. All the more reason to keep your distance—'

'So what I'm inclined to do now is tell him he's the subject of an investigation by NYPD, and potentially other representa-tives of the alphabet. And maybe in exchange he'll give me an idea about what happened to Vialoux.'

He thought at the very least the suggestion might irritate her.

But Loretta Flynn, apparently amused, said, 'He's aware he's a target. Arrogance is his best feature, as far as I'm concerned. Being surveilled by police doesn't seem to dissuade him from doing business.'

'Well, if he's being surveilled, does he have an alibi for last night? Between, say, eight and midnight?'

'I'm not going to get into it with you.'

'OK. I'm happy to ask him myself. And if he's so unbothered about New York's finest following him around, I can't see how I'd cause him any distress. Which begs the question, why are you sitting here trying to warn me off?'

He saw the tendons in her neck tauten and then fade. She said, 'I just want to be clear that if he ends up dead, you will go to prison.'

'I doubt it. But I'm pleased that in some cases you're prepared to investigate murder. You might have the budget for it if you weren't sending three cars and four people to talk to me on my lunchbreak.'

Flynn said, 'You were undercover with the Italian mob. Tony Asaro.'

'Nice try. But no comment.'

'I heard when you ended the operation you took two hundred thousand dollars from Asaro's wall safe.'

'Two-fifty, thereabouts. Allegedly.'

'So not the kind of issue you'd want the law to look into with any kind of vigor.'

'Indeed. Fortunately, I'm well outside the statute of limitation on robbery.'

'Yes, but not on trafficking. That's a Class A felony, with no expiration date. And we might argue that in taking the proceeds, you were rendered complicit. I suspect we'd hand it over to the feds. The Southern District of New York has an admirable track record in such matters.'

Marshall didn't answer.

Flynn said, 'Stay out of my way. I'd recommend just sitting quietly and hoping that Mr Lewis ends up incarcerated. Otherwise, I give you my personal assurance that I will have you instead.' She nodded at his door. 'You can get out now.'

TWELVE

The protesters on Fifth Avenue had been reduced by weather to the hardy few, all of them soaked and pretty hoarse by now. Marshall stopped at the Strand Books kiosk for shelter from the weather and called Nevins on his cell. It went to voicemail.

Marshall said, 'I just met your friend Loretta Flynn. Call me back. I'm eager to discuss.'

He assumed his theory was correct: that Nevins had made a query on D'Anton, and Flynn had then warned him off. She hadn't denied it. She hadn't even claimed she couldn't comment. And Nevins had been evasive on the D'Anton topic earlier.

He waited for another break in the rain, and then walked down to Forty-second Street and went into the public library. His library card was a recent and valuable acquisition, and he regarded himself as some kind of model patron. He always used bookmarks. Never had he dog-eared a page. He was fastidious in his treatment of paperbacks, and never creased the spine. And he never kept a book past its due date. He didn't want some paltry surcharge being logged against his membership, awkward sums growing progressively inelegant with compound interest. He reserved thirty minutes on one of the public computers, and ran a search on D'Anton Lewis.

Google Images had a cached headshot, ten years old or thereabouts, from when he was on the staff of some Wall Street trading company Marshall had never heard of. Since then, he didn't seem to have done much, at least as far as the internet was concerned. No Twitter or Instagram or anything convenient like that. The News tab on Google came up with the story Jordan Mora had mentioned – D'Anton buying the town house from that billionaire sex trafficker, Jerry Erskine. Price undisclosed, but thought to be in the neighborhood of thirty million dollars.

He searched Loretta Flynn. The first hit on Google was the NYPD website. She was second in charge of the seventeenth precinct, just as she'd told him. There was a smiling headshot of her in dress blues, alongside an italicized blurb about her passion for helping the community. The text with its humble-service theme was rather somewhat counterposed to Marshall's own impression of her. He guessed *ruthlessly pragmatic* wouldn't have much value as a PR term.

He thought about calling Jordan Mora, but he didn't want to give an impression of coming on too heavy. Although she might know whether D'Anton had always been the kind of guy to carry a ten-inch dagger in his coat, or if it was a recent lifestyle choice. He could hear himself saying that to her, seeing her smile.

The call history on his phone still had the number for the bagel place. He typed it into Google, and the search results showed him a street-view image of the premises. He opened the Maps window and had a look around. The bagel shop was on a corner site. There was a florist's next door and a twenty-four-hour Minimart directly opposite.

Marshall called the number again.

'Bagel shop.'

'Is Frank there?'

'Who are you, pal?'

'I'm coming to see him. He can pick a time, or I can.'

The guy hung up.

Marshall googled Ray Vialoux. A few news items had appeared in the last few hours, describing in brief the shooting at the restaurant. Nothing yet about poor Lydia in the house across the street. He scrolled through search results and found Vialoux's website. APEX INVESTIGATIONS. The homepage had a mission statement about achieving best results, and some detective-related imagery. A digital camera the size of a cinder-block, and a floppy disk sitting on some splayed documents. The CONTACT US page had Vialoux's name and cell number, and his company address over in Park Slope. Beneath the text was a photograph of the office frontage, pre-arson. Marshall closed the browser and walked out of the building, threading through tourists looking everywhere except where they were going.

Harry Rush's office was in an old red-brick building in Washington Heights, way up on 155th Street. It looked like some kind of cultural intersection point. There was a Mobil station next door on the corner with Broadway, and the Church of the Intercession was directly opposite. The sidewall of Harry's building had a five-story-high painting of an eagle that looked to be swooping down on the Mobil.

Rush Law was on level five. Marshall took the stairs up and went into Harry's reception area. Harry's administrator, Marlene Delacroix, was behind the desk, and Harry's bodyguard and driver, Chiat Money, was sitting on one of the client chairs, reading a magazine. In the corner, a shirtless man wearing torn fatigue pants was filling up a hot-water bottle from the watercooler.

Chiat saw Marshall enter and lifted his chin.

'Hey, Chiat. How you doing?'

Chiat shrugged. 'Usual. Groovin' smooth as a motherfucker.'

'That's good.'

Marlene was reading a book by Lena Dunham. Without looking up she said, 'You can go in. He knows you're coming.'

Harry was at his desk, on the phone. Marshall closed the office door and sat down in the visitor chair, opposite. Harry had his eyes shut, brow gently furrowed. He said to the phone, 'Yeah. Yeah. Of course.' Trying to wedge his way into something tedious. 'I think the fact . . . I think the fact you threatened to do that to him with the knife, and then the body was found essentially in that configuration . . . yeah. That's the immediate obstacle. OK, you call me back then.'

He put down the phone, let his breath out through pursed lips. He was a black man closing in on fifty, very tall, very fit, very well-tailored. He had on a tan suit with a tan tie, gray shirt matching the gray in his hair – buzzcut turning salty at the margins.

Marshall said, 'You heard what happened?'

'Yeah. The cops ran through it. Unbelievable. But you're OK?'

Marshall spread his hands, like the fact of his presence was sufficient response. 'Do you know what he was into?'

'Vialoux? Shit, no.'

'But you put him onto me.'

'What do you mean?'

'Ray said he went to you first, and you told him to talk to me.'

Harry shook his head. 'No, all he did was ask for your details. All he said was he needed to talk to you. I never knew what his problem was.'

Marshall didn't answer.

'Look, don't sit there like you got a bone to pick. Have a coffee, chill out.'

'I already had coffee.'

'All right, well. I'm not your problem.'

Marshall said, 'They'd set up surveillance across the street from his house.'

'What? Who did?'

'Whoever nailed him.'

He told him about Lydia in the house across the street.

Harry ran his hands through his hair. Veins stood out on his forehead.

Marshall said, 'He told me he had debts he couldn't service. He was part of a gambling ring someone called D'Anton Lewis got him into.'

Harry shrugged. 'All right.'

Marshall said, 'And I wondered if you know Vialoux, maybe you know D'Anton, too.'

'I know *of* him. He's not cut from nice cloth, put it that way.'

'Yeah. I got that impression.'

He told Harry what had happened.

Harry said, 'Shit, he threatened you?'

'Cock to throat, were his exact words.'

Harry opened a drawer and removed a letter-size envelope, tossed it toward him. It spun midair and then hit the desk, slid and then stopped with one corner cantilevered. Marshall sat there for a moment, not moving. Then the urge to make corrections ran in a prickle across his shoulders and down his spine. He slid the envelope fully onto the table. Strict, parallel orientation and a generous two-inch offset, edge with respect to edge.

Harry said, 'That's your fee for last month.'

'What do you know about D'Anton?'

The door opened, and the shirtless guy stuck his head in from the waiting area. Harry said, 'Charlie, just give us a minute. I won't be long.'

The door closed.

Harry said, 'Look. I don't know anything. All I know is other people's speculation that he's into heavy shit.' He shrugged. 'Story you just told me, that'll mix into the pot with everything else I heard, frankly make me even more certain he's a guy best avoided.'

Marshall didn't answer.

Harry said, 'And shit, mob guys? Frank Cifaretti?' He shook his head. 'Sorry, no way.'

'Vialoux's dead. I mentioned that, right?'

'Yeah, and I don't want to join him. And I don't want photos of my family showing up in the mail, because I did the wrong thing, or knocked on the wrong door.'

'He told you about the photos, huh? What else did he say?'

Harry shook his head. 'It's not worth it to me, I'm sorry. I don't want to be mixed up in something's gonna cost me.'

They sat looking at each other for a few seconds. Marshall had a line forming, something about how being a family man demanded a different kind of selfishness – generosity in a personal sphere closing you down to the broader world – but he knew he couldn't say it. Harry had a different kind of calculus to make, one that Marshall knew he'd probably never understand.

He went and sat outside the church for a while, watching the traffic go by on 155th Street, and then he started walking. Three blocks down Broadway, his phone rang. It was Hannah Vialoux.

'Hey. Everything all right?'

'They said it was you who found Lydia. Why didn't you tell me? You just left?'

He had the answer right there in his mind, but he couldn't say it, couldn't tell her he felt a tension being back in the house, being around her. Like everything was set on edge by history. He said, 'I'm trying to find who did it. That's all.'

'Esther Lopez says she saw one of them. She said she spoke to you, too.'

'That's right.'

'They've been following him for weeks. I remember now. They've been following him probably for six weeks. The boys saw him being watched.'

'What? What boys?'

'No, Boynes. *Boynes*. Their daughter committed suicide. Ray looked into it, I think I told you earlier. He was at their house, and they saw that man watching, sitting in his car. I remembered, because of the description. Shiny hair, and that smile on his face. They said he just sat there, smiling.'

THIRTEEN

When he reached her street there were still a couple of patrol cars parked down the block outside Lydia's. He saw Bruce Linney in his front courtyard, chaining his daughter's bike to the fence. He went up the steps to the Vialoux place, and Hannah had the door open when he reached it.

'Oh, God, you're soaking . . .'

He stepped inside and let her take his coat off, her hands on his shoulders bringing back more memories. He heard someone on the stairs and glanced up, saw Ella's feet disappearing to the second floor.

Hannah hung his coat on a hook. 'They told me about Lydia. I can't even . . . I can't get my head around it. It's weird, I'm almost *calm*. Like I can't even fathom how bad it is, and I've just . . . like my brain's given up on it. I don't know. She'd always wave. Whenever I saw her, she'd always wave.'

He let that have a second, not sure how to commiserate with any meaning, other than to offer his silence. He said, 'Come and tell me about this smiley man.'

They sat at the kitchen table.

'I can't remember what I told you. Did I tell you about the Boynes?'

'Briefly. You said their daughter committed suicide.'

'That's right . . . it was just so sad. You seem to hear of it more and more, but Jennifer – their daughter, I mean – she'd seemed very normal, very happy, apparently . . .' She shrugged. 'Then one morning, she didn't come down for breakfast. Ginny went up to check on her, she was . . . she'd hanged herself in the closet. Just . . . well.' She smiled sadly. 'Awful. Her parents, they said on her Facebook there'd been abusive messages, so they'd asked Ray to look into it, in case there was a note or something on her computer. He never found anything. But anyway, I'm rambling. The reason it came back, Ginny Boyne called this afternoon to say she'd heard what happened. She's so nice, honestly. And I remembered Ray had been over at their place one evening – must've been six weeks ago. I think what happened, Martin had met him at the door, and he just happened to see this car pull up at the curb and then sit there, watching them. I don't think Martin paid it any notice, but then apparently when he saw Ray out, the same car was still there, two guys up front just watching them. Martin's not – I mean, Martin's not the biggest guy, but Ginny said he went over and asked them what they were doing. And I remembered today, hearing the description from Esther, Martin said the guy looked him right in the eye, and smiled, and drove away.'

'And how did you hear about it? Did Ray tell you?'

'No, Ray didn't say anything. Ginny Boyne, she called me the next day to check everything was all right. So nice, honestly. Not like she didn't have her own worries.'

'Did you ask Ray about it?'

'Yes, I did. I think at first he didn't even remember, but then he said they were just trying to serve a summons on him. I mean, it seemed pretty harmless. I guess I just forgot about it.'

'Do you remember him going to court?'

She shook her head. 'He might've not told me. He was talking to me less and less, but . . . you'd think if it had been a summons, why wouldn't they do it as he was coming out of the Boynes'? They saw him go in, all they had to do was give it to him when he came out again.'

'You never saw any little smiley guys?'

'No. That's what the police asked. I don't remember seeing anyone like that. Or anyone else.'

Marshall said, 'Do you have the Boynes' number?'

He stood in the kitchen door watching her on the phone in the hallway, Hannah standing with her back to him, leaning on the wall, twisting her hair around a finger. He could see pretty clearly what had drawn him to her all those years ago. She still had it.

He looked at the floor to get his mind back on task, glanced back up as Hannah said, 'Ginny, he's here now, if that's OK?'

She looked back at him across her shoulder, extending the handset. Their fingers brushed as he took it. Another small fact he had to work hard to ignore.

He put the phone to his ear, and Ginny Boyne said, 'I'm not sure how much help I can be. I didn't actually see it.'

A quiet voice, but matter-of-fact. Tiredness, blended with determination. He'd heard it before. Other voices, other miseries. The bereaved, learning to cope.

He said, 'That's fine. Of course. Is your husband available to speak?'

'No, unfortunately. He's in New Jersey on business. He won't be home until late, I imagine. Generally he gets in about eleven on travel days.'

'What about tomorrow?'

'Yes, that's fine. Are you with the police? Hannah said you're an investigator.'

'Ex-police. I'm a friend of Ray's.'

The present tense grated, but he felt he had a greater duty to manners than accuracy.

He said, 'Did you see the men who were watching Ray? I understand there were two of them in a car—'

'No, I didn't. I'm sorry, I wish I could be more help—'

'Don't apologize. I completely understand.'

'Martin saw them, but I think I was inside at the time. It's . . . well, you can probably appreciate, it's been a horrible few weeks. We were so lucky to have Ray shine a little light onto everything. He was wonderful, really. Absolutely a blessing. If you get here before . . . no, tomorrow's Saturday, isn't it? We'll be here all day. Just come when you're ready.'

She gave him the address, and Marshall thanked her and ended the call. He dialed his neighbor, Vera Boykov.

'This is Vera.'

'This is Marshall.'

She lowered her voice: 'This is Marshall.'

He said, 'I won't be home until late, so I won't be able to feed Boris.'

'Understood. But you are not Boris-feeder anyway, yes? Even

if you are present. Food for him, this is non-imperative. So the challenge is as follows: how do I convey to *you* this is the case?'

'Have a nice evening, Vera.'

He set the phone back on its wall cradle. Hannah was standing in the kitchen door, arms folded, watching him.

She said, 'Something I was going to say earlier. Why did you tell Nevins about us?'

About us: the phrase had a resonance – the special resonance of precise meaning in a vague term.

He thought: here we go.

He waited a moment, making sure he could trust himself to say the right thing. 'I couldn't not tell him. I was there when Ray died. And we worked together. There's about zero chance they'd ignore the possibility I was involved. And I wouldn't help things by not telling them about the affair.'

Affair.

She shifted her weight as he said it, one foot to the other, uncomfortable with the term. He had that urge again to tell her this was why he'd been wary coming back. Subtext seemed to color every interaction, like a secret lens augmenting his vision, showing the past in the present moment.

She said, 'Yes, but how would it *harm* things? How were they ever going to know about it anyway? The only way they were going to know is if *one of us* said something.' She shrugged. 'I just find it funny, I don't know why you thought you couldn't trust me. I mean, why would I say anything? Why would I want to tell them I'd failed, and been unfaithful? There was nothing in it for me.'

He looked at the phone on the wall, like maybe it could take him back a few minutes to an easier conversation.

He said, 'It had nothing to do with trust. All it had to do with . . .'

It was hard laying it out plain and innocent while she was studying him like that, alert for weaknesses in the claim.

He said, 'Ray was dead, they were looking into it, I thought that probably meant they'd be looking into me.' He shrugged. 'I thought it was safest to be upfront.'

He knew it was just a re-phrasing of what he'd said first time around, and he worried they might end up stuck in some kind of loop. He recalled what Jordan Mora had said, how Vialoux had told Hannah that Jordan was male.

Some kind of odd dynamic.

He wondered what that meant, what the implications were, day to day.

She said, 'I just didn't quite understand the principle. I mean, you're being upfront about that, but not about the tracker in his car? Maybe if we're more consistent, I won't need the worst parts of my life laid out for inspection by strangers.'

Worst parts.

Marshall thought that was probably calibrated for sting.

He said, 'Look, I'm sorry. Maybe I should've thought about it more. It was one in the morning, and my friend was dead. My brain wasn't working that well.'

He knew that was a stupid thing to say. His friend dead meant her husband dead. He didn't need to be outlining the emotional toll.

But Hannah just looked at him quietly.

Then she said, 'Stay for dinner. I'm doing meatballs.'

Ella didn't come down. He and Hannah ate at the table, the third plate untouched, unremarked upon. Halfway through the meal, the phone in the hallway rang. Hannah got up and answered. It was all one-way traffic. He heard a yes, an OK, a thank you, and then she was back in the room with him.

She said, 'Police are still short-staffed, apparently. They said there'll be a car free about eleven.'

'That's fine.'

'You don't have to stay, I mean it.'

'It's no trouble.'

'And feel free to have a shower, obviously. You still look wet. I'll give you some of Ray's clothes . . .'

'No, it's fine. I'll head home when the night watch shows up.'

She nodded. 'I didn't mean . . . I shouldn't have said what I said before.'

He would've preferred to forget it, rather than crawl back underneath for the sake of needless repairs.

'Don't worry. It's fine.'

'I appreciate everything you've done. It's amazing.'

quietly, sipping his coffee, thinking about what he'd do if the
man in the mask appeared again at the window. Or what he'd
do if someone tried to enter the house. Nice to sit there with
his musings. A terrible kind of solace.

Ten o'clock now. He went around turning off downstairs lights
and returned to the living room. Footsteps upstairs, and then
switch-clicks: the filtered hallway glow made progressive concessions to shadow, and then the house was dark and quiet. He sat
very still, willing something to reveal itself on the street.

Time dragging by in silence. A mobility scooter went past on
the south sidewalk, the same one he'd seen earlier: Kurdish flag
flying from the rear. The driver was wrapped in a hooded coat like
an Arctic dog-sled rider. The only motion out there in the cold.

Another quiet stretch of nothing. Twenty minutes. Twenty-
five. Then from upstairs, he heard a door tick against a latch.
Feet on the stairs in a nimble patter, and then Ella went past the
door to the hallway. She paused, and stepped back into view.

She said, 'You're here.'

'Yeah. You heading out?'

'Good guess.'

Marshall said, 'Safer to stay in until this is all wrapped up.'

She looked at him, just a shape in the dark. 'Thanks for the
advice.'

Then she went out.

The door thumped shut as he called to her, and he heard her
feet on the steps. Flat rhythm in descent on the wet concrete.

Safer to stay in. He could've put it in slightly firmer terms.
He got up to follow, thinking he'd try Round Two at persuasion,
and then a car edged into view at the curb. Bass music coming
from inside, louder for a moment as Ella opened the rear door
and climbed in, and then the car took off with a long and rising
snarl of exhaust.

He turned from the window and saw light from upstairs, went
into the hallway and saw Hannah on the landing.

He said, 'Sorry, I should've argued harder.'

Descending now. 'There's no telling her what to do, I promise.'

She stayed on the bottom stair, eyes level with his. She
was wearing a bathrobe, and she let it open. She was naked
underneath it.

'Don't worry about it. He was my friend.'

She didn't answer, and the conversation hit a lull. The c and chime of the cutlery seemed to heighten the awkwardn

She said, 'It's nice having company at dinner for a chang

'Yeah. I know what you mean.'

He wasn't quite sure why he'd said that. He liked his solitu In a way, he thought maybe it was essential, at least for some like him. He was wired differently, that was pretty obvious. I undercover work and its requisite paranoia had made h rigidly particular in certain aspects of his life. And as far as understood it, having a partner demanded some capitulatio now and again. That didn't sound like him. His habits and h attitudes weren't elastic, and he knew enough about relationship to recognize that aspect of himself as a potential major short coming. And he accepted that. He was happy with it. But why pretend otherwise?

He helped her clean up, and then she told him she was going to do some work, take her mind off everything. She said she was in front-end web development these days, what they called UX design.

'UX?'

'User experience. Making websites look nice, basically.' She smiled. 'Making cut-throat companies seem approachable.'

He nodded. He couldn't help thinking maybe that was the perfect role for her. Putting a happy veneer on something that wasn't what it should be.

'I do a lot of it from home, which makes things easier. Especially under house arrest.'

She went upstairs, and Marshall was left alone on the ground floor.

He paced quietly, living room to kitchen and back again, thinking about what he should do next. From upstairs, he heard an argument that centered on Ella's non-attendance at dinner. Something from the girl about how it felt a bit too soon to play happy-family. Marshall could understand that. He couldn't fault it at all.

He made himself coffee and took it through to the living room, sat with the lights off, looking out at the street. Darkness setting in. The whole scene glossed by the recent rain. He sat

'Hannah . . .'

She came toward him, laid her arms on his shoulders. 'Come upstairs.'

Close enough he felt her breath on his mouth. Then her lips touching his, her body pushing against him. He laid his hands on her hips under the robe, skin smooth and bed-warm, pushed her away gently.

He said, 'I don't think this is a good idea.'

Her hands slid off his shoulders. The shape of her stood facing him in the dark. She folded her arms, drawing the robe around her.

He said, 'Sorry. I just don't think it is.'

She backed up a step, above him now.

'Maybe you better go, then.'

He had a feeling this was the best offer he'd ever turned down. But it was complicated. He didn't think he had it in him to lay things out in a way that made sense to her.

He said, 'It's not that I don't want to. It's just kind of complicated.'

She shook her head. 'No it isn't. You either want to, or you don't. The door will lock behind you.'

He watched her walk away from him, up the stairs, and then he got his coat and went out.

FOURTEEN

He sat on her front steps in the dark, using a lot of will-power just to stay there and not ring her bell. The sensation of the moment still vivid and electric. More there to be had, if he'd only stand up and turn around.

Twenty minutes past eleven, a patrol car arrived and parked at the opposite curb. Marshall recognized the driver from last night. He gave the guy a wave and headed off toward Fourth Avenue.

It was just him and a couple of rats at the Forty-fifth Street Station. Platform rats, not down-on-the-track rats. They knew they were in charge at this time of night. They came up to him and stood twitching in silent and unrushed appraisal, and then carried on with their business. Marshall caught an N train up to Atlantic Avenue and then a Q all the way down to Brighton Beach, walked back north on Coney Island Avenue.

Thirty minutes past midnight and not a lot happening. Occasional traffic and the storefronts all dark and shut up. He saw a guy come out of a bar and head uptown, weaving and unstable, as if navigating some hidden slalom. Across the street, a homeless man reclined on the front steps of a dental practice, propped up on his elbows with his legs stretched, like catching sun on the beachfront a few blocks south.

Marshall walked up to Neptune Ave and went into the Minimart on the corner, opposite the bagel place. He poured himself coffee at the self-serve station, went over to the cashier and slid money through the window. The number of scuff marks on the Perspex suggested that not all patrons were this civil. The cashier's attention was on a Spanish sitcom playing on a TV back there, and Marshall figured if you did want to rob the place, you could probably make decent progress before the guy noticed.

He took his drink over to the bench at the coffee station and stood looking out the window. The exterior of the Minimart was covered with magazine and concert advertisements, but between the scenes of Photoshopped glamor were slices of real life: the street, and the businesses on the other side of it. The bagel shop on the corner, the florist's adjacent. In front of the florist's was a van with FRANK'S FLOWERS printed on the side below a daffodil logo. The van's rear door was open and a couple of young guys were unloading boxes and carrying them inside. The bagel shop had a CLOSED sign up and metal blinds covering the windows, but he could see shadows moving around in there.

The Minimart's front door opened with a *ding*, and the homeless guy he'd passed a few blocks back stepped inside. He looked around the small space with its color-onslaught of packaged goods, and then he came over to Marshall at the coffee bench and stood looking at him.

Marshall said, 'How you doing?'

'Doing OK, thanks. Sorry to bother you. The coffee's two bucks, I'm at a buck eighty . . .'

He held out his palm: coins arrayed there, evidently insufficient. Marshall dug in a pocket for his cash and peeled off a two-dollar bill. He squared up the remaining money and confirmed correct sequence – lowest denomination at the outside of the transverse fold – and handed over the two bucks.

The guy pinched it by a corner, hesitant. 'You got anything smaller?'

'No, you're good.'

The guy said, 'Two-dollar bill's rare. I don't want to steal your good luck.'

Marshall looked at him. 'How rare?'

The guy shrugged. 'Pretty rare. They must be. I hardly ever get them. And people if they give me anything, they want to give me something small, you know?'

Marshall thought about that as he looked at the bagel shop. He saw a guy appear behind the glass front door and stand there for a moment like a silhouette in a shooting gallery, and then move away. He said, 'Maybe people are conscious of the rarity, and so they factor that into their donations.'

'You mean like less inclined to give out two-dollar bills? Because they're rarer?'

'Yeah. So you in turn would get a disproportionate impression of their rarity.'

The guy nodded slowly with narrowed eyes as if banking the theory for future rumination. Then he went to the cashier window and handed over the venerated bill and came back and poured himself a coffee. A phone on the wall behind the cashier rang, but went unanswered.

'You ever known a florist to be open at night?'

Marshall said, 'No.'

The guy shook his head. 'Me either. That one is, though: look at it.'

They stood there at the bench drinking coffee, looking at it.

The guy said, 'My experience of life is principally nocturnal. Sleep during the day when it's warmer, go out at night for food. I would say the idea of a twenty-four-hour florist is pretty novel.'

'I think you might be right.'

The phone behind the cashier's desk rang again. The cashier

made a noise, unintelligible but vehement, reached behind him without looking and took the cordless phone handset off the wall and listened. Then he rose wearily and came out through a door in his Perspex booth and said, 'Which of you is Marshall?'

Marshall said, 'I'm Marshall.'

The homeless guy looked on with an expression of naked awe as the phone was handed over, as if maybe it was God himself on the other end of the line.

Marshall put the phone to his ear, saw now that there was a figure in the door to the bagel shop, doing likewise.

'Yes?'

'Why don't you come over, instead of just standing there, looking? You can bring your coffee.'

There was no traffic on Coney Island Avenue. Marshall walked across four empty lanes under a full line-up of green lights and went into the bagel shop: a raucous entry with the ding of the mechanical bell and the door crashing shut behind him on an overzealous pneumatic arm.

He saw a counter over to his right, glass-topped and showing rows of empty stainless trays, clean and bright as morgue dishes. Tables in front of it and booths along the left wall, facing Neptune Ave.

The guys he'd seen unloading the flower van were behind the counter, leaning on it with their arms up on the curved glass, looking at Marshall as if they'd never laid eyes on someone less impressive. They appeared to have spent a lot of time at the gym, but only doing bicep curls. Good for carrying flowers, no doubt. There were two other guys seated in a booth, and Marshall recognized one of them: the mob man, Frank Cifaretti. He was fortyish now, paunchy and stubbled, wearing white Nike trainers and a rumpled tracksuit made to seem space-age. Some kind of shiny finish to it. He looked like an athlete who'd dozed off on the couch for six months and then woken up out of condition. The guy with him was going for a more classic look. Long hair in a ponytail, eyes half-hooded as he looked at Marshall across his shoulder, like he was too cool to stay awake.

Frank said, 'We like to keep an eye on the Minimart. Wouldn't

believe how many cops just *happen* to stop in for coffee. And
then they'll stand there two, three hours sometimes. Must be
fucken lovely in there.'

Marshall said, 'Coffee's not bad for two dollars.'

Frank Cifaretti said, 'Yeah, I'm sure. Benny, get the door
would you? Don't want to be robbed. Be a real shame.'

One of the flower guys came around the counter to the door
and clicked the lock, and Frank said, 'I see you show up just
now, I thought: surely, *surely* it isn't.' He spread his hands. 'Yet,
here the man is.' Then gesturing to him, beckoning. 'Sit down.'
Looking him in the eye now, voice a little lower: 'Sit yourself
down right here.'

The ponytail guy got out of the booth, and Marshall took his
seat. There was a cell phone and a couple of shot glasses and a
deck of cards spread out on the table.

The flower man called Benny said, 'Frank, I get you something? We still got some avocado.'

Frank gathered the cards, tamped them square. 'No, just give
me a . . .' He seemed to give this some thought. 'Give me a
salmon on cream cheese.'

'You got it.'

Frank said, 'We wouldn't normally do you this kind of courtesy, invite you in after hours. But you did us a real favor.' Lifting
his chin, grinning. 'When you were undercover. We heard all
about that.'

'Oh, you did?'

Smiling back a little, like letting the guy inflate his ego. Ponytail
and the other flower man were at a table beside them, flower
man sort draped in position, going for maybe a wilted daffodil
look. The guy with the ponytail was up on the table with his feet
on a chair, leaning forward elbows-to-knees as he studied
Marshall in profile.

Frank said, 'They had you with the Asaro crew, right? And
now they're basically taken care of.'

'So I hear.'

'Makes things . . .' He stirred a hand, looking for the word.
'Makes things a little easier, commerce-wise. Not having the
competition. It frees up resources. Around here, Brighton Beach,
this used to be Russian territory, and now we're moving back in,

as you can see.' He pointed at him, clicked his fingers. 'Hey, you still got any of the money left?'

'What do you mean?'

Frank came forward a little, conspiratorial. His hair and beard were of uniform length, like his head had been carefully glue-painted and then dipped in grayish bristles. He said, 'I heard you took some cash out of Tony Asaro's safe when you called it quits. Two, three hundred grand, something like that?'

Marshall said, 'Nice that my reputation got here first.'

'Yeah. It got here about ten years ago, and I'm tired of it.' He licked his lips as if tasting the phrase, sat back and shook his head. 'I hate the thought of a guy going around with a story he thinks gives him some cachet. When really he's not worth anything.'

Marshall smiled, happy to let the guy feel like he was stacking points. There was a door behind the counter leading to a back-room, and presumably the flower shop next door. He watched Benny come around the glass counter carrying a plate and then set it down on the table in front of Frank.

'Boom. There you go.'

A halved bagel, a thick load of cream cheese and salmon on each slice.

Frank said, 'You got any capers?'

'Oh yeah, sorry. I'll bring them over.'

He went out through the door behind the counter, and the four of them sat there for a moment in the quiet.

Frank spread his hands. 'So.' He scrolled his bottom lip out, dropped his voice a little: flat, bored, low: 'What do you want? Take it you're the man's been calling us, huh?'

Marshall said, 'You sit here all night, playing cards?'

Frank didn't answer. A car went past, its motion described by yellow light in the metal blinds.

Marshall said, 'Ray Vialoux's dead.'

Frank smiled. 'Old Vialoux, huh? Well, that's good.' Trying to get a reaction. 'He's the sort of guy, he's a real spot-on defin-ition of human trash, isn't he? Or he was.'

Marshall sat there. In his periphery, he saw the ponytail guy had a gun in his hand, hanging between his knees: a SIG P226.

Marshall said, 'Surprised you didn't hear about it. Thought if you're in here eating salmon bagels you must be the big dog. But I guess not.'

Frank ran a hand around his jaw, a slow tour as if sculpting a reply, but then he just sat there quietly, watched Benny as he came back with his jar of capers.

'Sprinkle them on there from a height. I like them to fall kinda random.'

They all watched as Benny tipped out a few from about eighteen inches.

Frank said, 'Yeah, look at that. Beautiful.'

He picked up a half-bagel and bit into it, eyes on Marshall.

Marshall said, 'Are you going to help me, or are you going to pretend you don't know what the deal is?'

Frank chewed, looked at his bagel. 'Dish ish goob.' He swallowed, shrugged. 'There's no pretending.' He smiled. 'This is all coming to me a hundred percent authentic.'

Marshall said, 'Vialoux got shot through a window while I was sitting talking to him.'

'Front-row seat, huh? Nice.'

Marshall said, 'He told me a guy called D'Anton Lewis got him into a game you're running. And apparently he ended up with a debt.'

Frank shrugged.

Marshall said, 'I know you have a patience problem. I'm worried you got tired of waiting, and had him whacked. That how it went?'

Frank didn't answer. Benny was at the table with the other two now, leaning way back in his seat, matching the vibe of the other flower man.

Marshall said, 'I found this place because I hit redial on his home phone.'

Frank smiled. 'Shit. Yeah, they always said you were smart.'

'So was he just calling up for recipes or something?'

Frank shook his head. 'Use your cranium, pal. I'm not stupid enough to hit a guy who owes me money. He was paying it down, and now I'm seventy-k in the hole. Do some fucking math, Jesus Christ.'

He took another bite. Benny's phone rang. He answered, and listened, and then said, 'Yeah, well, I told her to cut them about an inch up from the base. Problem is, they seal over, don't take in any water. If she's gonna ignore pro advice, that's what happens.'

Marshall said, 'Who's the shooter?'

Frank chewed.

Benny said, 'All right, she knows best,' and hung up.

Marshall said, 'Witnesses saw a little guy who smiles a lot. You know anyone that friendly?'

Frank shrugged. 'Vialoux was police. I don't give a shit about that guy. And, you know. Tell me a story surprises me. He got into something hot and got burned. What'd he think was gonna happen?'

Grinning at him as he chewed wetly, mouth full of fish and cream cheese, the smell of it coming across the table.

Marshall said, 'You seem to have all the details about how I shut down the Asaros. Why do you think I won't have the same luck in here? This is a bagel shop and a florist.'

Frank slid his plate away. 'We got a camera put up, sole job's to watch the Minimart over there, see who's coming to check us out. You know how fucking tired I am of police? You think I look at pictures of these guys, going in for coffee every other day, you think I have any time for them? And Vialoux, shit. He used to have a badge, but that was the only thing made him police.'

'What does that mean?'

'It means take your story somewhere else.' He shrugged, mouth downturned, blameless. 'I don't care he's dead, I don't care who did it, I don't care if his wife or his mother or his aunt been shedding tears. I don't give a fuck. Don't show up here, think your CV's got the kind of weight's going to make people worry. I'm not worried about you, pal. I don't want to hear about Ray Vialoux, unless you got a funny story about what his face looked like with a bullet going through it.'

That got a few sniggers going around. Marshall sat there quietly, watched Frank shuffle his cards briefly and then set them down. In all likelihood, that was a unique deck. Never in history had such an ordering of cards been achieved, because the chance of any given composition was one-in-fifty-two, times one-in-fifty-one, times one-in-fifty, and so on, all the way down to one.

One-in-fifty-two factorial was the technical expression, and fifty-two factorial was something like eight times ten to the power of sixty-seven. A massive number. You could shuffle cards all day for the rest of your life and never replicate something composed by pure fluke in an idle moment.

He waited for quiet and said, 'All right, I apologize. I thought you were high enough up the chain, you'd know what's going on. Or are you just too scared to say?'

Frank seemed to find that pretty entertaining. He laughed again, turned a little in his seat so he could prop his elbow on the back of his chair. He said, 'We're not really a collaborative set-up. Surprised you didn't grasp that, all your undercover work.'

Marshall said, 'So what's it going to take?'

'Huh?'

Marshall said, 'What's it going to take? To get someone down here who knows the story.'

Frank wriggled in his seat, crossed his legs knee-on-knee under the table. He reached for the second half of bagel and took a chomp. The salmon topping leaned steeply and then settled as he pulled away.

Marshall said, 'You obviously got the picture. I can be kind of a handful to people in your industry.'

'Mmm, well. Our industry can be kind of a handful to your kind of people.' He shrugged. 'Sometimes guys get shot. You know. Sometimes they're just sitting there, someone clips them through a window.'

'What's it going to take.'

Frank shook his head, brow lightly furrowed. 'Huh?'

Marshall said, 'Let's not go through this again. What do I have to do to get someone down here who has a clue? You going to make a call, or do I need to come back tomorrow? Keep coming back until I see someone who looks like a boss walk in the door. Otherwise you can just tell me now what happened, and I can leave.'

Frank took another bite of bagel, a playful light in his eye, something coming together in his mind.

He said, 'I never seen someone shot that close. I mean, you know: I never seen someone shot in the head from across a table. What is this, five feet? And at least . . . well. At least a guy like you, upstanding and whatever, always operating on the right side of the line, there must be some part of you thinking at least the guy deserved it. Hopefully the family sees it that way too?' He laughed, mouth full of white and orange. 'Or are they a bit surprised by it all?'

Marshall said, 'Coffee over there's only two dollars. I can keep coming back. I can be a real pain in the ass.'

Frank shook his head. 'We been around forever. We weathered bigger storms than you bring in the door.'

Marshall spread his hands. 'Yet I'm still here. I guess you could shoot me.'

Frank didn't answer.

Marshall said, 'Cops might not buy it, given I'm just sitting here in a booth.'

Frank shrugged. 'We got throwdowns. Don't give me ideas.'

'Maybe I should. You don't seem to know how to get rid of me.'

Frank Cifaretti seemed to think about that for a moment. Then he leaned the other way in his seat, reached behind him and brought out a revolver – a little Colt Cobra .38, snub-nose. He thumbed back the hammer and said, 'It's not a mystery to me, pal, I promise. I squeeze, you go goodnight.'

'And then you go to prison. Or do you trust everyone to keep to the approved story? Trust they won't get into trouble somewhere up the road and trade out of it by saying what really happened. I guess . . . yeah. Come to think of it, I never heard of a Mafia rat. No one ever turns, do they?'

Frank didn't answer.

Marshall said, 'Tell me who the shooter is, I'll get out of here, make this someone else's problem. Otherwise, I'm quite comfortable, thanks.'

Frank didn't answer.

Marshall said, 'He owed you money, fine. I can accept maybe you wanted him alive. But I don't accept you know nothing about what's happened. You little scamps love talking.'

'Yeah, keep going. See what happens.'

Marshall said, 'You just told me all about how the law loves checking up on you, so let's not pretend you're going to murder me right here.'

Easy enough to say, but his subconscious didn't see it as a guarantee. The fear glands were working: blood pounding, a prickle on his scalp in two places, one for each pistol. Frank was looking at him along the barrel of the Colt, some wry plan seeming to form in the narrowed eyes. He opened the cylinder and held the gun upright, one tube covered with a finger. The five unsupported shells dropped out and rolled in ponderous separate arcs with a sound like marbles. He aimed the Colt at Marshall again, the cylinder still hanging out to one side. Five tubes with fresh air and one with a bullet.

He said, 'Tell you what: show me you can do a round, we'll point you in the right direction.' He grinned. 'I figure that's culturally appropriate, given the neighborhood. Russian Roulette. How it's meant to work, right? Borrow shit from other cultures, make it your own.'

He spun the cylinder. The tubes blurred soundlessly with the motion. The guy with the ponytail had his own pistol up now, the SIG aimed at Marshall's head from a range of about three feet. The two guys beside him were both shifting in their seats, concern manifesting as a need to get comfy.

Frank said, 'You know the rules? Spin, close it, pull the trigger. If dead Vialoux's so important, should be an easy decision, right? One in six. Hard man like yourself must've stared down worse odds than that.'

Marshall picked up one of the bullets on the table, weighed it on his palm.

'Yeah, there you go. One in six. Not bad, huh? To answer a question you want answered. Clear up something real important.'

Frank spun the cylinder again and made a V with his fingers, held it below his eyes. 'Watching me the whole time. Like we're doing it together.'

Marshall didn't answer, studied the cylinder going around, the blur gradually resolving into separate tubes as the motion slowed.

'Pass it here.'

Frank slid the gun across the table.

Ponytail guy leaned closer, the SIG two feet from Marshall's temple.

Marshall picked up the Colt in his right hand. He pointed it at the floor beside the booth. Blood still pounding in his head. He breathed deeply, trying to make space for clear thoughts.

He said, 'These are hard-nose rounds.'

'Yeah.' Amused, rubbing his jaw again. 'Didn't say it wouldn't hurt.'

Marshall gave the cylinder a test-whirl, watched the motion. He said, 'So the bullet's a decent portion of the cylinder weight. Isn't it?'

'If you say so.'

Marshall thought about it. He said, 'And gravity wants the bullet at the bottom of the cylinder. So the cylinder will spin faster when the bullet's in the bottom half. Like a kid on a swing. So when I stop the spin, the bullet's more likely to be in the *top* half than the bottom. Because the rotation's slower through the top part of the circle.'

'I don't have a clue, pal.'

Marshall looked at the gun again, aiming at the floor on a shallow angle, the cylinder hanging out to the left of the frame. He said, 'And then of course the cylinder has to move through ninety degrees when it closes, so the top half will actually be the right-half. Won't it? And Colt cylinders move clockwise when you pull the trigger. So it's pretty unlikely I'll shoot myself, all things considered.'

'If you say so.'

Marshall looked back at him, hoped the guy couldn't see the pulse going in his neck. 'If it's nothing to you, why don't I load another round?'

Silence.

Marshall said, 'Far as I'm concerned, two bullets will make the weight even more exaggerated. Even slimmer chance I'll shoot myself. But as far as you're concerned, the odds will go from one-in-six to one-in-three.'

They looked at each other. Frank with an amused light in his eye, but Marshall could tell he was trying to weigh it all up, trying to decide if it was worth it. A one-in-three chance he'd have a dead man on the premises.

Benny said, 'Frank, maybe we should just keep it at one . . .'

Frank reached and found a piece of bagel without looking

and put it in his mouth, eyes staying with Marshall the whole time.

Frank said, 'So what are you expecting? What do you think you're getting if you live through a one-in-three roulette shot?'

Marshall waited, putting it together. He said, 'I just want you to understand that I don't come down here for entertainment. I come down here because I have something I need to do. And if this'll convince you I'm serious, then let's go. One way or the other, I'm going to be a problem for you.'

Frank looked at him, not moving, and then something about the little speech seemed to send a current down a wire. His mouth twitched.

He said, 'All right. Load it with two.'

Marshall's hand shook a little when he picked up the bullet from the table. The brass slipped in his fingers and he fumbled it and grabbed it on the second try. He placed it in the tube beside the one already loaded.

He looked up, and Frank spread his hands. 'When you're ready.'

Marshall still had the gun in his right hand, pointed at the floor beside the booth. He reached across himself with his left arm and spun the cylinder, set it whirring on its spindle.

He looked at Frank.

'Actually, there is something you can tell me.'

Frank said nothing.

The cylinder spun on.

He could feel it wobbling in his grip as the rotations slowed, the offset bullet-weight becoming more and more apparent. He raised his left hand and with great care reached into his coat pocket and brought out the tracking unit from Vialoux's car, saw Frank Cifaretti's eyes move and settle on it.

Marshall said, 'Which one of you put this in his car?'

He glanced over at the guy with the ponytail, still looking at him past the steady frame of his own gun, pitch-black and boxy. Marshall tossed the tracker to him, a gentle underhand lob, the trajectory seeming lazy in its slow rise, finally peaking and then making its descent, an easy waist-high catch for the guy, and he took it in his left hand.

Not so easy though that he could do it without looking. A

second's distraction, but it was enough. Marshall flicked his wrist
to close the cylinder on the revolver and reached across the table
with his left hand to cup the back of Frank Cifaretti's head,
brought the pistol up and rammed it muzzle-first into the guy's
mouth.

The motion was just a straight-right punch with a gun on the
end of it. Frank had his mouth open slightly in shock, but
Marshall still broke teeth going in. The gun disappeared almost
to the hammer and Marshall thumbed it back, Frank's eyes wide
and lightning-bolted with capillaries, the gun muffling a shout
that seemed to vibrate up Marshall's arm. He looked over at the
guy with the ponytail, still aiming the SIG at him. 'Why don't
you put that down now?'

Nothing happened for a second.

Then Frank coughed, and blood and tooth chips oozed out
past the gun. 'Put it bown. Chrisshake, put it bown.'

Marshall said, 'On the ground's safest. Give it a little kick,
too.'

Benny had both hands in his hair. 'Chris, shit, put it down.'

The guy leaned and put the SIG on the floor, nudged it with
his toe and sent it skating along the aisle. He still had his
composure. Frank and the flower guys weren't taking things
quite so well. Marshall shoved Frank back against his seat with
the gun, the man's eyes so wide he looked like he was trying
to swallow it.

Marshall said, 'Why was Vialoux killed?'

'I bom't mow.'

His eyes were so wide, he looked like he'd been pushed
from a plane with no parachute. He said, 'Jeesh Chrysh, I
bom't mow. I bom't mow.'

'Who's the shooter? Tell me who the shooter is. The little guy
with the smile. Who is he?'

'Rangellosh guy. Ee worksh for Rangello.'

'I can't hear you. Rangello?'

'Mo! Farking risshen! Mikey Rangello!'

'Mikey Langello?'

'Yesh!'

Marshall said, 'I don't know any Mikey Langellos. Who
is he?'

'Fark. He runsh phings. He's bosh.'

'Where is he?'

'I'm bom't mow. Preesh. I bom't mow. He's farking AWOL.'

'What, you mean he's missing?'

'Mo!' He was jerking in his chair. 'Risshen! Mo one mows where he ish! Fark shake. Mo one mows!'

'So who's the smiley man. What's his name?' Shoving him against the chair even harder now, Frank's neck bending back over the upright. One mad-crazy eye drilling into Marshall, bloodshot and panicked.

'I bom't mow. Chrysh, preesh. Preesh. I bom't mow.'

'What. Is. His. Name.'

'I bom't mow! Fark. I bom't mow. I bom't mow. He's Rangellosh guy. Preesh—'

Marshall let him go.

He pulled the gun out of the guy's mouth, and Frank collapsed forward.

He panted, spat on the table, looked at the red drool for a second. Rorschach-in-blood that maybe told him something. He said, 'You're dead, pal. Show fucking dead.' He let the quivering subside and said, 'All you got out of that, you got a death warrant.'

Marshall slid out of the booth and stood up. The three guys at the next table were just looking at him. Ponytail man pretty calm, Benny and the other flower guy very pale and still.

Marshall said, 'I have two bullets. If you're going to follow, make sure you're third in line.'

He put the gun in the back of his belt, under the coat, and walked out. When he heard the door crash shut behind him, he started running: full sprint across the intersection, heading south on Coney Island Avenue. He saw headlights come awake on a cross street, a car moving off the curb and then swinging through a red light to follow him, and Marshall slowed as he saw Detective Floyd Nevins put his window down.

Nevins swung to the curb, eyes on his mirror, watching the bagel shop behind them.

He said, 'In.'

FIFTEEN

The car was a rusted yellow Volkswagen hatch that smelled like cigarettes. Nevins pulled them off the curb and headed south, still watching his mirrors. The dashboard had a little bobble-head figurine of a Batman villain – Riddler, Marshall was pretty sure – nodding along to the motion of the car.

Marshall said, 'Vehicle budget must be tighter than in my day.'

Nevins glanced at him. 'Small talk first, huh?' He was in jeans and a faded sweater and a Yankees cap. 'This is off the narc impound lot. I was hoping for something flashier.'

He made a right and went over to Ocean Parkway, headed back uptown. It took him another block to get to it. 'What were you doing in there?'

Marshall said, 'Asking questions. Same ones you have probably, except I scraped up the courage to go in the door.'

Nevins just looked at him.

Marshall said, 'Is this your version of working undercover?'

Nevins swung to the curb. 'If you're going to be an asshole, you can walk.'

'Do you want to know what I was doing, or not?'

The turn signal tocked faintly.

Then Nevins made some half-formed comment under his breath, no doubt offensive if afforded greater clarity, and pulled back out into the traffic lane. He sighed through his nose, as if cleansing himself of irritation, and said, 'You were setting a pretty good pace.'

'I was timing myself back to the subway.'

'What are you doing down here?'

'I told you. Same as you.'

'All right. So what am *I* doing down here? Don't take me in circles.'

'Vialoux said his debt was with a mob guy – Frank Cifaretti. I told you that. I remembered the bagel place is one of his fronts.'

'And then kept that recollection to yourself, obviously. And you didn't tell me he was mob, either. Or was that another instance of delayed memory?'

'It was an instance of assuming you'd run his name and then know what I know. Or did you decide to stop searching databases after being warned off D'Anton?'

No reaction. Which itself was a tell, Marshall thought. Like an unmarked cop car: suspiciously bland. He knew Nevins must have been told to leave D'Anton alone.

Nevins said, 'If there's a body back there, you're going to put me in a difficult position.'

'All you have to do is tell the truth. You saw me running, gave me a ride.'

Nevins looked at him, no trace of humor.

Marshall said, 'No one's dead. Relax.'

'So what happened?'

'I asked them about the little guy with the smile. Frank Cifaretti thought he might work for a guy called Langello. Mikey Langello. That's all he knew about it.'

'And you took him at his word, did you?'

He pictured Frank with the gun in his mouth, saying he didn't know why Vialoux was dead. Neck arched back and that one eye locked on him, terrified.

Marshall said, 'Vialoux was a mob hit, but those guys didn't know about it. It's something above their pay grade. And the guy above their pay grade's off the grid, apparently. Frank said no one knows where this Langello guy is.'

Nevins didn't answer.

Marshall said, 'I'm up in Flatbush. Come in for a beer.'

Boris emerged from the pet flap to greet them. He stood watching as Marshall unlocked the front door, and then trotted in again after Nevins. Marshall turned on the lights and went into the front room.

'Just give me a minute.'

He turned on the lamp and sat at the desk to consider his Pollock puzzle. Everything vivid and inviting under the glow. Straight away, he thought he saw a lineup, a shape and color match that ran voltage down his spine. He tried the active piece on the working edge but couldn't get a clean fit, tried again with

a ninety-degree rotate and came up short. Something there at a
deeper layer of puzzle-knowing that he couldn't make operative.
He backed off and went in again after a piece-swap, tried both
lateral working edges and then the two verticals, got it within
microns of a lineup but couldn't close the placement. He piece-
swapped a second time, encouraged by a tantalizing mental flash,
but the board let him down. No: that was a fallacy. Every aspect
of it was what you showed up with yourself. Your categories and
your patience and your vision. The board had no say. He tried
a fourth piece, seeing something on the lower lateral edge, but
then pulled out, knowing even from six inches that it was piece-
mirage, nothing there for him. But then something – *something*
– told him to stay with it, and on reflex he paired a working-edge
diagonal shift with a ninety-degree rotate, coming across to the
right of the frame almost without thinking and laid it down clean.
Two edge contact: convex-convex with respect to host shape.
Then still flowing off instinct, he made a take from the loose
reserves and came across to the *same* right-hand edge and placed
piece five on the first attempt: one touch, double-edge contact,
and again double-convex.

He leaned back, knowing he wouldn't hit another run that
smooth in one night, and Nevins said, 'You good?'

Marshall turned off the lamp and stood up. 'Yeah. I'm good.'

He found a couple of Budweisers in the fridge and took them
through to the living room. Nevins was over at the desk.

'Pollock, right?'

'Yeah. *Convergence.*'

'Yet to converge.'

Nevins gave the jigsaw a thorough scan, maybe assessing it
for post-retirement value. Marshall handed him a beer and Nevins
took a sip, eyes staying with the puzzle. He selected a piece from
the reserves and ran it down the left vertical working edge, found
a home for it near the base of the frame: two-sided contact,
complex shape and color interactions, concave-convex with
respect to host curvature. Inarguably a nice placement.

Marshall said, 'You didn't return my call.'

Nevins glanced at him.

Marshall said, 'I met Loretta Flynn. We had a nice talk this
afternoon, in the back of her car. I wondered why you were so

cagey when I asked you about D'Anton Lewis. I figured she must have warned you off.'

Nevins sifted through the reserves.

Marshall said, 'Did she tell you anything interesting? Other than avoid him?'

'She said D'Anton was very much within the scope of their current operation, and she would advise if anything relevant materialized.'

'I think that's how deputy inspectors spell, Fuck off.'

'Quite possibly.' Nevins chose a second piece.

Marshall said, 'Cifaretti was a good lead. I'm surprised you were down there by yourself. Or were you worried if you asked for backup, you'd be told to stay away from him, too?'

'How did Flynn find you?'

Marshall said, 'I assumed because you'd told her about me.'

'I told her you might try to speak to him, yes.'

'Right. Well, I knocked on his door, and then twenty minutes later I had three unmarked NYPD cars following me.'

'What did Flynn tell you?'

'To stay away, more or less. She said D'Anton had a mistress who tried to blackmail him, and then went swimming in the Hudson with no fingers.'

Nevins nodded. He was still trying to place his second piece. Marshall guessed Flynn had shown him the photo of the hand, too.

Marshall said, 'It didn't exactly persuade me he has nothing to do with Vialoux's murder.'

Nevins said, 'Loretta Flynn oversees trafficking cases. But she wouldn't tell me what her interest is in D'Anton.'

'The question is, if they're looking at D'Anton, are they looking at Cifaretti, too, for the same thing. Frank said they get a lot of cops drinking coffee at the Minimart, but I didn't see anything that looked like surveillance. And you were the only one who came to meet me when I left.'

'Yeah. And what was going on that you had to set a Guinness World Record for coming out of a store?'

Marshall said, 'I put a gun in Frank Cifaretti's mouth and asked him what the story is.'

Silence.

Marshall said, 'It was his gun, actually. They had some clever idea about playing Russian Roulette. I thought that was a bit risky.'

Nevins put the beer beside him on the desk. 'You think it's less than a one-in-six chance they'll find you and kill you?'

Marshall had some beer. He said, 'The smiley guy works for their boss. Whoever this Langello guy is.'

'You said that already.'

'I thought if I said it again, I might get a thank you.'

Nevins dropped his second piece on the reserves pile and turned from the desk. He looked tired and hollowed out. Marshall had asked in jest if he was working double shifts, making the most of his last few days on the job, but he wondered now if he'd landed on the truth by accident.

Marshall said, 'What do you think he was into? Vialoux?'

Nevins drank his beer.

Marshall said, 'He shouldn't be dead over a seventy-k debt. We've established that already. And Frank Cifaretti just told me he'd wanted him alive to keep paying. But then he also said it's his boss who's had Ray killed, apparently.'

Nevins said, 'Some people . . .' He faded off, and then said, 'Crises aren't tidy, are they? Things fall down all over the place. Marriage, job, gambling, whatever . . .'

Saying it with a kind of dull resignation, and Marshall wondered if he had inside knowledge, his own story of how life had picked him up and thumped him on the rocks.

Nevins said, 'I think whatever his trouble, he'd crossed a line bright enough, the debt couldn't save him. They weren't worried about getting back their seventy thousand. They just wanted him gone.'

Marshall didn't answer, thought back to his run-in with D'Anton Lewis.

Open you up, cock to throat.

He wondered what Vialoux had been doing with him, whether a job for a guy like D'Anton could put you on a hitlist with the mob. D'Anton seemed to consider murder a possibility. Why else did he need three bodyguards watching him cross a sidewalk?

Marshall said, 'What are you going to do when you retire? Cold turkey, or do you have a P.I. gig lined up?'

Nevins moved his tongue around his cheek for a second. Marshall watched him scanning the room. Two a.m. and the detective protocols still running in his brain, looking for detail that would mean something. 'Did you get anything out of D'Anton?'

'No. He told me to stay away from him. And then Loretta Flynn came and told me the same thing.'

He picked up a coaster from the coffee table and centered it under Nevins' bottle. In general, he preferred straight edges, because they lent themselves straightforwardly to a condition of order: parallel, or perpendicular. Coasters were an exception. It was a question of complimentary geometry. A circular coaster, with its edge concentric to the edge of the thing supported, was a deeply pleasing arrangement.

Nevins said, 'They'll be looking for you now. Cifaretti's people. You're somebody's full-time project, I guarantee it.'

'Cifaretti's a full-time project, too. For his dentist.'

Nevins' beer was three-quarters full, but he left it on the desk and moved to the door.

Marshall said, 'People have taken morbid interest in me before. And here I am, drinking beer on a Friday night.'

'Yeah. But it's like Russian Roulette, isn't it? How many times can you spin and not pay? These guys have long memories, and after Tuesday, I can't help you anymore. Think about that.'

'I've only known you for a day. I haven't developed a dependency just yet.'

Nevins opened the door.

Marshall said, 'Are we going to keep doing things in parallel, or are we going to help each other?'

'Up to you. Is there anything else you need to tell me?'

Marshall said, 'You weren't just going to sit there all night looking at a store with its blinds down. You saw me go in, and thought you'd see what happened. Well, as I say, I'm happy to confirm, the suspect is one of Mikey Langello's guys. I'll keep you updated with my progress. But maybe in the meantime you could call around, see if anyone knows where he is.'

Nevins went out, and the door seemed to swing shut behind him on its own accord. Marshall stood at the window and watched him get into the yellow VW and drive away. He stayed there a minute, finishing his beer, and then he turned out the light and went upstairs.

He made it halfway. He stood in the dark with his head level with the landing, and then he turned and came back down and switched on the desk lamp. The piece Nevins had placed on the puzzle was three inches up from the base of the frame. Marshall excised it carefully, lifting it with a thumbnail, no disruption to its neighbors, and returned it to the reserves. Then he switched off the light and went to bed.

SIXTEEN

What remained of Vialoux's office was on Sixth Avenue over in Park Slope, the ground floor of a three-story redbrick building, near the corner with Fifth Street. Marshall got there a little before nine thirty on Saturday morning. To the left were brownstone town houses, and to the right, on the corner, was a store advertising jewelry and watch repairs: *Lowenstein's*.

Vialoux's frontage was boarded up with plywood, and some enlightened soul had already thought to illustrate it with genital-themed graffiti. As if the arson just wasn't quite enough as an indignity.

Marshall backed up to the curb and surveyed the upper windows. No one visible. According to the gold lettering on the glass, the middle floor was an architect's office, and the top was an accountant's. He saw a light on in the jewelry place next door, but no one answered his knock.

There was a laundromat on the corner diagonally opposite. He crossed the intersection and went inside. Two women were at a work bench beyond the counter, folding clothes and chatting merrily in Spanish over the bored drone of tumble dryers. One of the women saw him and came over with a smile and a sing-song good morning.

'Laundry, or questions?'

He smiled, caught a scent of bleach that prickled through his whole airway. 'Sorry?'

'You look like police.' She nodded at Vialoux's office, visible through the window behind him. 'I saw you just now, looking at the damage.'

'Did you see what happened?'

She shook her head. 'It was during the night. We close at nine thirty. Wednesday, we open late, someone's here till eleven. Other than that, nine thirty.'

Marshall said, 'Do you remember people coming or going? Last couple of weeks in particular?'

She shrugged. One earlobe had been stretched and hollowed out by way of a plastic hoop, perhaps an inch in diameter. Marshall wasn't sure why people undertook such projects, but it was an impressive achievement given the small size of the opposite lobe. She said, 'Only since the fire there's been anyone over there, really. Police, I guess. Fire Department people.'

'Have the police talked to you?'

She looked him up and down. 'Thought I was talking to one now.'

Marshall shook his head. 'I'm a friend of the owner.'

She said, 'There were a couple came in yesterday, asked if we'd noticed anything. But . . .' She trailed off, shrugged. 'It's a street, isn't it? Ninety-nine percent of stuff, you don't even see it.'

'Did they take anything from his office?'

Shrug. 'People were in and out most of yesterday. So yeah, maybe.'

The woman at the bench said, 'I saw them take a file cabinet. All black from the fire but it must've been full of something. They had like three guys trying to move it.'

'Cops took it?'

'Yeah. Cops took it.'

Marshall said, 'You ever see the owner? Ray Vialoux?'

The woman at the bench said, 'I seen him now and then.' She looked up, amused. 'I don't understand, we're right across the street, we do dry cleaning. Why does he have to wear a crinkled suit all the time? Next time you see him, you ask him.'

'When did you last see him?'

The woman at the bench said, 'That was the one thing I knew, when they asked. I saw him Tuesday night.'

No hesitation.

She said, 'That's my closing night. I was locking up, heading out, I saw him going in his door. Only reason I saw, it was night-time, he was right there under his security light. He had kind of a package with him.'

'What kind of package?'

'I don't know. It was dark. Like one of those . . . maybe like a FedEx envelope?'

She mimed the dimensions.

Marshall said, 'So ten-inch-by-ten, something like that?'

'Yeah, well. Whatever this big is. It was an envelope.'

'All right. Thanks.'

'And now we get to ask you a question.'

'All right.'

'What's he doing in there that police asked more questions about who's coming and going than if we saw people with gas and matches?'

Marshall shook his head. 'I don't know.'

All three of them turned and looked out the window, like the boarded shop front could illuminate the topic.

Marshall said, 'You ever seen a little guy, dark hair combed straight back, smiles a lot?'

He got two shrugs in response. The woman at the bench resumed her work. As far as Marshall could tell, pants were folded manually, but T-shirts were handled by way of a plastic board, comprising a number of hinged panels. You laid the shirt on the board, and then operated the panels in logical succession, and the resulting folded garment was a thing of dimensional perfection.

Marshall said, 'Where can I get one of those?'

They sold them for thirteen-ninety, plus tax. He paid, and they bagged it for him, and he headed off along Sixth, looking for coffee. He found a place a few blocks away. They did cappuccinos, but like the coffee shop over in Sunset Park, they hadn't heard about flat whites yet. He stood in line and couldn't help feeling he was the odd one out. Everyone was young, very good looking, and dressed in Lululemon. Most people had an Apple product of some description. He took his coffee to-go, and walked back toward Vialoux's office, thinking he'd try a second time to talk to the jewelry people. When he got back to the corner with Fifth Street, he found Jordan Mora standing on the sidewalk, looking at the plywood.

She said, 'Spray paint's a nice touch, isn't it?'

SEVENTEEN

S he was in that tan coat Marshall liked, the one she'd worn yesterday when he met her on the street up in Jackson Heights. Jeans and knee-length boots and a turtleneck sweater. Hair a little messy in the breeze.

She said, 'Have you looked inside?'

'No. I should've brought a claw hammer . . .'

And he should tell her right now what had happened yesterday, his run-in with D'Anton, and the denizens of the bagel shop. It might make her re-think her association. He checked the street, saw people in activewear, people pushing strollers, people enjoying their Saturday in non-threatening fashion. He'd be OK for now.

She said, 'What?'

Light and amused, like she sensed some kind of punchline coming.

Marshall shrugged. 'Nothing.'

'All right.'

She moved past him and knocked at the door of the jewelry place. The window displays were empty. Black felt shelves with nothing on show. But the lights were still on, and beyond the counter, a door was open to a back room.

Jordan knocked again, and a woman came out of the back-room. She unlocked the front door, opened it wide enough to put an apologetic face in the gap.

'Hey. Sorry, we're actually closed.'

'Oh, sure. We just wanted to ask you about the fire next door . . .'

'I, ah . . . OK.' She leaned out for a better angle on Vialoux's office, as if confirming its burnt status. 'Are you police?'

Jordan said, 'No. Friends of the owner. Did you happen to see anything?'

The woman shook her head. She was fiftyish and heavyset, densely freckled. Curly red hair in a ponytail that didn't quite achieve total anchorage. A few errant strands were springing forward, antennae-like. 'No, this is my dad's place, I just came to pick up a couple things.' She allowed herself an eyeroll. 'If I can find anything.'

The expression seemed to invite complicity. Jordan smiled.

She said, 'Look, sorry to hold you up—'

'No, no. It's fine. It looks terrible, what happened. Lucky they managed to control it when they did, it could've been . . . yeah. Could've been something else.'

The door was closing slowly, the woman's smile growing as the gap in turn narrowed: defense against a charge of rudeness.

Jordan said, 'It's just – they need a couple photos for the insurance and I said I could do it, but obviously we can't get in the front with it all boarded up. I have a key, I thought maybe we could go through the back?'

The woman had to think about it for a second, but Jordan was hitting her with a broadening smile of her own, and the woman said, 'I guess if you're quick . . .'

'Thank you so much.'

They stepped inside, and the woman locked the door behind them. 'I was trying to find a couple of his prescriptions. God knows why he buries them at work. You should see the paperwork in that office, honestly. Here, come through . . .'

She led them into the back office. There was a scarred old wooden bench with lamps and magnifying lenses on articulated arms, and a set of tiered wooden shelves holding ranks of miniature tools – tiny saws, and picks and pliers made from blackened metal.

They went out into a rear courtyard shared between the jeweler and Vialoux's office next door. It was part of a long stretch of outdoor space, concealed from the street and formed from the adjoining rear yards of the town houses fronting Fifth and Sixth. There was a metal chair outside Vialoux's rear door, and a beer bottle crammed with cigarette butts. The chair was warped and rusted through in a couple places, as if showing the strain of holding up Vialoux and his problems.

The glass in the rear door had either melted or shattered, but it hadn't been boarded up: no public access, no need. Jordan reached through to free the lock and then stepped back as she pulled open the door. She turned to the woman and gave a smile that Marshall read as intending to convey finality.

'Thank you so much. We'll only be a minute.'

The woman looked hesitant now, as if she sensed that having granted frictionless access to a private business, she had some kind of duty of continued stewardship.

'I'll umm . . . I haven't seen a burned building before. Might as well take a look . . .'

Marshall followed the two of them inside. It reeked of smoke. The floor was covered with a soggy black pastry of ash and charred debris, maybe half an inch thick, perceptibly elastic underfoot. Jordan led the way through a narrow rear hallway, bathroom to one side and a kitchenette to the other, and then on into the main office space. Faint illumination from the white shards of glow between the plywood panels on the windows.

The jeweler's daughter said, 'Gosh. It's something, isn't it?'

Jordan played her phone light over the room. By the front door were the remains of a small reception counter, wood panels gone and just the steel frame extant. Vialoux's desk was in a similar state. Narrow metal skeleton presiding over a shallow pile of ashes, and the L-shape ruins of what would've once been a laptop computer. Against the wall was a file cabinet, matt-black with soot, drawers hanging open. Marshall checked each in turn. Whatever paperwork had been stored was now a modest pile of ash in each drawer. The file dividers had been reduced to feeble strips of metal. He toed about under the desk. The sprung bracket of a stapler. Long horsehair splays of denuded copper wire. A small picture frame, four-by-six, nothing left but a narrow metal edge. He wondered who or what Vialoux had kept there on his desk with him, whether it gave him any help or comfort in the last few weeks, or if its value had been lost before the fire. He moved closer to the door, heard glass crunching under his boots.

He asked Jordan for the phone light, and she handed it over.

Marshall shone it at the floor. The slurry at his feet purplish in the glare, a whorled sheen of oil on the water. He toed around carefully, found the edge of a piece of glass and levered it up with the lip of his boot sole. He brought the light in closer, studying the composition of the mess, saw a half-inch of charred detritus covering the glass. He dug around some more, widening the hole, keeping the light on his work, and for a brief moment saw blue industrial carpet before the soot-black water seeped in.

He said, 'I think I've seen what I need to see.'

When they got outside to the courtyard, the jeweler's daughter was suddenly talkative again, perhaps conversationally repressed by the vibe of the office, and now making up for lost observations. She told Jordan it was a good reminder of the importance of smoke alarms, and she was going to check her father's system was working, and her friend Heather had been doing up a place in Prospect Park, and a blowtorch had been left briefly unattended, and that was almost a tragedy too, and everyone was just one idle mistake from something you can regret, big time. Then something occurred to her, and it made her stop. 'All of this stuff, it's replaceable, but . . .' She shook her head, frowning, closing in on pithy insight, bedrock truth: 'You can buy another office, but you can't buy another life. You know?'

Jordan reiterated her appreciation, and they went out through the jeweler's shop, and the red-haired woman told them to be safe, and saw them off with a smile and a click of the lock.

Marshall said, 'Do you think she noticed we didn't take any photos?'

'Yeah. That's a point.' She stood looking at him. 'So what's the theory?'

He said, 'Let's sit down somewhere.'

EIGHTEEN

They walked to the coffee place Marshall had found on Sixth and sat amidst the Apple-and-Lululemon crowd at a table by the window: Marshall with his second cappuccino of the day, Jordan with a chai latte or something. She was quarter-profile to him, shoulder to the window, patient and reflective as she sipped, maybe a little amused as she watched Marshall arrange his cash: bills tamped square and with a single, crisp fold at the midpoint – transverse, obviously – denominations in ascending order, outside to in. He leaned sideways to slip the cash in his pocket – the motion flashing him back two nights to his meeting with Vialoux, that same action affording a second's prior warning of the looming and mortal threat – and Jordan said, 'Are you going to tell me now what you think, or do you need some more quiet brooding?'

Marshall said, 'They broke in because they were looking for something. Obviously. And they must've found it. I talked to the women in the laundromat. They said the police took a file cabinet with them yesterday. They wouldn't bother doing that if it was full of ash. Which means whoever hit Vialoux's office took the time to open one file cabinet, and not the other. And why would they do that, unless they'd found what they were looking for?'

Jordan said, 'They.'

'Same guys who got him at the restaurant. Timeline seems pretty clear. Fire occurred at ten or eleven o'clock, Thursday night. They obviously shot him and then came up here to his office.'

'Could've been theatrics. The arson, I mean.'

Marshall shook his head. 'Hired guys wouldn't do that. They don't pull the trigger and then hang around for extras. They were at his house before they killed him. The guy could've thrown a Molotov through the window, instead of just standing there, waving. And they could've done that here, too. Molotov, I mean. But they didn't. They went inside. They were looking for something specific, they knew he had it, and they found it.'

'So then why the fire at all? If they'd found what they needed, the arson was pointless. Other than as some kind of final insult that he was never going to experience anyway because he was already dead.'

Marshall said, 'What do people keep in file cabinets?'

'Well. Files, obviously. Paper.'

'Right. So they were looking for a physical document. And it's impossible to tell now what he had, and what he didn't have, and what might've been taken.'

Jordan had some chai latte. 'You said the timeline's clear.'

'Pretty clear.'

She said, 'But it's not logical, is it? If, like you say, they were hired to do a job. I mean, they were sophisticated enough to track his car, know his movements, but then when it came down to it, the best they could do was shoot him through the window of a restaurant, and then come up here and light a fire. Two birds, one stone would've been easier. Wait until he was in his office, kill him, take whatever they needed. Seems pretty obvious.'

'So what's your theory then?'

'I don't think these guys are hired. I think they're part of it. I think they're vicious enough, they thought they could fix the problem themselves, but they're too involved to do it properly. They've got something at stake, and it's making them reactive and impulsive rather than dispassionate.'

That made sense. He thought of D'Anton on the street in the rain yesterday, showing him the dagger he carried.

Reactive and impulsive rather than dispassionate.

He thought the man's behavior might fit that assessment.

She said, 'Do you agree?'

'Yeah. I think so . . .' Then he said, 'Full disclosure, I'm probably not the safest guy to hang around with.'

He told her about yesterday, meeting D'Anton and being warned off by Loretta Flynn from NYPD. The guys in the bagel shop down in Brighton Beach, and his game of Russian Roulette with Frank Cifaretti.

She absorbed it all in with the same patient and unperturbed expression she'd worn yesterday, when he told her about Vialoux. She sipped her chai latte and waited for him to finish, and then she said, 'I don't imagine he'll forget about that any time soon, will he?'

Marshall said, 'Depends when he sees a dentist. As long as he can stick his tongue in a gap, he'll want to get even.'

'D'Anton Lewis obviously knows something. Else why go straight to death threats when you asked him about it.'

'Yeah. And people of spotless innocence don't tend to be under active surveillance by NYPD. They think he killed a woman he was having affair with, in 2017.'

'Really?'

He told her about the woman recovered from the Hudson, the photo of the hand Loretta Flynn had showed him. The imagery brought a silence for a long moment.

Then Jordan said, 'It doesn't exactly surprise me. Maybe Vialoux did a job for him, and it pissed off the mob enough that this Langello guy had him killed – gambling debt or no.'

Marshall said, 'I liked that theory, too.'

'Liked.'

'Except I saw Vialoux the night he died. He seemed to think his only existential risk was a gambling debt.'

He watched her think about it.

She said, 'Maybe he thought he could get away with not telling you. Or maybe he thought he couldn't afford to.'

'What do you mean?'

She shrugged. 'If he respected you enough to ask for help, maybe he didn't want to own up to whatever he was doing.'

'I think my potential impression of him was the least of his worries.'

Jordan shook her head. 'You don't know that. You don't know what he was into. He might have thought that if he could just live another day, he could fix his problems and keep his reputation intact, too.'

Marshall didn't know where to take things after that. He sat drinking his coffee, imagination doing dark work, giving him that line from D'Anton:

Open you up, cock to throat . . .

He said, 'Did we cover the fact there're some mob guys after me?'

'Yeah. Anyone tries to shoot you, I reserve the right to reassess my proximity.'

'I was being serious.'

She shrugged. 'You don't have to walk me through it. If you want some gallantry points, you can go and lock yourself up at home, rule out collateral. But I'm happy to take the risk, if it means finding out what happened to Ray. But don't think I'm going to dive in front of a bullet for you.'

Marshall said, 'I'm pleased we cleared that up.'

Jordan didn't answer.

He said, 'What were you going to do if she asked for the key?'

'Sorry?'

'Our friend from the jewelry store. You told her you had a key to Vialoux's office.'

She said, 'I do have a key.'

Maybe his surprise was somehow evident: she said, 'I worked with him.'

He almost said, *Briefly.* But he didn't. He let the topic die, verbally at least, mutual agreement in their shared look. Something there that maybe he'd come back to, but for now he just said, 'I'm going to talk to a witness who saw the smiley man, and then I'm going to see D'Anton again.'

'Is that a statement, or an invitation?'

Marshall said, 'The invitation was implicit in the statement.'

She smiled. 'Who's the witness?'

He told her about the Boynes, Vialoux looking into their daughter's suicide. 'Apparently Ray was around there one night, they saw a nice little man with a smile, sitting in a car, watching.'

They were by the window, and the image was too suggestive for her not to look: he watched her scan the street, checking faces, checking vehicles. He almost told her he was happy to do all this alone, but he figured there was probably an injunction against that kind of reminder, covered when she told him not to walk her through it. In any case, she'd been a cop. She knew the risk of this kind of thing, these kinds of people. Also, Marshall thought, he really liked her company.

He said, 'And I need a car, too. Something big.'

NINETEEN

Jordan had one of those oversized smartphones with a screen the size of a paperback book. She searched for rental companies, and the Google app showed half a dozen in Park Slope alone. They walked over to a place on Third Avenue, and Marshall asked the guy at the counter for the biggest car available. The ensuing wince conveyed so much bad luck and apology, it seemed for a moment as if catastrophe had befallen the entire fleet.

Marshall waited, and the guy shook his head a couple times, and then explained that their last Dodge Grand Caravan had been driven off the lot only two minutes ago. The wince deepened, gaining crinkles, and the guy said that sometimes that's just how it goes. They still had a Chevy Tahoe, though, if that would do?

Marshall said that would be fine.

He showed his driver license, and paid with his Visa. He was averse to both practices – he preferred anonymity and cash – but he was cognizant that total stealth was unattainable, especially in this era: everything archived, computer power imbuing history with more and more detail, finer and finer resolution. At some point, Marshall thought, reality and knowledge would converge, and everything that ever happened would be a fact on a hard disk, sequenced to ones and zeros. Data – records – were the new religion, but he figured that even for a non-believer, a one-off visit to the church wouldn't kill him.

He drove out onto Third Avenue, Jordan up front beside him, and he told her his plan for the car.

She said, 'You should've paid extra, got the collision-damage waiver.'

He said, 'I think we'll be OK.'

'You think.'

'I'm not making you come with me.'

She seemed to consider that, the big SUV cruising along with a smoothness that made Marshall feel distant from the outside world. It was a nice car: gleaming black paint, chrome rims, smoked rear windows in case he wanted to give a ride to someone famous.

She said, 'Let's talk to the witness first.'

The mother – Ginny – had given him the address on the phone yesterday. Their place was in Sunset Park, a slightly tired brownstone a few blocks south of the Vialouxs. Marshall had to loop past three times before he found a curb space long enough for the Tahoe. A wind chime was hanging from the Boynes' eave, and it tinkled as they went up the steps, as if announcing their arrival. Or as if to say: go easy. Everything here is delicate.

Jordan pressed the bell, and it chimed faintly within the house, discordant with the wind-chime melody still picking out its careful notes.

Ginny Boyne answered the door. She matched the impression Marshall had formed yesterday, hearing her on the phone: someone who'd been through a lot, but hadn't lost sight of the way forward. She was shortish and petite, mid-fifties, a little stooped, but with a strength in her face – the slight squint making her seem focused, mouth firmly set but with a faint upward curl, like she still saw the light and humor in the world.

She said, 'You're the man from yesterday.'

He smiled. 'I'm the man from yesterday.'

They did the handshakes and hellos. Jordan introduced herself as a friend of Ray Vialoux's.

'Come in, come in. Don't worry about shoes. We're a shoes-on house.'

They followed her into the entry hall. The door to the living room was closed, and Ginny opened it slightly and peeped in.

'Is he there . . . yes. There he is. Come through . . .'

They followed. The chairs had been moved against the walls, making space for a large table standing on a spread of newspapers. Draped on the table was a paint-daubed bedsheet, and on top of that was a wooden board – perhaps three feet by four – constructed on which was a miniature artificial landscape. Through its center was a blue swathe of painted river, nicely textured with random strips of white papier-mâché – signs of chop and velocity, Marshall presumed. The adjoining terrain on both sides had been formed from what he thought was paper over chicken wire. A rugged landscape, well rendered. Sand and rocks down at the water's edge, larger pebbles that gave a sort of boulder-strewn effect to the lower slopes of the hills. One hill was gouged deeply through its side to form a sheltered valley, the coloring greener and more verdant, lots of cotton-wool shrubs and trees formed from little stubs of twig, topped with moss. All very impressive.

Standing on the far side of the table was a man in his mid-sixties. Ginny-like in his slenderness and hunched stance, but he was taller – Marshall's height, and maybe Marshall's build, once upon a time. He looked startled for a second as they entered, interrupting his quiet hobby. Then he smiled, polite and expectant, chin forward to see above spectacles sitting low on his nose, the whole visage grandfatherly and patient. He held a little plastic figurine in one hand, a fine-tipped paintbrush in the other.

'Mart, this is Jordan and Marshall. Friends of Ray Vialoux.'

'Oh, sure, hi. Sorry, let me put this down.'

He turned and placed the figurine and the paintbrush on a workbench against the wall behind him, turned back and shook hands with them, Jordan and then Marshall.

Ginny said, 'Starting to come together, isn't it?'

Marshall said, 'It's incredible. Must have taken you months.'

'Yes . . . I think the landscape's finalized. It's just a question of how I position everyone. The permutations can get a little overwhelming.'

He glanced behind him at the workbench. The surface was cluttered with dozens of plastic figurines, inch-high soldiers with strange armor and exotic weapons. Everything carefully painted, bright and precise down to the microdetail. Artillery, too: tanks and grenade launchers and gun emplacements, all showing signs of brutal and prolonged conflict.

Martin said, 'Hard to keep a steady hand during the paintwork, especially with so much infantry. That's where the really challenging stuff is. I'd actually intended quite a formal livery style, but it was just too difficult to sustain with any accuracy. But then the other day, I happened to be reading about the Bay of Pigs, and it just got me thinking maybe a guerilla theme would work better. There's a sort of requisite sloppiness to the look. So the challenge now of course is I have to go back through and make sure no one's too tidy.'

Maybe this is what it took. Maybe to distract from catastrophe, you had to dive into detail of another kind, absorb yourself with a project and all its attendant decisions. Marshall wondered how often the guy could glide through a blissful stretch of not thinking about it, not thinking about the fact his daughter was dead, or if it just always there, a dark basecoat to everything he considered. He noticed now that there was nothing on the walls: nothing except the occasional brass picture hanger, or a lonely nail.

Ginny said, 'They wanted to ask you about the man you saw. The night Ray was here.'

'Oh of course, that's right.'

He came around the table, stood at the front window with his hands on his hips. He glanced between Marshall and Jordan and said, 'Do you think the man I saw . . .' He swallowed, licked his lips, looked out the window again. 'Did he have something to do with it?'

Marshall didn't want to give him a straight *yes*, risk making him think he could've done more.

He said, 'We're not sure. But he'll be worth talking to, if we can find him.'

Martin nodded, looked at Ginny now. 'So when was it? Six weeks ago, maybe, something like that?'

'I think we worked out it was six weeks. The week after . . . well. It was the week after we lost her, wasn't it?'

Martin Boyne took a moment sucking on a front tooth. He bulged his eyes and then blinked carefully. He said, 'We had an idea Jennifer had been bullied, and that was why . . . Anyway. We wanted to make sure. Ray came and collected her computer. In case there was a . . . we thought there might be a message, or some kind of explanation.'

Jordan said, 'Did he find anything helpful?'

'No, in the end, he didn't. Nothing on the computer, apparently. It's all just . . . yes. Anyway.'

Ginny Boyne said, 'And Ray's daughter – Ella – she knew her, of course. She's known her since school, since they were this high. She even – she took the time to call me up and say how sorry she was, and that . . . well.' She stood beside her husband at the window. 'She was very certain no one had been giving Jen any trouble. So maybe it was just one of these awful things that happen. But sorry, I'm interrupting . . .'

The pair of them stood silently for a moment, unified in memory, and then Martin said, 'Yes . . . I was actually waiting for Ray in here – in fact right here by the window. I think . . . I guess, as you do, I'd been going around and around with things in my head all day, and I was just looking forward to talking to someone, really.' He ran a hand through his hair, looked behind him at the model terrain on the table before he turned back to the window. 'I saw Ray park and head over, and I just happened to see another car pull in to the curb over there . . .' He pointed on a diagonal, through the window. 'I guess because it was late and I saw the headlights, it made me notice. And then the fact that nobody got out. It was just parked there.'

Marshall said, 'What sort of car was it?'

'Oh . . .' He shook his head. 'I couldn't even tell you.' He shrugged. 'It was just a car. Nothing about it really stood out. It was just the fact it seemed to show up at the same time as Ray did.'

Ginny Boyne said, 'Sorry, I should have offered – can I get anyone a drink?'

Jordan gave her a smile. 'No, not at all. I'm fine.'

Marshall said, 'Thank you, we've just had coffee. Don't worry.'

'We'd offer you a seat, but it's more like a hobby room than a living room, right now.'

Marshall said, 'It's absolutely fine, don't worry.' Then to Martin, 'Did you get a closer look at who was in the car? Ginny mentioned on the phone, you saw Ray out when he left, and the car was still there?'

Martin Boyne nodded. 'I saw him to the door. He had Jen's computer with him, and I think . . . as I say, it had been on my mind all day, and I could see from the top step when I went outside, the car was still there. And it wasn't . . . it wasn't some-thing I'd ordinarily do, but things happen, and they rewire you, I think . . .'

He ran his hand through his hair again, as if embarrassed at the insight. Then pointing again, he said, 'Ray had left his car over that way, to the left, and the guys watching, they were over to the right more. I don't think . . . I'm not sure I even said anything to Ray. He went toward his car, and I went toward their car and . . .' He shrugged. 'That was it, basically.'

'Did you speak to them?'

He shook his head. 'I don't know what I thought I was going to do. I was really just heading over there without thinking, pushed along by all this frustration from other things. I'm not sure what I was going to do. Ask them why they were there, I guess. But I never had to make a decision. They obviously saw me coming, and they started up and drove off. Came right past, which is how I saw. The man in the driver's seat, he turned to look at me as they came past, and yeah . . . I guess as Ginny said, he just had this smile on his face. You know. Daring me to do something. But, well. I didn't, of course. I just stood there, and then I went back inside.'

His voice was different for the final line – duller, heavier – as if he saw his actions as a symbol for larger failure.

Marshall said, 'Do you remember anything else about him? Other than the smile? Hair, age?'

'Dark hair, I think. And he could've been . . . well. Forties, I guess. A white man in his forties. But just this bright smile, almost like a clown. And . . . unpleasant, somehow.' He shook his head, eyes on something in the distance. 'He just gave me this sense, it was like he could feel bad luck or misfortune. You know. Just this . . . misplaced sense of glee about him, really. Almost devilish.' He shook his head. 'Sorry, things are coming back in bits and pieces as I think about it.'

'No, not at all. That's great. And what about the man with him?'

'Yes, well that was the thing I'm trying to get clear. I don't think . . . I'm not even sure now . . . I'm not even certain it was a man. I think maybe it was a woman.'

TWENTY

Marshall saw Jordan's eyes cut across to him, but neither of them spoke. After a moment, Martin Boyne shook his head.

'Look, I'm sorry. I wish I had something more to tell you. Like I say, the car was moving before I got to them.' He shrugged. 'It was just an impression, really, as they went by. And the guy with the smile, he was turning to look at me as they passed. He was driving, so he was on the side nearest to me, and all I can really picture . . .' He shut his eyes, furrowed his brow. 'All I can see is his face in the window.' He shook his head. 'I can't even see it now, but I remember . . . I remember thinking at the time, it looked like a woman beside him.'

No one answered. The wind chime on the front eave touched out a few careful notes. Marshall saw Jordan glance at him again: a silent query as to who would do the prompting.

Marshall said, 'Can you remember what gave you that impression? What made you think it was a woman in the car?'

Silence in the room. Boyne was still looking out at the street, a gleam to his eyes from the window light. Or maybe something else: bright with memory, or a wish he could change things.

Marshall said, 'There must have been something you noticed at the time.'

Silence again.

Ginny Boyne took her husband's hand, shook it gently. The whole limb wobbled, as if boneless. 'Try to remember, darling. It could be helpful.'

Marshall said, 'Maybe hair? Body shape? Size?'

But Martin Boyne was shaking his head. He said, 'I'm sorry, I can't remember. It was weeks ago. It was a glimpse in the dark, weeks ago.'

He came away from the window and went back over to his workbench, started moving things around: nothing productive, just idle, awkward motion to get him through the moment.

He stopped and said, 'It's like when you wake up and you know you had a dream, but you can't remember the dream. That's what it's like.'

No one answered.

Martin said, 'I'm sorry, there's just been too much on my mind. I can't think about anything else.'

Marshall said, 'It's OK. We understand.'

Martin shook his head. He braced himself on the edge of the bench. 'We had to move my landscape down here. It used to be upstairs, in the spare room, but it was too close to where she was. I couldn't get anything done. I'd just stand there, thinking she used to be on the other side of the wall.'

He shook his head. All kinds of anguish and misery in that single gesture. A kind of dismal finality to it. He said, 'I'm sorry. I don't think I can help you.'

They sat in the Tahoe to debrief. Marshall had the wind chime framed by chance in his side mirror. Oddly compelling to watch the subtle motion.

He said, 'This changes things slightly. Lydia's neighbor – Mrs

Lopez – she had the impression there were two men in the house. The smiley guy told her they were nephews.'

'Maybe he lied. She only ever met one of them.'

'But why risk being caught out? They knew they'd have to leave Lydia's place eventually, and there was a reasonable chance someone would see them, so why risk drawing instant suspicion? And a male–female pairing is more innocuous, anyway. If he said son-in-law and daughter, or nephew and wife, or whatever, it's just slightly more common than two nephews. And common is good, as far as they're concerned. Common means forgettable.'

Jordan said, 'Maybe he just weighed it up and decided the odds were in his favor. Might've thought the best thing in the long run was to have people looking for two men, rather than a man and a woman. I can see the logic in that.'

Marshall didn't answer.

Jordan said, 'Does silence mean agreement?'

Marshall smiled. 'I still think my theory's better.'

Jordan didn't answer.

Marshall said, 'Does silence mean agreement?'

'What's your theory, then? Assuming Boyne was right, and he saw a woman in the car?'

'Obviously the woman's a third player. Maybe she hired them.'

Jordan thought about it. 'You think she tagged along on surveillance a couple times, and then gave them the OK?'

'Something like that. Tracked his car, followed him long enough to find out he owed money to the mob, maybe thought that would be a good cover for murder. Distract us from whatever else he was part of.'

'If they were mob guys she hired, they'd know about the debt already.'

'True. Even easier, then.'

'So who is she?'

'I don't know. But I think we should ask D'Anton Lewis.'

They headed north, the Saturday morning traffic flowing well. As they went up through the western edge of Brooklyn Heights, the Expressway gave them a nice view west across the river to Manhattan. Nice if you liked gray, Marshall thought. Gray sky, gray water. Rooflines of the skyscrapers stepping up and down like some volatile graph, a histogram of commerce and aspiration spanning the length of the island.

The Google app on Jordan's phone wanted him to take the Midtown Tunnel, but Marshall cut across early on the Brooklyn Bridge and then went up FDR Drive. They hit traffic at Midtown, but Marshall didn't mind. He was wired for unilateralism, single-mindedness. There was something very pleasing in saying no to a suggestion. He'd decided on a route, and that was the way he went. They made it all the way up to Seventy-third and Marshall stopped before the corner with Park Avenue.

He said, 'Do you mind driving?'

'I'm not on the insurance.'

'I meant, do you mind driving, and not crashing?'

'Hilarious.'

'If someone hits us, I'll say I was at the wheel.' He nodded up the street. 'I don't want D'Anton's guys thinking I've got him under surveillance.'

He told her again what he wanted to do.

She thought about it.

She'd looked calm enough on the drive over, but now he saw uncertainty taking hold.

'This is the guy who threatened to cut you from groin to neck.'

Marshall said, 'He employed more confronting language.'

She looked out her window.

Marshall said, 'You're not being conscripted for anything. But if you want to talk to D'Anton, I think this is the best way of getting in the door.'

She didn't answer.

Marshall said, 'The freedom doesn't have a timer on it, either. You can just drive away, if you want.'

'Don't worry. I'm not going to do that.'

'How'd you get a key to Vialoux's office?'

She shrugged, innocent. Then she said, 'All right. Jump out.'

Marshall climbed down and got into the rear seat behind the driver's, hidden by the smoked glass. Jordan walked around the hood and slid in behind the wheel. She got her door closed, and an NYPD traffic cop pulled up alongside, shouted for her to move off the red curb.

'Not off to a good start . . .'

She waved an apology and signaled to pull out. The cop held back and left a gap for her, roof bar flashing, making a spectacle of the infringement. Jordan went straight across the intersection, staying westbound on Seventy-third, and the cop turned left onto Park, downtown.

Marshall slid across to the right-hand seat and tapped the window. 'This is him coming up. The white place.'

He could see a doorman outside D'Anton's, standing in the alcove. They'd stepped up security since his visit. He recognized the guy from yesterday.

Jordan said, 'We're just heading straight through?'

'Yeah, keep going. I don't think that guy will let us in, somehow . . .'

Jordan cruised past doing maybe twenty-five. D'Anton's doorman had his back to the alcove wall, looking at something on his phone. There were no curb spaces big enough for the Tahoe, so Jordan looped the block. Fifth to Seventy-second, and then back around the corner off Madison. The parking situation was unchanged. The doorman was still on his phone.

Jordan said, 'You think he's on the same message?'

'Yeah, possibly. Or maybe he's writing a novel.'

'Yeah . . . *East Side Alcove*. Shall I go around again?'

Marshall checked the time. Coming up on twelve midday. 'Better wait. He might realize something's up.'

She found a spot a block over, on Seventy-second Street. They waited there for twenty minutes, and then tried again for a third pass. The doorman was off his phone by now, but he didn't seem to pay attention to them. Black SUVs were pretty ubiquitous in this part of town. A curb space had opened up near the corner with Fifth, and Jordan parallel-parked. It took her three tries to line it up and swing in.

Marshall said, 'Smooth.'

'Thanks. It's like trying to park a container ship.'

She adjusted her mirror. 'Would they post a security guy if the boss isn't home?'

Marshall said, 'Be the smart thing to do. Make people waste their break-in effort while he's buying groceries.'

'Is he the guy you put in an arm lock?'

'No. But I doubt he's a big fan of mine.'

They sat there in silence for a while, Marshall sideways on the bench for a view out the rear window. Midday turned into one o'clock. He watched her browsing through news items on her giant phone.

He said, 'What's Jack doing today?'

'My son? Jake?'

He felt the quick, internal plunge of a social misstep. 'Sorry. Jake.'

She smiled. 'He ditched me for his rich friend. They have a place in Montauk. Jake got invited for the weekend. He said he needed a day off school yesterday, but funnily enough, he's feeling great today.'

'I bet he is. I wouldn't mind a friend with a place in Montauk.'

'D'Anton might have one.'

Marshall said, 'Yeah, he probably does.' He glanced back at the house. 'If he's under surveillance by NYPD, they're hiding it well. There's nothing on the street. No one's driven past more than once, other than us. And I didn't notice anything yesterday, either.'

'They might be set up in an apartment.'

'Maybe. They'd need a hell of an operations budget. This isn't a cheap neighborhood.' He put his face to the glass to see the windows above them. 'Be a nice assignment though, wouldn't it? Some plush apartment on the Upper East Side.'

'Bringing back fond memories of being undercover.'

'No. Not really.'

'How long were you in?'

'Two years. Give or take.'

'And you're . . .'

Marshall glanced at her.

She said, 'You're all right. Obviously.'

He smiled. 'I guess so. Although there's no point of comparison. There isn't another version of me out there somewhere who never went undercover.'

True in a strict sense, atom-for-atom, but it wasn't the whole story. There were people *like* him. Maybe in the absence of his experiences, he'd be more like Bruce Linney, the guy down the street from the Vialouxs. Infinite patience, no strange rules in his head he was compelled to obey, a peculiar affinity for T-shirts with dumb lettering. #DAD. But Marshall figured there was nothing minor in his history that could be edited for a more domestic outcome. He'd have to run the tape back twenty or twenty-five years and then lay down fresh material.

Jordan said, 'I remember when I was still in training, they had a couple of guys who'd been undercover come and talk to us. I don't know if they'd picked them to give a full-spectrum picture, or if it just worked out that way, but one guy seemed fine, the other guy had done it pretty hard. Said he was addicted to meth, didn't really have contact with his friends or his family. Didn't have many teeth, either, I seem to remember.'

Marshall said, 'I've chipped a few, but everything's basically intact.'

It came out sounding a little glib. But then he thought about it, and decided maybe it wasn't bad, for an off-the-cuff remark. *Basically intact.* Fairly succinct and honest, on a couple of levels. He was somewhere on that continuum between the guy who was fine and the guy who definitely wasn't.

Jordan said, 'Funny that was his recollection. Boyne, I mean. He knew it was a woman in the car, but he couldn't explain why he had that impression. Like you say, there must have been something, some detail, that he noticed at the time.'

'Yeah. But it's also like he put it. Sometimes you wake up after a dream, and all you can remember is that you had a dream. If someone put a gun to your head, you wouldn't be able to give them any details.'

Jordan said, 'If someone was quizzing me at gunpoint about a dream, I think I'd just make something up.'

'Yeah, I guess I would, too, actually. You think we should have pushed him a bit harder? Boyne?'

She shook her head. 'His wife had already talked to him about it. He must have tried to remember what happened before we got there, surely. So I imagine whatever memory he had of it is already recalled. Interesting though that he was quite hesitant. I wasn't sure if he was just trying to reconstruct everything, or if maybe there *was* some detail he remembered, but he didn't want to say. Almost as if he was thinking, *No, that can't be right.*'

Marshall didn't answer, thinking that one through for himself.

Jordan's eyes stayed on him for a moment, and then she went back to her phone browsing. It was two o'clock now.

She said, 'What if he doesn't show today?'

'D'Anton? I'll just keep coming back, I guess. Until he decides he needs to come outside.'

Another hour of inactivity. Rain resumed. Soft roof-patter, a slow dribble down the glass. Then at 3:20, a second man stepped out of D'Anton's to join the first. The two of them took up position like they had yesterday, one man facing east and the other facing west, a two-man human corridor on the sidewalk outside the alcove. Then a flash of headlights as a black SUV turned in off Madison Avenue.

Marshall said, 'All right. Go time.'

TWENTY-ONE

Jordan started the engine and swung the Tahoe into the traffic lane. Marshall was twisted in his seat, looking out the rear window. 'Hold here a second. We'll wait until he steps out.'

The SUV pulled up level with D'Anton's front entrance.

It was the same Lincoln Navigator that Marshall had seen yesterday, and it was the same guy who got out of the front passenger seat and opened the rear door. For a long moment, he and the two sidewalk guards stood at parade rest, an almost photographic stillness. Then D'Anton Lewis emerged from the alcove. The overcoat was tan today, well fitted, brown brogues sharp at the toe and polished to a honeyed gleam. He raised an umbrella as he came down off the step and started across the sidewalk toward the waiting SUV.

Marshall said, 'Now.'

Jordan put the Tahoe in reverse and hit the gas.

They took off backward, a jolt and a high-rev roar, and then a short half-block sprint, the front of D'Anton's Lincoln zooming closer in the rear window, and Jordan touched the brake and brought them to a soft halt with the Tahoe's rear fender three feet from the other vehicle.

One-way street, cars parked on both sides. Nowhere for it to go, unless they planned to reverse all the way to Madison.

Marshall opened his door and climbed out.

D'Anton was at the rear of the Lincoln, umbrella still raised.

Marshall closed his door. 'Sorry. Me again.'

The security team hadn't moved yet, no doubt a little wary: wary of Marshall, wary of taking action that might provoke employer disapproval, especially after D'Anton's feedback on their maneuver yesterday.

Marshall said, 'Don't tell me you forgot. We were talking about Ray Vialoux. And I think I gave one of your guys a sore shoulder . . .'

Progress: the man was moving now. He came over to where Marshall was standing by the rear of the Tahoe, hands in his pockets, exhaust misting past his knees. Marshall had to give it to him, he knew how to walk up to someone: calm, unhurried, face a little slack so the only thing on show was disapproval. That same gliding motion he'd used yesterday, like his whole world operated without friction. Even the umbrella contributed something, spired at its peak with gothic sharpness.

D'Anton said, 'I thought we understood each other. I don't want to talk, you want to keep your good health.'

'Yeah, what was your line? Cock to throat, something like that?'

D'Anton didn't answer.

Marshall said, 'Stabbing me on the street probably isn't worth it, right?' He glanced around, looking up, taking in all those windows, all those potential witnesses. 'And maybe I'm filming you from behind the tinted glass.'

D'Anton shrugged. 'I have a long memory.' He smiled, almost tender, making a fond promise to himself. 'I'll find another time, I'm sure.'

Marshall shook his head. 'No need. We can clear this all up right now. What was Ray Vialoux doing for you that got him killed?'

D'Anton stood there looking at him.

Marshall said, 'Your image is important, right? You want people to take you seriously. But you can't stab me here, we've covered that.' He turned, glanced at the Tahoe. 'And you can't drive anywhere. You could walk wherever you're heading, and I could follow, and we could make it a spectacle.' He shrugged. 'Or I guess you could go inside, and I can keep coming back, and people will start to think you're trying to avoid me.'

D'Anton said, 'Your image seems important to you, too. Hard to come striding up to people, be a pain in the ass, if you're in a wheelchair with two broken legs.'

Marshall said, 'Broken legs? Better than being stabbed in the balls. Two meetings, you're softening already.'

D'Anton was moving the umbrella slightly, twisting it back and forth. The spiked circumference passing left and right across his forehead and the gaze below it even sharper.

Marshall said, 'You're still thinking it through, huh?'

He tipped his head, aiming at the white town house.

'Let's go inside. That's the easy way to do it. Otherwise people will start asking why I'm following you around, wonder what you've been doing that it's worth my effort. Police tend to wonder these things, you know? Especially given my history.'

The security guys were still standing, watching, so patient and unmoved they seemed like set-dressing for the interaction. Recordings of suited men, overlaid on the street by way of hologram.

D'Anton moved away, heading for his front door. When he reached the curb, he stopped and turned back, nodded at the Tahoe. 'Is Ms. Mora joining us, or is she just a chauffeur?'

He knew the man wanted a reaction, dropping the fact he knew her name, but Marshall just said, 'Yeah, she'll come in for a talk.'

D'Anton said, 'I'll give you ten minutes. Consider that a tremendous courtesy. You're not a policeman anymore.'

D'Anton went into his white palace, followed by one of the security guys on the sidewalk. The other man took up guard duty in the alcove, and the third guy got back in the Lincoln. Marshall waited outside for Jordan to park the Tahoe, and when she walked back and joined him, she said, 'You first.'

Saying it with half a smile, but Marshall thought trepidation was definitely warranted. Easier to stab and maim inside your own home, rather than out on the street.

But nothing happened. They entered the foyer unimpeded. It was an impressive space. Double-height ceiling, curved stairs accessing a wide balcony cantilevered from the second level, a security guy at the balustrade keeping watch, solemn as a pall-bearer. The floor was marble, patterned with some kind of intricate geometric art, and against one wall were two life-size mannequins dressed in Batman costumes. Muscled body armor, and the full cape and cowl, molded out of what looked like thick black rubber.

A white-gloved butler was waiting for them at the bottom of the stairs.

'Sir. Ma'am . . .'

The guy gave a tight smile and a tight little bow, a ten-degree incline before resuming strict vertical. His gaze went back and forth a couple times between Marshall and Jordan, as if in pre-emptive reproach of any unbecoming conduct.

'If you'll follow me . . .'

They followed.

The guy set a brisk pace down a white hallway, framed landscape paintings on both walls, delicate scrollwork along the cornicing. There were open doorways to either side. On the right was an office, and then a library with low, fat furniture and leather-bound volumes shelved floor to ceiling. On the left was a long kitchen area, industrial-grade, large enough for restaurant catering.

They came out into a parquet-floored living room, French doors giving a view of a small planted courtyard. Beside the French doors, D'Anton Lewis was sitting on a high-backed red-leather sofa, opposite a pair of red-leather armchairs. In the center of the room was a wooden coffee table so dark and notched and scarred it looked to Marshall like it got here on the *Mayflower*.

He said, 'I like your Batman gear. You wear that at night?'

D'Anton Lewis gave a sub-zero smile. He said to the butler, 'Thank you, Jeremy.'

The butler did his ten-degree bow. 'I'll be in the study, sir, should you need anything.'

He departed with a prim and fading clack of shoe leather, and D'Anton said, 'One was George Clooney's suit, from the 'ninety-seven film, and the other was from the 'eighty-nine original. Michael Keaton wore it. They'd deteriorated a lot when I bought them, so I had them remolded. They break the rubber down and blend it with resin and then set it on plaster molds.'

Marshall said, 'Did they still have a copy of the heads, or did you get them in for a re-cast?'

D'Anton smiled but said nothing, sitting there quite placid, like any prior tension was distant and forgotten. Marshall took one of the red armchairs, and Jordan took the other.

Marshall said, 'You had me checked out.'

D'Anton made a show of sliding back his cuff to check the time. He wore a gold watch that Marshall thought would present a risk of theft by amputation. He was almost like a parody of a gentleman. The polished shoes, the trousers blade-sharp through the creases, a three-button waistcoat on over the shirt.

D'Anton said, 'Nine minutes. You're lucky I started the clock when you walked in.'

He rubbed his hands together carefully, as if checking he still had all his fingers. 'I apologize for yesterday. I'll concede it was unnecessary. I had various things on my mind and . . .' He looked away, came back with a smile that seemed more knowing than sympathetic. 'Pressure sometimes manifests as rudeness, doesn't it?'

Marshall nodded. 'Death threats could be regarded as unseemly.'

D'Anton glanced around the room, apparently out of interest. Maybe the house was big enough, he didn't come in here too often.

He said, 'I assure you nothing we're dealing with warrants facetiousness.'

Marshall said, 'You threatened to kill me yesterday. I'm just trying to bring the pressure back to a civilized level.'

D'Anton looked again at his watch, but made no comment on time elapsed. He said, 'To answer your question, yes. I did have you checked out. Or rather, I knew who you were by virtue of your knowing Mr Vialoux.'

'Oh, yeah? How does that work?'

'Basically, you spend half-a-million dollars per year on counter-intelligence, and you find out who the friends of your friends are. And you also find out if they hold positions that might pose . . .' He looked away. 'I don't know. How do we put it? A conflict of interest, I suppose.' Looking back at him. 'The short answer being, I have some paperwork pertaining to you.'

'Right. And you decided I'm the kind of guy you can afford to confide in.'

'Well, not necessarily. All those redaction marks in your file, I wasn't sure if they were covering up honesty or deception.'

'Which would be of most comfort to you?'

'Yes, very clever.'

Marshall said, 'Do you know what's happened to Ray?'

D'Anton nodded. 'I have a copy of the police report. I understand he was shot right in front of you.'

'Exactly. There's no mystery about the *how*. We just need to know the *why*. And the *who*.'

D'Anton looked at him.

Marshall said, 'What are you mixed up in?'

D'Anton shook his head slowly. 'Who says I'm mixed up in anything.'

Marshall said, 'Loretta Flynn, from NYPD.'

'Ah, Loretta. You've met her, I take it.'

'We had a nice meeting in her car after I saw you yesterday. She was worried I might shoot you or something. But she wouldn't go into why she's so interested in you. Apparently though, she runs drug-trafficking investigations, so I'm tempted to put two and two together.'

D'Anton smiled indulgently. 'Guilt and suspicion aren't the same thing.'

Jordan said, 'You keep a lot of security around. For someone who's committed to honest business.'

D'Anton put a foot up on the coffee table. Maybe it wasn't from the *Mayflower*.

He said, 'My wife is missing. I'm trying to find her.'

TWENTY-TWO

Marshall didn't answer that right away, thinking there might be some follow-up exposition, but the man was comfortable with silence. He looked like he might sit there wordless on his red sofa all day. Beyond him through the

French doors, Marshall saw a security man make a loop of the courtyard. He recognized him from yesterday, but it wasn't his friend with the sore shoulder.

Marshall said, 'How long's she been gone?'

'Ten weeks.'

'That's a long time to be missing.'

'I'm aware of that.'

Jordan said, 'Has there been a ransom demand?'

'No.'

'So what exactly happened?'

D'Anton shook his head slowly, mouth downturned, as if baffled by the simplicity of it all. 'She went out one day and didn't come back.' He checked the time again. 'She was hospitalized for depression and anxiety five years ago. Her health now is excellent, but she still sees a therapist in Boston once a month. Last appointment, she left here in the morning and didn't return.'

Jordan said, 'Did she attend the appointment?'

D'Anton nodded. 'We contacted the clinic. Apparently there were no concerns.'

'Has she been back since?'

'No. She canceled the following appointment.'

'How did she get to Boston?'

'By train. Amtrak from Penn Station.'

Jordan said, 'Did she have a return ticket?'

'Yes. Apparently it was never redeemed.'

Marshall said, 'It might be a separation. Without the parting sentiments.'

D'Anton said, 'We've been married twenty-three years. She never gave me any indication of being unhappy.'

'So have you notified the police?'

D'Anton shook his head. 'No, I haven't. As I'm sure you've gathered, my relationship with NYPD is antagonistic. To say the least.'

Marshall said, 'And I assume you don't want them in close proximity to your drug-running enterprise, or whatever the hell you're up to.'

D'Anton checked the time.

Marshall said, 'How are we doing?'

D'Anton said, 'You've obviously formed some conception of

me as a person with unsavory connections. And I'm not
commenting one way or the other.' He looked back and forth
between them, and then smiled. 'But whatever negative view
you've formed, make sure you don't forget it. Know that when
I say none of this goes to the police, I mean it.' He shook his
head slowly. 'None of this goes to the police.'

They didn't answer. The same security guy did a tour of the
little courtyard.

Jordan said, 'So you took it to Vialoux, rather than the
police?'

D'Anton nodded. 'I'll agree it's circumstantial, but hopefully
the facts of the matter are clear. My wife is missing. Mr Vialoux
attempted to find her. Mr Vialoux is now dead. I'm fairly
convinced there's some connection there, irrespective of your
disparagement of the scenario as . . .' He looked out at the
courtyard. 'Some kind of divorce trial-run. But I think it's
fairly simple. Find who has my wife, you'll find who killed
Mr Vialoux.'

Marshall said, 'What did Vialoux think happened?'

D'Anton seemed to consider the decor for a moment. Then
he said, 'My professional landscape is very difficult to navigate.
Industry standards change. What I mean by that is they deterior-
ate. Connections and information-sharing are detrimentally
ubiquitous. People see how others operate, and traditions suffer
as a consequence.'

Marshall said, 'I don't know what any of that means.'

D'Anton said, 'What I mean is that I used to be able to go
about my business, and I felt that the risk was mine alone. There
wasn't hazard by association. But as I say, things change. My
family is at tremendous risk. And now I'm fairly confident that
my wife has been kidnapped by the Italian mob.'

Marshall let that announcement have a few seconds' silence.
Then he said, 'But there's been no ransom, and no contact.'

'Correct. But the message is still clear. It's the unspoken that's
most powerful. Stop what you're doing, or we can keep this up.
Your whole world will just silently erode.'

Marshall didn't answer.

D'Anton said, 'Mr Vialoux had mob contacts through his
police work. As you do too, I'm sure. I thought that experience

might be enough to get me what I needed. In the case of Mr Vialoux, it wasn't. But now I'm thinking, maybe second time lucky.'

Marshall said, 'Italian mob's got a few members. Who are we talking about in particular?'

'A man named Michael Langello.'

Frank Cifaretti's boss. MIA Mikey.

D'Anton said, 'What do you know about him?'

Marshall shrugged. 'Never met him. But I understand he's senior on the chain. One of his people is a guy called Frank Cifaretti. Vialoux seemed to think he was the source of most of his problems.'

He told D'Anton about Vialoux's gambling debt.

'I see.'

'So you didn't know anything about it?'

D'Anton shook his head, studied a cuff link: silver, intricate, evidently to his satisfaction. He said, 'Hard to repay a debt when you're dead, isn't it?'

'So I gathered.'

D'Anton looked up. 'Which means that obviously it was something else that got him killed.' Silence for a beat, and then he said, 'Like perhaps he was investigating a disappearance, and the only way to make him stop was to make him dead.'

Marshall said, 'How far did Vialoux get with it?'

'He had inferences, but no proof. He assumed based on my business activity and commercial interests that Mr Langello was responsible. But . . . and modesty aside, my activities have proved disruptive in our particular sector—'

'Congratulations.'

'—so it could have been one of a number of parties. But our belief is that Mr Langello is responsible for the disappearance.'

'Have you asked him about it?'

D'Anton shook his head. 'Mr Langello's whereabouts are a mystery, too.'

Just like Frank Cifaretti told him.

Marshall said, 'I thought you said you're paying half-a-million a year in counterintelligence. Do you have to buy the premium package if you want people found?'

'It's not a question of money. It's a question of whether your name appears in a government database. If it doesn't, they can't help you.'

Quiet for a beat.

D'Anton said, 'Her credit cards haven't shown any charges since the day before she went missing. Her appointment was in the afternoon, so she was going to spend a night in Boston afterward, but she never checked into the hotel.'

Marshall thought about all of that, and D'Anton watched him, one hand patting out a rhythm in half-tempo clockwork on the sofa arm.

Marshall said, 'We'll need a photo at least. Date of birth, social security, address for the clinic in Boston. The more information the better, obviously.'

D'Anton lifted his chin, raised his voice: 'Did you hear that, Jeremy?'

From the hallway behind them: 'Yes, sir.'

D'Anton stood up. 'Jeremy will assist you. Wait here. I'm out of time, I'm afraid.'

Marshall said, 'Have we reached our ten minutes?'

D'Anton's smile was one of cool detachment, like a sales assistant being told, *I'll think about it.* He said, 'Have a nice afternoon. Jeremy will be with you shortly.'

He walked out, and the sound of his shoes clipped away neatly down the hallway. From the front of the house came the dull thud of the giant front door closing, and then a moment's silence, and then the familiar shoe-sole rhythm resumed in ascending volume as the butler approached and entered the room. He handed Marshall a sheet of paper, slightly curled, still warm from the printer.

'Ms. Lewis' passport, sir. You'll see I've written the clinic address there, too.'

The passport image was a copy of the information page. The date of issue was 2018. Renee Lewis was black, born in 1981 in Spokane, Washington. Always something of a photogenic feat, Marshall thought, looking good in a passport photo, but she'd managed it. She was attractive, and the smile she wore looked almost premonitory. Subdued and slightly sad even, as if she knew that at some stage her headshot would be information in a missing persons case. On the reverse side in handwritten block

capitals were the details for the therapist: Dr Ruth Davin. A
phone number, and an address on Beacon Street in Boston.

The butler said, 'Sir, ma'am. If you'll follow me . . .'

Marshall folded the page in half as he got to his feet – a
rare but nonetheless precise longitudinal fold – the better for
inner-coat-pocket transport. He'd read that the world record
for sequential paper folds had been set by a woman called
Britney Gallivan, who'd folded a four-thousand-foot length of
paper twelve times. Marshall had only ever managed a few
dubious sevens. He fell into step behind Jordan as she followed
the butler out of the room, into the hallway through which
they'd entered.

They had a head start on him, more considered on Marshall's
part than it appeared, and his twelve-foot lag meant neither of
them noticed when he sidestepped to his right through the first
of the three open doors between the hallway and the kitchen.

Brisk and quiet along the length of the room. Cool and perfect.
Stainless benches without a spot or blemish. At the third door,
standing with his shoulder to the frame, a baseball bat in one
hand, hanging by his leg, was the bodyguard he'd met yesterday:
his armlock victim.

Marshall stood quietly behind him, looking past the guy's ear
as first the butler and then Jordan came along the hallway. The
human brain is a pattern-hungry organ, and the space between
them implied an order of appearance. The butler–Jordan gap
should've been matched by the Jordan–Marshall gap, had he been
tailing them. Except he wasn't, and Marshall saw the guy stiffen
with the realization that something wasn't right – as instantly
apparent as a missed step in a dance – and he leaned forward
and said into the guy's ear, 'He's standing right behind you.'

He saw the live-wire jolt go through him: a microsecond, well
suppressed. He looked back at Marshall across his shoulder,
bemused more than anything. Like a guy in a concert line,
shoulder-tapped by a ticket-scalper. He eased away slowly in a
half-turn, the bat still hanging at his side.

Marshall said, 'I thought the sound might be a giveaway. You
know: three people, you should've heard three sets of footsteps.'
Smiling a little now. 'Just heading out to batting practice, are
you?'

The butler and Jordan had stopped and turned to watch. The guy with the bat smirked. 'Get lost, pal.'

He was a big mound of a guy, six-three or -four, domed brightly by a shaved skull. Muscle turning to fat as it crept waistward through his fifties. No question he posed some damage potential, and Marshall knew he should've just left it there and walked away. But there was something about the feeling of holding his ground, facing up to the guy. The same feeling he'd had earlier, out on the street, confronting D'Anton. Even though he was just a man with his hands in his pockets, he felt in that moment aware of his past and his experiences, his conflict faculties, such as they were, and he felt they counted for more than anything this guy had in his favor, bat in hand or not.

Marshall said, 'What did you have in mind? Shot to the side of the knee? I'd need crutches for a long time. Or were you thinking something more permanent? Swing at the head?'

'Get lost, pal. Before you find out.'

The butler said, 'Sir, I think it's time to leave.'

Jordan said, 'Marshall, let's get out of here.'

Marshall said, 'What I don't get is why you're hesitating now.' He shrugged. 'We'd all be looking at you after you hit me, so what's the problem? Stage fright?'

He took a step closer to the guy. 'Would've felt pretty good, surprising me, right? And surely it'd be even better, looking me in the eye while you take a swing?'

The guy didn't answer.

The butler said, 'Sir . . .'

Marshall said, 'Yeah, I'm coming. Don't worry.'

He kept his eyes on the man with the bat, looked at him evenly, four feet between them. The best move the guy could make would be to jab him: no room for a swing, but a lancing blow would be hard to evade. Same with a headbutt. Marshall would lose some front teeth if the guy connected with it clean. Good as it was to face up to him like this, part of him wondered why he took the risk. Some deeper inclination had pushed him into this. He could've come up behind him, landed a punch in his kidney, taken the bat, maybe given it to the butler to hold on to. That would be a nice finish. But there was something even better about doing it like this, letting him know what could have happened, seeing in the man's face that he didn't have it in him to try anything now.

Marshall nodded and said, 'All right, then.'

He turned and walked away, following Jordan across the foyer. The butler stayed ahead of them and had the door open as they reached it. Marshall looked back as he went out, saw the man with the bat standing watching him, no doubt seeing a movie in his head about what should've happened. And then they were out onto Seventy-third Street, into the cold and the faint scent of mossy stone: the scent of the Upper East Side after rain.

Jordan said, 'What on earth was that about?'

Marshall said, 'I met him yesterday.'

'Yeah . . . I figured.'

He spent a moment putting something together for her, but wasn't sure it worked – not as she'd hear it, anyway. Some things in life, they only made sense in your own head. He could open a Jackson Pollock jigsaw puzzle, assemble it in faultless sequence, one piece after the other one through a thousand, and the satisfaction wouldn't equal the fleeting rush of looking that guy in the eye and seeing that he didn't have enough back there.

He said, 'You probably wouldn't get it.'

'No. I'm sure I wouldn't.'

They reached the Tahoe, and Jordan got in behind the wheel again, Marshall up front beside her.

Jordan closed her door and said, 'Something about him. He's lying, isn't he?'

'D'Anton? Yeah, he's full of shit.'

He leaned forward to check his side mirror. The alcove guard was out on the sidewalk, watching them. Marshall said, 'Let's get out of here.'

TWENTY-THREE

Jordan went left on Fifth, downtown, and then cut back east on Seventy-second Street. She said, 'You go first.'

Marshall said, 'He told us she's been gone for ten weeks.

That's a long time to be missing. And he seemed pretty relaxed about the whole situation. Wife abducted by the mob apparently, but all he's done is get Ray Vialoux to look into it.'

'No offence to Vialoux.'

'No, I just mean you'd expect a more dramatic response. If she'd been gone that long and her whereabouts was a genuine mystery, he'd be thinking she's dead. Especially if he's heard nothing. And especially given we're dealing with people who are . . . you know. They obviously see some utility in the occasional homicide.'

'One way to put it.'

'Yeah, but you know what I mean. They killed Vialoux, they killed the woman across the street from them – Lydia – so why abduct D'Anton's wife, rather than just kill her?'

She said, 'Maybe they're not as pragmatic as you are.' She thought about it for a block, and said, 'Might think they can hold her a while, encourage D'Anton out of whatever business he's in. Give her back after six months, once he's in an approved line of work.'

She was attractive, no question. And he liked the fact there was plenty going on in her head. Good to have someone who could catch and throw it back. What he needed to do was ask her to dinner, but he didn't want to pop the question too early. Better to wait until closer to the time, make it seem more natural, like it was just the obvious way for the day to unfold.

He said, 'It's still a big liability, keeping someone prisoner. Especially for that long, two and a half, three months.'

'So you think she's just left him?'

Marshall said, 'Would you want to be married to him?'

'I don't think so.'

'Yeah. Me either. And I think his wife reached the same conclusion, and walked out. And he's spinning it to us as something more, try and find out where she's gone.'

There were people on the sidewalk carrying Halloween masks, a couple of guys with bullhorns waiting at a light. Maybe the Fifth Avenue protest was booked for an evening session.

Jordan said, 'The question is, did he spin Vialoux the same story.'

Marshall shook his head. 'I don't think so. Otherwise Vialoux would've told me. But he didn't sit down and say his life was coming apart because of a gambling debt, and he was stressed out of his mind trying to recover a kidnap victim from the Italian mob. Kind of thing he would've mentioned.'

'Yeah. Probably.'

They came to a stop, traffic backed up for the on-ramp at FDR Drive, a two-block waiting line.

Marshall said, 'I think she went off on her own volition, and D'Anton asked Vialoux to find her. Or at least try to contact her, and I don't know . . . negotiate conditions of return.'

'And now he's dead, D'Anton's trying out a different story.'

Marshall said, 'Something like that. Although I think the mob angle probably has a grain of truth to it. If he wants us to find her, there's no point sending us in the wrong direction.'

'So she ran off with the Italian mob?'

'Yeah, potentially. Might've come to an arrangement with them. Set her up with a place, and in exchange she gives them D'Anton's trade secrets or whatever. It'd explain Vialoux's role, too. If D'Anton knew the mob had put her somewhere, he could've got Ray in as an intermediary, sweet-talk them into giving her back, rather than as an investigator, per se.'

Jordan said, 'The credit-card detail wasn't right. He said there'd been nothing on it since the day *before* she went missing. She either started using cash for everything, or she swapped over to a clean set of cards.'

'Yeah. Which backs up the theory that she had help. They could've set her up with a whole new wallet. New ID, cards, bank account. All she had to do was walk out the door and she's away. And maybe too they had some agreement they'd look after her if D'Anton sent people looking.'

She said, 'Mob version of witness protection.'

'Potentially.'

They crawled onward. People blasted their horns, as if they could only see one car ahead, and the source of the holdup was a mystery.

Jordan said, 'Or maybe she was looking after herself, found a couple of guys to help her with the problem.'

She looked over at him. 'Martin Boyne thought it was a woman in the car that night, with the smiley man. We should see if he recognizes her.'

Ginny answered the door.

They hadn't called ahead, but she said, 'Oh yes – come in, come in,' as if in her mind a follow-up visit had been inevitable.

The house smelled of roast chicken, and from the rear Marshall heard a cable news commentator going on about something: a sustained dose of bewildered indignation. The door to the living room was open, and he saw a number of figurines and artillery pieces had been positioned on the model landscape.

Jordan closed the door behind them. 'We won't take up too much time. We just have a photo we want to show your husband.'

'Oh, sure. Let's see where he's got to now.'

She left them by the front door and went upstairs, the wind chime outside touching out a melody, polite and subdued as hold music. Marshall heard muffled voices, a brief back-and-forth, slightly querulous in pitch. Then Ginny came back down with Martin Boyne in tow, the man's faint smile somewhere between nervousness and strained patience.

He said, 'Hello again.'

Jordan said, 'Sorry, I know you told us you don't have much recollection of the man in the car . . .'

Marshall showed him the copy of Renee Lewis' passport.

Boyne took the paper from him, held it carefully at the edges like some kind of treasured artefact. He studied it in silence for a moment, tilting it minutely this way and that.

'I think . . .'

He looked at his wife, and then at the paper again. More tilting.

'I think. Yes, I think I've seen this person before.'

He looked up at Marshall, as if to imbue his words with greater certainty.

Marshall said, 'You saw her in the car that night? With the smiley man?'

Boyne nodded. 'I think so. Yes, I think this could be her.'

TWENTY-FOUR

Jordan said, 'So what do you want to do with it?'

They were back in the Tahoe, still parked at the curb outside the Boynes', just after six pm. Sky dark and starless, lights on all up and down the street.

Marshall said, 'It's no use to the police yet.'

She seemed to consider that in the quiet for a moment, both of them looking out the windshield. 'I don't think that's quite true. Drug-trafficker's wife absconds, kills the P.I. sent to look for her. I think they'd find that pretty interesting.'

Marshall said, 'We primed the witness. We gave him the context, and then showed him the photo.'

'The context was always going to be clear. Last thing we talked about with him was the fact he saw a woman in the car with the smiley man. Then we show up with a photo of a woman. He would've put it together.'

Marshall didn't answer.

Jordan said, 'If you were still a cop, and someone brought you this, wouldn't you want to act on it?'

Marshall said, 'I'd prefer they brought me something that they'd worked on themselves for a bit longer.'

She didn't answer at first. Then she said, 'I'm not sure that view is necessarily representative.'

Marshall said, 'You can take it to the police if you want. I'm going to keep running with it.'

'All right.'

He wasn't quite sure what she meant by that, but he decided he didn't mind. She could do what she liked.

He said, 'I need to check Hannah Vialoux's doing OK. She's a couple blocks over.' Then, to make sure she didn't get the wrong impression, he said, 'After that, do you want to get some dinner?'

He'd deliberated over the wording, and felt that was the best way to say it. *Get some dinner* felt more relaxed and unserious than *Have dinner with me*.

She didn't respond for a second or two, and Marshall felt like he'd driven a car off a ramp: airborne, waiting for the tires to hit the ground again.

Then she said, 'Yeah,' and nodded. 'OK.'

Marshall said, 'Great.' He studied his side mirror for a second, playing it cool, tires back on the ground but still having to work to keep it straight.

He said, 'There's a place up in Williamsburg that's quite good. Sage.'

She was nodding, smiling a little too, like she sensed the cognitive effort that went into his proposal, the myriad options available to him when contemplating a simple question.

She said, 'All right. I'd like that.'

He sat there in satisfied silence – hopefully mutual – while they drove over to the Vialoux place. No luck with parking this time: everything was taken. Jordan told him to go ahead and she'd circle until he was done.

'You don't want to come in?'

'She thinks Jordan Mora's a man. I think I'll wait a bit longer for the gender reveal.'

She was halfway up the block by the time he knocked at Hannah's door. She opened it an inch, security chain still attached.

'Marshall, I'm fine.'

'I just wanted to check in.'

'Great. I'm still alive. As you can see.'

He'd been worried it might go like this. She went to close the door, but he caught it in time.

'Excuse me, let go.'

'Can I come in?'

'Let go, please.'

He didn't want to turn it into a scene. He took his hand off the door. It only had an inch to travel, but it still closed with a slam. He waited there on the top step, not sure if she was done with him or not.

She opened the door. No chain this time.

'You don't need to keep checking up on me.'

'I think we've covered that.'

She didn't answer. She shook her head, looked away, exasperated. She wasn't blocking his path though, and he figured if he took a charitable view of that, he was OK to enter. He stepped inside. Hannah closed the door.

Marshall said, 'Is Ella home?'

'No, she isn't.'

Silence for a beat. They looked at each other.

Marshall said, 'Are we going to talk about what happened, or is every interaction going to be sort of tense and awkward from now on?'

She folded her arms, turned away from him. 'I don't need you to be a smartass. You can leave if you're going to be like that.'

He thought it was a reasonable question, derived from an accurate observation. The problem was, he thought, the skill wasn't in the insight, but in saying it right, taking the edge off it.

She said, 'I guess somehow I just got the wrong idea about what was going on. And . . . well. It's been a pretty weird time. My head's in a funny place.'

'It's fine. We don't have to make it . . . you don't have to explain anything.'

She said, 'You're the one who just asked are we going to talk about it.'

True. But only because she'd made a point of seeming affronted. He wondered if she resented him for turning her down, or if she just felt guilty for making a move so soon, Ray only dead a couple days. He'd felt bad for a long time, being with Hannah, betraying his friend. The fact he and Vialoux were police was another layer of perfidy. You don't go behind the back of that kind of team. And then on top of all that was the issue of what he'd put at stake. He could've broken up a family, broken the thing that he himself might never have. He felt he owed it to Vialoux to not only find out what happened, but keep his hands to himself.

Marshall said, 'All I wanted to say . . .'

He wasn't sure if telling her all that would improve the situation or not.

He said, 'It's fine. Everything's fine. I just wanted to check you're all right.'

'Don't worry about it.'

'Give me a call if they don't send a night watch.'

She shook her head. 'I think they've given up on guard duty.

But like I said, it's fine. I can look after myself. We have locks . . . as you can see.'

She had the door open now. He stepped outside. Jordan had already looped the block in the Tahoe. Hannah watched the car coming along the street on its second pass.

She said, 'I'll let you know about the funeral.'

She pulled the door closed, paused with it half-open, nodded at the SUV. 'Enjoy your evening.'

TWENTY-FIVE

They returned the Tahoe to the rental place and took the subway up to Williamsburg. Sage was a few blocks down Graham Avenue. The Saturday night crowd meant they had a thirty-minute wait to get in, but they ended up with a table for two by the window. Marshall liked being out at this hour in this part of town, full-dark, but early enough the sidewalks were still busy. He liked to keep an eye on the street for security, but it was interesting too, seeing the different characters, the cast that made up a night scene in the city. Bearded hipsters, people with toy dogs and puffy winter gear, like parodies of South Pole expeditioners. Teenagers head-down and eyes-to-iPhone, as if dodging the crowd via directions on the screen.

'You been here before?' She was looking at the menu.

'Yeah, a few times.'

'What do you recommend?'

'I've only ever had the massaman curry. Beef.'

She smiled. 'Why break a good habit.'

'Exactly.'

They ordered drinks, and some spring rolls for starters. When the waitress moved away, Jordan asked him how people end up undercover with the mob.

Marshall smiled. 'I'm not sure there's a typical induction process. I had a longish, unpleasant slide into it. Got involved because of my uncle, really. He was always around made guys, hung out on the edge of the Asaro family for a long time. He had a gambling debt with them that he couldn't get on top of, and it reached the point, they weren't going to let him out of anything unless I did a job for them. They knew I was a cop, obviously thought I could be of some use. In the end, I said yes.'

He tended to be pretty circumspect about his work, but it was easy, somehow, talking to Jordan. He liked how relaxed she seemed about it, quiet and patient and interested, watching him over the top of her water glass, swilling it a little.

He said, 'It went downhill from there, basically. I was documenting everything, logging evidence, so NYPD liked the arrangement. But I was just getting . . . I didn't like where it was heading. Morally, I guess. And it's no kind of life, that's for sure. You can't live for that long with your paranoia dial cranked up to eleven all the time. That's what it's like. I was certain I was going to be made, and I felt essentially stuck in this holding pattern of being debriefed, and then going back in for another round. On and on, you know. In the end . . .'

He thought about how to put it, one of those moments where brute facts had to be elided for the sake of social niceties, or a pleasant dinner. Although, seeing her there across the table, he had the feeling he could tell her anything and she wouldn't hold it against him. He went with the polite version anyway, and said, 'Tony Asaro had a place on the Upper West Side, in the Langham there by Central Park. I went in one day, blew my cover, that was it.'

Blown his cover in quite a literal sense, actually. He almost said that, wondering if it would sound clever or just sort of morbid. He decided to leave it out.

He said, 'They got Tony on tax evasion in the end. He went to one of those prisons that looks like a weekend retreat for middle management.'

She laughed. Their drinks arrived: pinot noir for Jordan, micro-brew beer in a can for Marshall. He tried to ignore the parallels, the weird feeling that hit him. He saw himself with Vialoux the other night. The restaurant, the window table, and then the figure with the gun . . .

He broke himself out of it with a smile, forcing himself into something brighter, still watching the street in his periphery.

He said, 'Anyway. That's my life. How's yours been?'

She laughed again, quieter this time, and then looked away, maybe weighing up the question, and he felt dumb for being so offhand about it.

She said, 'Well, I always thought mine was unconventional, but I think my perspective just had a re-alignment.' She looked at him. 'I grew up in a commune, actually. Back in New Zealand. Until I was twelve, anyway. Then I think my mother had enough of it, and we went to live with my grandmother.'

Marshall said, 'Twelve years, that's definitely giving it a fair chance.'

'Yeah. She was there fifteen, actually. Three before she had me. I don't think she minded sitting in a circle playing guitar, but fetching water from a well and making stuff out of flax hit its limit eventually . . .'

She had some wine, smiled around the lip of the glass, and he could see in the movement of her eyes she was making the same assessments he was: what to include, and what to omit.

She said, 'It was part of why I came overseas. Got to a point, I really just wanted some distance on everything.' She shrugged. 'Haven't been back.'

Marshall nodded, nothing to offer on that immediately, and he realized in a detached sort of way that he wasn't in any rush, either. Something extremely pleasant about shared silence in candlelight with this sort of company.

They dealt with the spring rolls, and the waitress came back and took their entrée order. Marshall went with the massaman curry again, no sense at all in seeking out alternatives, given he'd found something essentially above reproach. Jordan had the stir-fry vegetables. He wanted to hear more about commune-living, but didn't want to go in too heavy with the questions. He told her about his Jackson Pollock project, his thousand-piece *Convergence* jigsaw, recounted his session at the desk the other night, the way he'd managed to lay that piece down clean, no lineup, just something telling him it was right. He liked the way she listened so intently, cutlery poised but waiting for him to finish. Something about his explanation that put a light in her eye, making her smile. He didn't know what it was, but it was good being listened to like that, someone seeing the magic of the world in the same way he did.

He would've liked to stay there another hour or two maybe, draw it out, just sit there watching her talk. He thought if they ran a city-wide test somehow, scanned everyone's brain and took a reading of contentedness, he'd be right up at pole position, no question. But they were through coffee now, and the wait line was out the door, and when the waitress brought the check, he thought it may as well have had a timer on it, bright red numerals counting backward.

They had an awkward back-and-forth for a moment, both of them making moves to pay, but Marshall came up trumps. He had cash, and he'd known it would give him an edge in this situation, the fact he could lay down the full amount and then just walk away from it, hostage to chivalry. They threaded out past the line at the door, and then they were on the sidewalk in the cold again with the Brooklyn night lights and the crowd, and Marshall hoped the evening still had more to give him. They started walking back up toward the subway station at Graham, and he said if she had time, they should get a drink somewhere. There were a few places down Metropolitan he wanted to try. Jordan told him that would be great.

Then she said, 'Jake's away for the weekend, of course. So . . .'

He waited for it.

She said, 'Yeah, whatever. We can find a place, or you can come over, and I'm sure there's something in the cupboard . . .'

'Ok, great. Yeah. Let's do that.'

She said she'd get them a cab, given he bought dinner, and Marshall told her he'd prefer to take the subway if that was all right. His MetroCard expired at midnight, and he wanted to capitalize on its final hours. He wasn't quite sure if she saw it his way or not, but she smiled and said that was fine – he'd be stupid not to take advantage, obviously.

She only had pinot noir in her apartment. Marshall wasn't really a wine drinker, but he deliberated carefully, and he decided this was one of those times when it was in his interest to make an exception. They had a couple of drinks, Jordan telling him more about commune-living, something about how the philosophy of the place was essentially doomsday prep, but then that principle ended up subordinate to a resurrectionist Christian doctrine, and that puritanical element served as a kind of bug light for the social fringe: anti-vaxxers, people with unyieldingly strict ideas about gender roles, and some other stuff Marshall didn't really keep up with. Not due to lack of interest, but simply because he had other things on his mind right then. They were on the sofa by that point, things heading nicely in the right direction, Marshall thought, and at nine o'clock Jordan had finished her second wine, and she put the glass down and said, 'That's enough of that.'

Marshall said, 'What do you want to do now?'

And Jordan looked at him and said, 'Hmmm.'

That was an hour ago. Now he was alone in her bed, feeling unimprovably happy. The pressure of the last few days gone, at least for now. No sound in the apartment except the faint hiss of shower water, Jordan in the bathroom through the wall. He thought he could lie there all night, watching the ceiling, listening to the water, give his brain a holiday. Nothing but white noise, radio between stations.

He searched through bedding debris and found his underwear and shirt. The wine had grown on him, actually. He went into the living room and poured them each a half-glass to finish the bottle. He sat on the sofa, still feeling pretty good about everything, and a minute later Jordan came out of the bathroom wearing a towel.

'I've turned you into a pinot man, have I?'

'Don't know if I'd go that far. But it has its merits.'

She sat down at the table. He remembered her sitting there yesterday when he visited, and it was nice to superimpose the two Jordans in his mind – this one right here in front of him, and the one from yesterday – appreciate the supreme good fortune that got him from one situation to the other.

He said, 'I wouldn't mind some more of that Eric Clapton Jake had on yesterday.'

'I wouldn't mind some, either. Except it's in his room, and I'm forbidden to enter under any circumstances. And he has a sixth sense for other people setting foot in there.'

Marshall said, 'I guess talking is fine, then.'

She laughed. 'What's the plan of attack for tomorrow?'

'Find D'Anton's wife. We can figure out the details tomorrow.'

'Yeah. We'll sort it out over coffee.'

He smiled at that, and they drank some wine, and Jordan said, 'What does it say under all the redaction marks in your personnel file? Or whatever D'Anton was talking about?'

Marshall said, 'I don't know. I think that's the point of redactions.'

She was still looking at him, though.

Marshall said, 'When I blew my cover, they thought I'd taken some cash out of Tony Asaro's safe. Internal Affairs was looking at it for a while, didn't charge me in the end. It would've got written up on a DODA form and then blacked out if it was related to covert stuff.'

'What's DODA?'

'Disposition of disciplinary action.'

She said, 'So did you?'

'What?'

'Take any money?'

'They didn't think so.'

She paused, looking at him as she sipped her wine. 'OK.'

Marshall said, 'Can I ask you a question, too?'

She looked at him for what felt like a long moment, and then said, 'Uh-huh.'

Marshall said, 'Did you have an affair with Ray Vialoux?'

She didn't answer.

Marshall said, 'I just thought . . . well. If you only worked a handful of jobs with him, why would D'Anton Lewis remember you so well? He must've had some reason to check you out. And the fact you still had a key to his office. It didn't seem like the kind of thing you'd have unless you knew him pretty well.'

Jordan had some wine. She said, 'Any other clues?'

He shrugged. 'I'm not making anything of it. I'm just asking the question. I thought right from the start, the fact you were prepared to find out what happened, I wondered if maybe you and he were an item.'

She said, 'Is that why you're trying to find out what happened? Were you having an affair with him, too?'

That had an edge to it that he hadn't heard before.

She said, 'You forgot to ask if that was why my marriage

ended. Maybe my husband left me because he found out about me and Vialoux.'

Marshall said, 'I hadn't thought of that, actually.'

'Slower than usual, then.' She looked around, as if weighing up the situation somehow.

She said, 'What was the plan . . . wait until after sex, and then hit me with the hard questions?'

He didn't answer.

She said, 'Look, this has been great. But I think we should call it a night.' She put her glass down, and the sound of it hitting the table seeming to punctuate her line, reinforce the finality.

Marshall nodded slowly. There was some minor comfort in the fact he hadn't seen this as an outcome of his questioning. It felt exculpatory, in a way. The problem was, he realized, he'd seen everything as part of the same mystery, intrinsic to the central question of why Ray was dead. He should've seen where the line was, the divide between the pertinent and the personal, the stuff that was none of his business.

She was in the bedroom now, and when she reemerged, she had his coat and his trousers draped on one arm, the other hand still holding the towel together. She dropped the clothes beside him on the sofa.

'It isn't midnight yet. You can still get another ride out of your MetroCard.'

But it was midnight by the time he got down to the station. With a sort of irrational hope, he ran the magnetic stripe through the turnstile reader, and the little green text window said INVALID. The metal push-bar didn't budge. For a vexing and unpleasant second, the message seemed to resonate with life more broadly, a galling applicability to the present moment. Then he bought a single fare, and placed his change in a cup beside a sleeping homeless man, and waited in the midnight quiet of the empty station, nothing but furtive rat motion for five whole minutes. Then shadows moved, and with the stilted syntax of a prototype robot the automated voice told him that a train was arriving, and sure enough it did, and a moment later Marshall stepped on.

Thirty minutes past midnight wasn't late in New York terms. When he got to Flatbush, there was still a decent crowd out on

Clarendon Road. When he turned down his own street, heading south, it was quieter: no one else on the sidewalks, and only occasional traffic.

He didn't notice the SUV until it was alongside him, the driver timing the approach so the vehicle came abreast of Marshall at a clear stretch of curb, no parked cars to shield him.

The SUV's rear door opened while the vehicle was still rolling, and when it came to a halt just ahead of Marshall, a man slid out and stepped up onto the curb in front of him. It was one of the guys from last night, at the bagel place: the guy with the ponytail. He had a gun in one hand, hanging against his leg, and he raised the weapon to gesture at the open door.

'In.'

TWENTY-SIX

The guy was twelve feet away, which meant there was little hope of taking the weapon off him. Far more likely to get a bullet in the chest before he closed the gap in any meaningful sense. Behind him were street-front town houses, effectively a solid wall. No prospects there, escape-wise. His only option really was to turn around and run for it, back toward Clarendon. Except this guy was a few years younger and several pounds lighter than Marshall, and he had better footwear, too – trainers as opposed to Doc Martens – and all of that together sounded like a recipe for being chased down and shot in the spine.

Marshall said, 'How'd you find me?'

'Drop your phone on the ground and get in the car. Or I'll shoot you right here. Your choice.'

He had his tone just about perfect. Flat and indifferent, like it was nothing to him whether Marshall was a passenger or a murder victim.

Marshall waited.

The guy shook his head. 'Don't make me count, pal. I won't do it out loud. I'm just going to drill you.' He gestured with the gun. 'Take your phone out, put it on the ground, get in the car.'

Marshall placed the burner on the sidewalk, and got in the car.

Ponytail followed close, cutting off his exit but standing hip-forward, keeping the gun back out of grab-range. That same SIG pistol from last night. He knew what he was doing. The worst way to handle a weapon was to give the other guy a chance to have it.

'Far side. Move.'

Marshall slid across the rear bench, the right-hand side of the car, behind the empty front passenger seat. Leather, and a piney scent of air-freshener. Mini-television screens built into the front headrests. Oddly luxurious, he thought, given the circumstances. He recognized the driver: Benny, from the bagel shop last night.

The guy with the gun jumped in behind the driver's seat and said, 'Go,' as he pulled his door shut.

Benny got them rolling. He was tense: upright in his seat, arms locked at ten and two on the wheel, triceps standing out with the effort.

Marshall said, 'What's the plan? We going to a meeting, or are you dumping me somewhere?'

Ponytail said, 'Shut up, pal.'

He was sideways in his seat, back propped against the door, the gun pulled in tight against his hip as he aimed at Marshall.

'You're better to pretend you never found me. Penalties for abduction are pretty high.'

'Hold your left hand out. Slow.'

From up front: 'This fucking GPS, honestly. It always wants an actual address. How do I . . . I just want a general area, you know?'

'Pull over and figure it out. Don't fuck around with it while you're driving.' Then to Marshall. 'Left hand up. *Now!*'

The car swerved gently on the shout, and Benny said, 'Chris, Jesus.'

The guy called Chris didn't answer. He was holding handcuffs, one bracelet hanging open like a claw.

'Left hand up. Now.'

Voice back to its chilly norm. Something in his eye that said the night had been long enough already.

'I'm not going to argue the point. I'd rather put one through your head and out the window than have to sit here watching you.' He shrugged. 'Your choice.'

Marshall held his left arm out.

The guy cuffed his wrist, cinching the ratchet tight and then keeping hold of it.

'Lean forward. Head against the seat.'

He should've argued for longer. He'd be dead if he couldn't use his hands. But the guy was keeping the gun back well out of reach, close in by his hip.

Marshall said, 'I get motion-sick if I can't see a window.'

'Don't test me, pal. Lean forward.'

Marshall leaned forward. He felt the guy's gun against the back of his neck, shoving his head against the seat in front of him.

'Put your right hand behind you.'

He did so, and felt the cold grip of the second handcuff bracelet as it clicked into place.

Trapped.

'There. No moving, no fucking talking. All right?'

Benny said, 'Oh, finally. Here we go. It's like a whole different screen and menu and shit. You can actually select the place, though. It's got like its own icon on the map.'

Chris said, 'Put it on mute, will you? I don't want to keep hearing that stupid voice all the time.'

Marshall said, 'Is this a local abduction, or are you taking me across state lines, make it federal?'

He took the punch on his cheek, the blow knocking his head sideways against the door, making his ears ring. Hot copper taste in his mouth. Blood dripping off his bottom lip: one-Mississippi, two-Mississippi . . .

'Yeah, nothing to say now, huh?' Leaning closer. 'Shut. The fuck. Up.'

'Chris, dude, don't fuck him up too bad. I don't want the car getting messed up.'

'You shut up, too. Eyes on the road. We get pulled over, you're getting a dead cop in your trunk.'

'Man, just chill . . .'

'All right, quiet. I'm calling him.'

Him would be Frank Cifaretti. Broken-tooth Frank from the bagel shop, looking for payback from last night.

He heard Chris say, 'Yeah, it's me. We picked him up on that street.'

Pause.

Then: 'I don't know. Just walking. It was pretty easy. He's with us now. You want to talk to him?' Chuckling to himself. 'All right. We'll call you when we get up there.'

Up there.

The bagel shop was south, downtown. He wondered where they were taking him. Upstate, maybe, or over to Jersey. Somewhere unpopulated, quiet enough for score-settling and burials. He let his breath out gently, trying to stay relaxed, focused.

Chris's voice went softer, faux-sympathetic. 'You doing OK there? I heard a great big sigh.'

'I told you I get motion-sick.'

'Yeah, well. Keep doing the breathing. You'll be OK.'

'Whatever. Not my car.'

'You keep your head down, too. You understand? You put your head up, I'm going to put one through you.'

'How'd you find me?'

'Be quiet.'

Marshall said, 'Did Frank find a dentist? His teeth didn't look too good.'

'I'm sure you're going to find out all about it. Hush, now. Just like we talked about.'

Marshall said, 'You remember he asked me about money? Asked what I took from Tony Asaro?'

Nothing.

Marshall said, 'He was right. I took about a quarter mil, three hundred thousand. But if you want it, you're heading in the wrong direction.'

Quiet.

Then: 'Get it when you're dead, won't we?'

'Yeah. Except you'll have to share. Because I'm going to tell Frank about it when I see him. Or do you think he'll let you have it? Bonus payment for not getting pulled over by a state trooper?'

'Shut the fuck up.'

Marshall said, 'If we're heading over to Jersey, you're better to go up FDR Drive, take the George Washington Bridge. Brooklyn-Battery's a toll road. They'll have cameras.'

A long moment of soft road noise.

Then Benny said, 'Shit, sorry, I can't work this thing while I'm driving . . .'

He felt them brake, swing to the curb, and Chris, dangerously convivial, said, 'What I don't get, how's a man, how's someone get to be your age, thirty-four years old, you don't learn to drive without a GPS? Have some pride in the knowledge of where you live, Jesus Christ . . .'

Marshall said, 'So we are going to Jersey?'

He took the punch on his cheek again, the force of it putting him against the door, and then Chris had a hand in his hair, gun jammed in the back of his neck.

'Shut up, or I swear I'm gonna drill you right here.'

'Dude, please don't fuck him up too bad, not in the car. I'm trying to keep it nice.'

Chris right in close to him now: breath in his ear, a whiff of body odor. 'How's that help the motion sickness? You feel better?'

Marshall spat blood. Lights from passing traffic flitting in the edge of his vision, strange shapes and flashes, ringing in his ears. He said, 'You killed anyone before, or is this a first?'

Chris said, 'This guy, honestly . . .' Faded off into a laugh that sounded forced, and now they were moving again, Benny stepping on it hard, making up for the delay.

Marshall said, 'You're going to think about it. You're going to think about me all the time. You'll be doing something completely innocent, eating dinner, watching TV with a beer, feel like life's pretty good, and you'll remember the guy you drove out to New Jersey so he could be killed. And you'll wonder if maybe that was a bad idea. I'll be off in sweet nowhere, and you'll be living with it.'

A brief spell of quiet, and Marshall thought maybe he had some traction. He was trying to time his next remark, line it up for maximum impact, and then the hand in his hair gripped even tighter, and his head was yanked backward, the gun still jammed in his neck.

'You think it'll be sweet, huh? Why you trying to talk us out of it then?'

'It's the getting there I'm worried about.' Voice sounding weird with his throat stretched, thin and croaky.

'Shut up. Listen. All right?'

Spit flecks hitting his cheek.

Benny said, 'Chris . . .'

Chris said, 'You are not a guy. You are not a guy I'll think about and go, "Oh gee." You are a job. You're a fucking job, and all I'm going to think about, I'm going to be relieved and thankful it went off without a hitch. OK?'

'Chris, honestly, I'm trying to keep it real nice. If there's like a mess or anything you have to wipe it up real fast. If you leave it, it soaks in the leather . . .'

Chris, still right in his ear: 'Yeah, you're getting the hang of it now. Nice and quiet. Good for you, too, keeping your head down. Slows the aging process, better blood flow. Pops out all your wrinkles.' He laughed. 'Always want to be looking fresh.'

He almost went another round with him, tell him again about the money, try to get it in his head that murder was a bad idea. Or blow on the ember that was already taking hold. But he didn't want to get hit again. Better to let the pressure drop. He probed his cheek with his tongue. Torn-up and bloody, but it wasn't free-flowing. No point trying to qualify for sutures. Although, there was no telling how much time he had. It seemed they were Jersey-bound, but that could mean some old warehouse over on the riverfront, or rural country out west. Which would be how far? Thirty, forty miles. So maybe forty, fifty minutes' drive, this time of night.

The road acoustics changed: lighter, more echoic, and he knew they were on the Brooklyn Bridge. He kept his head down, obeying Chris's edict, felt himself tilting with the curve as they came down off the ramp onto FDR Drive.

He said, 'I wasn't kidding about being motion-sick.'

Benny said, 'Maybe we should find somewhere to let him spew.'

'All right. Everyone shut up.'

Marshall said, 'It's smoked glass. No one's going to see if I sit up.'

'You want to get hit again? Huh?'

'Can you crack the window a little?'

'I'll crack your fucking head a little.'

It was like trying to coax someone out on a tightrope, a little bit at a time: gently, gently by the hand. Balance and timing. Lead him out over the drop, and then let him go.

The car stayed quiet for a few minutes, smooth progress up the east side of Manhattan, and this time it was Benny who spoke: 'Chris, honestly, if I can't get this thing clean, Lynette'll flip . . .'

Chris said nothing.

Benny said, 'I'm gonna give him some air. Just an inch.'

Chris said nothing.

Marshall heard the window mechanism, discreet and precise and subdued. He sat slowly upright, leaned back in his seat, his face in the chilly flutter of night air coming through the gap.

Benny said, 'We gotta drive all the way back again, remember? No good if he spews, and we have to ride with the smell all the way home. The blood . . . you always feel sick on blood, you know?'

Chris said, 'I'll ride with Frank. Doesn't bother me.'

He had his back to the door again, gun in close by his hip and aimed at Marshall. That sleepy-eyed look on his face.

'I'm watching you, pal. Don't think you can go taking liberties now.'

Marshall made a show of breathing deep, taking in a cleansing dose of night air.

'I'm just sitting here trying to keep the man's car clean.'

'Right. If that's all you want to do, we'll get on just fine.'

They went up Harlem River Drive, brick project buildings over to the left beyond the southbound traffic lanes, Yankee Stadium somewhere over to his right. His best hope now was to somehow make them stop the car, but they were less likely to do that in a built-up area. More chance of being noticed, more chance of a friendly traffic cop pulling up to check all's OK.

He slid lower in his seat, trying to take the pressure off his cuffed wrists. The steel was biting in against the bone. He slid left a little, and beyond the edge of the front passenger seat the GPS screen was visible on the vehicle's dashboard: a street map at an oblique view, a white chevron on a blue line showing their progress on the recommended route. Thirty-two miles to go. Which meant thirty or forty more minutes, Marshall guessed.

He couldn't see the intended destination, but it was a westward trajectory. He said, 'Funnily enough, being punched in the head didn't make me feel any better.'

Nothing.

Marshall said, 'In fact, I think I might be a little worse.'

'You'll be just fine, pal. Don't you worry. Frank'll know how to cure you.'

He seemed to think that was pretty funny.

Marshall said, 'All right. I'm going to be sick whether we stop or not.'

'Chris, we should . . . I'll pull over and let him do some spring cleaning.'

Chris didn't answer. Marshall closed his eyes, did a few deep nose-breaths, like trying to sooth some ferocious gut turmoil.

Chris said, 'Guys throw up all the time, don't worry about it. Especially this kind of situation. All you have to do, just make sure you don't throw up on me. Keep all the good stuff to yourself.'

Marshall didn't answer. He did a couple more deep breaths, releasing each one audibly, and with purse-lipped caution, wanting Benny worried about the condition of his vehicle. They crossed the Hudson up at the George Washington Bridge, just as he'd suggested, and Benny's GPS directed them onto Route 4, a northwesterly bearing, New Jersey suburbia going past to either side of them.

Benny said, 'It's actually pretty good. There's like a yes-or-no setting for if you want to drive on toll roads.' He looked at Chris in the mirror. 'I told it no. That's why it's not taking us on the Pike.'

Chris said, 'You're a genius.'

Marshall watched the night going by. He knew he couldn't make a move yet. Too much traffic to risk letting him out of the car. He breathed through his teeth, squeezed his eyes shut, giving them his best impression of a man trying not to lose his stomach.

'Don't you spew in my car, man. Don't do it.'

Chris said, 'I don't think the odds are good, Benny. I think he's going to do it.'

Benny said, 'You keep it together, I'll put a good word in with Frank.'

Chris laughed. 'Yeah, he'll go easy, leave a couple teeth in.'

Thinner traffic now. Fewer lights going by in the opposite lane. Benny drove faster on the quieter road, the rotor-like flutter in Marshall's open window gaining tempo.

Marshall said, 'I got a jigsaw puzzle I'm working on.'

Chris said, 'Yeah? Good for you.'

'Jackson Pollock.' He tried for what he hoped looked like an apprehensive smile. 'Any chance I'm going to finish it?'

Chris said, 'Don't ask me hard questions.' Then he said, 'Who's Jackson Pollock?'

Benny said, 'He's that guy, they have him in the Met – no, in MoMA. Or whatever the place is, they have the helicopter hanging where you go up the stairs.'

Chris said, 'MoMA.'

'Right, yeah. We went with Lynette's aunt. He's the guy, he does paintings, they sort of look like random spatter, you know? Like it's happened by accident, but he's done it that way on purpose.' He worked on the thought for another half-mile or so, nodding as he built up his theories, and said, 'It's all sort of balanced and planned out, which is cool. You look at it, you might see a little area and think it's just scribble or it's nothing, but it's actually doing something for the bigger picture. You know? He's done everything for a reason.'

Marshall said, 'Yeah.'

TWENTY-SEVEN

The challenge was keeping his attention on the here-and-now, concentrate purely on what he needed to do. But he kept being taken on these little mental detours, a helpless observer of the fact that if he'd played things differently, he'd still be in Jordan's apartment, in her bed: at or near the zenith of modern urban comfort. He wasn't sure if it was an evolutionary flaw, the fact he was in this much peril and still being distracted by what might've been, or if there was some existential benefit to unconscious musing: remind him every so often of what was at stake, and thereby encourage survival.

He watched his window. Route 4 became Route 208. Beyond the highway's shelterbelt of trees, he caught glimpses of suburbia, low and undistinguished, everything homogenized by nighttime. Small, bright nodes of commerce at the highway interchanges. Motels and gas stations and diners. Businesses catering to the long-hauler.

At Franklin Lakes, Route 208 turned into Interstate 287, easing them westward. They stayed on it for a mile or so, and then Benny took an offramp, curling them under the highway and into a northbound sideroad.

Nine miles to go, according to the GPS.

Forest country. Headlights flashed past southbound, one pair and then another, and then they were alone, tunneling into a darkness that felt total and uncharted, the SUV like some wayward satellite, hurtling without end.

Eight miles.

Eight minutes, Marshall guessed.

Close enough, they might decide there was no point stopping.

So do it now or don't bother.

He slumped against his door. Nothing ahead except the empty road, the dashed centerline a steady Morse Code through the spill of headlights and the carriageway seeming to hover on shadow, ditches running parallel to either side. He jerked upright, wild-eyed and panicked, as if overcome by something hideous, and he saw in Benny's backward glance an expression of equal horror: the horror of knowing that something bad was going to happen to his car.

'No, no, no. The window, the window—'

The glass was coming down, more than enough room now to stick his head out of the car.

But he didn't.

He retched and convulsed, leaned forward, and released the mouthful of bloody spit he'd been building for the past twenty minutes. The wet slap of contact with the floor was clear and unmistakable, even above Benny's shouting – 'Shit, no, no, no, no, no' – and he fell hard against the seat in front of him as they braked, the SUV coming to a halt on the right-hand shoulder, fishtail and smoke and a squeal.

'Get him out, get him out, get him out—'

Marshall swayed, summoned a shocked look, as if gut contents were on the rise once more, and Benny shouted again for him to use the window. Marshall collapsed forward, made a gagging noise that was barely audible amidst Chris and Benny's shouting:

'*You* didn't want to stop, *you* get him out. Get him out of my car, or you fucking tell Lynette—'

'We're almost there, just *drive*—'

'Dude, *get him out of my car.*'

'Mother*fucker*—'

'Fuck *you*—'

'Fuck *you*—'

He heard Chris's door open and then slam as he jumped out, and Marshall knew he had five or six seconds to get this right. He rose as best he could in the confines of the cabin, standing hunchbacked with his head and shoulders crushed to the roof, tortuously awkward with his hands cuffed behind him. He heard Benny say, 'Hey, get down – sit down,' not seeing it yet.

Chris was coming around the back of the car, grit-crunch of footsteps, three seconds maybe from opening Marshall's door. With a desperate off-balance lurch, he got his right foot and then the left up on the seat cushion. He stumbled briefly, head and torso flat against the roof, turned to face the open window like some strange and wingless bird: legs a shaky A-frame, cuffed hands cocked oddly behind him like a stump of tailfeather.

Benny seemed to get it now, realizing that such urgent and decisive motion was not commensurate with a state of limp and feeble nausea. He shouted again for Marshall to get down, and then called for Chris to wait.

But it was all happening too fast, and with Chris no doubt running hot from the argument, the shout probably sounded like one more pejorative, rather than a warning. He was right there now, standing by the rear tire, and Marshall heard the *thunk* of the outside handle, and then the door began to open.

Marshall crouched lower and stepped forward, saw the surprise come into the man's face at the unexpected scene: Benny looking panicked back across his shoulder, and Marshall up on the seat.

Chris had the gun in his right hand, but aimed at the ground
– arm lowered to accommodate the swing of the door. His instincts
were fine: he brought the weapon up as he stepped back, trying
to give himself more space as he lined up a target, but Marshall
was already in motion, scything with his left leg, a swing-kick
on a wide, savage radius.

It was a clumsy move: poor stance, poor visibility, poor
balance, but the one redeeming factor was the open window,
giving him a broader sweep, rotational momentum he wouldn't
have otherwise achieved. He caught Chris on the point of the
chin with the instep of his boot, and saw his jaw shunt back
a full three inches. The gun was still thirty degrees below level,
and the shock of impact made him squeeze off a round, the
scene glimpse-lit by the flash, roadside trees in black and
yellow.

Marshall jumped down from the rear seat onto the roadside,
off-balance in the dark, adrenaline and desperation keeping him
upright, a vague man-shape ahead, teetering, on the cusp of a
fall. Marshall kicked him again, a groin impact this time that
doubled the guy over, kicked him a third time, a vicious blow
summoned up out of fear and fury. He heard the guy wheeze,
but didn't stop, couldn't afford to stop. Again, again, again, and
the man went headfirst on his back into the roadside ditch. A
metallic skitter as the gun followed likewise.

Benny was still behind the wheel of the SUV, and Marshall
heard him shouting – 'Chris, Chris!' – and then something else
that was lost as the engine revved and the vehicle took off, tires
spitting road gravel and the rear door flapping closed with
the boost, a flash of headlights as another car went past in the
opposite direction.

Marshall slid down the bank of the ditch, careful to keep his
feet. Chris was supine and groaning.

'Where's the key? Where's the handcuff key?'

The guy was trying to feel for the gun, moving his arms feebly
like a ditchwater snow angel. Marshall heard the scrub of locked
tires, looked up to see the SUV skid-stop on the shoulder, two
hundred yards away. The dome light came on as Benny jumped
out, and Marshall saw him open the rear door of the truck.

'Key. Where's the key?'

Chris said, 'Nnnh.' Still learning to talk with a broken jaw and a three-inch overbite.

Marshall crouched by his head, straddling it with a foot at each ear, and with his cuffed hands grabbed the guy by the ponytail.

'Nnnh! Nnnh!'

He eased himself vertical, jaw clenched with the effort, breath hissing in his teeth. On the road to his right, he heard a door slam. He looked toward the noise, saw the SUV's rear taillight vanish briefly as Benny passed in front of it. Another door slam as he got in behind the wheel. Marshall sucked air, huge frantic gulps, and then surged toward the road-side bank of the ditch, dragging the guy with him. Legs burning as he made the climb, slow-motion agony. Every fiber at its white-hot limit. He yelled with effort, and got a foot up onto the roadway. To his right in the distance, the SUV's lights were sawing back and forth across the width of the road as Benny tried to get himself turned around.

Marshall stood there gasping, willing more out of muscles that had already given him everything. The guy was wet with ditch-water, but the gain in weight felt exponential. It was like trying to haul a parachute full of sand. He gave himself a final standing lungful, head pounding to his heartbeat, and then he leaned forward like a mountaineer attacking the last hundred feet of Everest, and ran with everything he had.

When he reached the far shoulder, he kept going, down into the roadside ditch, and with a crazy, frantic burst of effort, he powered himself up the far side, the broken and catatonic cargo dragging behind him, Marshall panting and spitting foam like a flogged racehorse. Ten feet beyond the far bank, his legs wobbled and gave out.

He fell to his knees, hunched and gasping, as if in penitence to the forest before him. Shadows forming now, shadows from headlights, growing more distinct as the SUV's engine in turn grew louder. White glare behind him, and long stripes of tree-shadow stretching off into the depths, everything rotating about its respective tree-axis as the car approached. Dark spokes turning about some terrible and awesome fulcrum.

The car halted, and everything went still.

'Key. Give me the damn key . . .'

The guy called Chris gaped and said nothing.

Marshall turned and felt blindly with his cuffed hands. He heard a door open and then slam, and then another car went past on the road behind him: the same twirling shadow pattern, but briefer.

'Come on, come on. Where is it?'

Wallet in his right trouser pocket.

Phone in his left pocket.

He glanced behind him toward the road, saw a flashlight beam twitching left and right, scouring the far shoulder.

'Chris! . . . Chris!'

The guy's coat pockets were zippered. Marshall found the tab for the side pocket, tugged it down gently.

Nothing but lint. He worked his way north and found a breast pocket, tugged the zipper down.

And found two handcuff keys on a split ring.

Benny was down in the far ditch now. Marshall ran crouched, deeper into the trees. Awkward and lurching, like some lab-cooked humanoid, making its escape. Twenty feet, thirty. The night air freezing and piney.

He dropped to his knees in the pitch-black lee of a gnarled trunk, searched by touch for the lock barrel on the left handcuff bracelet.

There.

Shiver-fingers lining up the key.

One stab. Two. Three.

Come on.

Fourth stab. A scrape of metal as the key sunk home, and then a click that unlocked more than just the bracelet: adrenaline, elation. He rose to his feet and unlocked the second bracelet as he walked, moving parallel to the road, the SUV off on his right. He saw the twitch-motion of Benny's flashlight crest the far ditch and then come across the road to Marshall's side.

'Chris! Chris, what the fuck? Where are you?'

Marshall paused at the tree line.

He breathed deeply, evenly. Calmer now. He watched the torch sweeping wide arcs, way off to his right. Marshall crossed the ditch, far less demanding without a passenger, and then walked across the road. Invisible in the dark. Benny's torchlight sweeps still frantic, but safely distant. Marshall slipped into the tree line on the far side and worked his way back in the direction of the stopped SUV, red taillights guiding him. He knew he wasn't far from where they'd first pulled over, and that meant he wasn't far from where Chris had dropped the gun.

He stood still and scanned the length of the ditch below the car. Nothing. He hadn't built up the night vision. He crouched and waited for it to sharpen, the torchlight still flicking randomly on the opposite side of the road, Benny calling Chris's name.

Marshall waited, silent, safe in the trees. He heard Benny say, 'Shit,' and then the flashlight went out. Darkness for a second, two, and then light began to filter between the trees, an accelerated dawn as another pair of headlights came along the road, soft note of tires growing louder. Marshall didn't move. He could see now where Chris had fallen: scour marks in the bank from where he'd been dragged up onto the road, patterns richly textured in the glare. He scanned the ditch again, alert for any hint of gleam.

And there was the gun, ten feet away, just lying in the mud.

The shadow-motion slowed and then went still as the car came to a halt up on the road, level with the parked SUV.

Muted purr of an electric window, glass descending.

'Everything OK?'

Benny said, 'Oh, yeah . . . I, ah.'

The sound of the idling motor was low and smooth and patient, like the car could sit there all night until the man offered up a decent story.

Benny said, 'I saw a dog run in front of me, I'm worried I might've hit it.'

'You need some help?'

'No, no. I'm fine. I'm just looking around. I don't think . . . I just want to make sure. I'm hoping it got away clean. I'm pretty sure it did . . .'

Engine noise.

Then: 'All right . . . take care.'

By the time the car had pulled away, Marshall had retrieved the SIG and climbed up the bank and onto the road. He laid the gun across the warm hood of the SUV and sighted in. Not easy in the dark. It was all guesswork. Benny's flashlight was back on, the beam skitting left-right in the trees.

Not long now.

'Holy shit. How'd you get over here? Chris! Oh man, oh shit. Where is he? Chris? Where is he? Oh man . . .'

He kept saying it as he scrambled up the bank toward the road – oh man, oh man, oh man.

Marshall waited, focused on his breathing, making it gun-ready. Nice slow heartbeat. He sensed the quiver-pause rhythm of the muzzle, matching his body tremors. He saw the man's head crest the top of the bank, and then his torso came into view. The flashlight was underslung on the barrel of what looked to be a ten-gauge Ithaca shotgun. Marshall let him get all the way up onto the road, and then shot him twice in the chest. Trees in prickly visage with each flash. He came out from behind the hood of the SUV and stood for a moment looking down at Benny, lifeless and crumpled in the bottom of the ditch. Visible in dead repose by the glow of his own flashlight.

Marshall slid down the gravel incline and picked up the shotgun, used the flashlight on the barrel to find his way back over to Chris, half-hidden beyond the tree line. His phone and wallet were lying where Marshall had left them. He put the wallet in his coat pocket and picked up the phone. It wanted a fingerprint for access.

He tried Chris's index finger. No good. The device shivered in rebuke. He tried the guy's thumb.

The imagery refreshed, and brought up the home screen.

Marshall opened the history, found the call Chris had made from the car, when they'd first picked him up. No name attached to it.

He held the screen by the guy's face.

Chris said, 'Nyuh . . .'

'Is this Frank's number? Frank Cifaretti? Look at it.'

He could see he wasn't going to have much luck. The guy's focus was about ten miles away.

'Help . . .'

Marshall said, 'What were you going to do to me? Once you'd driven me out here?'

No answer. A car went past, nightmare shadows through the trees. Then dark and quiet again, no sound except the guy's breathing, shallow sips of air, rapid and feeble.

Marshall said, 'Yeah, I thought so.'

He put the SIG in his belt and picked up the shotgun and walked back to the road.

TWENTY-EIGHT

He could sympathize now with Benny. It wasn't easy getting the car turned around. The ditches cut into his maneuvering space. Pulling a one-eighty meant a cumbersome five-point turn. But he got himself heading in the right direction, and the GPS unit seemed unbothered by the violent interlude and the change of driver, the chevron symbol leading him onward through the dark.

The SUV was nice to drive. Responsive and quiet, and the steering wheel had a button for everything. Stereo volume and station, cruise control, hands-free calling. He'd been worried about the phone timing out, not letting him back in again without a fingerprint, so he had it playing a video off the guy's Facebook feed: highlights from *Seinfeld*, Marshall was pretty sure, the sound low and just the canned laughter audible every so often.

It took seven minutes to reach the GPS's programmed destination. The chevron disappeared, and a message on the screen told him he'd arrived. It wasn't clear what exactly he'd arrived at. This stretch of road appeared no different from the previous eight miles, dark and dense forest to either side, regular as wallpaper. Then he rounded a bend, and he saw the clearing beyond the left shoulder.

It was a graveled parking lot. He braked and swung in off the highway, details emerging piecewise in the slow sweep of the headlights. The mouth of a hiking track, a public bathroom, a low wooden sign with a Department of Environmental Protection logo. He stopped for a second and read it. There was a little stylized map, and an extensive range of symbols describing various prohibited activities. Maybe when they found out about all of this, they could add a couple to the list: no kidnapping, no murder.

The map had a you-are-here arrow, and emanating from its tip were two lines meandering away from each other at a right angle, more or less. One line was labeled TRACK and the other was labeled FIRE ROAD.

He took his foot off the brake and let the car roll on, and a second later the headlights found the entrance to the fire road. It was just a gravel track, deeply rutted, wending slightly uphill as it disappeared into the trees. There was a barrier arm supported by a bollard at each shoulder, but Marshall couldn't see a lock. As far as he could tell, there was nothing to stop someone just swinging it aside.

The phone in the console beside him issued a sustained burst of canned laughter. He had it face-down so it wouldn't light up the cabin. He held a hand up level so he could see it against the light of the windshield. Still a faint tremor. The phone issued another round of tinny laughter. He breathed carefully a few times, oddly distant from the jubilation. Then he backed the car around and parked where he had a sight-line to both the highway and the mouth of the fire road, shut off the lights but kept the engine idling.

He figured Frank Cifaretti and his people were on to a pretty good system: drive someone out here at midnight, bury them up the top of the fire road in the offseason. Probably be months before anyone else even went up there. He checked the phone. No messages. Still eighty-six percent battery. Chris had obviously been diligent with his charging. Marshall opened YouTube, and found a highlights reel of Jean LaPierre and Larry England at the 'ninety-seven Jigsaw Masters in Spokane. LaPierre had been tailing with a twelve-piece deficit, but then made it up in the closing seconds of the final quarter. The puzzles that year were all Claude Monet, and England seemed to hit a wall right at the finish. LaPierre though stayed cool through the whole thing, operating with surreal form and laying down pieces in no rush whatsoever.

Marshall had the shotgun leaning against the seat in the passenger footwell, the SIG pistol in his lap. Every so often he hit the turn signals, one side and then the other, using the glow to check he was still alone. The Masters replay was into the final minutes, the commentators almost drowned out by the crowd, Saul Tarrant shouting he'd never seen someone lay down a piece-chain that smooth.

He watched cars go past: shadows through the trees, and then the long blade of white out on the road, red taillights fading off into nothing. He worked the turn signals, and checked his mirrors in the jaundiced glow. Empty parking lot all around. The little dashboard clock numerals read 1:22. Marshall saw headlights, starry at first in the distance, and then dazzling as the car swung into the parking lot. It came broadside to him as it turned, materializing out of the glare, and Marshall saw it was the van from the flower shop last night. FRANK'S FLOWERS.

He started the engine and flicked on his lights. The van sat idling. Tempting to ram it. That would give them a fright. But there was no telling how many people were inside. He didn't want to be stuck out here with a written-off SUV, having to face three or four people with automatic weapons. Except, why bring four people? It'd be Frankie C, and one other guy, maximum.

He thought about it another second, wondering too what questions were being posed behind the black glass of the other vehicle. Probably wondering why he was still sitting there.

Marshall had the SIG held low in his right hand. He reached across himself with his left, picked up Chris's phone and composed a text message: WE'LL FOLLOW YOU.

He sent it to what he'd guessed was Frank Cifaretti's number – the number Chris had called when they picked him up.

Nothing for a moment. Both vehicles sat waiting.

Then Marshall saw the glow behind the windshield of the flower van as his message was received. Driver's side: Frank Cifaretti was at the wheel.

The light vanished. The flower van rolled on, nosed up to the barrier across the fire road. Marshall swung the SUV around and pulled in behind it.

The van's front passenger door opened. A man climbed out.

Shortish, medium build, dark hair combed back and gleaming.

He walked up to the barrier arm and swung it open with a faint screech of metal, and when he turned to walk back to the

van, Marshall saw the expression on his face: strange in its open-
ness and innocence. Bright eyes and a red-lipped smile.

The smiley man got back into his seat and shut the door, and
the flower van proceeded slowly up the track between the trees,
grit crunching beneath its tires.

Marshall let the brake off, and followed.

TWENTY-NINE

T he sign at the parking lot had indicated the fire road curved
only gently, but the actual formation was more accom-
modating of nature: frequent switchbacks, as dictated by
tree-size, or gradient.

Marshall gave the flower van a thirty-yard lead. He drove left-
handed, the SIG pistol in his right hand in his lap. They rounded
a bend, and the track ascended at a steeper gradient, the van
ahead of him wallowing and bumping in the ruts, losing traction
every now and again. He'd see it slow, and then regain pace with
a scramble of tires and a spray of gravel.

He checked the phone. No response to his message. He had
it replaying the Jigsaw Masters video to keep it awake, and he'd
found a little button that let you turn the sound off.

They wound through a series of tight turns, the van moving
out of sight on each bend, just a crimson smudge of taillights
between the trees. The track was only a couple miles long, which
would mean a fifteen- or twenty-minute drive at this speed. The
windshield was fogging up with his breath. They came out onto
higher ground, a straight section maybe two hundred yards long,
and the phone in the console began to vibrate with a call, shivering face-down on its screen-glow.

Marshall checked it.

Frank Cifaretti's number. He didn't answer. Maybe they'd
think Chris just hadn't noticed. Which was the truth, in a sense.

The van stopped.

Marshall stopped, thirty yards behind it.

The phone in the console went quiet.

Ten seconds. Twenty.

Then Marshall heard a rattle from the glove compartment. Benny's phone, obviously. It carried on for ten or fifteen seconds, and then Chris's phone in the console took over.

Marshall looked around. Hard enough turning the damn car out on the road, let alone on a narrow fire track. He thought about ramming them again, but he didn't like the idea of being swaddled in airbag, trapped behind the wheel as people shot at him.

The console phone gave a sharp double-buzz. Text message.

ANSWER YOUR FUCKING PHONE.

It vibrated again with another call.

Frank Cifaretti's number.

Marshall waited for it to quit, and then he set the headlights to high beam. The woods and the van lit up in a brighter, panoramic sweep. All they'd see from their end would be white glare. He took his foot off the brake and let the SUV roll forward, idle speed, one or two miles per hour. He set the button on the steering wheel for cruise control, and then he opened his door and slid out, pushed the door gently closed again behind him.

He let the SUV draw ahead of him, and then he stepped behind it, looping around the rear fender and breaking away to his right, off the track and into the trees.

Two miles per hour was about a yard per second, meaning the SUV would take half a minute to close the distance to the van. Marshall stayed abreast of it, matching its progress as he threaded through undergrowth.

Twenty yards to go. Fifteen.

Marshall stopped, shoulder to a tree, and lined up the SIG pistol on the flower van's passenger window.

Ten yards.

He saw the door open, the little guy with his smile slip out and raise a shotgun: a fluid and practiced move, the weapon compact and pump-action, aiming for the SUV's windshield. He was sidestepping to widen his angle, moving toward the trees, Marshall tracking him, waiting for the guy to hold still, too risky to shoot a target moving across him in poor light.

The guy's first round blew the glass out of the SUV's passenger window, the noise like a bomb going off, Marshall still holding, waiting for a stationary target. He watched the guy pump his second round, the gun staying shoulder-high and steady, the man still coming sideways toward the trees, and then something told him that the picture wasn't right.

The smiley man jerked the gun around. Surely instinct more than actual vision, murder-hunch acquired through murder-habit. He was aiming for the trees now, and he dropped to the ground as he fired, buckshot and splinters ripping through foliage as Marshall moved back behind cover. Another shot, the fading roar of it like a jet fly-over, leaf- and bark-confetti coming down all around him.

Marshall glanced and saw the little guy getting to his feet, turning, running for the van as the driverless SUV crunched against its rear fender. Marshall aimed the SIG and fired, saw the little guy dip as if he'd stepped in a rabbit hole. Marshall fired again, but the guy was still up and moving, shadow a long dark stripe in the beam of the flower van's headlights, gait an awkward limp-lurch, like some wind-up figurine. Marshall broke cover and sprinted, reached the flower van in time to see the little guy disappear into the trees on the far side of the track, pistol in one hand and the other clutched to his upper thigh. He'd ditched the shotgun. It was on the ground behind him. Frank Cifaretti was still in his seat at the wheel of the van, hands raised, eyes shut, breathing hard.

He said, 'All right. Just take it easy. Please. Just take it easy.'

Like all he'd wanted was moderation. Marshall leaned in through the open passenger door to see the rear load space. Pliers, hammers. Three half-gallon bottles of bleach. Two shovels. A bag of four-inch nails.

'Keep your hands up, Frank.'

'OK, OK. I'm just sitting here.' His front teeth were gone. 'Sitting' was 'shitting'. He'd obviously found a dentist.

'I didn't . . . I didn't even want to come out here, all right? Just . . . you don't need to point it at me.'

The rear of the chassis had been raised up by the contact with the SUV, the back wheels almost off the ground. Marshall kept the SIG raised, sweeping the trees, moved across to his left and opened the SUV's passenger door. He leaned in and killed the ignition, felt the vehicle settle back off the van's rear fender as the load came off the gears. He picked up Benny's shotgun from the footwell and turned on the flashlight on the barrel, stepped back to the front of the van and swept the trees with the light. No sign of the smiley man. Marshall opened the breech and dumped the shells on the ground. Frank was still doing as he was told, sitting there with his hands raised and breathing hard, like he thought the roof was about to cave in on him.

Marshall said, 'Come here. This way.'

'Look, I'm not doing anything, OK? I'm sitting here. I'm fucking sitting here.' Chin shiny with spit.

'Yeah, and now I'm telling you to move. Come on. Fast.'

Frank started to slide across the bench toward the passenger door, and Marshall helped him, grabbed him by the collar left-handed and dragged him out.

'Hey, wait. Waitwaitwaitwait. Shit—'

Marshall clamped a hand on his mouth and shoved his head back against the side of the van. Two wide eyes looking back at him along his arm. Marshall held the SIG in tight by his shoulder, wanting the muzzle in the picture, too.

'I've seen what you've got back there, so don't tell me you were bringing me out here for a hike.'

Frank had both hands on Marshall's wrist, but wasn't having any luck moving it.

'All you have to do is walk, you understand? Walk, and keep your mouth shut.'

Frank didn't get it yet. Marshall let him go. Then he stepped away and picked up the empty shotgun and passed it to him.

'That light goes out, I'll shoot you. You drift, I'll shoot you. You say anything . . . what do you think's going to happen?'

Frank shook his head, mouth ajar, slack with dawning horror. 'Come on.'

'I don't have much time. Hike, or a bullet. What do you want?'

He had the SIG raised again, two-handed grip and aiming at his face, but Frank was looking past it, looking Marshall in the eye, and whatever he saw in there seemed to dissuade him from protest.

He said, 'Jesus Christ . . .'

Just a whisper, weak under the weight of a hard lesson: that sooner or later the world comes back at you with its equal and opposite force. Marshall grabbed his shoulder and spun him around, fired the SIG at the ground, a double-tap. Twin cracks echoing out over the terrain, fade-time long enough to count. Thunder slowly dissipating.

'Oh, God . . .'

'Walk.'

He shoved him between the shoulder blades, Frank's head lolling back and then forward, slow-motion whiplash, the empty shotgun cradled in his arms.

'Walk.'

He waited by the van's fender until Frank had reached the trees on the far side of the track, and then he sprinted in a crouch, moving to within ten feet of him.

'Walk. Hurry. Go on.'

The ground coverage was dense in places, but Marshall stayed low, arm raised to protect his face from low foliage, Frank's light up ahead twitching at random as he moved.

A nine-mil pistol round to the thigh wouldn't make anything easy, especially a getaway at night in near-freezing cold on sloped and forested terrain, and Marshall knew the man would be making stories out of facts: the sound of the double-tap, a kill shot, and now the flashlight drawing nearer.

As it turned out, he'd only made it three hundred yards. The woods lit up with the flash of his pistol shots, three rounds spaced and careful, and Frank Cifaretti went to his knees with a scream. The woods lit up again – a blink and then gone – as the little guy fired a fourth time. Marshall waited a beat, nurturing that mind's-eye image of the flashes, fifteen yards away at his ten o'clock. He swung his aim in the dark, and squeezed the SIG's trigger three times.

The light of each shot formed a microsecond still-frame, and he saw the little guy first crumpled at the waist, and then falling, and then prone.

Then dark again. Quiet.

Marshall waited, crouching. Ragged breathing up ahead and his heartbeat thumping in his ears. Acrid gun smoke. He eased his way forward and picked up the empty shotgun from where Frank had dropped it, aimed the flashlight at the man now lying face-up on the ground. Marshall picked his way over to him through the undergrowth. The man's gaze holding on Marshall's, eyes rolling to stay with him. Marshall crouched. The guy's mouth seemed to have a natural upward curl, the effect heightened by raw skin around his lips, as if reddened by licking.

'You going to tell me how all this happened?'

No answer. The guy lay there just breathing quietly. Blood on his teeth and in the spittle that flecked his chin. He had a chest and a stomach wound to add to his leg problem.

Marshall said, 'You tell me what's been happening, we can get you some help. Otherwise you can just lie here, take your chances.'

No answer. His eyes moved from Marshall's now, looking up at the sky, as if ready for whatever came next.

'You going to tell me anything? I figure you got about fifteen minutes to try and make some good in the world.'

The man's eyes slid back to him, and for a second Marshall thought he'd provoked some kind of epiphany, some kind of change of moral direction in the last moments of his life. But he just lay there looking up at him, the smile on his face starting to grow, and Marshall wasn't sure if he'd lost all comprehension, or was instead more firmly wedded to whatever rule had got him here. Too late in the game to change, maybe. Or just clinging on to whatever wreckage was available, flawed principle or not.

It only took another minute, and then he stopped breathing. Dead with that same strange expression. The smile and a distant, hopeful look. Maybe even curiosity. Like he'd always known dying had another angle, and here it was.

Frank Cifaretti was obviously worried about joining him. Marshall put the flashlight on him, saw Frank struggling to his feet, panting and swearing. Face bright with sweat, sinew and tendon about to pop through his skin.

'Get me . . . I gotta get out of here. I can't die in here . . .'

Marshall held him by the upper arm and walked him back out to the track. Frank limping and groaning, bent almost double. Marshall set him down by the flower van, propped up against the front wheel. Frank tipped his head back, eyes shut, mouth open.

Marshall sat down beside him. 'You going to tell me anything, or are we going to sit here in silence, contemplating?'

'I didn't . . .' He shut his mouth and swallowed, breathed carefully through his nose while he composed something in his mind. He looked down at what was happening under his hand – blood oozing through his fingers – and then looked at the sky. He said, 'I didn't want to bring you out here.'

Marshall said, 'So why are we both out here?'

Frank shook his head. 'You gotta do so much. You gotta do so much to . . . to make them know that you're serious.'

Marshall wasn't quite sure what he meant.

Frank looked at his hand again. 'Shit. This is . . . I think this is bad.'

'You want me to call?'

Frank shook his head, looked down at his hand. 'I got about five minutes.' He sighed through his teeth. 'I said to Gaby as I left, when they called me, I said . . . I said, Why am I doing this shit? You know. Go out, take the trouble to . . . to make something worse. And you know what she said?'

Marshall shook his head.

'She's reading a book, she looks at me over the top of the book, she goes, "Yeah. What's the point?" I didn't have anything to say and I don't know why it didn't stop me.'

'Why didn't you tell me you knew him?'

Frank sat there panting, getting his breath back from his little speech. 'What?'

'I asked you last night about your little smiley friend.'

'Marco.'

'That his name? Marco?'

'Little Marco.'

'Right. You told me maybe he's one of Mikey Langello's guys. And now I think you know him pretty well. Given you drove out here with him.'

'He called me up.'

'Who did?'

'Mikey the L. Langello. He told me this guy Vialoux . . . he said he was turning into a problem, and he was sending a guy down to sort it out. To take care of things.'

'To kill him.'

'I don't know what he meant. He just said to me, he told me he was sending a guy down, and I needed to let him do his thing.

He said whatever he needed, I had to . . .' He shook his head: exhausted, frustrated. 'What's the fucking word?'

'Do as he said?'

'No. No, I want to say like housing.'

'Accommodate.'

'Yeah.' Relief in his voice. 'We had to . . . we had to accommodate him.'

'What was his problem?'

'Huh?'

'What was his problem with Vialoux?'

'I don't know . . .' Shaking his head. 'I don't know. You just . . . when the man calls up, you say yes. You tell him no problem.'

'And who was helping him?'

'What?'

'Who was helping Little Marco?'

Frank was out of breath again. He sat with his eyes shut, panting.

Marshall said, 'He killed a woman across the street from Vialoux. Did he tell you that? A witness said there were two guys.'

Frank was shaking his head. 'I knew he was set up there, across the street. He was . . . he was in there a couple days. He sends me this text, he says, "Bring me some drinking straws." I'm thinking, What the fuck? But whatever. I buy him some straws, I show up there, Jesus Christ, I thought it was an empty house. But the woman, she's basically dead.' Still shaking his head. 'There wasn't anything . . . I'm sorry. It was all out of my hands.'

That wasn't true. He could have stopped everything right there. But it was useless to make the point now.

Marshall said, 'Do you know D'Anton Lewis?'

'D'Anton? Yeah, yeah . . . D'Anton.'

'Do you know his wife, Renee?'

'Huh?'

'Do you know Renee Lewis? D'Anton's wife?'

He shook his head. 'No. Get me the . . . in the van. In the van there's a box. Gaby always does . . . there's a box in the glove compartment . . .'

It was tempting to tell him to forget it. But he wanted to keep Frank on-side, keep him talking. Marshall looked as directed, found a Glock 9 and a Tupperware container of lettuce salad. He went and sat down next to Frank again and passed him the container.

'Get the . . . take the lid off for me.'

Marshall removed the lid. The salad looked pretty good. Bits of tomato and cucumber and little cubes of cheese that might've been feta. Maybe a Greek salad, although he wasn't sure if you were allowed lettuce in a Greek. There was a fork in there for him, too.

'She always makes me this healthy stuff. I didn't think . . . she worries about me. She worries I only eat bagels.'

'Do you?'

Frank said, 'Yeah. I been hitting them pretty hard.'

He had his right hand on the wound and the other on the fork in the container. 'Jesus . . . arm's not working . . . get something on the fork for me. Load me up.'

Marshall speared some tomato and cucumber, passed him back the fork. Frank grabbed it shakily.

'How do I find Mike Langello?'

'Mikey L. Mikey the L.' He put the forkful in his mouth.

'Yeah. How do I find him?'

'He's not well. Guys say he's not well.'

'Not well how?'

'I don't know. Getting like the shakes, and shit. Some kind of attacks.'

'But where is he?'

'He's up in Boston.'

'Boston. Where in Boston?'

'I don't know. Oh, man.' He was shivering now. 'Here, load me up again. I can't . . . I can't make this thing work.'

Marshall built him another forkful of salad. Frank took it shakily.

'How do I find Mikey Langello?'

Nothing.

'Frank?'

Frank didn't answer. He sat and chewed his salad, eyes closed and face tilted skyward, as if tanning himself by the dim light of the moon. He stabbed vaguely for the container. 'Give me one more. There's time for one more. Are you still there?'

'Yeah. I'm still here.'

'That's good. I didn't . . . I didn't think it would go like this.'

Marshall put some feta cheese and tomato on the fork. 'Yeah. Me either.'

'You gonna stay here a minute?'

He paused before replying, and he thought about asking if they'd afforded Lydia any semblance of decency or kindness in her final hours. But there was no point in a lesson at this stage in his life. Lessons needed hindsight, and Frank would be dead soon.

Marshall said, 'Yeah. I'll stay here for a minute.'

He used the light on the shotgun and picked his way through the woods to Little Marco. Nothing in his pockets other than cash. Made sense. He wouldn't want to be picked up on suspicion of murder and have his driver's license in his pocket. Marshall counted the bills by the light of the torch. One hundred fifty-three dollars. Six twenties, three tens, three singles. Good bill-diversity. Marshall put them in value-order, applied a transverse fold, and then pocketed the money and walked back out to the track. He got into the SUV and reversed it twenty yards or so, set the brake and got out with the engine still running and the high beams lighting up the scene.

He opened the rear door of the flower van. There was a duffel bag in there too, with a towel and a change of clothes. Torture must be hot work. He unloaded the bleach containers and poured some on the corner of the towel, used it to wipe down the guns he'd handled. Fingerprints were his main concern, but the bleach would degrade any DNA he might've left. He cleaned the SIG pistol, and then Benny's shotgun. Fumes prickling his whole airway. Frank's salad container and fork got the same treatment, and then the areas of the flower van he'd touched: passenger door, glove compartment, rear door handle.

He fetched Chris's phone from the SUV and cleaned it for prints, and then used one of the hammers from the flower van to smash it to pieces, poured bleach on it for good measure. Nothing of interest in the guy's wallet. Wipe, discard, bleach. The handcuffs got the same treatment. He stood there quietly for a minute, long-shadowed in the glare of the SUV's headlights, thinking about what he may have missed. His boots would have to go. He must have left about ten thousand viable impressions. The crime-scene techs could take their pick. He gave the van door a final wipe, and then transferred the bleach containers and the towel to the SUV, climbed in and reversed slowly down the fire track toward the highway.

Four thirty a.m. and no traffic. The bleach towel made a sharp odor, and he drove with his window down to keep the air breathable. He retraced his route, past where he'd left Chris and Benny on the shoulder, and fifteen minutes later he was coming into Franklin Lakes. Marshall stayed south on Route 208, and turned off when the exit sign announced Paterson, New Jersey.

He'd never been to Paterson, but he sensed it was big enough for his requirements. He headed directly south. The town center was off to his right, a few blocks away. Low rise and brick. The Passaic River was somewhere over there, too. Probably responsible for the whole place, the way rivers often were. He drove across a highway and then a rail overpass, into an area of tired-looking clapboard housing. Sixties vintage, maybe. Weeds, some vacant lots, the odd broken window. He turned off the main road and parked at the curb and sat listening to the radio for a while. Six am, lights started coming on behind windows. Marshall bleach-wiped the center console, the steering wheel, the dashboard, and then the inside of the door. He got out and wiped down the outside handle, and then went around to the other side of the vehicle and poured bleach in the footwell where he'd released his theatrical vomit. He wiped down the bleach containers, and left the car with its windows down and the bleach-wiped key in the center console. A nice acquisition for somebody, even if it did smell like a hospital ward.

Five blocks north was a commercial stretch that was just starting to come awake. He saw a gas station, and a hardware store, and a diner called Sam's. It had a fried egg for a logo, and Marshall gathered they knew how to cook a breakfast. There were a few people in there already, but he thought he'd give it thirty minutes. Let the clientele build up, make him less memorable. He wandered along the street to kill time, found a pawnshop a couple of blocks away with a few jigsaw puzzles in the front window. Definitely worth coming back later for a more thorough review.

It was seven o'clock by the time he'd made it back to the diner, and there were half a dozen patrons now. Marshall took a window seat, sat there for a moment with his eyes closed. Something heavenly about being safe, headache notwithstanding.

'Get you something to drink?'

He opened his eyes. A waitress standing there in the aisle.

'Cup of coffee would make my day.'

'Hard night?'

He looked at her, realized that by talking he was probably undermining any hope of being forgotten. But something about having just killed three people and seen a fourth catch the train as well, he thought an idle conversation would be nice.

He said, 'How do you know I didn't just roll out of bed?'

She smiled. 'Did you?'

'No.'

'Well, there you go. I get you anything to eat? Or you still thinking?'

Marshall turned the menu over, perused it for a moment, and told her he'd have pancakes. He reached in his pocket for the recently procured money, laid out one of the twenties: loose on the table for now, but he'd position it somewhere meaningful, in terms of the available geometry. Maybe open under his cutlery, with the longitudinal axes in logical correspondence. Or folded in a square, a makeshift coaster for his mug with the side-length matched to the diameter of the mug-base. He'd think about it. The main thing was, even if this was as far as he got with the whole thing, at least Little Marco was paying for his meal.

THIRTY

He found a shoe store a couple blocks over. Even better, it transpired that they had a sale on. Marshall bought a new pair of Doc Martens, and six pairs of socks, donated the old shoes to a homeless man camping outside the front

window. A good score for the guy, Marshall thought. Ample
sole-depth remaining, and the lace-fray was barely discernable.
Marshall threw in a pair of socks, too. He found a gas station
and bought a bottle of water and a packet of Tylenol, and checked
himself out in their bathroom. The inside of his left cheek
was raw and copper-flavored, and his saliva was bright red. The
cheek was about twice its normal thickness. He took two Tylenol
with water to dull the headache, and then broke in the new
shoes with a walk over to the Paterson bus station. It turned out
to offer that rarest of public facilities: a payphone. Its copy of
the White Pages had been through a lot – tears, water damage,
burn marks – but the P section was more or less intact, and
Marshall found the confidential tip line for the New Jersey State
Police. He told the operator he'd been camping near the top
of the fire road and heard gunfire, walked down for a look and
saw a guy sitting dead beside a van.

He caught a bus from Paterson over to Manhattan, and was
home by one o'clock. His burner phone was in the gutter, not
far from where Chris had made him leave it on the sidewalk.
It was dead now from rain exposure. Marshall guessed Chris
probably was, too.

It rained through the afternoon. He slept until four o'clock,
woke to find the headache was improving, and the bruising to
his cheek was now vividly described in blues and purples. He
had a couple more Tylenol and worked on his Pollock jigsaw,
battling the lower right quadrant. No joy today. He couldn't see
the lineups. He gave up and sorted out the new socks he'd bought,
cutting them out of the packaging, removing the plastic tags,
re-bundling them. Then he just sat there thinking about his Vialoux
case. D'Anton and Renee Lewis, the mob man Mikey Langello.
All the little overlaps he'd heard . . .

Five o'clock, he broke a new burner phone out of its box, and
called Jordan Mora. No answer. He called Harry Rush.

Harry said, 'You're still alive, then.'

'Yeah.'

'You still angry I want nothing to do with pissing off mob guys?'

Marshall said, 'You heard of a guy called Mikey Langello?'

'Langello? Yeah. He was running the Brighton Beach outfit
for a while.'

'Not anymore. He's AWOL.'

Quiet for a while. Harry said, 'I already told you I want nothing to do with it. You'd be well advised to keep your distance, too. And you still need to come and collect your fucking jigsaw.'

He tried Hannah Vialoux.

'Hello?'

'Hey. Just me.'

Silence.

He said, 'Marshall.'

'Yeah, I know. I was starting to . . .' She sighed. He heard it catch in her throat.

'What is it?'

'Nothing. I'm just glad you're all right. I had a call . . . it was stupid, but I had a call last night, one of the cops who was here Friday. He said you hadn't left any details and they still needed a statement from you. I told them your address.'

So that's how they'd found him.

Marshall said, 'Don't worry. I spoke to them this morning.'

'Oh, good. Yeah. It was still . . . they shouldn't have even asked. It could've been anyone. Honestly, it's like . . . people put you at ease with a bit of authority, you tell them anything. I didn't even click until this morning, couldn't believe how stupid I was—'

'Hannah, it's fine—'

'And then you weren't picking up your phone. I kept thinking . . . I was worried something might have happened—'

'Hannah. It. Is. Fine. I'm fine.'

Now in hindsight and in the silence, he could hear how hard his tone had been. He laughed, trying to kill the moment, but it sounded brittle and awkward. The side of his head throbbed with renewed vigor.

He said, 'Don't go around and around thinking about that kind of thing. Just forget about it.'

Nothing.

Then she said, 'So which cop was it?'

'What do you mean?'

'Who wanted to talk to you?'

'I don't know. I spoke to Nevins.'

'When?'

'This morning.'

He hated how he could do that to her. Lies flowing out like mercury.

She said, 'I called him just now, he said he hadn't spoken to you.'

'Hannah, please relax. I left him a message. Everything is fine.'

Silence again. Then she said, 'What is going on?'

'Nothing is going on. But you can do us both a favor by forgetting about this. Just don't worry about it. Please.'

She didn't answer.

Marshall said, 'I was just calling to check that *you're* OK.'

'Yeah. I'm still alive.'

He thought he heard a smile.

She said, 'Look, I just . . .'

'You don't have to – everything's fine. Honestly.'

'You don't know what I'm going to say yet.'

'All right.' He thought he probably did, though.

She said, 'I was going to say: I'm sorry how I acted the other night. It's just been . . . it's been a pretty strange time.'

'Yeah. I know. It's fine.'

'The funeral's Tuesday morning. Tuesday at nine.' She told him the address.

'I'll be there.'

'All right. Great.'

He hit a block for a second, nothing to say. He watched a raindrop crawling down the outside of the glass. Inching, inching. Stop-start. Diverting one way and then back the other. He knew how it felt.

He said, 'Look, I have to . . .'

'Yeah?'

He was going to tell her he kept a gun on the edge of the sink while he showered, use it as subliminal evidence that maybe they weren't going to be compatible. That really, it wasn't even worth trying. But he wasn't quite sure how to confess that without it sounding a little off. He didn't want her thinking he was Timothy McVeigh. Then again, he hadn't felt a need to confess all of that to Jordan . . .

He said, 'Don't worry. I'll see you Tuesday.'

'OK. See you Tuesday.'

He disconnected, and tried Floyd Nevins' number.

'Detective Nevins.'

Marshall said, 'I wasn't sure if you'd pick up on a Sunday.'

'Is that why you called?'

'No. It was just something that occurred to me as it was ringing. That maybe you wouldn't pick up.'

Nevins didn't answer. Faint clangs and clashes from his end, maybe kitchen noise. Then he said, 'Hannah Vialoux is worried about you.'

'She mentioned that. Far as I can tell, I'm OK.'

'I'm relieved.'

Marshall said, 'Have you solved it yet?'

'I can't go into details with you.'

'That sounds like a long way of saying no. Did you ask if anyone knows where this Langello guy is, exactly?'

'I asked.'

'And what did they tell you?'

Nevins dodged the question: 'Have you solved it yet?'

Marshall said, 'Yeah. I think maybe I have. I'll call you tomorrow.'

The first train to Boston on Monday morning was at seven a.m. out of Penn Station. Marshall got there an hour early and bought his ticket at the Amtrak window. He went over to Dunkin Donuts and bought a coffee, and then wandered the concourse. He liked these moments, the feeling of being a normal member of society. Blessedly mundane, unremarkable. That said, he was probably the only person wearing concealer to disguise facial bruising. He went over to the payphones on the Amtrak concourse, and called the NYPD's seventeenth precinct. He had a burner phone with him, but the coffee transaction had left him with change that he needed to jettison: there was no way to carry coins of varying denominations in a manner that wasn't irritating. Plus he liked the novelty factor of using a payphone. Penn Station was one of the very few places in New York that still had them.

A desk sergeant picked up, and Marshall asked for Loretta Flynn.

'She's not in yet.'

'It's urgent. Can you put me through to her cell phone?'

'What's the nature of the call?'

'I can't discuss it.'

'Right.' The word drawn out so thinly, the *t* was almost lost. Marshall wondered if it was intended to convey skepticism, or just tiredness.

The sergeant said, 'I'll need a name.'

Marshall said, 'D'Anton Lewis.'

Silence on the line for thirty seconds while he was transferred. Marshall stood with his back to the console, watching the crowd. Then the line clicked, and Loretta Flynn said carefully, 'How can I help you?'

Marshall said, 'It's not actually D'Anton, and it's not actually urgent, but I figure we should talk anyway. I was going to suggest another meeting in the back of your car. But this is probably a little easier.'

It took her a moment to recognize his voice. 'Don't waste my time.'

'You need to improve your surveillance of Mr Lewis. The current system isn't working.'

The rustle of an exhalation. 'I'm hanging up the phone now.'

'OK. It's one of the few things that's easier to do than to say. But if you hold on, I have more to tell you.'

Silence, but he hadn't heard the beep yet. She was still there.

Marshall said, 'Funnily enough, I think he's being less than honest with you. Or has he told you about his missing wife?'

'What are you talking about?'

'I asked him yesterday about what happened to Vialoux. D'Anton told me his wife's been missing for a couple months, and he asked Vialoux to find her. He thinks whoever has her also killed Vialoux. Possibly an ex-mob guy called Langello. I thought it's the kind of information you might find useful.'

He hung up before she could respond, went over to the Hudson News and used his remaining change to buy a copy of the *Times*. The crowd was coalescing now, waiting for the track announcement. It was quite a spectacle. People all packed together, faces upturned, as if the departure boards described a future beyond that of a simple train ride. Then at five minutes to the hour the track number appeared, and he joined in with the swarm.

He was down the back in coach class, but he found a window seat. The train headed east into Long Island City and then turned north, following the river, the day just breaking. Weak light and a threat of rain. The old guy next to him was heading up to Cambridge, visiting grandchildren. He had four of them apparently, and he gave Marshall a biography on each as they headed up through the edge of Brooklyn. Marshall smiled and nodded, but he knew he wouldn't have the stamina to make it through the entire family history. He looked out his window. Rust and dereliction out at the margins of the city. Still interesting though. He liked seeing everything, the outputs of bygone efforts, bygone lives.

His neighbor went off to the snack car, and when he came back he took a seat across the aisle, and the woman by the window on that side got to hear all about the grandchildren, too. Marshall read his *Times*. He watched the trackside landscape slowly changing, looking more like New England now, by turns suburban and then rural. Trees kinked and brittle in the cold. Like a blood-vessel diagram, a picture of the back of your eye. He had his printout on Renee Lewis with him, and he went over it again. The passport image, and the address for the therapist's clinic she'd been visiting. Dr Ruth Davin. Beacon Street, over in Back Bay. Nice part of town.

It was almost eleven thirty by the time the train pulled in at South Station. The old guy followed him down the aisle to the door and gave him some more details on the grandchildren. He'd told the lady in the other window seat he had one grand-daughter at college and another on a waiting list, but now they were both in a Master's program at MIT. Marshall shook the guy's hand and told him to enjoy his stay, and headed off west on Essex Street, through the bottom of the financial district. It felt five degrees cooler than in New York, and people up here always seemed to be doing it tougher. Homeless guys sleeping on the sidewalk, hanging out in storefront doorways. Little knots of them on street corners, blowing into cupped hands for warmth and then proffering them in the hope of coins. Marshall dealt out cash from Little Marco's roll. He walked along the south edge of the Common and then up Arlington Street past the public garden, headed west again along Commonwealth Ave. He liked this part of town. Brownstone apartments overlooking the street with its tree-lined median and the statues of the venerated. Alexander Hamilton, and then some other guys whose plaques he'd have to read in order to remember.

He turned north and went all the way up to the Charles. Stiff cold wind coming in off the water. Plenty of traffic on Storrow Drive, following the riverfront, but not many people out walking. A few courageous souls in coats and woolen hats. Cambridge looking bleak and subdued under the heavy cloud. The MIT buildings were directly opposite, the far side of the river, and he thought of his friend from the train. Maybe right now, one or even two granddaughters were over there, grinding through a Master's program. Couldn't exactly fault the man for saying so, truth or otherwise. Marshall knew better than most people there were worse crimes than embellishment, padding out the CV of a loved one. A nice kind of deceit, really. Something good for someone you loved. Rather than something bad for someone you hated.

He walked over to Beacon Street and found Ruth Davin's office. It was in a four-story redbrick building that also had a cardiologist and a fund manager. They all had their names and post-nominals in authoritative gold lettering on the street-front door.

The remaining units seemed to be private dwellings. Marshall went in and took the stairs up to Dr Davin's office on the third floor. He wondered if the fund manager ever came in, have a session on the couch when the markets dipped. Maybe book in to see the heart doctor when things got really dire.

The reception area looked like an appropriately low-stress environment. Lots of low leather furniture, fat and shiny. A couple of side tables with vases of flowers. Flower paintings on the walls. Everything very conducive to positivity, Marshall thought. Or conducive to thinking about flowers, anyway. The reception counter was on his right, a door behind it open to what looked like an administration area. A desk back there and another flower painting on the wall. To his left was a closed door. The consultation room, presumably. Straight ahead was a window that faced the public alley that ran behind Beacon Street. Double-hung glazing with brass fitch catches on the rail. He went over for a closer look. The catches would pop open with a knife blade. If he had to, he could come up the fire escape and let himself in that way.

'Good morning. May I help you?'

A woman was standing behind the counter. Thirtyish, red-haired, very polished. She must have been in the office. Totally silent. They obviously took discretion seriously.

The clock on the wall was at five seconds to midday. Marshall didn't want it to catch him mid-phrase. He let it get to twelve, and said, 'Good afternoon. Is Dr Davin available?'

'No, she's in session, and then she has another appointment until one thirty.' She gestured at an iPad set up on a pedestal on the counter. 'If you'd like to enter some details you can arrange an appointment. Have you visited us before?'

Quiet and somehow reassuring. Like she thought whatever inner trouble had brought him here might manifest, break through the facade.

Marshall said, 'No, I haven't.' He brought out his printout on Renee Lewis. 'Actually, I just had a couple questions. You might be able to help me.'

'Oh. OK.'

He went to pass her the paper, poised for his have-you-seen-her routine, but then he stopped.

He looked at the iPad, thought for a moment.

'Sir?'

'Sorry, just thinking.' He folded the paper and pocketed it again. Smiled apologetically. 'Maybe it's easier if I make an appointment.'

'Sure. Of course.'

She gestured again to the iPad on the counter. 'If you just touch the new client icon . . .'

He did so, and the iPad screen refreshed and showed a list of questions. Name, date of birth, address, gender, preferred pronouns, telephone number. Stuff about his medical history when he scrolled down. He entered his name as Michael Langello, and selected he/him from the pronouns menu. There looked to be about seventy different options. In the phone number field, he

entered the number for his current burner. The address section
he filled with streams of random symbols: dollars and pounds
and carets and exclamations. What he hoped resembled the output
of a computer gone haywire. He left all the medical history
questions blank. The iPad didn't seem to mind. It let him click
through to the next screen and read Dr Davin's debt collection
policy. Heavy stuff. If you didn't pay, they sent someone after
you, apparently. He ticked the box to say that was all fine, and
it gave him some more dropdown menus with available appointment hours. Marshall selected one at random, tomorrow afternoon
at three p.m., touched the little icon that said CONFIRM. The
screen refreshed and showed him a green tick.

'All OK?'

He looked up, saw her smiling at him from across the counter.

'Yeah, thank you.' He tried to imbue his own smile with a
battler's quality: down on his luck, but making the most of it.
Getting there. He stepped away, and saw her own expression
softening a little, Newton's law in human terms: the force of
perceived courage bringing an equal magnitude of sympathy and
admiration. He felt the burner phone in his pocket buzz, no doubt
a confirmation text for his appointment.

He headed for the door. 'Thanks for your help.'

'No trouble.'

He stopped suddenly, like he'd just remembered something.
He winced, touched his brow. 'Oh, sorry. Man, I'm just not
thinking at the moment.'

He'd caught her returning to the office. She moved back to
the counter, looked at him pleasantly.

He issued what he hoped sounded like a self-deprecating
chuckle, ran a hand through his hair. 'Sorry, with everything
going on, the brain's in a bit of a blur.' He twirled a finger, as
if trying to catch himself up with his own reality. 'I moved house
a couple days ago, but I'm still . . . I can't remember if I put in
the new address or the old one.'

'Oh . . .' She sat down, shook a mouse to wake up a computer
screen. 'What was the name, sorry?'

'Langello.'

He spelled it for her. If she recognized it, she gave no
indication.

'And what should the address be?'

Good question. Marshall said, 'Nevin Place.'

He leaned on the counter as she typed. The edge of the monitor was right there by his elbow.

'Nothing's come up . . .'

'Oh damn . . .' He invented another street: 'I must've put the old place. Mora Way . . .' He spelled that for her, too.

More typing.

'No. Sorry.' Shaking her head slowly. 'I can't see anything.'

Marshall said, 'Oh, damn, really? So what comes up under my name?'

'Let's have a look. Langello . . .'

He watched the keyboard as she typed *Langello*, watched her hand moving to the mouse, the double click, and Marshall touched the corner of the monitor, swiveling it towards him a fraction, and then leaned over for a view of the screen. Subtle and reflexive, he hoped. The automatic gesture of any reasonable person being thwarted by I.T.

There were two entries under Langello.

Marshall's was the first, the address field full of random symbols: dollars and pounds and carets and exclamations, like some kind of coding error. The next entry showed an address on Bloomfield Street, Dorchester.

Langello, Michael.

Marshall said, 'Well, I don't know what's happened.'

'It looks like some kind of error maybe.'

'Oh, yeah. Look at that.'

He pulled his phone from his pocket, as if about to answer a call. She was looking at him enquiringly, patient, accustomed to working with the harried. Or maybe skeptical and hiding it well, running the math on the likelihood of having two patients called Michael Langello.

He made an apologetic gesture, as if hostage to the whim of his imaginary caller, headed for the door. 'I guess I'll sort it out tomorrow at the appointment. Thanks for your help. Times like these, it makes a big difference.'

THIRTY-ONE

It was enough to make him throw out his old theory. He'd assumed Renee Lewis had called up the mob, got in touch somehow with Langello's crew, asked them to keep her in hiding from D'Anton. Mob version of witness protection, like Jordan had said. With the smiley man sent out to run interference, prevent her from being found.

But it was simpler than that, obviously. They had the same therapist. Renee Lewis and Mikey Langello, both seeing Dr Davin. He could picture them in that flower-themed reception area with its leather furniture, the whole place devoid of stress. Show up open-minded with a sharing sort of attitude, maybe you start chatting to people. Small talk about all those flower paintings, and then one thing leads to another. Coffee, wander along Beacon Street, and before you know it, you're leaving your husband. Moving up to Boston to be with an Italian mob guy, albeit one who's getting himself squared away for seven hundred dollars an hour, or whatever people had to pay for the privilege of a leather waiting area with an iPad on the counter.

He walked down to the Back Bay subway station. Actually, they didn't call it the subway in Boston. It was called the T, and your MetroCard was good for nothing. You needed a CharlieCard, or a CharlieTicket. That was the downside to traveling outside New York: having to learn these different systems, different rules. He liked to move through the world with a certain fluidity and confidence, operate out of reflex. There was an irksome inefficiency about standing there looking at the route map, deciding what color line he should be on. But he got it figured out. He took the orange line and then the red down to Fields Corner, and from there it was only a short walk, ten minutes, over to Bloomfield Street.

The address from the clinic led him to a two-story white clapboard place with a chain-link fence across the dirt yard, and a flag hanging from a pole above the porch. There were a lot of flags on this street. It seemed to be a flag kind of town. He stood there for a minute, just watching. No one at the windows. No car in the driveway. The fence was low enough he could step across it without opening the little gate, and he crossed the yard with its dreary flowerbed below the porch-front balustrade and creaked up the steps and rang the bell. Silence inside. Down the street, a dog had started barking, as if wired by cosmic error to the button.

'Hey.'

Behind him.

He turned and saw a woman on the porch of the house across the street. Fiftyish and saggy. Clothing torn and hair manically tousled, as if her home were subject to some horrendous micro-climate.

She said it again: 'Hey.'

Marshall didn't answer.

'She doesn't need anything. Don't be trying to sell her shit.'

She had a cigarette sloping out one side of her mouth, the barrel wagging in ferocious amplitude with her speech.

Marshall said, 'I'm not selling anything.'

'What?'

'I'm not selling anything.'

She spread her hands. 'So what're you doing?'

The door opened, and he turned back to face it, saw a woman maybe eighty years old standing there with a walking frame.

Marshall said, 'Hello. Sorry to intrude. I'm looking for Michael Langello.'

She stood holding on to the walker, shaking a little, very stooped. 'He's not here.'

From behind him: 'Harriet, don't let him sell you anything. You don't need anything they want to sell.'

Marshall said, 'I'm not selling anything. I'm just trying to find Mr Langello.'

'What's he done?'

'Do you know him?'

'What's he done?'

'A woman's missing. I need to know if he's seen her.'

She nodded solemnly. Her hair was dead white, hanging

dead straight to her shoulders, as if trying to match the geriatric
limpness of everything else. She said, 'Are you a good man?'

'Excuse me?'

'I said, Are you a good man?'

'I think so.'

'You think so.'

From behind him again: 'Harriet, I'm gonna come over.'

'No, don't worry. I'm just talking to the man.'

'What?'

The old woman closed her eyes. 'I said I'm just talking to the
man. Don't trouble yourself.'

'Don't let him sell you anything.'

Marshall said, 'I'm not trying to sell you anything.'

The eyes opened. 'Who told you Mikey's here?'

'This is the address he gave his doctor.'

'Right, well.' She stood straighter, blue veins standing out in
her hands. 'This is his mother's house. I'm his mother.'

'Do you know where I can find him?'

She reversed away from the door carefully with the walking
frame. 'You're the first person I've talked to this week. Come in
for a moment.' She shunted forward a fraction and then back
again, trying to get herself turned around in the hallway, and he
thought of Benny in the SUV, trying to maneuver on that narrow
road in the middle of the night.

She said, 'Give a lady five minutes and I'll see you on your
way.' She looked across her shoulder at him. 'Follow. That's it.
Shut the door after you.'

She led him to the kitchen. Outdated but immaculate. Dull metal
bench with a metal faucet, brutishly practical. Like a wash station
at a morgue. The refrigerator had a big chrome handle on it, as
if repurposed from a Buick. Magnets all over it, advertising every
conceivable service. She found a packet of cigarettes and a lighter
on the counter, put a cigarette in her mouth and fired herself up.
Every tendon in her hand straining as she flicked the wheel.

'Sit down. No one likes an awkward stander.'

He sat down at the little Formica table, and she joined him.
'Who's the woman. The woman you said's missing.'

'She's from New York.'

She nodded slowly. 'Might want to give folks more detail than that. If you're trying to find her.'

'Her name's Renee Lewis.'

'And who are you? That you're looking for Renee's gone missing.'

'My name's Marshall.'

'Police?'

'Ex-police. I was with NYPD.'

She worked on that with a few nods. 'Known a couple Lewises in my time. Knew a Carol Lewis, and I knew a Lewis Tennant. Never met a Renee. Not once.' She looked at him. 'But you think my Mikey has.'

'Maybe. I just want to ask him.'

'All right.' In the slow nod and distant gaze Marshall saw a sad desire to avoid details.

She said, 'He moved up here, I thought that'd mean I see him all the time. But I don't. He's even got a man brings me groceries. Won't even do that himself.' She pointed at the window. 'You see that window?'

Marshall looked over. The window above the sink. 'Yeah. I can see it.'

'The catch is broken. It needs a new catch. I said to him, I told him to come down and see to it. I said, don't send someone down. Come do it yourself and talk to your mother at the same time. He comes down, this is two months ago. He comes down and he takes the old catch off, but he doesn't have a new catch to put on.' She pointed at him with the cigarette. 'That's the catch. If you know what I mean. Anyway. That's as far as he got and he hasn't been back. I went over to Dodson's, I bought a catch myself. You know how long it takes to walk over there, with this thing? The frame?'

'Quite a while, I imagine.'

'Yeah. You're imagining correctly. Took me an age. And it won't even fit. Goddamn me if you can get it on there, in the holes.'

Silence. She sat smoking, looking at him.

Marshall said, 'How about this.'

She leaked smoke. 'I'm listening.'

'I fix your window, you tell me how to find your Mikey.'

She nodded. 'I was thinking something along those lines.' She rose shakily. 'I'll put coffee on. The thing I bought, it's under the sink there. And if you look in the workshop, there's tools and everything. Arthur had all sorts.'

He found the window catch in the cupboard under the sink. It was a standard sill-mounted bracket with a lever handle that could move through ninety degrees. According to the packet: TWO #8 SCREWS INCLUDED! A minute later he identified the problem. The existing screw holes on the lower sill were set too close. The pitch was out by maybe an eighth of an inch.

She said, 'Yeah, that was the other goddamn thing. You ever seen a screw like that? Jesus Christ.'

Marshall said, 'Yeah. It's a square drive.'

'Nonsense is what it is. How you take your coffee?'

'Black with a little cream.'

'Black with a little cream. All right.'

She showed him the stairs to get down to the workshop. He took the screws with him. A portion of the subfloor had been dug out to create the necessary headroom. There was a workbench with a vise and a circular saw, and a pegboard with various tools. An old chest of drawers filled with screws and nails in various lengths and gauges. Sitting on the bare dirt around the excavation were neon lights daisy-chained with multiplugs and extension cord. Marshall flipped the switch at the bottom of the stairs, and the lights all blinked on in hesitant sequence. Pale glow, and a faint sizzle of electricity. It looked like the mouth of some cross-border smuggling route. He dug through drawers, and amongst the decades-old detritus, he found a torn and empty packet of #8 hex head nuts. Then a minute later he found an actual nut. He wound it onto one of the latch screws to check the gauge, and then found a square-tip screwdriver that fit the screw head. He took needle-nose pliers and a rat-tail file off the pegboard and went back upstairs. It was a ten-minute job with the file to open up the right-hand screw hole on the aluminum sill, working it hard on one edge to create an oval. He lined up the handle bracket again, making sure the widened hole would accommodate the necessary screw pitch, and then he dressed the hole smooth as best he could with the tip of the file.

'You're a man knows what he's doing.'

'Some of the time.'

He drank the coffee she'd made him, and then he went outside to finally attach the new handle, standing below the open window to see the underside of the sill. Fiddly, damp-fingered work. He fixed a screw through the widened hole first, driving it through the bracket and then onto the nut held steady with the pliers. Then he jiggled the handle bracket until he'd lined up the second hole, and homed the screw.

He went back inside and the woman said, 'There. You missed your calling.'

Marshall pulled the window closed and tested the latch. 'See how it's got two settings there on the lever? You can have it fully closed, or you can have it a fraction open for air.'

'Yeah. I ain't a total idiot.'

He sat down at the table again and lined up his tools. File, pliers, screwdriver. She sat watching him, smoking.

'What are you going to ask him?'

'I don't know yet. I'll think about it while I'm heading over.'

She smiled at that. 'You're a truth-dodger. But you fix a good latch, I'll give you that.'

Marshall smiled.

'Whatever you're gonna say to him, you ask why he hasn't come to visit his mother. All right?'

'All right.'

'Lady shouldn't have to look beyond her own blood and family to find a good man. Here.' She reached behind her for a scrap of notepaper on the counter and passed it to him. 'Wrote it down for you.'

One of the fridge magnets was for a cab service. Marshall used Mrs Langello's phone to make the call, and then waited for it at the curb, twenty minutes all up, the woman across the street coming outside every ninety seconds or so, telling him no one around here wanted to buy what he was selling.

The address the woman had given him was for Maple Street in Cambridge, and it was a forty-minute ride getting up there. A beautiful old neighborhood. Two- and three-story homes on generous sections, grand and dripping oak trees on both redbrick sidewalks. Mikey Langello's place was an upmarket version of his mother's. Two-story New England clapboard on a large section with a rich, well-tended lawn. White stone driveway, and a white picket fence in place of chain-link. A vine-covered pergola covering a redbrick path from the mailbox to the front door. The rear of the property was sectioned off with a vine-covered wooden fence.

'Timed it well, bro. Gonna rain soon.'

'Yeah, I think you're right. Thanks for the ride.'

He paid the guy with the last of Little Marco's cash, and stood watching the house from the sidewalk as the cab pulled away up the street. No discernable change since he'd arrived. No face at a window, no twitching blind. He walked quietly up the redbrick path, the yard sweetly garden-scented and damp with a mist just strengthening to rain. No buzzer at the front door. He knocked, and then listened to silence. He knocked again, looked around carefully in the alcove for signs of surveillance. A little buttonhole lens above the lintel. He knocked again, and tried the handle. Locked. Marshall checked the street briefly, and then went around the side of the house. The fence had a gate that accessed the rear yard. He reached over and found the latch and let himself through, closed the gate quietly behind him and walked around into the rear yard.

There was a redbrick patio with a metal table and chairs, and an outdoor fireplace in such distressed condition it could have been the chimney of an original dwelling, since demolished. Pretty flowerbeds all along the perimeter fence, and a black plastic compost bin over in a corner.

Renee Lewis was walking from the bin to the house. She was carrying a metal bucket, and she dropped it when she saw Marshall. She raised her hands as if to cover her mouth, but then held them at her sides. Fists clenched, as if clinging to her own composure. Jaw clenched too, and her nostrils flaring as she breathed.

She said, 'Do it.' Eking it out through locked teeth. She shut her eyes. 'Get it over with and goddamn you.'

He saw himself for a moment as she had: tall and grim and coat-clad. 'I'm not going to hurt you. I'm not here for that.'

She opened her eyes. 'Did D'Anton send you?'

Marshall shook his head. 'He's looking for you, though.'

'Who are you?'

'I'm a friend of Ray Vialoux's. I was, anyway.'

She swallowed. She was attractive. Shortish and heavy, but with the sort of smooth and balanced features that would probably remain ageless until she hit seventy.

Marshall said, 'Who else is in the house?'

She swallowed again. Throat muscles slender and precise. 'He's out. He'll be home soon.'

Meaning Langello.

Marshall said, 'I'm not here to hurt you. But we're going to sit down. And you're going to tell me everything.'

THIRTY-TWO

He did a little tour of the house with her, confirming they were alone, and then they sat together in the ground-floor living room: Marshall in an armchair with a view through the half-open blind to the front yard and the road, Renee Lewis opposite him in the center of a long sofa. Alone and nervous, self-consciously erect on an expanse of white leather, she looked like something captured for the purpose of study.

Marshall said, 'I want to be clear about what's happening. I'm not a repo man. I'm not taking you back to your husband. I'm not here because I want to know about your personal life. I'm here because the man you hired has killed people. So I need to get the story straight. Do you understand?'

Her hands were on her knees. She studied each in turn. 'What's your name?'

'Marshall Grade.'

'Are you a police officer?'

He shook his head. 'Just someone trying to find out what happened.'

'I didn't want anyone hurt.'

'I've heard that a lot.'

'How did you find me?'

He told her. Dr Davin's clinic, Langello's mother, here.

She said, 'Well, let me be clear, too.'

'All right.'

'Do you know my husband?'

'D'Anton Lewis?'

'Yes.'

Marshall nodded. 'I've met him.'

'I've been trying to leave him for a long time.'

'Why?'

She looked at him blankly for a second, and then laughed faintly, as if the answer was self-evident. She said, 'Because he's terrible.'

'So you traded in a drug dealer for a mob man.'

She took a moment to answer. He wondered if she thought the line was too uncharitable, or just too accurate.

She said, 'That's a pretty heartless way to put it.'

'Why. Did he say he's changed?'

'He's retired. And he's a good man.'

Marshall didn't answer. The cab driver had been right. The rain was coming down now.

She said, 'There's a Bible story. Jesus comes back as judge. And his judgment . . . He has most contempt for the people who are neither good nor bad. There's a certain purity in choosing one thing or the other.'

'Was that how he sold it to you?'

She was still sitting there, carefully upright.

'There aren't many people who can keep me safe. But he's one of them.'

'Did you meet him at the clinic? Dr Davin's?'

'His appointment was before mine. I was in the waiting area one day, and I saw him come out of his session. I recognized him. D'Anton had had meetings with him. But I hadn't actually met him before. I had my appointment, and I came out, and he was still there, at reception. He'd waited for me. He said something like . . . two New Yorkers in Boston, why don't we get a drink. Something like that. Something . . . simple.' She smiled faintly. 'But it worked.'

Marshall didn't answer, wanting her to feel the pressure of the silence.

She said, 'It's funny when you know someone by reputation.

And then you meet them, and see them up close, and they're just . . . He was nice – he *is* nice. Funny, considerate. But interesting, too. Right away he was interesting.'

'Why. Because he's keeping it legal, but he still talks to hitmen now and again?'

She looked at him.

Marshall said, 'You know a guy called Little Marco? Smiles a lot.'

She said, 'It's from a surgery. The smile.'

'How do you know?'

'Michael told me. He was brain damaged as a child. Marco was. There was a problem with the birth, and he ended up with facial droop. He had surgery to fix it, cosmetic surgery to lift his mouth, but they overcorrected.'

Marshall said, 'It's nice these guys talk to each other about their problems.'

She shrugged. 'You can sneer. Michael was . . . he's turning his life around. He's gained an awareness of himself through therapy. He's interested in people. He asked him what had happened.'

'You paid him to kill Ray Vialoux. So he wouldn't find you.'

She was shaking her head. 'No. No, we didn't. I told you, I didn't want anyone hurt. Neither did Michael.'

'The reality's quite different. He killed Vialoux, and he killed a woman along the street from him.'

She had her hands edgewise on her thighs as she stared down at her lap, and he thought of Vialoux on the night he was killed, making that same gesture, like he could see the whole dilemma right there in front of him.

She said, 'He was working for my husband. And it was imperative that he didn't find me. He went to the clinic on Beacon Street. Vialoux, I mean. Somehow he learned that Michael and I were both patients. Or maybe someone had seen us together. I don't know. Dr Davin called and asked if I was all right, because apparently Vialoux had told them I was missing. He'd left a card with his details, told them he was an investigator from New York. I think they were pretty concerned. Mikey called him and said he needed to stop looking, but this guy seemed to think . . . I don't know. He seemed to think there could be some kind of amicable solution. But you can't have anything amicable with D'Anton involved. I don't think he understood that. Or, I guess maybe he did. I think maybe he realized if he didn't find me, D'Anton wouldn't be happy. And then it would be him who was in danger. Vialoux.'

'So you got Little Marco onto him.'

'No. Not in that sense. Not in the sense you mean. We . . . we're here because we want a different kind of life. And . . .' She closed her eyes. 'You go out in the yard, walk around the block, it's a long way from what we used to be part of. We had to protect that. We need to protect all of this.'

Marshall didn't answer.

'Mikey told him . . . he said he didn't want to be following up on the guy, keeping tabs on him, seeing how close he was. He wanted this Marco guy to take care of it.'

Marshall said, 'That has pretty clear connotations. In your old life, at least. Maybe not in this zip code.'

She shook her head again. 'I heard him talk to the guy. Mikey never said kill anyone. It would defeat the whole point. We're trying to avoid attention. He just said . . . he wanted this guy to keep tabs on Vialoux, or whoever D'Anton sent, stop them from trying to find me.'

'And why did you think that wouldn't be a fatal exercise?'

'Sorry?'

'What made you think no one would be killed.'

'I . . . because I told him. I told him what I just told you, that the whole point was avoiding attention. And . . .' He saw her mouth start to shake. Her voice took on a warped quality. 'I didn't want this to happen. I didn't want this to happen. He probably had kids, a family.'

She sat sobbing, face in her hands. He sat there quietly, not about to offer any comfort.

She said, 'I had a bad feeling about the guy. From the way he looked. He was just such a strange man. Mikey had him in the kitchen, and this guy was just sitting there dead still, very straight in his chair, and just sort of blank. Even though he always had this smile, there was nothing in his face. It was just . . . empty somehow. And . . .' She closed her eyes, shook her head again. 'Funny the things that stay in your head. I was in the house, but I left Mikey to talk with him. I heard him ask the guy, Marco, if he wanted a drink, and Marco told him, yeah, he'd like a glass of milk.' She shrugged. 'Unusual I guess, but whatever. But then, it seemed like he didn't even touch it until he was leaving. They finished talking, and he got up, and just drank the whole thing. I'm not saying . . .' She shook her head. 'I wasn't freaked out by a guy drinking milk. I just mean the way he did everything, it seemed robotic. And it made me think . . . it gave me this horrible feeling that once you point him in the right direction and let him go, maybe he wouldn't stop.'

Marshall nodded. 'I think that's what's happened.'

She was shaking her head again, lips clamped together, tears falling. 'I don't know where he is and I don't know how to stop him.'

'He's stopped. But he left an awful lot of damage.'

She nodded. 'I worried from the start this would happen.' Her voice was steadier now. 'But Mikey said it'd be all right. He said he'd been told what to do, and he'd do it. There were people in Brooklyn that were going to help him out.'

'Frank Cifaretti's guys?'

'Yes. I think so. Frank.'

She passed her tongue across her top lip, catching some tears. 'Mikey said Vialoux had a gambling debt. They were going to use that to pressure him . . . you know. Basically show him that if he kept making trouble, life would be difficult.'

Marshall nodded. 'Life's impossible for him now. And pretty difficult for his family, too. Without him around.'

'What happened to the woman? The woman on his street.'

Marshall thought about that for a moment. He said, 'I think she deserved better than after-the-fact sympathy from someone who's complicit.'

She swallowed. 'I . . .' But she didn't seem to have anything. After a moment, she said, 'What was I supposed to do about him?'

'Sorry?'

She jutted her chin, spoke with her lower teeth showing. Forceful. 'What was I supposed to do about him? About D'Anton?'

Marshall didn't answer.

'You can't stop someone like him. There's no getting away. So what was I supposed to do? He gets exactly what he wants and there's no stopping him. He's . . . he's abusive and controlling. You have no idea. So what was I meant to do about that? Other than make a deal with someone who could . . .' She thought about it. 'Fold the mirror back a little, show him what it's really like.'

He let that have a few seconds' silence.

She said, 'And don't say, "Go to the police." If it's good enough for you without them, it's good enough for me, too.'

Marshall said, 'When were you last in New York?'

'I don't know the date.' She shrugged. 'Months ago. It would have been a Friday. I left for an appointment and just never went back.'

'A witness saw you in a car with Little Marco in Brooklyn, six weeks ago.'

She shook her head. 'Not me. Six weeks ago, we were in Europe. Mikey said we should get away for a while. Forget about everything.'

'Light the fuse and walk away, you mean.'

She didn't answer.

Marshall said, 'Did you take any photos?'

She nodded. 'Most days.'

'Show me.'

He followed her to the kitchen. She unplugged a smartphone from a charging station and tapped and swiped for a moment. She handed it to him. Photos of European-looking scenes, countries he'd never visited. The images were all date-categorized. There she was on London Bridge. Standing alone, and then posed with Langello in the next shot. More London, and then maybe some seaside England, and then maybe some seaside France. Marshall scrolled on. Weeks of pleasant living. He set the phone down on the counter. She didn't move to take it. She stood with her arms folded, watching him.

'What's going to happen now?'

Marshall shrugged. 'Usual stuff. I tell the police. They investigate. Eventually they show up and ask you about it.'

Her mouth was moving, but there was nothing coming out. She swallowed and tried again. 'He wasn't meant to kill anyone. We didn't want him to kill anyone.'

Marshall said, 'Bit like playing with matches though, isn't it? You wanted a small fire, but got a big one instead. I think plenty of people would say, I told you so.'

He left her standing in the kitchen and went out the back door, let himself through the gate in the side yard. As he crossed the front lawn toward the street, a silver Lexus sedan swung into the driveway. A man at the wheel who he guessed was Mikey Langello. He saw Marshall, and his face went slack with dread. The Lexus skidded to a halt.

Marshall stopped and stood there.

Langello clambered out, awkward, trussed for a second by his seatbelt, and then fighting the door. He was a tall guy, fiftyish, plenty of meat on his shoulders and arms. Bulge of his gut tautly smooth beneath the polo shirt belted into his trousers. He kept his eyes on Marshall still standing in the middle of the lawn, and ran for the house.

'Renee! Renee! . . . Shit.'

But he'd left his keys in the car. He slipped on the wet grass and went down on his knee for a second, sprinted for the Lexus. By the time he'd made it back to the house with the keys, Renee Lewis had the door open.

'Renee, Jesus.'

He hugged her, pushed her back inside as he pointed at Marshall. 'Get the fuck out of here.'

'Mikey, he knows about everything.'

'What?'

'He knows what happened.'

Langello held her at arm's length for a second, like trying to re-focus the picture. He ran a hand through his hair. 'Jesus, just . . . get inside, will you?'

He pulled the door shut behind her, and resumed pointing at the street. 'You deaf or something?'

But the dread hadn't left his face. Marshall had expected more steel from a mob boss. Although, thinking about it, maybe it was a different kind of fear. Scared more of what Marshall represented, as opposed to Marshall personally. Scared by the fact that people could still find him. Like despite what he'd told himself, starting a clean and honest life, things had a way of coming home.

'Marco didn't stick to the brief.'

'What?'

But he could see behind the man's eyes it was making terrible sense to him.

Marshall nodded at the house. 'Did you think you were going to walk in and find her dead? Be pretty horrible, wouldn't it? I don't know how people even begin to cope with something like that.'

The guy's chest was heaving as he breathed. He still had his arm raised, aiming at the street. Tempting to kill both of them. Bring some balance to the saga. But what sense would that make? Excessive force as penance for excessive force.

Marshall said, 'Visit your mother. God knows why, but she misses you.'

He walked across the yard and headed off down the pretty street, along the redbrick path and under the oak trees in the light rain.

He caught a cab back down to South Station and bought a ticket for the three pm train to New York. Business class this time. He felt he'd earned it. His car was full of corporate-looking people with laptops and little hands-free earbuds for their phones. He waited until they were rolling, everyone focused on their Excel spreadsheets and their emails, and then he called Nevins.

'How can I help you?'

Marshall said, 'I'm up in Boston.'

'Good for you.'

'I know what happened.'

It took an hour to lay it all out for him. Everything except his shootout in the woods last night. They'd put it together eventually. The New Jersey cops would tell NYPD they had a few of their clients in the morgue. No need to have his name attached to any of that. He ended the call, and the scene around him was unchanged. People still working away on whatever they were working on. New England blurred past. An announcement was broadcast that Chip was back on duty in the snack car. People began to come past him down the aisle, food-bound. Marshall stayed put. The landscape shadowed. Lights came on. He had his own line stuck in his head:

I know what happened.

A bold and certain claim. It made him comb back over what he knew. He ran through the story again, turning it over in his mind like a stone from a river. Looking at the details and blemishes. Was one strange fact just an oddity of how the thing was formed, or was it something fatal to the structure of the theory?

People and events. Hannah Vialoux. Jordan Mora.

Some kind of odd dynamic, Jordan had said.

The Linney guy across the street. The window vigil. What else had he seen?

The smiley man, and the woman with him in the car. Surveilling Vialoux, the night he visited the Boynes.

It must've been another woman.

Seven pm when the train reached Manhattan, city lights heaped like dragon's treasure along the length of the island, and Marshall wondered if that really was the end of the matter, or if maybe there was some other layer to it.

THIRTY-THREE

R ay Vialoux's funeral was in Greenwood Heights. Even without the casket and the flowers and the mourners, it all looked pretty funereal, Marshall thought. Heavy gray sky, wind clacking the branches of the trees. He stayed near the back of the group, people largely anonymous with their coats and umbrellas. The priest kept going mute, words snatched away in the gusts. It was an unusual mix of tradition and new-trend. Vialoux had requested a green burial, apparently. Environment-friendly. No embalming or formaldehyde. The casket was biodegradable, or so Hannah had told him, and even the hole had been dug by hand. The backhoe method wasn't compatible with the green philosophy. It surprised him that this was what Vialoux wanted. Even the burial aspect. If he'd had to guess, Marshall would've said Ray wanted to go straight in the furnace.

A couple of guys he vaguely recognized from twenty years ago gave eulogies. Vialoux on patrol and not taking any shit.

Vialoux on patrol and getting the better of guys who thought they had everything figured out. He could see Hannah and Ella up there in the front row, holding hands, holding it together. A detective Marshall didn't know got up and gave a reading from a Richard Price novel, about a detective going to see a psychic to help solve a murder. It got a few subdued laughs going around the group.

The priest read the committal prayer, and Marshall stayed back as the casket was lowered into the earth, people moving forward to see Ray go. He watched Hannah throw a handful of earth on the coffin, and then she threaded through the edge of the crowd to where he was standing.

'Thanks for coming.' Red-eyed but composed.

'No trouble.'

'Is that makeup?'

He touched his face out of reflex. He'd applied fresh concealer this morning, to disguise the bruising. 'Yeah, I slipped the other night. Didn't want to show up looking like a rotten grape.'

He could see she had more questions, but she kept them to herself. They stood side by side watching the last of the dirt-throwers. It wasn't a huge turnout. Maybe twenty people, priest included. No sign of Jordan Mora.

She said, 'There's a number you have to call at police plaza, so they can process all the pension stuff. It says on the website, I looked it up, you're entitled to pallbearers if you're ex-PD. But they said they wouldn't. They wouldn't provide them.' She shook her head, lips sealed, eyes brimming. 'It meant so much to him. The job. And they couldn't even give him pallbearers. I said to them, "He was shot through a window, for goodness' sake. If that happened to a serving officer it'd be national news, but with this . . ."' She shook her head, looked away. 'All I got, it was just no ma'am, sorry ma'am and . . . what was it.' She looked at the ground. '"We have to review the circumstances and the individual." I mean . . . come on. What could the circumstances be that they can't even do him that small courtesy. Given how much it would've meant to him.'

He put his arm around her and held her for a moment, wondered what they had on file about Ray Vialoux over at One Police. One day, they'd be vetoing pallbearers for Marshall, too. He watched

Ella drop a handful of dirt. Then the Boynes: Ginny and Martin. Pale with grief and cold. People were breaking up now into little knots. Friends, ex-cops, wider family.

Hannah said, 'Are you going to find him?'

He wasn't sure at first how to answer that.

She said, 'Or have you found him already?' Gaze holding pointedly on his bruised cheek.

Marshall said, 'The police are with him.'

Technically true, he figured. Provided the New Jersey cops had followed up on his call. He wasn't sure about the average daily intake of false tip-offs in respect of dead bodies.

She said, 'So who is it?'

'A hired man.'

He saw a muscle working in her jaw. 'A hired man. Who the police are with.' She nodded. 'Glad you're still upholding principles. I thought maybe on the day of my husband's funeral, you might be a little more forthcoming, but I'm sure Ray would like to see you still keeping your mouth shut.'

She walked away from him. Stopped after a few paces and turned back. 'Sorry, by the way.'

By the way.

It made it unrelated to what she'd just said, and the confusion must have showed in his face. She smiled. 'There's coffee and sandwiches back at the house. Make sure you come over.'

He gave her a twenty-yard lead, and then he began to follow, people drifting with him, heading for the cemetery lane along which six or seven vehicles were parked. The rear car was a black SUV with tinted windows. Marshall recognized it. He saw the curbside rear door open, and D'Anton Lewis climb out. He closed his door, eyes on Marshall, and then took a moment to stand there and button his coat. Marshall waited on the grass and let the man come over to him, D'Anton moving slow, as if time elapsed according to his own rhythm. He was careful to stand much too close, give himself a downward angle.

Marshall said, 'What you can do if you want to be a real gentleman, you stand with the mourners, at least make a show of paying respects. Rather than wait in your car and then make a nuisance of yourself.'

'Oh, I'm sorry. I thought we were just standing here, talking.'

'Mmm. Were you intending to stop here? Or am I in your way?'

'I thought I'd get an update from you.'

'Oh yeah? On what?'

D'Anton took a breath in and out through his nose. Unrushed, almost forlorn, as if disappointed at having to spell things out. 'Have you had any success locating my wife?'

Marshall nodded and said, 'Uh-huh,' and saw in the man's eye that he'd surprised him with that. 'I found her yesterday.'

Silence.

Then D'Anton's lip curled, indulging him, like this was all one big joke. 'And where is she?'

Marshall kept eye contact. 'I'm thinking of the place right now.' He put a finger to his temple, tapped it. 'It's right here. But I'm not going to say it.'

'I wouldn't play that game, if I were you.'

Marshall said, 'I think I'll be OK.' He nodded at him. 'Got your coat all buttoned up. Won't be able to get your dagger without tangling yourself.'

D'Anton smiled, rolling with it. He said, 'I'm surprised you haven't gathered yet that I can cause trouble for you.'

Marshall shrugged, kept his voice pleasant: 'Yeah, well, likewise. And I've got a pretty good track record, actually. If there weren't so many people around, I'd be tempted to throw you in the ground on top of Vialoux.'

It seemed to add to the man's amusement. He said, 'How is it that I always get my way, do you think?'

Marshall shook his head. 'I don't know. I don't really care, to be perfectly honest. I'm not telling you where your wife is. I think she's a liar, but I think she's telling the truth when she says you're a piece of work. Excuse me.'

He stepped past him and walked across the lawn to the cemetery lane, and when he looked back, D'Anton was still standing there, watching him.

He took the subway down to Fifty-third Street in Sunset Park and reached the Vialouxs' place just before ten thirty. The little house made the turnout seem larger than it was. The entry hall was standing room only, loud with overlapping conversation. He saw Bruce Linney talking with a couple of ex-cops he recognized. Linney had swapped his #Dad shirt for a suit and tie. He and Marshall traded nods. And over by the stairs was Martin Boyne, wearing an expression of pale fear, like he knew eventually he'd have to talk to someone.

He saw Marshall and smiled nervously. 'Hey.'

'Hey, Martin. How you doing?'

'Pretty good, I think.' The nervous smile again. 'Despite it being a funeral.'

'Yeah. I know what you mean. Is Ginny here too?'

'Yes, Ginny's here. Try the kitchen, maybe. She always leaves me to fend for myself at these things . . .'

He stopped at the bathroom on the way, sat down on the lid of the commode and took off his boots. He was wearing the socks he'd bought in Paterson: plain white, but they had a little embroidered L or R on the outside of the heel to denote left or right as appropriate. The sock-shape was the same for both sides – identical stitching, as far as he'd determined – so in truth the lettering implied a false status of chirality. But he still liked to have things around the right way, and he had a feeling that something was off.

The left sock was OK. A little embroidered L by his ankle. He checked the right. Shit, *another* L. Two left socks. It must've happened when he did the re-bundle, after cutting off the packaging. It hadn't occurred to him to check the pairings. He sat there for a moment, thinking about the best way forward. Soft hubbub coming through the door. At least he'd known something wasn't right. And he realized now there was only one option. He peeled off his socks and folded them carefully and put them in his inner pocket. Left side, obviously. Then he donned his boots barefooted and went looking for Ginny Boyne.

She was in the kitchen, as Martin had guessed, standing in a foursome that also included Hannah Vialoux. Hannah saw him coming and broke away, and the other two faded off as well, that idle drift Marshall had seen people do, smiling and concertedly distant, as if pulled by social currents they were helpless to resist.

But Ginny held her ground. She smiled at him. 'Hello again.'

'How you doing, Ginny?'

'I'm all right, thank you.' She gestured with the mug she was holding. 'I have coffee, so things could be worse . . .'

They covered all the basics: how it had been a nice service, and the speakers had done well, and the bit from the Richard Price novel had been funny and relevant, and it was good how it hadn't rained, despite threatening to do so.

Marshall said, 'Thank you again for taking the time to speak to us on Sunday. Much appreciated.'

'Oh. It's no trouble.'

'Sorry to labor the topic—'

'No, no. Not at all—'

'We're still trying to square up a few details. In terms of Ray's movements the last few weeks.'

'Oh, sure. Yes, of course.'

'Do you remember the night he visited – I know you said you don't recall too many details—'

'Yes. It's all a bit foggy, sorry.'

'That's OK.'

'You mean the night he collected Jennifer's computer?'

'That's right. Do you happen to remember what he was intending with it? It was a laptop, right?'

'That's right . . . I think . . . he was going to take a look at it that evening, and then get a technician to help him if needed. But he told us in the end he gained access himself, and there was nothing on it really, let alone a note or a letter. Almost like she hadn't used it.'

'Why did he think that?'

'Excuse me?'

'Why did he think she hadn't been using it?'

'Well, apparently there just weren't many recent files.'

Hannah was back now. 'Not interrogating you, is he?'

Ginny said, 'No, not at all. Just talking.'

Marshall said, 'I was on the way out, anyway. Nice to see you both.'

He got two *Nice to see you*s in reply, Hannah's a little cooler than Ginny's.

'Where's Ella? I'll just say goodbye.'

Hannah nodded toward the front of the house. 'Said she's going out for some air.'

He found her sitting on the front step, smoking a cigarette. Marshall sat down beside her.

She said, 'Are you coming for a smoke, or are you trying to have like a real meaningful talk?'

He glanced at her. She smiled faintly. 'You know . . .' She deepened her voice: 'Your dad and I were buddies, you can count on me, ra-de-ra.'

Marshall grinned. 'I'd hoped all that stuff was implicit.'

'Oh, right.'

She offered him the cigarette pack. Marshall waved it off. 'No thanks.'

She said, 'You're probably close enough anyway to get it secondhand.'

'Yeah. Probably.'

Silence for a while. A car went past. An appropriately solemn pace. A couple more smokers joined them on the front steps. Ex-cop types.

Marshall said, 'I was just talking to Ginny Boyne.'

'Oh yeah? She's real sweet.'

'She said you were really kind when their daughter died. People always appreciate those things.'

She looked at him for a few seconds. 'That's kinda random. But OK.'

'Well, it's true. It makes a difference.'

She said, 'Yeah, I mean. Least I could do, I guess. It didn't really make any sense. Hard for everyone who knew her, so I can't imagine what it was like for her family.' She shrugged. 'Well. Now maybe I do.'

He let her work on her cigarette for a moment, and then said, 'You ever seen this smiley man?'

'Huh?' She glanced at him.

'Apparently there was a guy following your dad around.'

'If he was only following him around it wouldn't have been so much of a problem.'

He waited.

She said, 'The guy who killed him, you mean?'

'Yeah. Little guy. Always grinning. Weird little dude, apparently.'

She shook her head, looked away. 'You got a real gift for

timing, don't you?' She tugged her cuff back, checked her watch. 'Funeral was only what, hour ago, you're already back at work.'

He shook his head slowly, keeping eye contact. 'I wasn't trying to cause offence. I'm just trying to get all the details squared away. So we can know what happened.'

'The police already asked me about that stuff.' She clicked her fingers. 'The Nevins guy. Detective Nevins.'

Marshall nodded. 'Sure. I just thought I'd ask. I remember when I talked to Martin and Ginny, they said they'd seen the guy. And Martin had seen a woman with him too.'

She shrugged. 'What do you mean?'

'So it wasn't you that night? In the car with the little guy who's always smiling?'

She shut her eyes, shook her head. 'What the fuck, man. Honestly.'

Quiet. He sensed the attention of the two other smokers. The quality of the stillness out here.

'I have to ask the question.'

'No you fucking don't. In fact . . .' She shook her head again. 'Get out of here. Do without this shit, honestly.'

Something there in her eyes that looked to him like fear, worry. But he got to his feet. As he turned to walk away, he saw Hannah had come outside, too.

She said, 'I couldn't have put it better, frankly.' She gestured with her chin, aiming up the street. 'Get lost.' Then: 'Ella, for God's sake, put that out.'

Marshall stood on the sidewalk, looking between them. He settled on Ella, her lips pursed in a slow draw on the cigarette, and regarding him with faint interest now.

She said, 'Anything else?'

'Yeah. One question.'

'One question.' Voice deeper, mimicking him.

Marshall said, 'When you called the Boynes, after their daughter died—'

'Jennifer. Her name was Jennifer.'

'Jennifer, right. You called and spoke to Ginny after she'd died. Is that right?'

She nodded. 'Uh-huh.'

'And you told her you were sure she hadn't been bullied. You said that wasn't the reason she killed herself.'

'Yeah. So?'

'So how did you know that?'

'Huh?'

'How could you be certain that wasn't the reason?'

She blew smoke, no rush, nothing in her face. 'Because she told me, you idiot.'

She flicked the cigarette in the gutter and trudged up the steps to the front door. Hannah watched her inside, and then came down, stood in front of him on the sidewalk.

'What are you insinuating?'

'I'm just trying to ask a question.'

She pinched the bridge of her nose, looked at the ground. 'Just get out of here. You're not helping anything.'

He didn't answer. He turned and walked away, and when he glanced back, she was already up the steps and through the door.

THIRTY-FOUR

A brief walk in the rain, and then the clatter-squeal of the subway. It was twelve thirty by the time he made it home. Three NYPD patrol cars and three unmarked detective's cars were double-parked on his street. He was pretty confident about who they were after. He went up his front steps and found the door already open. Floyd Nevins and two uniformed officers were standing in his living room.

Nevins said, 'We have paperwork.'

Marshall took off his coat and shut the door. 'I'm sure you do. What are you looking for?'

'More evidence you might have withheld. Pertaining to the Ray Vialoux murder investigation.'

'More, huh?' He hung his coat on the back of the door. 'What was the initial evidence I withheld?'

Nevins said, 'You're allegedly in possession of a tracking device recovered from Mr Vialoux's vehicle.'

Hannah must've ratted on him.

Sorry, by the way.

It made sense now.

He sat down at the desk and studied his puzzle. Habit was habit. He took a piece from the reserves, sighted the lineup, and then homed it on the working edge, third try. Not bad, as far as placements went. But probably one was enough, given the circumstances. It would be hard to concentrate with Nevins and the two cops looking over his shoulder. He heard more people upstairs, someone else in the kitchen.

'How many people did you bring?'

'Six, all up.'

'I'm flattered you thought I'd be such a handful.'

'We had some last-minute add-ons. Inspector Flynn is here with some people.'

On cue: footsteps from the kitchen, and then a voice said, 'Nice to see you again.'

He turned from the desk as Loretta Flynn entered the room.

Marshall said, 'Is this petty retaliation, NYPD-style?'

'No. This is work, NYPD-style.'

'I think that's a stretch.'

'Why? Have you not heard of search warrants?'

'I have. But this is just a shakedown to keep me away from your man D'Anton.'

Flynn just smiled.

Nevins said, 'Where were you on Sunday night?'

'Upstairs. Sleeping cozily in my bed.'

'You haven't been out to New Jersey, by any chance?'

'Why do you ask?'

'Frank Cifaretti and some of his people were found dead yesterday.'

'How did you hear that?'

'Organized crime unit at the FBI notified us. Given he's a person of interest in the Vialoux case.'

Marshall nodded. They looked at him.

Nevins said, 'No comment?'

Marshall said, 'My thoughts and prayers are with the organized crime community at this difficult time.'

Nevins said, 'One of the people with him was identified as

Marco Perrin. We think he might've been the man hired to hit Vialoux.'

'Little Marco. The smiley man.'

'So you haven't been out to Jersey?'

Marshall said, 'This all sounds like a serious criminal matter.'

'It is.'

'So I'd prefer not to comment.'

'It's a simple question.'

Marshall shrugged. 'And you've heard what I have to say.'

Silence.

Then Flynn said, 'We found your safe, obviously. Do you want to tell me the code, or do we need to bring in a gas axe?'

He smiled. She wanted the stolen cash, from his undercover work. Severance pay, as he liked to think of it. The few hundred grand he'd taken from Tony Asaro, after his shootout that ended the whole thing. Money that might keep him alive in years to come. They didn't have the probable cause to search for that alone. If they did, he'd have been searched already, years ago. Easier to piggyback on this thing.

She said, 'Something funny?'

Marshall said, 'No. I'm just wondering if you really want me to open it.'

'If it's that complicated, I can give you the options again.'

He stood up from the desk and slid his chair in, turned to face her. Maybe five feet between them. She hadn't moved, but the two uniforms had their hands on their guns now, thumbs hooked on the grip in that faux-idle cop fashion, like that's just how they happened to be standing.

Marshall said, 'Maybe you could all give me a moment to talk to the inspector.'

Flynn nodded, looking at him. 'Yes, that's a good idea. Give us a moment.'

The two uniformed cops passed between them as they went outside. Nevins waited a second, and then he shrugged, and went out after them.

Flynn waited for the door to close, and said, 'What is it?'

'I thought you're too senior to be out serving warrants.'

'Oh, you know. Nice to get out from behind the desk every now and then.'

Marshall said, 'You're not investigating D'Anton. Are you? You told me you were warned I'd try to make contact. But I waited outside his house the other day for an hour before I saw him, and no one tried to intervene. Because no one knew I was there. There's no surveillance.'

'Is that right?'

'I went back two days ago to confirm, and again no one stopped me. Which I thought was interesting, given that I was supposed to stay away from him. Or did I misinterpret you?'

Loretta Flynn didn't answer.

Marshall said, 'So I figured the reason you showed up when you did was because he called you. So do you have him logged as a confidential informant, or is it a more casual arrangement? I would hope not. It would be quite inappropriate.'

She smiled.

Marshall said, 'What's he got on you?'

She shook her head. 'Is that it? Is that all you wanted to say?'

'I can say it again, to different people, if I have to. But if you leave right now, I'm happy to err on the side of reticence. By which I mean I won't tell anyone you obstructed a murder investigation in order to do a favor to a drug-trafficker.'

Loretta Flynn nodded slowly, like she was taking care to process his statement. She said, 'Why don't we go upstairs, and you can open your little safe?'

'Why don't I tell you the code, and you can do it yourself?'

He recited the combination.

'There's a gun in there, but don't freak out. If you dig around through all the stolen money, there should be a permit, too.'

She told him she'd seen guns before, and she was pretty sure she'd be able to keep it together.

She turned and went upstairs, and Marshall opened the front door. Nevins and the two uniformed cops were standing on the sidewalk.

Marshall said, 'You want coffee?'

Nevins looked at him levelly and then nodded, holding eye-contact. 'Yeah. Let's have some coffee.'

He came back inside and followed Marshall to the kitchen, watched him prepare the little Bialetti percolator.

'You worried I'm going to make trouble?'

Nevins folded his arms, leaned his hip on the edge of the counter. 'I'm skeptical about your harmlessness, put it that way.'

'All I can do right now is brew your coffee too strong.' He set the percolator on a stove element and lit the flame. 'You haven't asked me much about this evidence I allegedly stole. I'm starting to think you're just playing tag-along with Loretta, hope I'll be intimidated.'

Nevins was peering at him, leaning in a little. 'Is that makeup? What did you do to your face?'

'I slipped.'

'You slipped.'

Marshall shrugged. 'It's wet, it happens. You talked to D'Anton Lewis yet? Or is Flynn still keeping him off-limits?'

Nevins didn't answer that. They stood for a few seconds listening to the percolator heating up. Low rumble like a far-off jet inbound.

Nevins said, 'Maybe it hasn't occurred to you, but a bit of preemptive honesty will serve you better than waiting to be arrested.'

'What, for the dead gangsters in New Jersey? Thanks for the advice.'

'You think they won't find you?'

'No, they'll definitely find me. Because you'll definitely tell them I visited Cifaretti the other night at the bagel place. But there's a difference between finding someone, and finding evidence that they're guilty.'

He stood there and let Nevins look at him as he in turn looked at the percolator. The rumble building, as if from the heat of relayed attention: Nevins to Marshall to the water in the stainless vessel.

'So you won't say you didn't do it.'

Marshall said, 'I don't have to. It's called burden of proof, not burden of denial.'

The percolator reached temperature. Marshall removed it from the element and took two mugs from a cupboard and placed them on the counter. Not a move he was accustomed to. A one-cup pour was his standard. The challenge with this was he didn't have anything to validate the spacing. If he'd had tilework he could've used the grout lines as a reference. Nothing here, though.

This was a by-inspection job. He got the handles pointing in the same direction, and then imposed what looked to be a two-diameter mug-separation, centerline to centerline. He poured coffee in each, generous allocations of two-thirds capacity, and then worked back and forth with little thimblefuls to finish things off with precision.

'You want cream or sugar or anything?'

Nevins shook his head. He picked up a mug. 'If you'd kept me in the loop, we could've found him, and he'd still be alive, and he could've told us exactly what happened.'

'Who, Little Marco? You think he'd be that helpful, do you?'

'Maybe. Maybe not. But what good is your solution? Kill them all. Terrific. Maybe in your mind that's some kind of useful resolution. Personally, I don't . . .' He looked away. 'I don't see how there's any sort of moral or intelligent dimension to it.' He shook his head. 'I don't know . . . I'm not even sure you realize the story's not about you.'

'Oh, Jesus. Give me a break.'

'No, fuck you. It's nothing to do with you. You put yourself in the middle, but it's not about you at all: it's about the guy who died, and his family. Vialoux and his family. And Lydia across the road, and the people who knew her. Her family. They all had a right to know what happened. And now whatever they find out will always be a few details short, because you went ahead and did what suited you.' Pointing at him now, slightly flushed.

Marshall said, 'But the story is about me, isn't it? I was right there at the beginning. I could've been shot through a restaurant window, too. But I wasn't, and now I'm the guy figuring out what happened.'

Nevins scoffed, tipped his head back. 'Holy shit . . .'

'Frankly, I knew Ray Vialoux pretty well for a long time. I think if he heard the guy who clipped him ended up dead somewhere in New Jersey, he'd be happy. Especially on the day of his funeral. I think he'd like that.'

Nevins didn't answer.

Marshall said, 'World's the way it is whether you know about it or not.'

'Uh-huh. And what's that got to do with anything?'

'Well. This Marco guy, you think he only hurt and killed two people in his whole life? You think Vialoux and the lady across the road – Lydia – you think they were it?'

'I'd hardly think so.'

'Yeah, me too. But you're not going to figure out who all the others were, are you? Do a full audit and make sure everyone he came in contact with gets to hear the full story of every fuckup? Guy's dead, and it sounds like he deserved it. And I don't see how that's changed by people knowing about it or not.'

Nevins just drank coffee.

Marshall said, 'Any case. It's not about the guy who pulled the trigger. It's about whoever paid him to do it.'

'Right. And you have that figured out, too?'

Marshall shook his head. 'Not yet. There's another – what did you call it? Another moral or intelligent dimension. I think this thing has another immoral, unintelligent dimension to it. But I'll give you a call when I find it.'

'Wonderful.' Nevins poured his coffee in the sink and set the mug down on the counter.

'Too strong?'

'Yeah. Probably bad for my blood pressure right now.'

He went back outside and joined the two uniformed cops on the sidewalk. The other three were just coming down the stairs: two more uniformed officers, and Loretta Flynn bringing up the rear.

Marshall went through to the living room. 'Find anything good?'

The uniforms ignored him and headed out, but Flynn stopped on the bottom stair. She looked at him as he sipped his coffee.

Flynn said, 'You'd have done yourself a favor if you'd left something. I get the feeling that until you're in prison, you'll do exactly what you want.'

He nodded. 'Oh, I see. You think because I'm investigating a crime in a way you don't approve of, I should be behind bars?'

'No, you should be behind bars for killing those people two nights ago. But that's New Jersey's problem. No doubt you'll be talking to them before long.'

'No doubt they'll ask me some questions. But I don't imagine I'll be talking to them. I'm not a total idiot.'

Flynn said, 'Well, if you want to prove it, stay away from D'Anton Lewis, like I told you to.'

'Here I was thinking it's in your interests to have him clipped.
He can't extort you when he's dead.'

She gave a little derisory breath through her nose, somewhere
between a scoff and a sigh. 'Not everyone on this planet is
corrupt. I'm sure it was thrilling to think you'd uncovered a
conspiracy.' She came down off the bottom stair and stood in
front of him with her arms folded. 'But I'm happy to confirm
I'm not being blackmailed. I'm not on the take. I don't have
some . . .' She shook her head, dreaming up offences. 'I'm not
boosting my pension with some drug-money kickback scheme.
Contrary to your assumptions . . .' She raised her voice, jutted
her lower jaw slightly as she spoke: 'I. Am doing. My job.'

Marshall nodded. 'Congratulations on your institutional loyalty.
But D'Anton Lewis had information pertaining to a murder
investigation, and you prevented access to him.'

She said quietly, 'And why would I do that, do you think?'

Marshall sipped his coffee.

'Come on. You're the ex-undercover guy. The man who's seen
everything. Why would I prevent access to him?'

He looked at her. He was prepared to accept she wasn't on
the take. And there'd been no denial when he said she wasn't
investigating D'Anton. Which meant . . .

Marshall said, 'Who's he testifying against?'

She held his gaze for a long moment. Then she turned and
walked away.

'Who's D'Anton testifying against?'

She paused at the front door. 'Pleasant as it is talking with
you, I'd rather keep my job and not get into the details. I'm sure
you understand.'

He shook his head. 'No, not really. I look at you, I think,
Here's another piece of the police machine who thinks doing her
job is equivalent to doing the right thing.' He shrugged. 'So what
if he's a protected witness? You held up a murder investigation
because it suited some unrelated strategy. So don't go around
thinking you operate with some kind of . . . I don't know. Just
because it's on NYPD letterhead, it doesn't make it virtuous.'

She nodded, smiled faintly, like she understood his point. 'You
can give me a call when they bring you in for the New Jersey
killings. I know some good lawyers.'

THIRTY-FIVE

He closed and locked the door and stood watching from the front window as the police got back in their respective cars and drove silently away. He sat at the desk. The loose reserves were down to less than a hundred pieces now. Nearing completion. He made himself home two more pieces on the working edge, and then he went upstairs to assess the damage.

It resembled the aftermath of a freak storm, or a haunting. Every door and drawer was hanging open. He went around rectifying things. They'd left the safe open, but his gun was still there. And his permit. No cash for them to confiscate. Not in here, anyway. He locked the safe and checked the bathroom. They'd removed the top of the toilet cistern, but replaced it imperfectly. A thin fillet of darker paint was exposed where the lid wasn't sitting level. He jiggled it home. The phone in the kitchen rang. He went downstairs and answered. It was his neighbor, Vera.

She said, 'A visitation.'

'Yes.'

'From members of the state. Representatives.'

'Yeah. They're gone now, though. How's your day going?'

'No complaints. That is, none that I would voice to a neighbor. To a tenant.'

'That's good.'

'So what is it, makes you man of interest?'

He didn't want to get into it with her on the phone. 'Mistaken identity.'

'They think you are not the man you are. Or they think another man is you.'

'That's right.'

'Which is why you are here, and not there. With them. A backseat ride.'

'Exactly. Vera, sorry, I have to go. I'll come over next week and tell you all about it.'

'Everything is all right?'

'Yes, everything is all right. Thank you very much for checking, though.'

He went to hang up, but had an idea.

'Sorry, you there?'

'Yes.'

He said, 'Do you have a computer?'

'Several.'

Marshall said, 'Who do you go to when you need one fixed?'

'Few are fixed. The theme is malfunction.'

Marshall said, 'So you don't have someone you take your computer to?'

'When desperate, in moments of desperation, yes. I visit Larry.'

'Where's Larry?'

'Newkirk. Newkirk Avenue. I have found him competent.'

'All right then.'

'When searched for on Google, Larry's business, he has four-point-nine stars. I agree with this rating of him.'

'Great.'

'Something needs fixed?'

'No. I just need to ask him a question.'

She nodded slowly. 'You play with cards close to stomach.'

'Chest. Yeah.'

'Chest. Yes. Everything is OK?'

'Thanks, Vera. I'll see you.'

He hung up, and stood for a few seconds with his hand on the phone on the wall, just thinking. Then he used his burner to call Jordan Mora's number. Still no answer. The call went to voicemail.

'Hey. Just me. Marshall. Give me a call when you get a chance.'

He went outside and stood at the curb, wanting to be sure the police had genuinely departed. But the cars on the street were all familiar. Nothing that looked like law enforcement, or pre-arrest recon. He could hear Vera – faint but trenchant Russian coming from her upstairs office. Barely a pause. He wondered if she was giving an online lecture. He watched the street for another couple of minutes, and then he turned and slipped down the narrow alleyway between his house and Vera's. He moved quietly into her rear yard and opened the little access hatch to the subfloor. When he'd moved in, she'd requested his help with a broken pipe beneath her kitchen. It was the gray water discharge line from her sink, and it had separated at the elbow joint. An easy fix, as it transpired. The original plumbing had been replaced with PVC, and all he'd had to do was slot the section back in and silicone the gap. He'd also taken the opportunity to nail an eighteen-inch square piece of plywood to the underside of two floor joists, thereby creating an eight-inch-deep cavity between the plywood and the flooring above. It was here that he stored his proceeds from this undercover work: the cash bundle triple-wrapped in black plastic, ribboned cross-ways with gleaming black duct-tape, like a gift from the anti-Santa.

He checked that his package was undisturbed, and then crawled back out. As he closed the subfloor hatch, he felt the burner phone buzzing in his pocket with a call. He checked the screen: Jordan Mora's number.

He answered quietly. 'Sorry, just give me a second.'

He slipped along the alleyway to the street and went back inside his own place, locked the door again behind him.

'You still there?'

'Yeah, I'm here. I saw I missed a couple of calls. I thought it was probably you.'

He said, 'Did you think at the time it was probably me and decide not to answer, or did you just think of it now?'

Quiet. He thought he might have misjudged that one.

She said, 'I couldn't decide whether to go to the funeral or not. In the end I thought maybe it was safer to stay away.'

'It was all right. As far as funerals go.'

She said, 'Look, I'm . . . I have the afternoon off. Or, I mean – I can take it. I thought we could maybe do something. If you're free?'

'I . . .' He wasn't sure how much to tell her on the phone: Boston, the trip out to New Jersey with Cifaretti's crowd. He worried the more he told her, the less inclined she'd be to want to see him. Maybe this was all the kind of stuff he'd need to say in person. And they'd either arrest him, or they wouldn't. Might as well play the odds, see her while he had the opportunity.

He said, 'That'd be great. Why don't you . . . do you want to come over, and we can grab some dinner?'

'OK. That sounds nice.'

He gave her his address and she said she'd be around later that afternoon, five-ish. He ended the call, and for an entire second felt relieved, buoyant with the anticipation of seeing her again, and then he was back to pondering just how long he had before there were more police at his door. It'd be FBI, most likely, for an interstate offence, with multiple corpses. The crime scenes were a bleach swamp, so he doubted they'd have evidence beyond the circumstantial. But they'd still bring him in and hold him for a while. He needed to be out and free long enough to chase down the last of this Vialoux matter, get to the bottom of his bad feeling . . .

He checked the front window again. Still nothing that looked official. He called Ginny Boyne.

'Sorry to keep pestering you.'

'No, no. You're not a bother. Don't apologize.'

'Do you remember, did Ray give you a receipt or anything? When he took Jennifer's possessions?'

'I don't think so . . . no, he didn't. There was no need. We trusted him with everything, obviously.'

Marshall said, 'Sure, of course. Do you happen to have a serial number for the computer, anything like that?'

'Probably. We have all of her things, packaged together.'

'Terrific.'

Quiet for a long moment. She said, 'I thought you were trying to confirm Ray's movements.'

'Yes, I am. This is all part of it.'

'I'm just . . .'

'Yes?'

She said, 'It seems like . . . aren't we going a little off-track?'

'Like I say, I'm really sorry to keep pestering you, but it is important. Every little detail is important with these things.'

'I just don't see how it's relevant.'

'Ma'am.' Slipping into his old cop voice. Like stepping through a door in his mind, and there was the uniform right there on its hanger.

He said, 'It could be really important. If you can tell me the serial number, it would be greatly appreciated.'

Silence. Then: 'You'll have to hold for a moment.'

'Thank you. I can wait.'

It was five minutes before she came back on. 'Do you have a pen?'

'Yes. Go ahead.'

She read out a long serial number for him. 'The docket in here, the warranty, it says it's a Microsoft Surface. If that's any help.'

'Thank you. That's very helpful. One last question.'

'Yes?'

'Can you confirm for me again the date your daughter died?'

Ginny Boyne said, 'I didn't realize it was going to be such a detailed excavation.'

He didn't know what to say to that.

She said, 'August ninth. She passed August ninth.'

Then she ended the call.

Marshall got up from the desk and went through to the kitchen, hunted through cupboards and found the old copy of the Yellow Pages that Vera had left him. He opened it at C and found computer repairs. Dozens of them. Twenty-five places between here and Sunset Park alone. He saw a number for Computers by Larry. Newkirk Avenue. That would be Vera's go-to man. Mr Four-point-nine stars on Google.

Marshall called the number.

No answer.

He tried the next number on the list. Lev's PC repairs.

'This is Lev.'

'Hello. I'm looking to buy a computer secondhand. The seller tells me you deleted the contents for her a couple of months ago.'

Shit, that wasn't the term. It was called something else . . . reformatting. That's right: you reformatted a hard disk.

The guy said, 'I'll need some more info than that, pal.'

'It's a Microsoft Surface.'

'And what was the customer's name?'

'Uh . . . I don't know. I'm buying it online, I just have a username.'

'I'm not sure I have time for a mystery.'

'I have the serial number if that helps? She says she brought it in sometime between August ninth and August twelfth . . .'

'Well, she's mistaken. I was out of town first half of August. Have a nice day.'

He kept at it.

He tried more numbers, and got a litany of 'no's. He tried Larry's again. Still no answer.

Three thirty, there was a knock at his door.

It wasn't the police, and it wasn't Jordan.

It was Ella Vialoux.

THIRTY-SIX

In her dark, baggy sweater and baggy jeans, arms hanging at her sides, she was almost penguinlike. She lifted her arms a little and let them fall again, looking up at him flatly with her jaw pushed slightly to one side. Marshall wasn't sure if the gesture meant *Bring it on*, or if it was intended more as self-deprecation.

She said quietly, 'I just came to say, I didn't mean to be an asshole.'

'It's fine.' He stood aside. 'You want to come in?'

She smiled faintly. Dim light coming out of the dark. 'I was only planning to say it once.'

'That's fine. We'll think of something else to talk about.'

She stepped inside. 'I don't have your number. I got your address off that note you left.'

'Right. Cool.'

'Hey, this is whatshisname. From the MoMA.' She was looking at his Pollock puzzle.

'Yeah. Jackson Pollock. I've had him there so long, I call him JP now.'

'Oh, man. You need to work on your jokes. Your face is all bruised, by the way. Down the side.'

'Yeah, I know. I slipped. You want a drink or something?'

She shrugged. 'Yeah. Glass of water would be good.'

He poured one for each of them, and they sat at the kitchen table, Ella hunched slightly and turning her glass slowly on its coaster like a three-a.m. drinker looking down through a Johnny Walker. She said, 'Yeah, so, anyway . . .'

As if summing up an explanation playing out in her head.

Marshall said, 'I wasn't trying to get in your face or be an asshole, either. I'm just trying to find out what happened to your dad. Why it happened.'

She didn't answer.

He said, 'I'm not insinuating anything. I'm not accusing anyone of anything.'

She nodded slowly. 'It sorta felt like . . . I was just worried you thought I had something to do with it. I mean like. Maybe you thought Jennifer killed herself because of something I did. But she didn't. Only she knows why, but it wasn't from what I did.'

'OK.'

'She was so nice. Honestly. Just kind of a bit like. I don't know. She always seemed a little bit afraid of life or a bit vulnerable or something. But super nice, super kind. A bit like her mom, really. Like you can imagine things buffeting her around. She often . . . she kind of went around with this look a lot of the time like she was just hanging on. I mean, maybe a bit stressed or something. But she was so smart. We had classes together sometimes. This is at high school, I mean, so up until last year, really. She was so quiet, people used to think . . . it was easy to think maybe she didn't know what was going on. That she was a bit slow or something. But she always understood things. She just took things in quietly.' She smiled. 'She was like this undercover expert in all kinds of stuff. You could ask her a question, and you'd get this whispered but certain answer.'

'When I talked to you this morning, you said she hadn't been bullied. She told you that?'

'Yeah, well . . . I just thought. I mean, I'd known her for like almost fifteen years or something. Since we were six or seven, probably. And I could tell something was up. You know. We had people we both knew from school, so I'd see her quite often at parties and whatever. She was just quieter, even quieter than normal. I said to her, this would've been a couple of months before, you know. A couple months before she died, I just said to her straight up, is everything OK? And I remember she said . . . she basically just brushed me off, really. Said don't worry, it wasn't anything to do with anyone we knew. She literally said, she wasn't being bullied or anything. So I was like, well, you know. What's going on. And she said it was just something for her to figure out. She said yeah, she had a problem, but no one could help her with it.'

'Did you talk to her about it again?'

'No. That was it. The next thing . . . that was the last time I spoke to her. After that, it was too late. She was gone. She was dead.'

She blinked carefully. 'Uh.' She cleared her throat. 'Sorry.' She drank some water.

'No, don't apologize. I'm pleased you're telling me all this.'

She said, 'Even though she'd been sad, it was still such a shock. You know. You don't expect it. Even when things are rough.'

'Yeah. I know what you mean.'

'That's why I called Ginny. I thought, you know. If I'm wondering why it's happened, they're going to be wondering like ten times or a hundred times more, so at least I could tell them why she *hadn't* done it. You know? At least I could rule something out for them.'

'Sure.'

'Dad was like . . . he was drinking way too much. He just seemed . . . it was weird. It was like he was just dead set on something going wrong. I thought, I had this idea . . . if he helped the Boynes, maybe it would help get him back in the right direction. Make him more like himself. For a few days, you know, for a little while, I think maybe it worked. He had sort of a project, and he was doing something with a real purpose. But then, you know. There was nothing on her computer that explained anything. It was all just normal stuff. Homework projects on Paul Revere and Martin Luther King and shit. He said he had this special P.I. software he could run that searched for certain words like dead and die and whatever. But nothing came up. Nothing that was like a goodbye letter, I mean.'

Marshall didn't answer.

Ella said, 'I remember when I called Ginny, this was a couple weeks after Jennifer died, and I said maybe my dad could look

into it. You know, like how he used to be a cop, and now he's
an investigator. And that was when she said, you know, she and
Martin, they're not that good with digital stuff, so maybe dad
could try and get into her computer and see if there was like a
note or a clue. They were just . . . she was so grateful, it made
me sad. I mean. Like they'd been through so much, but she still
didn't think the world owed her anything. She was like that . . .
it was exactly the same last week. I spoke to her again, she said
she'd found like a hard drive of Ginny's, and maybe Dad could
look at that, too. Dad was down in like, Brighton Beach or
something, maybe Coney Island. I went around and picked it up
from her and . . . oh, man. Every time I see her I want to cry.'

Marshall let her have a moment, and then said carefully, 'What
hard disk?'

'It was in Dad's office. It would've got burned up in the fire.'

'Tell me exactly what happened.'

She studied him, concern coming into her face. 'Why, what's
the problem?'

'When was this?'

'Why is this important?'

'Please just tell me.'

'It was . . . I don't know. Tuesday. She called and said she'd
found a hard drive of Jennifer's. And could my dad take a look
at it, like he'd done with the computer. Like I said, he was in
like, Brighton Beach or something, so I went and picked it up
from the Boynes and took it home for Dad.'

Brighton Beach. Probably down at Frank Cifaretti's bagel
place, trying to renegotiate his debt. Except . . .

'How did you know your dad was down there?'

She was back in her three-a.m. drinker's pose, staring at her
glass. 'Yeah, well. That was the other thing I needed to tell you.'

He waited.

She said, 'I had a tracking thing in his car. I spent so much
time worrying about him, and I knew Mom was stressed out, too,
always thinking about him, so in the end I thought . . . I dunno.
I thought it would be a good idea to know where he was. And then
obviously Mom found it in his car, and gave it to you. And
I thought . . . at first I thought you were just some kind of . . . I
dunno. I didn't know why you were there. So I thought it was

pretty funny, you know, that thing keeping you busy for a while. But then . . . well. Mom said she'd told the police about it, and I thought about it, and . . . I'm glad you're not in any trouble.'

'They searched my house with six cops, but didn't find anything. It was actually kind of funny.'

He thought she was laughing, but she wasn't. She sat sobbing into her hands, shaking, hunched into herself. He sat there patting her shoulder telling her it was all right. She took a breath and let it go with a sigh, and it sounded like all her hope, all her happiness was riding out on that one breath.

He said, 'It's all right. It'll be all right.'

'I'm going to miss him so much.'

'I know. But that's how the good people keep on living. People missing them. Keeping them alive in their thoughts.'

She didn't answer that, and he knew in her case, missing her dad would be complicated. Loving Ray Vialoux was a careful exercise in *à la carte*.

She rubbed her face. 'Ugh. Man. Sorry to . . . I didn't mean to come here and be all dramatic.'

Marshall poured her some more water. 'This isn't dramatic. Trust me.'

She took the glass from him and downed the lot. Wiped her mouth, a clumsy motion with an oversize sleeve, like a little kid. 'What the hell happened. Honestly.'

Marshall said, 'I think I know.'

'You think you know.'

'Maybe today, maybe tomorrow, I'll know for sure. And I'll be able to tell you all about it.'

She sat looking at him. She said, 'What's with this other hard drive?'

'I'm not sure yet.'

'Yes you are. You just don't want to say it.'

He remembered the woman at the laundromat who'd seen Ray going in his office door with the package.

He said, 'I'm not going to keep any secrets. I just want to make sure I've got it right before I tell you.'

She didn't answer.

He said, 'You want to hang out here for a while, or you can take off if you want . . .'

'Yeah. I'll take off. I didn't mean to get you in trouble.'

'Don't worry. You didn't. I'm glad you came over. You've made things much clearer.'

No one came for him.

Ella left, and then Jordan showed up at five o'clock. Marshall was at his desk where he could see the front window, Yellow Pages open on the Pollock puzzle. Jordan knocked, and he got up and opened the door for her. She came in smiling, looking nice, looking relaxed and pleased to see him.

'Cool place.' She set her handbag down by the door, nodded at the desk. 'I pictured you with different hobbies, though.'

'Oh yeah? Like what?'

'I don't know. Reading true-crime or something.'

'I'm reading the Yellow Pages. Almost as good.'

'I just didn't think of you as a jigsaw-puzzle man.'

'It's on hold until I finish the phone book. Gets real good about seven hundred pages in.'

She laughed. He was glad it was this easy. He didn't want them chipping away at an iceberg all evening. But it was a strange experience to be standing here, moving easily through the small talk and all the while knowing that a SWAT team might kick down his door. It was like an out-of-body experience, in a way: the part of his brain in charge of self-preservation looking on as the rest of him went about a normal date night.

She said, 'So how have you been? You made it through the funeral . . . Hey, what've you done to your face?'

He was going to give her his standard, dumb line: that he slipped. But her expression was one of deep and authentic concern, and he didn't have it in him to bullshit. He sat down on the sofa.

'Actually, it's been a funny couple of days . . .'

He told her what had happened on Sunday night, getting picked up by Chris and Benny on his way back home, and then driven out to Jersey. That got her sitting down at the desk, and he saw the horror coming into the face as the color left it.

He said, 'Sorry. I didn't know whether to tell you or not.'

She didn't answer for a moment, like the shock had caused a lag in her brain. Then she seemed to catch up with a frown, and

a swallow, and a shake of the head. 'What? No. Oh my God.'
She leaned forward, studying him with concern. 'What happened?'

He told her about Frank Cifaretti and the smiley man, Marco
Perrin, in the dark in the woods. She didn't interject. She sat
there pale and attentive, and when he was finished, she just
sat there shaking her head, staring at him.

'You told the police?'

'I told them where to find them.'

He smiled. She didn't. She said, 'I'm so glad you're OK. Oh
my God.' She tented her hands over her mouth and nose. 'I'm
so glad you're all right.'

'Like I say, I didn't know whether to tell you about it or not.'

'No, I mean . . .' She was still shaking her head. She closed
her eyes and went still. He figured the story alone would be a
lot to take in, but then there were all the corollary issues that
went with it. Like whether he was the sort of guy who was
ultimately safe to be around. Hopefully it would be a few more
days, maybe a few more weeks, before she seriously engaged
with that question.

She said, 'I'm just glad you're OK.'

'I think I am.'

'And I'm glad you told me.'

'That's good.'

Quiet between them for a minute. Faint rain pattering on the
roof. She said, 'But were we right?'

'About what?'

'Was it D'Anton's wife who hired him? Little Marco?'

Marshall nodded, told her about finding Renee Lewis and
Mikey Langello, the ex-mob guy, up in Boston.

'They say they hired Little Marco to stop Ray from tracking
them down. They didn't want D'Anton finding them.'

'Fair enough in principle.'

'Yes. Except Little Marco got carried away.'

She came over and sat down next to him, put an arm around
his neck. 'Carried away. I guess that's one way to put it.'

'Yeah.'

They listened to the rain for a while. She thrummed the fingers
of the draped arm on his chest. She said, 'So that's it, then.'

'Maybe. Maybe not. That's why I'm reading the Yellow Pages.'

She looked at him, turning to see him in profile, and he felt her breath on his cheek. She said, 'What are you thinking?'

Marshall said, 'I'm almost too scared to say.'

'No you're not.'

He didn't answer.

She said, 'Why?'

He spent a moment on that. Then he said, 'I just want to be sure about it.' He shut his eyes. 'I really like this cuddle, though. It's nice.'

'Yeah. It's pretty good, isn't it?'

He leaned over and found her mouth and kissed her. She tasted pretty good, too.

But she broke away. 'You need a shower first. You have sawdust in your hair. And . . . cobwebs, I think.'

'I had to crawl under a house.'

'Right. Well, it looks like it.'

He ran a hand through his hair. He said, 'So as far as you're concerned . . . would you say a shower is essential? Or just recommended at this stage?'

She studied him again. 'I would say it's absolutely imperative.' Talking in his ear now. 'If you want things to go any further.'

He went upstairs.

Tempting just to do a thirty-second rinse, but if he started granting himself concessions, there'd be no end to it. He'd descend into a life devoid of form and order. He unlocked the safe and took the Colt with him through to the bathroom, folded it in its protective towel on the edge of the sink while he showered. After a minute, Jordan came upstairs, stood there in the hallway looking in at him through the open door.

'Interesting set-up. Most people go with the door-closed option.'

'It's a security precaution. I like to be able to see people coming.'

'Right.'

He said, 'On that note, I think there's probably room for two in here.'

She appraised the layout. 'Oh, do you think so?'

She started taking off her clothes, making it a show, both of them amused. She came toward him, down to her underwear now, working hard to keep a straight face, and then she paused and looked behind her, back down the stairs.

'I can hear your phone.'

'Damn. How's that for timing.'

'It's not illegal to ignore it.'

'Yeah. Exigent circumstances.'

He grabbed a towel and wrapped it around his waist as he went back downstairs. The phone was still there on his desk, quivering on its back with the incoming call, screen alight in pulse-rhythm to its silenced ringtone.

He sat down at the desk and answered.

'Hello?'

'Hey. This is Larry, from Computers by Larry. I have some missed calls from you?'

Marshall said, 'Yes. Thanks very much for getting back to me.'

'Sure.'

'I have a question about a laptop I'm looking to purchase. I understand you may have serviced it.'

'Oh, sure. Do you happen to have the device serial number at hand?' Sounding like the kind of guy who ran a business with a four-point-nine-star Google rating.

Marshall said, 'Yes, I do. Sorry, give me second.'

Shit, he was dripping water all over his Pollock puzzle. He found the piece of paper, read out the long code to the guy, twenty or thirty characters.

'It would've been around maybe ninth or tenth of August. Something like that.'

'All right. Give me a sec.'

Keys tapping.

'Uh, yeah. This looks to be it. Microsoft Surface. I ran a re-format and a Windows re-install.'

'OK, great.' He had to swallow. 'Can you tell me who brought it in for you?'

Pause.

'I, umm. What is this about exactly, sorry?'

Marshall waited.

The guy said, 'It's just . . . I really value confidentiality, and you know. Things like this, it can affect customer trust and confidence, and, well. That kind of thing, it translates to our general reputation and Google rating and all sorts. We have like four-point-eight stars.'

Marshall said, 'Four-point-nine, I heard.'

'Oh really? Well, yeah, there you go.'

He sat there for a moment.

'Sir?'

So close.

Close enough he thought he could bend the bars of honesty a little, slip through to the other side of the mystery.

Marshall said, 'I'm an investigator. I've been hired to look into the murder of a man called Ray Vialoux. You may have seen it in the news.'

Pause. Then: 'I, uh . . . oh my God. Sure. I think maybe I have. The thing at the restaurant.'

'That's right. Anything you can tell me could be crucial.'

Silence.

Marshall said, 'Larry,' putting a little extra into it as he said the guy's name. Making him part of the story, integral to progress. 'Can you tell me who brought it in? The computer?'

The guy said, 'I guess . . . I guess if it's something that serious . . .'

He trailed off, and then he laughed: quiet, brief, slightly nervous, and yet somehow rich with implication. The sound people give when recalling something strange, or uncanny, or unsettling, and maybe they shouldn't go into it.

The guy said, 'Yeah. I remember.'

THIRTY-SEVEN

Marshall called Nevins.

'Yes?'

'I said I'd call you when I solved it.'

'Uh-huh.'

'This is the call.'

He told Nevins what he'd discovered.

Nevins said, 'Don't do anything.'

'Well, that's why I'm calling. I am going to do something.'

'Please don't.'

Marshall said, 'It's an ostensibly free society. I can go and talk to people if I like. I'm asking if you'd like to come with me.'

'It needs more work.'

'There's nothing to be worked. The computer guy made the I.D. The evidence is all burned up in Vialoux's office. All there is to do is ask the question.'

Nevins swore. 'I'm at the supermarket. Meet me . . . do you have a pen?'

'Yes.'

Nevins gave him an address. Fourth Street, down in Kensington. Not far. He said, 'I'll be home in thirty minutes.'

They caught an Uber.

Nevins had a tidy but narrow three-story clapboard house that wouldn't have looked out of place in a seaside town on the way up to Boston. Bluish-gray siding and white trim on the window-sills. A cockatoo weathervane way up at the third-story apex.

Marshall knocked, and a young guy of about thirty answered the door. Very fit and good-looking, very on-trend. Dark oversize spectacles, wavy hair combed just so, expensive tailored shirt belted into smoothly ironed chinos, rolled up to show a hint of ankle above polished loafers.

'Hey. Is Floyd in?'

Inside it smelled like Mexican cooking, maybe chili con carne. The guy leaned away from the door and called, 'Floyd? He's here.'

Nevins came down the stairs in his suit, gun and badge on his belt. The young guy stood aside to make room.

'Please be careful.'

Nevins said, 'Always am.'

'Please be extra, extra careful.'

Nevins said, 'Please save me some chili.'

'How long will you be?'

Nevins looked at Marshall. 'God knows.'

*   *   *

They rode in Nevins' car: Nevins driving, Jordan up front beside him, Marshall in back.

Nevins looked at him in the mirror. 'Don't try and sell it to me.'

'I'm not. All I said was you can come along if you like. And here you are. So I obviously sold you on that.'

The Boynes' street had no curb space. Nevins double-parked. They went up the Boynes' front steps, and Marshall knocked, and the three of them stood quietly in the cold. Just on seven p.m. Sky pitch-black with the cloud cover, and the street shiny with rain and car-gleam under the streetlights.

The door opened.

Ginny Boyne looked out at them through the gap, eye jumping to take in the trio one at a time.

Marshall said, 'Sorry. Me again. We were hoping to speak to Martin.'

She let them in, but she didn't offer them a seat. They stood in the narrow entry hall, and with brow furrowed and gaze downcast, Ginny Boyne called to her husband. Footsteps in the upper hallway, and then Martin appeared. Halfway down the stairs, he hesitated, taking in the four of them. Then he descended the last few treads. Quiet in the house. A TV playing faintly. Martin Boyne stood performing slow but complicated re-arrangements of his clasped and white-knuckled hands.

Marshall said, 'Evening, Martin.'

'Hello.'

Marshall said, 'Why did you delete the contents of your daughter's computer?'

The hands went still. The head swiveled to look at him. 'Excuse me?'

'The day after your daughter died, you took her laptop computer to a service center on Newkirk Avenue, and had the hard disk wiped, and the operating system reinstalled. Why would you do that?'

Silence.

'What did you think was on her computer? What was so important that it had to be deleted immediately?'

A long pause. Martin Boyne licked his lips.

Ginny said, 'Mart, what's he talking about?'

Martin Boyne's eyes were still on Marshall, a faint and not-unkind smile on his face, like this was all a regrettable misunderstanding, albeit with a funny side.

He said, 'I don't know what you're talking about. I don't know what he's talking about, sweetheart.' A whisper.

Marshall said, 'I think you do. On August tenth, the day after Jennifer died, you took her computer to have the contents of the hard disk erased and the operating system reinstalled. Why was it so urgent that you did that? What did you think might be on the computer? What did you think she may have recorded about what was happening to her?'

'Mart, what is this nonsense?'

'And what was on the second hard drive?' He looked now at Ginny. 'You found a hard drive last week, and you gave it to Ella Vialoux. That's right, isn't it?'

The information seemed to startle her. She leaned away from him. 'I . . . what does this—'

'Yes or no? You found a hard drive, and you gave it to Ella to pass on to Ray to examine.'

'What does this—'

'Please answer the question.'

'Yes! For goodness' sake. What does this—'

'Thank you.' He looked now at Martin. 'So I ask you again. What was on that drive that you didn't want found?'

'Mart, for goodness' sake. What is going on?'

Marshall said, 'It was your hard drive, wasn't it? The computer was hers, but the hard drive was yours. And what was on it, Martin? What was on it that you didn't want found? That nobody could ever see?'

Martin was looking agitated now, a twitch at the corner of his mouth. He said, 'I . . . this is nonsense. This is rubbish. Absolute rubbish.'

He turned and began to ascend the stairs.

Marshall drew a breath, and shouted, 'Martin!'

Giving it everything, a house-shaking blast, the vocal equivalent of a phonebook smashed against a table, and he saw the four others jump visibly.

Martin stopped. He turned and looked at him. Two steps from

the bottom, and eye-level now with Marshall. More confident with the added height.

He said it again: 'This is rubbish.'

'Are you going to have the courage to tell the truth?'

No answer. Just faint TV noise.

Marshall said, 'Ray Vialoux had your secret hard drive, and you had to get it back. Is that right? It was essential that you got it back, or destroyed it. So you called the man you saw following him. Didn't you? The night Ray came to the house, you saw the smiley man following him. He looked devilish. You remember telling me that? He looked like the devil. But then you had a crisis, and you thought maybe you should call him. Frank's Flowers. It was right there on the van, wasn't it? Call the devil and ask if he could help.'

'Martin, what is this nonsense?' Ginny Boyne looking desperately between Marshall and her husband.

Marshall said it again: 'Are you going to have the courage to tell the truth?'

Martin licked his lips, dipped his head. 'Well, yes I am. This is . . . this is crazy talk.'

Marshall said, 'Did you get what you wanted? Is that what you asked him to do? Kill Vialoux, and torch his office? Or did things get out of hand?'

He saw a flicker in his eye, saw for a second the man's desire to tell him the same thing Renee Lewis had: that no one was supposed to die. That the smiley man started, and just didn't stop. Because evil doesn't have a leash on it. But maybe that was a lesson Martin Boyne knew well enough for himself.

He said, 'Leave now. All three of you. This is obscene. You come in here . . . this is obscene.'

He turned and continued up the stairs, and his decisiveness seemed to give his wife some strength, too.

'Yes, please leave. This is . . .' Her mouth quavered. 'This is disgusting. Truly disgusting.'

She spread her arms, ushering them toward the door, and from upstairs Martin shouted, 'I'm calling the police.'

Calling the police.

The phrase touched something in Marshall's memory, some

dim connection, and then he saw Ginny Boyne's look of confusion, and that was enough: Marshall pushed past her, shoved Nevins aside, sprinted up the stairs three at a time.

Light and shadow through an open doorway – an office – and he entered the room to see Martin Boyne standing in profile: eyes shut, hands clasped below his chin, lips moving in whispered recital. Prayer, or preparation. Farewell to this world, and a petition to the next, maybe: In his hands was a revolver, the hammer pulled back.

Marshall crossed the room in two frantic strides and saw Boyne's eyes open in bloodshot panic as Marshall slapped the gun away from the underside of his jaw. The shot went through a wall with a bang and a plume of gypsum dust, and Marshall grabbed the gun two-handed and shouted for Nevins.

But that was it.

Boyne didn't have the strength. He released the weapon and fell limply to his knees, panting quietly, hunched as if rubber-limbed. Marshall could hear Ginny screaming, and he called, 'Clear. We're clear.'

Nevins was in the room now. He looked at Marshall, and in that glance was the certainty that he had the whole story. Gut-instinct proof: more persuasive and conclusive than anything logged as formal evidence. Certainly Ginny Boyne interpreted the same message. She stood in the doorway and screamed, hands covering her ears, as if protecting herself from the pitch of her own anguish.

'What did you do? What did you do to her? Martin? What did you do . . .'

Then Jordan was there too, an arm around Ginny's shoulders and whispering in her ear, pulling her gently away from the room and back along the hallway.

Marshall dumped the shells from the gun as Nevins handcuffed Martin Boyne. He didn't resist. He remained kneeling, shoulders heaving as he breathed. Marshall crouched in front of him as Nevins called 911.

'Are you going to tell me what happened? Are you finally going to have some courage?'

Nothing. He sat quietly breathing. He licked his lips. The same expression of placid curiosity that he'd seen on Little Marco as he died in the woods. The truth was right there behind his eyes, deep in the mis-wired circuitry of his wretched head, and Marshall had the strange and awful impulse to break open the man's skull, as if it might yield the facts of the matter. He looked up and saw Nevins looking back, almost like he'd read his mind, or maybe shared that same thought. A crazy notion reserved for the sane. Marshall got up and went back downstairs. Ginny Boyne and Jordan were in the living room, Ginny in an armchair in the corner, and Jordan crouching beside her. The model landscape still center-stage. Ginny shaking with grief, face in her hands. He wondered if this was all a total revelation to her, or if her life had been a long campaign of denial, erroneous self-counsel: No, it can't be happening.

He crouched in front of her. 'Ginny . . .'

She looked up, tear-streaked.

'Can you tell me what's been going on?'

'I . . .' She let her breath out through gnashed teeth, tears still falling. 'I can't . . .'

'You can tell us. Did he hurt Jennifer? You can tell us.'

She put her face in her hands again. She sat like that for a long time.

'Ginny?'

She looked up. Features warped and crumpled, as if summoning the memory of something awful. She said, 'Sometimes at night . . .'

'Sorry?'

She looked up again. 'Sometimes at night . . .'

But she couldn't finish the thought. She closed her eyes and just sat there shaking her head, face wet with tears, Jordan rubbing her back.

A minute later, Marshall heard sirens, saw the red and blue light in the windows.

An on-call night-shift detective took their statements. Marshall gave her the background, and the blow-by-blow of what had happened tonight. She told him she wasn't in a position to run down details, but the day watch would be taking over in the morning. Boyne would be held for a psych evaluation following the attempted suicide, and then questioned about the death of his daughter. As of right now, he wasn't facing charges. He was being detained for his own safety.

Marshall gave his statement and then stood outside to wait for Jordan. It was a good turnout: ambulance, two NYPD patrol cars, and a detective's ride. He watched the two paramedics and a uniformed cop bring Martin Boyne out the front door and down the steps on a stretcher. Boyne as blank and waxy as something out of Madame Tussaud's. He watched the paramedics load him in the ambulance, and then drive away. The cop drove off, too. No one else out on the street. This was just New York normal. Every metric of weirdness for what had happened had been exceeded before.

Nevins came outside and stood looking at him.

Marshall said, 'What?'

'How did you know he'd try to shoot himself?'

'I would have, if I was him.'

Nevins was still looking at him.

Marshall said, 'Ginny looked so surprised when he said he was calling the police, I remembered – she mentioned once that they only have a downstairs phone. He could've had a cell, I guess. Shame I didn't think of that.'

'Why? You prefer another corpse?'

'In this case, yeah. Chances are, he won't admit anything. And there's probably no evidence left. The best solution now is for him to not be on the planet.'

'The best solution would've been to work the evidence for another couple of days, and then knock on his door.'

'Yeah, well. Evidence disappears, doesn't it?'

Nevins didn't answer.

Marshall said, 'Sometimes guilt does, too. And if you get people . . .' He thought about it. 'If you catch them with their conscience at its blackest, sometimes they tell you something.'

'You just told me he's not going to say anything.'

'Not with his mouth. I figure though if you run upstairs and try to shoot yourself in the head, you're probably guilty of something.'

'Yeah, exactly: something. All we're probably going to know was that it was bad. Whatever he was doing to her. Bad enough, she ended up hanging herself.'

Marshall shook his head. 'You were as convinced as I was. You saw what happened.'

'Yeah. Like I say: convinced that he did *something*.'

'The lack of information isn't my problem. It's a problem with the universe.'

'Depends if you think Marco Perrin being murdered is a problem with the universe, or a problem with whoever killed him.'

'I don't see any problem at all with him being dead.'

'Yeah, I had a feeling that might be your opinion.' He looked back at the house, shook his head. 'I want to know what it takes to get the better of a guy like that, you know?'

'Who? Smiley Marco?'

'Yeah. Someone that evil, what does it actually take?' Looking at Marshall now. 'Someone better, or someone even worse? You know what I'm getting at?'

Marshall said, 'I'm surprised you've been around this long, haven't learned what counts as a good result.'

'No, I think I have a good understanding of the concept.'

Marshall shook his head. 'We're meant to buy into this myth that the law is one size fits all. It's bullshit. You know, anything else in life – anything complex – you hear all about how you need different solutions to suit different problems. Well, I agree. And the fact that there's such a thing as a career criminal, it's obviously proof that the justice system doesn't cover all scenarios. And every now and then . . .'

He thought about it, Nevins watching him carefully. Nevins said, 'Yes?'

'Every now and then, the solution is a guy like me.'

Nevins said lightly, 'I think we're beholden to quite different principles.'

Marshall nodded. 'Yeah. You're beholden to a system that takes forever, and a lot of the time doesn't help anyone. I'm . . . I wouldn't say beholden. I like the idea of people getting their comeuppance sooner rather than later.'

'Careful what you wish for, huh?'

Marshall shook his head. 'No, I already got mine. I was under-cover for two years. I told you that. Trapped with the mob for two years, because the people on the official channels wouldn't listen when I said I needed to be pulled out.' He shrugged. 'Basically, I paid the price for not taking things into my own hands sooner. And I don't want to be one of those people who had to learn a lesson twice.' He looked around for a moment, putting the rest of it together. 'Doing things my way has got you every piece of substantive information in this case. And I'm sorry I didn't bring it to you on a platter. I can imagine that must be frustrating.'

Nevins smiled emptily. 'No, what's frustrating is knowing you'll get away with killing four people in New Jersey the other night.'

'Oh, well. Tell the FBI you saw me sprinting out of Cifaretti's bagel shop. It might change my good fortune.'

'So you did do it?'

Marshall shook his head. 'No. I'm just observing that that piece of circumstantial evidence is not in my favor.'

Nevins said, 'Rest assured, I told the FBI something similar. And I told them all about your means and motive.'

'And they didn't believe you? It's hard sometimes, isn't it?'

Nevins said, 'I don't know that they didn't believe me. They said the scene examination implied a narrative consistent with internal dispute. In other words, it looks like they thought Little Marco was a liability, so they took him out there to get rid of him, and everyone started shooting at each other.'

'Sounds plausible.'

'No, I think the evidence is less consistent than they imply. But what they told me is they've been under pressure, as is always the case, and they're pleased to have a straightforward resolution. Because pressure means money, doesn't it? And now they can cross Cifaretti off the list and attribute the death to some other dead guy, and they don't have to spend six or seven figures taking you through the courts. So you can bitch all you like about the people on the official channels. But you're off the hook because someone at Department of Justice decided the budget spreadsheet would look better if they left you alone.'

Nevins looked at him a long moment. Marshall could see he had something else to say, but in the end he kept it to himself. He turned and walked away towards his car.

Marshall said, 'It's your last day.'

Nevins stopped and turned back. 'What?'

'You told me Tuesday's your last day.'

Nevins nodded. 'Last day shift. I'm still on call until the end of the week. This might've been my last case. Thanks for the messy ending.'

He got into his car and drove away.

THIRTY-EIGHT

They caught an Uber back over to Marshall's place in Flatbush. The cat was waiting for them.

Jordan said, 'Who's this?'

'Boris. Belongs to the neighbor.'

He followed them inside.

Marshall said, 'You want a drink?'

'Yeah. I think I better.'

She followed him to the kitchen.

'You might be out of luck in the wine department. I have beer, though.'

'Beer's fine. Don't bother with a glass.'

He popped the caps off two bottles and handed one to her.

Jordan said, 'I'm not sure if you're meant to say cheers or not. After something like that.'

'Yeah, I know. You feel like dinner at all? I can make something.'

She said, 'I don't know. I've got this . . .'

He waited.

'I've got this weird feeling that nothing's the right thing to do. Like I'm meant to just stand here all night and reflect on it.'

'Yeah. But then what do you do tomorrow? Are you meant to carry on being somber?'

She drank some beer, looked at him past the tilted bottle. 'You mean, if eventually you're going to get back to being normal, why not just do it now?'

'Yeah.'

'Well. There's no logic, is there? It's a feeling. It might last, or it might not.'

He didn't answer.

She said, 'How do you feel about it?'

'I don't know . . .' He gave it some thought. 'I guess the best measure of it is . . . it's like: how absorbed are you by the thing that happened, and how often do you just think about normal stuff?'

'Yeah. And where do you fit into that?'

'I'm still thinking about the awful stuff.'

She said, 'Me too.'

Boris came in, and served as a good focal point. They both looked down at him, shiny cat eyes looking back a little disappointed at the lack of cat food, and it seemed to break them out of the topic. Jordan put her beer down on the counter. 'I'll freshen up. Then maybe some Uber Eats.'

'What's that?'

'Uber Eats? It's like regular Uber, except only your food rides in the car.'

'I see.'

She went upstairs, and Marshall used his burner to call Hannah Vialoux. It rang through to voicemail, and Marshall left a message asking her to call him back. He went to press END, and then hesitated. He said, 'We know what happened, now.'

He clicked off, and just stood there for a moment, thinking about everything. He finished the beer and took another one from the fridge.

He said, 'I should've known it was him from the interview.'

Quiet.

Then: 'What?' Calling from the upstairs landing.

He said, 'The first time we talked to him, he was off. Boyne, I mean. He couldn't remember anything. He couldn't remember anything about the car, he couldn't remember anything about the smiley guy's passenger. But then we showed him the photo, he suddenly decides it was Renee Lewis. I should've known he was full of shit. He was just making it up as he went.'

A long pause. Then she said, 'You got him eventually.'

'Yeah. Sort of.'

Jordan said, 'I think you should do some of your puzzle.'

'Yeah. I think I should, too.'

He took his beer through to the front room and sat at the desk, closed the Yellow Pages and relegated it to the floor. Puzzle space only now. He should've been here when he stepped through the door. He turned on the lamp. The working edge was shrinking. Maybe eighty pieces remaining in the reserves. Call it eighty square inches of image, yet to be infilled. Almost there. He had the desk space now to separate the reserves, see them each as disparate and essential components. Unity inevitable. All it involved was Marshall's vision, Marshall's talent. This close to the finish, he could almost make the lineups by inspection, no need for trial placements. He sat there for a moment, silent, hands to knees, sight-matching the colors, and when he finally moved, he made a clean, first-try placement on the right-side vertical working edge and then followed up with a quick second. The third piece gave him more trouble, nothing there for him initially despite a strong hunch, but he made a confident float-placement: setting the piece down inside the active zone but with no contact just yet. It would come. The parameters now were too constrained for there to be any real question. It was all just a matter of time.

The front door crashed open with a bang that shook the house. Marshall leaned away, arm raised out of reflex, looked back in time to see the door with its mangled locks bounce back off the adjacent wall.

And then D'Anton Lewis stepped inside.

Pistol in one hand and a sledgehammer in the other.

He leveled the gun at Marshall. 'Don't move.' He smiled. 'You're great just sitting there. Put your hands up. Come on, hands up.'

Marshall raised them. D'Anton ducked forward slightly to see up the stairs. 'Company, I take it?' Smiling still. 'Sorry to interrupt your evening.'

He heard Jordan say, 'Oh, shit . . .'

D'Anton said, 'No, no: don't worry. I only need a moment of your time. Stand there, though. Where I can see you.'

He leaned the sledgehammer against the doorframe, careful, like returning an umbrella after an evening stroll. Then he opened his coat and brought out the bone-handled knife, jiggled it casually as if taking its weight for the very first time. Gleam of the blade in the light of the desk lamp.

He said, 'Shame I had to ask the question twice.' He lined the gun up on Marshall's face. 'So are you listening now? Are you listening *real* good?'

'What do you want?'

'Where is she? Where is my wife?'

'Boston.'

'Where in Boston?'

'Cambridge. I don't remember which street.'

'I think you can.'

'No, no, listen. Listen to me. Everything you need is here. It's on my phone in the bathroom. It's just upstairs. Everything you need is in the bathroom.'

D'Anton ducked and glanced upstairs again.

Marshall said, 'There's no password or anything. You just slide the cover back and it's ready to use.'

D'Anton said, 'Get it.'

Marshall slid his chair back.

'No, not you. Sit down. Sit the fuck down. She can get it.' He stepped back, widening his angle, ducking down a little more. 'That the bathroom there? Behind her?'

Marshall said, 'Yes.'

'All right, get it. Ten seconds, come on.' Louder now: 'Ten! Nine! Eight! Seven! Six! Five! Four! Three! . . . Yeah, that's it. Come on down. Bring it here.'

He heard Jordan descending the stairs, glanced behind him to see her proffering her giant smartphone.

D'Anton returned the knife to his coat. 'All right, throw it to me.' Clicking his fingers. 'Careful.'

Jordan lobbed him the phone, and D'Anton caught it one-handed. Juggled it briefly to get it up the right way, found the button that lit up the screen.

'You said there's no password.'

Marshall had been expecting the bang, but when it came, the sound was still a shock: impossibly sudden and loud. D'Anton was standing right beside him, in profile to Jordan. He took the bullet through the ear and fell sideways against the edge of the table, the free-fall weight of him shunting it sideways, breaking a leg, sending everything to the floor. Marshall was left sitting there like some fluke-fortunate earthquake survivor:

untouched, but with debris all around him. A medley of blood and brain and jigsaw. A Pollock in its own right.

He ran a hand through his hair. 'Oh, man . . .'

'Are you OK?'

He glanced back at her. Wide-eyed, pale, clench-jawed. She still had the Colt raised, smoke coming off the muzzle. He hadn't returned it to the safe when they visited the Boynes. Still in the bathroom, wrapped in its towel. Violations of protocol, paying dividends. He said, 'Yeah. I'm all right.'

He looked at his puzzle again. No salvaging it. The breakup was total. He said, 'Shit. I can't believe it.'

The phone in the kitchen rang.

Marshall said, 'You mind getting that? It'll be Vera, next door. Just let her know everything's OK.'

He stood up from the chair and stepped out through the open door into the dark and the nighttime cold. At the far curb a few doors up was a black SUV. Marshall headed over. The driver's window descended before he got there. One of D'Anton's body-guards was at the wheel: the guy with the sore shoulder. The guy he'd tousled with during that first meeting.

'What happened?'

'He's dead. Come and wait inside, if you want.'

'He's *dead*?'

'Yeah, we shot him.'

'Oh, fuck . . .'

Marshall turned and headed back to the house, heard frantic motion behind him: seatbelt click and whine, a door opening and slamming, and then the guy sprinted past him and up the front steps, through the open door.

'D'Anton, D'Anton!'

The guy went to his knees, felt for a pulse. Jaw and then wrist.

'D'Anton, holy shit. What have you done . . .?'

Unclear if the question was for the dead or for the living. The guy started chest compressions, panting through his teeth to the rhythm. From the kitchen, Marshall heard Jordan say, 'Yes, we're OK, we're both absolutely fine. Yes, we're absolutely fine . . .'

The cat standing there looking at her, wanting something to eat.

Marshall shut the front door as best he could. D'Anton had done a good job. One swing with the sledgehammer, and both locks had blown out through the timber. He shoved it back against the latch, watched the bodyguard for a moment. His shoulder seemed to be holding up OK with the CPR. Marshall stepped around him and picked up his burner phone from the mess on the floor. He called Nevins.

Eight rings.

Then: 'Detective Nevins.'

Marshall said, 'I wasn't sure if you'd pick up after hours.'

Nevins sighed. Line-crackle. 'Is that why you called? To verify my after-hours policy?'

'No. I've got one more for you.'

Silence.

'One more what?'

Marshall said, 'What do you think?'